# THE
# LYLE
## OFFICIAL
# ANTIQUES
## REVIEW 1986

# THE LYLE OFFICIAL ANTIQUES REVIEW 1986

COMPILED & EDITED BY
ANTHONY CURTIS

The publishers wish to express their sincere thanks to the following for their involvement and assistance in the production of this volume:

KAREN DOUGLASS (Art Editor)
JANICE MONCRIEFF (Assistant Editor)
ANNETTE CURTIS
NICHOLA FAIRBURN
JOSEPHINE McLAREN
TANYA FAIRBAIRN
FRANK BURRELL
ROBERT NISBET
EILEEN BURRELL

Distributed in the United States by Perigee Books,
a member of The Putnam Publishing Group,
200 Madison Avenue, New York, NY 10016.
Distributed in Canada by
General Publishing Co. Limited, Toronto

Library of Congress Catalog Card Number 74-640592

ISBN 0-399-51179-2

Printed in the United States of America

1    2    3    4    5    6    7    8    9    10

# INTRODUCTION

This year over 100,000 Antique Dealers and Collectors will make full and profitable use of their Lyle Official Antiques Review. They know that only in this one volume will they find the widest possible variety of goods — illustrated, described and given a current market value to assist them to BUY RIGHT AND SELL RIGHT throughout the year of issue.

They know, too, that by building a collection of these immensely valuable volumes year by year, they will equip themselves with an unparalleled reference library of facts, figures and illustrations which, properly used, cannot fail to help them keep one step ahead of the market.

In its sixteen years of publication, Lyle has gone from strength to strength and has become without doubt the pre-eminent book of reference for the antique trade throughout the world. Each of its fact filled pages are packed with precisely the kind of profitable information the professional Dealer needs — including descriptions, illustrations and values of thousands and thousands of individual items carefully selected to give a representative picture of the current market in antiques and collectibles — and remember all values are prices actually paid, based on accurate sales records in the twelve months prior to publication from the best established and most highly respected auction houses and retail outlets in Europe and America.

This is THE book for the Professional Antiques Dealer. 'The Lyle Book' — we've even heard it called 'The Dealer's Bible'.

Compiled and published afresh each year, the Lyle Official Antiques Review is the most comprehensive up-to-date antiques price guide available. THIS COULD BE YOUR WISEST INVESTMENT OF THE YEAR!

**ANTHONY CURTIS**

# CONTENTS

# Acknowledgements

Abridge Auctions, *(Michael Newman), Market Place, Abridge, Sussex*
Anderson & Garland, *Anderson House, Market Street, Newcastle*
Banbury Auction Rooms
Banks & Silver, *66 Foregate Street, Worcester*
Barbers Fine Art Auctioneers, *(Chobham Ltd.), 102 Lower Guildford Rd., Knaphill*
Bearnes, *Rainbow, Avenue Road, Torquay*
Biddle & Webb, *Ladywood, Middleway, Birmingham*
Bloomsbury Book Auctions, *314 Hardwick Street, London*
Boardman Fine Art Auctioneers, *Station Road Corner, Haverhill, Suffolk*
Bonham's, *Montpelier Galleries, Montpelier Street, London*
Bracketts, *27-29 High Street, Tunbridge Wells*
J. R. Bridgford & Sons, *1 Heyes Lane, Alderley Edge, Cheshire*
British Antique Exporters, *206 London Road, Burgess Hill, W. Sussex*
Brogden & Co., *39 & 38 Silver Street, Lincoln*
Wm. H. Brown, *31 St. Peters Hill, Grantham, Lincs*
Butler & Hatch Waterman, *86 High Street, Hythe, Kent*
Capes, Dunn & Co., *The Auction Galleries, 38 Charles Street, Manchester*
Chelsea Auction Galleries, *71 Lots Road, London*
Christie's, *8 King Street, St. James's, London*
Christie's, *502 Park Avenue, New York, NY 10022*
Christie's, *Cornelis Schuytstraat 57, 1071 JG, Amsterdam*
Christie's East, *219 East 67th Street, New York, NY 10021*
Christie's & Edmiston's, *164/166 Bath Street, Glasgow*
Christie's S. Kensington, *85 Old Brompton Road, London*
Coles, Knapp & Kennedy, *Georgian Rooms, Ross-on-Wye*
Cooper Hirst, *Goldway House, Parkway, Chelmsford*
Dacre, Son & Hartley, *1-5 The Grove, Ilkley, Yorks.*
Dee & Atkinson, *The Exchange Saleroom, Driffield, Yorks.*
Wm. Doyle Galleries Inc., *175 East 87th Street, New York*
Dreweatt, Watson & Barton, *Donnington Priory, Newbury, Berks.*
Hy. Duke & Son, *40 South Street, Dorchester, Dorset*
Elliott & Green, *Emsworth Road, Lymington, Hants.*
R. H. Ellis & Sons, *44-46 High Street, Worthing, Sussex*
Farrant & Wightman, *2/3 Newport St., Old Town, Swindon, Wilts.*
John D. Fleming, *Melton House, High Street, Dulverton*
Fox & Sons, *5 & 7 Salisbury Street, Fordingbridge, Hants.*
Geering & Colyer, *Highgate, Hawkhurst, Kent*
Rowland Gorringe, *15 North Street, Lewes, Suffolk*
Goss & Crested China, *(N. J. Pine), 62 Murray Rd., Horndean.*
Andrew Grant, *59-60 Foregate Street, Worcester*
Graves, Son & Pilcher, *38 Holland Road, Hove, Sussex*
Giles Haywood, *The Auction House, St. John's Rd., Stourbridge*
Heathcote Ball & Co., *47 New Walk, Leicester*

Hobbs & Chambers, *'At The Sign Of The Bell', Market Pl.,* Cirencester
Honiton Galleries, *High Street, Honiton, Devon*
Edgar Horn, *47 Cornfield Road, Eastbourne, Sussex*
Jacobs & Hunt, *Lavant Street, Petersfield, Hants*
W. H. Lane & Son, *64 Morrab Road, Penzance, Cornwall*
Lawrence Fine Art, *South Street, Crewkerne*
R. K. Leonard & Son, *512 Halderness Road, Hull*
Locke & England, *Walton House, 11 The Parade, Leamington Spa*
Thos. Love & Son, *St. John's Place, Perth*
R. K. Lucas & Son, *9 Victoria Place, Haverfordwest*
Mallams, *24 St. Michael's Street, Oxford*
Martel Maides & Le Pelley
May, Whetter & Grose, *Cornubia Hall, Par, Cornwall*
Military Antiques, *2 Market Street, The Lanes, Brighton, Sussex*
Morphets, *4-6 Albert Street, Harrogate, Yorks.*
Neales of Nottingham, *192 Mansfield Road, Nottingham*
D. M. Nesbit & Co., *7 Clarendon Road, Southsea, Hants.*
Onslows
Osmond Tricks, *Regent Street Auction Rooms, Clifton, Bristol*
Outhwaite & Litherland, *Kingsway Galleries, Fontenoy Street, Liverpool*
Phillips, *The Old House, Station Road, Knowle, Solihull, W. Midlands*
Phillips & Jolly's, *The Auction Rooms, Old King Street, Bath*
John H. Raby & Son, *21 St. Mary's Road, Bradford*
Reeds Rains, *Trinity House, 114 Northenden Road, Sale, Cheshire*
Russell Baldwin & Bright, *Ryelands Road, Leominster*
Sandoe, Luce Panes, *Chipping Manor Salerooms, Wotton-under-Edge*
Robt. W. Skinner Inc., *Bolton Gallery, Route 117, Bolton, Mass.*
H. Spencer & Sons Ltd., *20 The Square, Retford, Notts.*
Stalker & Boos, *280 N. Woodward Avenue, Birmingham, Michigan*
Stalker Gallery, *2975 W. Maple Rd., Troy, Michigan 48084*
Street Jewellery, *10 Summerhill Terrace, Newcastle-upon-Tyne*
Stride & Son, *Southdown House, St. John's Street, Chichester*
Sworder's, *19 North Street, Bishops Stortford, Herts.*
Theriault, *P.O. Box 151, Annapolis, Maryland, 21404*
Vidler & Co., *Auction Offices, Cinque Ports St., Rye, Sussex*
Wallis & Wallis, *Regency House, 1 Albion Street, Lewes, Sussex*
Ward & Partners, *16 High Street, Hythe, Kent*
Warner, Sheppard & Wade, *16-18 Halford Street, Leicester*
Warren & Wignall, *The Mill, Earnshaw Bridge, Leyland, Lancs.*
Peter Wilson & Co., *Market Street, Nantwich, Cheshire*
Woolley & Wallis, *The Castle Auction Mart, Salisbury*
Eldon E. Worrall & Co., *15 Seel Street, Liverpool*
Worsfolds Auction Galleries, *40 Station Road West, Canterbury*

# Royal Doulton Character Jugs

WHEN Mrs Doreen Clarke tuned into the nationally syndicated Gloria Hunniford Show on a wet and windy spring afternoon, she could hardly have foreseen her impending good fortune. Mrs Clarke was to learn that the jug sitting on her sideboard — a jug produced in 1940, and therefore not in the true sense of the word an antique — was a rare and highly desirable piece.

She immediately contacted Gloria Hunniford, and was directed by Anthony Curtis, the show's resident antique expert and editor of The Lyle Official Antiques Review, to seek the advice of one of the world's leading Doulton experts, Mick Yewman. Mr Yewman confirmed that, indeed, her jug was a a rare one. The jug was instructed for auction and network radio sent a crew to record the sale. There was great excitement when the bidding outstripped the existing world record for such a piece, and went on to make an all-time high of $4,800. The ensuing publicity revealed the existence of many valuable and interesting jugs and sparked off a widespread interest and a demand for more information on Doulton Character Jugs.

With a view to supplying that information, we consulted the expert, Mick Yewman who, after approximately forty years of collecting, dealing in and discussions on every aspect of

Royal Doulton, Doulton Burslem, Doulton Lambeth Wares and their collectibility, is still smitten by the 'bug'.

Mick Yewman can remember the days of the late forties and fifties when there was no enthusiasm or interest shown by anyone in the antiques trade for these jugs which today fetch hundreds even thousands of dollars. They were, at the time, the province of the second hand dealers and, of course, since they were in current production, the china retailers.

He recalls an instance when, on holiday in Cornwall, he walked into a shop displaying about sixty Royal Doulton Character Jugs in varying sizes and all from new stock. He asked the price of the large size John Barleycorn jug, made a few hasty calculations, then asked for a price on the entire stock!

The manager was called, (chiefly, one suspects, to establish that the customer was of sound mind), a small discount was negotiated and a deal struck. All of these jugs were subsequently withdrawn from production in the late 1960's and that particular collection is now worth a considerable amount of money.

We asked Mick to lay down some guidelines and his comments are as follows:

WAY back before the turn of the century, the brilliant businessman and patron of the ceramic arts Henry Doulton, later Sir Henry Doulton, predicted that one day, all of his products would be collectible — and he was proved to be right, for Doulton has become a household name on a worldwide scale.

The Doulton Pottery was established in Lambeth, London, during the early 1820's by John Doulton and John Watts and was known as Doulton & Watts. When John Watts retired in the 1850's, the pottery came to be known as Doulton & Co.

In the early days production centered around a wide variety of stoneware items such as blacking bottles, ink bottles, jam jars, paint and acid vessels and some decorative figural flasks and jugs. Later productions, continuing into the 1920's, included vast quantities of stoneware pipes and all kinds of sanitary wares in both stone and earthenware.

It was around the 1870's that production of the decorative stoneware vases, pots, jugs, jardinieres and dozens of other attractive shapes and designs began. Most of the artists employed at that time were former students of the Lambeth School of Art and these include such well known names as George Tinworth, Hannah and Florence Barlow, Eliza Simmance and very many more spanning the following period of twenty years or so.

The Doulton & Co., Burslem factory came into existence when the Staffordshire works of Pinder & Bourne were taken over by Doulton in 1882.

In the late 1890's, Charles J. Noke left the Hadley factory of Worcester and joined Doulton, where, after building a new china works in the early 1900's, he took over the position of Art Director (1914). It is from around this period that we see the start of the production of many of their wares ie.,

Figurines, Seriesware, Kingsware etc. Indeed, figurines are still produced there today.

Charles J. Noke introduced Character Jugs in the early 1930's and his son, Cecil J. Noke, who succeeded him as Art Director in 1936, played a very important part in their development.

Today, in the United Kingdom alone, there are as many as four to five thousand collectors and dealers focusing their attention on these Character Jugs. Indeed, enthusiasm and interest has developed on an international scale involving tens of thousands of collectors and dealers throughout America, Canada, Australia, New Zealand and many other countries of the world.

The first Royal Doulton Character Jug, titled 'John Barleycorn Old Lad', was produced in the early 1930's from a design and model by Charles Noke. As the popularity of these jugs grew, many new characters were introduced including 'Sairey Gamp', 'Parson Brown', 'Dick Turpin' and 'Old Charley'. Some of these jugs are still in production today but many of the earlier designs were taken out of production during the sixties.

'JOHN BARLEYCORN' Character Jug Large — designed by C. J. Noke — Introduced in 1934, withdrawn by 1960 — AS D5327.
*Auction Valuation* **$120**

**'SCARAMOUCHE'** *Character Jug Large –*
*designed by M. Henk – Introduced in 1962,*
*withdrawn by 1967 – AS D6558.*
*Auction Valuation* **$600**

**'SIMPLE SIMON'** *Character Jug Large –*
*designed by M. Henk – Introduced in 1953,*
*withdrawn by 1960 – AS D6374.*
*Auction Valuation* **$575**

**'MEPHISTOPHELES'** *Character Jug Large –*
*designed by C. J. Noke and H. Fenton – Intro-*
*duced in 1947, withdrawn by 1948 – AS D5757.*
*(Rare)* *Auction Valuation* **$1,800**

**'JOCKEY'** *Character Jug Large – designed by*
*D. Biggs – Introduced in 1971, withdrawn*
*by 1975 – AS D6625.*
*Auction Valuation* **$300**

One of the first to be withdrawn was the Churchill character jug made during the Battle of Britain as a tribute to the great leader. Designed as a Loving Cup by C. J. Noke, it is cream colored with two black handles and the base bears the inscription *'Winston Churchill Prime Minister Of Britain 1940'*. This jug came into production in 1940 and was withdrawn within one year to eighteen months later. There has been much speculation as to why this particular piece was withdrawn but it is generally accepted that Churchill was not pleased with the 'likeness' portrayed and let it be known to the chairman of the factory that he would prefer production to cease. The resulting scarcity has established this jug as an extremely rare and desirable item, coveted by collectors throughout the world. A fair estimation of the price at auction today would be between five and ten thousand dollars.

**'DRAKE'** *Character Jug (Hatless) Large – designed by H. Fenton – Introduced in 1940, withdrawn by 1941 – AS D6115.*

*Auction Valuation* **$4,800**

**'CHURCHILL'** *Character Jug (as Loving Cup) – designed by C. J. Noke – Introduced in 1940, withdrawn by 1942 – AS D6170. Wording on the base: 'Winston Spencer' Churchill Prime Minister of Britain 1940. This Loving Cup was made during the Battle of Britain as a tribute to a great leader. Very Rare)*     *Auction Valuation* **$10,000**

Another character jug worthy of note, is that known as *'Drake'*, designed by Mr. H. Fenton. Introduced in 1940, the rim of the first version depicts only the character's hair, while the later version features a hat. The jug without the hat is known as the *'Hatless Drake'* and bears the wording on the back *'Drake He Was A Devon Man'*. It has been said that the first version was a pilot but this is unlikely to be true for production was retailed in the china shops of the day at a selling price of less than one dollar! (I have, in fact, met someone who bought a *'Hatless Drake'* from Blundells of Luton, in 1941). Production was limited however, and this is a very rare jug. In auction rooms today, the hatless version realises between $4,500 and $5,250. Two have recently been sold at the Abridge Auctions, Essex — one for $4,800 (a world record price at the time of sale) and the other for $4,500. The hatted version is less sought after and consequently sells for between $90 and $100.

It is impossible to discuss Royal Doulton Character Jugs without mentioning the red haired, brown haired and white haired *Clowns*. Again, these were designed by H. Fenton: the red haired and the brown haired introduced in 1937 then both withdrawn in 1942, currently fetch in auction between $3,000 and $3,600. In my own opinion, the brown haired is the rarest of the clowns. The white haired version was intoduced in 1951 and withdrawn by 1955. In auction today, this would make between $1,000 and $1,100. Whilst the latter example does not reach the lofty heights of the prices realised by the red and brown haired versions this still represents a remarkable return on investment in a jug which could have been bought as recently as the 50's for, at most, less than ten dollars.

'CLOWN' *Character Jug (Red Hair) Large – designed by H. Fenton – Introduced in 1937, withdrawn by 1942 – AS D5610. (Rare)*
*Auction Valuation* **$3,000**

One of my personal favorites is the character jug, of which there are three versions, designed by H. Fenton, depicting a Cockney Costermonger and known as *'Arry'*. These were introduced in the mid forties and all were withdrawn by 1960. One is predominantly brown in color; another is the same color but with brown buttons on his hat and collar and is referred to as *'Brown Pearly Boy'*; yet another with blue collar and white buttons is known as the *'Blue Pearly Boy'*. Prices fetched at auction today are as follows: *'Arry'* – $135 to $190, *'Brown Pearly Boy'*– $750 to $1,000 and *'Blue Pearly Boy'* – $3,000 to $3,750. The prices for the latter reflects the result of a very limited production.

Finally, let me draw your attention to *'Arry's* partner . . . *'Arriet'*, which was also withdrawn from production by 1960. This jug is predominantly brown with the addition of a green hat and handle. Again, there is a version with blue collar and maroon hat sporting a green feather known as *'Blue Pearly Girl'* which is extremely rare. At current auction prices *'Arriet'* would realise between $135 and $190, and *'Blue Pearly Girl'* anything from $3,750 to $5,250.

'ARRY' *Character Jug (As Blue Pearly Boy) Large – designed by H. Fenton – Introduced in 1947, withdrawn by 1955. (Very Rare)*
*Auction Valuation* **$3,750**

**'SMUTS'** *Character Jug Large – designed by H. Fenton – Introduced in 1946, withdrawn by 1948 – AS D6198. (Rare)*
*Auction Valuation* **$1,725**

**'OLD KING COLE'** *Character Jug (Yellow Crown) Large – designed by H. Fenton – Introduced in 1939, withdrawn by 1940 – AS D6036. (Rare) Auction Valuation* **$1,500**

**'THE CAVALIER'** *Character Jug (Goatee Beard) Large – designed by H. Fenton – Introduced in 1940, withdrawn by 1942 – AS D6114. (Rare) Auction Valuation* **$1,800**

**'GRANNY'** *Character Jug (Toothless) Large – designed by H. Fenton and M. Henk – introduced in 1935, withdrawn by 1940 – AS D5521. (Rare) Auction Valuation* **$1,200**

17

'REGENCY BEAU' *Character Jug Large –*
*designed by D. Biggs – Introduced in 1962,*
*withdrawn by 1967 – AS D6559.*
                *Auction Valuation*   **$750**

'UGLY DUCHESS' *Character Jug Large –*
*designed by M. Henk – Introduced in 1965,*
*withdrawn by 1973 – AS D6599.*
            *Auction Valuation*   **$500**

Discussing a subject embracing such an enormous range and variety of material, I have concentrated mainly on some of the rarest and most expensive examples but there are many others ranging from the current production models selling at around $40 each, to the out of production examples ranging in price from $90 to $225; from $500 and up to thousands of dollars.

Established collectors are invariably well informed and it is impossible to over emphasise to new collectors, the importance of gathering as much knowledge as possible before venturing into a field where some small detail such as the color of buttons, triangles or hair can represent the difference between hundred and thousands of dollars. This valuable information is however, readily available, fascinating to assimilate and quite apart from the undeniable visual appeal of Doulton Character Jugs, a great bonus to collectors is the Doulton backstamp and numbering system which makes each item readily identifiable.

Of the many books specifically on the subject of Doulton jugs there are one or two I would particularly recommend and these are as follows: A 'must' for dealers and collectors alike, is the publication *'Collecting Doulton Character And Toby Jugs 1985'* by Jocelyn Lukins, to whom I owe a debt of gratitude for supplying the photographs accompanying this feature; *'The Character Jug Collectors Handbook 1984'* by Kevin Pearson, which is a price guide to buying all of the jugs now withdrawn; *'Royal Doulton Character And Toby Jugs 1979'* by Desmond Eyles, a former Historical Advisor with Royal Doulton, and finally, any of the publications by the man whom I believe was responsible for initiating the interest in dealing in and collecting all Doulton wares through his many books on all subjects from the late sixties, Richard Dennis of Richard Dennis Publication.

**MIKE YEWMAN**
(Abridge Auction Rooms, Essex, England)

# Mirror
# Mirror

IN the Middle Ages, mirrors were of metal highly polished for, although the method of backing glass with a metallic substance was understood in principle, the glass was so poor and the impurities so many that, in practice, a face reflected from it would have resembled that of a plague victim seen on a foggy night.

In 1507, however, things changed when two bright young men from Murano near Venice, used an amalgam of mercury and tin to perfect the process of silvering and were granted a monopoly on the production of mirrors by this method for twenty years.

Apart from the imported product, Britons had to content themselves with pieces of polished metal until 1615, when Sir Robert Mansell applied for a patent to make mirror glass by applying a thin coat of mercury backed with tinfoil. So much in demand was his product that, within a very short time, he had over five hundred employees 'making, grinding and foyling'.

The mirrors produced by Sir Robert Mansell were, in fact, quite small hand glasses which, although vastly better than those of polished metal, were frequently disfigured by ugly black spots. This was a result, curiously, of England's dwindling forests. In an effort to conserve the nation's timber resources, wood was prohibited as fuel for manufacturing purposes and the substitute, coal, reacted with the lead flux during the heating process.

The glass, too, was far from perfect and it was not until 1665 that the Duke of

Buckingham, who established the Vauxhall Glass Works at Lambeth, perfected a method of pouring molten glass into shallow trays to produce a satisfactory mirror glass in sheets up to three feet six inches long.

Hanging mirrors were highly prized possessions at this time, becoming increasingly important in decorative schemes when hung above side tables or chests. Wooden frames, often of deal from three to six inches wide, became popular in about 1675 and were often highly decorated with intricate veneer work or more elaborate confections of tortoiseshell or silver.

*A fine Charles II carved limewood mirror, 64in. high. (Christie's)* **$14,750**

The standard design was of square construction with a semi-circular cresting.

By the end of the seventeenth century, mirrors were being made much taller than ever before, since it was fashionable to set them on the wall, often in pairs with matching tables, between the three long widows which were a typical feature of large rooms of the period.

Apart from the aesthetically pleasing effect this produced, it was also by far the most practical manner of hanging mirrors, allowing light from the windows to illuminate those desirous of viewing themselves in the days before frames concealed flattering strip lights.

Generally speaking, styles followed the Venetian mode; rectangular frames surmounted by pierced or other decorative cresting whose extravagance was limited only by the depth of the original purchaser's pocket.

More exotic finishes include floral marquetry, tortoiseshell, Chinese lacquer and chased, embossed silver. There was also a particularly popular finish, usually assembled on site due to its fragility, which consisted of cut shapes of glass — particularly sapphire blue glass — set in patterns around the border with small, white glass rosettes at the corners.

'Verre eglomise' was yet another highly regarded finish in which the underside of the plain glass border bore a painted design backed by gold or silver leaf on a base of green, black or red.

Mirror frames, in Queen Anne's day, were usually little more than inch-wide strips of convex beading set around the bevelled glass; the half round cornices being filled with mirror and taking graceful curving forms of ogee or cusp.

Gilt was becoming increasingly popular as a means of decoration, and sophisticated classical friezes were also coming into vogue.

One of the architects of this style was William Kent, who started life as a coach-builder in the North Riding of Yorkshire. One day, feeling 'the emotions of genius' — his words — welling in his breast, he set off for London at the age of nineteen determined to set the fashionable world to rights.

He caused quite a stir in the salons of London with his paintings, landscape gardens and interior decoration. He was consulted on every aspect of design, from furniture and glass to silver and plate, attacking each problem with verve and gusto in the attempt to create something 'audacious, splendid and sumptuous' — his words again.

William Kent reigned supreme in his age, though a few notables such as Walpole thought him 'immensely ponderous' and, later in the century, Robert Adam likened his work to 'that of a beginner'.

Large mirrors (pier glasses) set between windows continued to be popular throughout the eighteenth century, some reaching to enormous heights. Equally popular were Chimney Glasses — three mirrors, placed horizontally across the mantelshelf, often with a painted landscape above.

The sudden surge of interest in mirrors was a direct result of reduced prices following the introduction of mass production methods of manufacture. So advanced were British techniques, moreover, that great quantities of mirrors were now being exported to Italy, where it had all begun.

This period produced a multitude of smallish wall mirrors, those whose frames reflected architectural styles taking the lion's share of the market.

The broken pediment with an elaborate centerpiece was particularly popular when it enclosed classical entablature or, occasionally, a female head crowned with feathers.

The sides of frames were often quite plain with gesso edgings of floral sprays or corn husks, while more elaborate examples were to be found on which draped and folded material was simulated. This style was balanced at the base with a finely carved scroll apron, often incorporating a shell design.

In the 1740s, frames began to reflect the influence of the Louis XV rococo styles, and there are many mirrors of a transitional period owing allegiance to both this and the architectural styles.

Gradually, the flowing lines of the rococo style began to dominate — a development which was accelerated by improved glass production leading to lighter mirrors which no longer needed massively built frames to support them.

*A fine George I giltwood mirror with rectangular bevelled plate, 5 7¾in. high. (Christie's)*
**$11,500**

Chippendale, whose use of carving was brilliant, was well to the fore in the development of new styles, and this may have owed something to the fact that his father had long been noted for his superb mirror and picture frames.

Chippendale insisted that the carving, of gilded pine, should be very vigorous with boldly opposing C scrolls and garlands of flowers in high relief.

This style continued to be made throughout the nineteenth century, but the decoration was generally, by then, of gesso and not carved wood, — a point to watch when buying, since the latter are worth only a fraction of the genuinely carved pieces.

As a contrast to the rather flamboyant styles which were popular in the mid eighteenth century, a rather less ostentatious and — more to the point — far less expensive mirror was also produced.

*One of a pair of George I giltwood wall mirrors, circa 1715, 6ft. 8in. high.*
**$34,500**

The design basically resembles that of the earlier, walnut, narrow frames, though this was made of mahogany with fret cut decoration above and below but plain sides. There is sometimes a small shell design top centre but by far the most popular motif took the form of a gilded bird with outstretched wings.

The mirror itself is finely bevelled and usually surrounded by a narrow strip of gilt beading.

This is a very simple, yet pleasing, mirror whose popularity was underlined by the fact that they were made throughout the nineteenth century and are still being made today, though this could equally be because they are relatively easily made.

Early in the eighteenth century a notable architect, Sir William Chambers, saw fit to

*A late George II giltwood chinoiserie mirror with tall pagoda cresting, 6ft.6in. high, circa 1755.*                    **$14,000**

publish a book of oriental designs, having recently returned from China where he was duly impressed by the decorative styles he saw.

The vogue reached its height around the middle of the eighteenth century, when it was deemed the height of elegance and good taste to line the walls with hand painted papers and drape Chinese embroidery at all the windows.

Everything that might ever find its way into a room was, naturally, designed to blend with the wallpaper and Chippendale was, as usual, one of the first to turn his attention in this direction.

Some of Chippendale's designs, depicting long beaked birds, pagodas, grotesque figures and intricate tracery were almost impossible to carve in mahogany, it being too hard, and, as a result, most mirror frames in this style are to be found in gilded pine. Never modest in his claims, Chippendale made it clear in his catalogue that even the most intricate of his ideas could be faithfully executed by his skilled craftsmen — the implication being that all others were likely to fall by the wayside.

Obviously, there had been some backstabbing going on, the carvers from rival firms doubtless blaming their own shortcomings onto the near impossibility of translating Chippendale's fine drawings.

The bold rococo, gothic and Chinese decorative styles fell rapidly by the wayside once Robert Adam got into his stride during the last quarter of the eighteenth century.

His genius lay in the way his simple geometric designs created a subtle elegance which suited the period — or, possibly, even helped to shape it.

One of four sons of a Scottish master mason, Robert Adam was basically an architect who believed it within his province to design all furnishings and interior decorations in order to achieve an overall consistency of style. He particularly favored painted and gilded decoration, but sometimes employed the use of marquetry which, incidentally, was most probably executed in the workshops of his great contemporary, Chippendale.

The gilt Adam-style mirror has fluted pillars with acanthus leaf capitals and is surmounted by a lyre motif set amid carved foliage — a simple yet elegant piece.

Adam's confessed aim was to '. . . sieze the beautiful spirit of antiquity and to transfuse it with novelty and variety', a goal which he undoubtedly reached and one whose attainment earned his bones a place in Westminster Abbey after his death in 1792.

At the end of the 18th century, circular convex mirrors were introduced from France,

*One of a fine pair of George I walnut and parcel gilt mirrors, 53in. high. (Christie's)*
**$32,000**

gaining in popularity to reach their height during the Regency period. Ranging in diameter from about eighteen inches to three feet, they have deep cavetto borders — quite narrow on early examples — which are decorated at intervals with gilt balls or, occasionally, rounded flowers.

The mirrors themselves are surrounded by reeded black fillets, and some fine examples have candle branches fixed to the sides of their gilt frames.

By far the most important feature of any of these mirrors, however, is the full-relief gilt eagle, set with wings extended, amid foliage at the top. This is often balanced by means of a token amount of foliage or scrollwork at the base.

This style was particularly well suited to use in Regency rooms for, in general, furniture of the period was inclined to be on the low side — a feature which left plenty of room on the walls for the display of exotic mirrors.

Another, more practical, feature of the convex mirror is the panoramic view it gives of the room in which it is hung. By hanging it near her chair, the mistress of the house could keep an unobtrusive eye on everyone in the room while, at the same time looking to see that the parlormaid was not making rude gestures behind her back.

Our 19th century forebears must really have loved looking at themselves if we are to judge by the vast numbers of gilt gesso ornamental mirrors which are to be found in today's salerooms and shops.

Toward the end of the 19th century, mirrors tended to get themselves tacked onto pieces of furniture, notably dressing tables and sideboards, causing hanging mirrors to lose much of their importance and, therefore, much of their style.

**ANTHONY CURTIS**

# Antiques On The Move

IF antiques are your passion then the sleepy English town of Burgess Hill will surely capture your imagination. Nestled in the rolling green landscape of tranquil Sussex county, Burgess Hill is nevertheless strategically located between Britain's two major antique centers, London and historic Brighton. It is no coincidence that Britain's foremost wholesale antique experts, British Antique Exporters Ltd, is situated in this small community. Combining an ideal work environment for the company's artisans and its close proximity to major markets, Burgess Hill has played host to BAE's evolution into the cornerstone of the world's antique shipping trade.

In a day and age when high standards have been forsaken by many firms in favour of so-called "efficiency", BAE have succeeded in combining elements of traditional craftmaking with superb organization. This combination was revealed to me during my latest visit to Burgess Hill, when I toured the BAE's premises, a veritable Aladdin's cave of treasures from centuries past. It is difficult to believe that the offices and workshops co-exist within the same corporation. The offices reflect the high-tech attitude of BAE management, while the pervasive odor of wood and leather in the workshops characterizes the traditional craftmaking of the company artisans.

According to Norman Lefton, BAE's Chairman, the key to the company's success may be found in one word. "Specialization" he repeated for the benefit of my tape-recorder, "That's the secret."

My tour round the workshops revealed the extent of this policy. A staff of highly-skilled craftsmen are employed by the company, and each is an expert in at least one field. In the

*A fine 19th century figured mahogany linen press on bracket feet.*

interest of authenticity, the artisans prefer to keep restoration work to a minimum. When necessary, however, only the highest standards are applied.

Not only are the traditional crafts of upholstery and cabinet-making employed but so are many of the skills which have generally passed into history. That of the glass beveller, the carver and even a marble worker who will cut, edge and polish a piece of finely figured marble if necessary, to bring a piece back to pristine condition using traditional techniques and expertise.

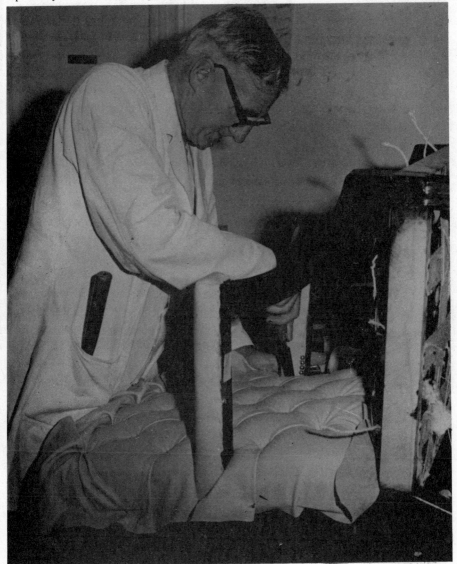

*Even experienced upholsterers concede that deep buttoned work using leather requires the hands of a master craftsman.*

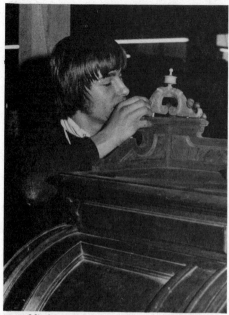

*Missing carving is replaced with skilled hands.*

*A simple reglueing of joints can make all the difference.*

I also watched the culmination of two weeks of work on a fine Regency rosewood table that required French polishing. Speaking with one of the company's veteran French polishers, I learnt that in order to achieve the highly valued patina characteristic of French polish, the craftsmen has to allow twenty-four hours drying time between each application of polish. Also in evidence was the painstaking technique of preparing and dyeing leather for upholstery, a task that is rarely undertaken in these quantity-conscious days.

"It's almost like sending your children away" says David Balmer, "you take care of them, make sure they are as perfect as you can make them, and then send them off."

Thankfully, David's children are well taken care of on their journey. Indeed, the technique of specialization extends not only to the restoration department, but also to the efforts of the packers.

With containers of antiques travelling as far afield as Australia and the United States, packing techniques must be of the highest standard. As Lefton admits, packing is an art in itself.

"You'll stand looking at the goods that have to go into one of these containers and you'll say 'no way' ", marvels Lefton, "but they do it every time."

It is essential that BAE maximize both their own and their clients' investments. That means transporting as many antiques in each container as possible. A typical forty foot container would hold approximately one hundred pieces of furniture, and sixty smaller items. Container loads of Georgian, Victorian, Edwardian and 1930's pieces leave the Burgess Hill premises every day for worldwide destinations. The 'safe arrival guarantee' that the company offers is a reflection of their confidence in the packers.

One of the most unusual features of the

*A skilled upholsterer at work on a fine 18th century wing chair.*

BAE set-up is the extent of on-going market research undertaken to support the decisions regarding shipment of goods. Although clients state a preference for the material they need, many of the decisions lie in the hands of BAE personnel. Client markets are thoroughly researched so that it is known what goods are desirable.

Norman Lefton concedes that one of the "perks" of the business is the extensive travel required of him. Changing tides in the world-wide market have dictated that much of his recent research has taken place in the USA, which Lefton refers to as "a burgeoning market."

"America is huge. Tastes vary from city to city, state to state," Lefton told me, "and it's vital to know what the tastes are in places as far apart as New York and New Orleans, Boston and Miami Beach."

Helyn O'Hare is in charge of Customer/Company liaison. "We don't guess what the customer wants, neither do we forget about the goods as soon as they leave Burgess Hill," she says, "we thrive on feedback."

BAE encourages clients to return detailed information on the condition and saleability of each antique received in the shipment. According to O'Hare, the vast majority of the feedback is positive.

*The ever popular roll top desk.*

Another one of the BAE's considerable assets is its purchasing power. This enables the company to buy and sell antiques at highly competitive prices. Company buyers are continually on the road, using their specialized knowledge of the British antique market, as well as the benefits of client market research, to acquire for the BAE exactly the right goods. If this isn't enough to satisfy the most pernickety antique afficionado, Lefton backs up his system with the highly innovative BAE Courier/Finder Service. It was the Courier/Finder system that initially attracted me to the BAE.

In the late 1970's I was a newcomer to the British antiques scene, unfamiliar with the labyrinth-like route that one took in the search for many items. Lefton was only too glad to point a disorientated American visitor in the direction of the Courier/Finder Service.

*Homeward bound American roll top desks lining up for despatch.*

*Even the smallest scratch doesn't escape the attention of the French Polisher.*

The service enables interested dealers to benefit from the specialized knowledge of the
company buyers, who journeyed with me on
my search for my particular speciality, fair-
ground gallopers. For the visiting dealer with
an inevitable limited schedule, the BAE
Courier/Finder Service is a godsend.

Response to the huge worldwide demand
for high-quality antiques, expertly restored
and perfectly packed, served to propel BAE
into the twenty-first century. Despite decades
of experience in the antique shipping trade,
the company itself rejects the notion that
their administration is old-fashioned. Proof
positive may be found in the company
administrative headquarters, where computers
hum, bleep and clatter with hidden precision.
Indeed, BAE is fully computerized to facilitate efficient delivery and excellent worldwide
communications.

*Carefully packed and ready for loading.*

*"It all goes in like a giant jigsaw puzzle"
said the chief despatcher.*

Lefton escorted me through the premises
as I made ready to leave. With the help of
BAE, and particularly the Courier/Finder
Service, my fortnight in England had been an
enormous success. On the way to my waiting
car we stopped briefly at the packing terminal
where I observed the meticulous loading of
huge numbers of securely fastened antiques
into twenty foot containers. BAE's Chairman
would hardly admit to being a romantic, but
he could not resist a few sentimental parting
words. "You know, we pack all sorts of different goods in these containers, but there's
one thing we always include," he said
dreamily, "and that's a little love."

**MARK JENKINS**

*A good William & Mary period figured
walnut chest on stand.*

# And So To Bed

IT was most probably the crusades which were responsible for the fact that early beds were enclosed, tent-like structures. This gave a degree of privacy to the occupants and excluded draughts — a not unimportant feature in the naturally air conditioned rooms of pre-16th century Britain.

It was in the 16th century that wood began to be used to replace some of the drapes surrounding the beds, carved corner posts putting in an appearance for the first time, and a carved, panelled headboard extending to a height of about four feet.

As the century progressed, the panelling on the headboard was extended upward to the tops of the posts and a wooden tester, often with a carved frieze, was added to support the drapes.

Another style dating from this time has the posts at the foot standing on heavy square bases independent of the bedstock.

As time passed, the posts at the head of the bed disappeared altogether, the wainscote being sufficiently sturdy to adequately support the tester. The roof of the bed, too, underwent a change, being panelled in wood instead of covered with fabric.

These changes in style caused this type of bed to weigh several hundredweights, beside giving the impression that it was a small room placed within a room.

The posts at the foot were still quite slender however, and the bedstock had the original rope supports.

It is usual for the back to have only its upper panels decorated, those at the base, which normally would be hidden behind mattresses and pillows, being left plain.

The drapes were still an important feature of beds during this period, being as flamboyant as they ever were. There are records showing that black drapes, however, were used by families in mourning.

The drapes on some of the early beds were really spectacular; those made for Catherine of Braganza as a present from the States of

*An Elizabethan oak tester bed with box spring mattress, 7ft. wide overall, circa 1580-1603.* **$31,000**

Holland being an embroidery of silver on crimson velvet which cost, even then a mammoth $12,000.

James I, it appears also liked to sleep in some style for his bed curtains, tester, quilt and valance were all of gold flowers worked on a velvet ground. This set the Royal Purse back some $10,500

Lesser mortals began to turn away from drapes — and at those prices, who can blame them? — concentrating more on the woodwork, since, in those happy days a good oak bed, with carving cost as little as $25.

Bed posts took on greater importance now they could be seen and they reached their maximum girth during the early part of the 17th century.

Where the mattresses had earlier been supported on a mesh of rope, it was now placed on a base of wooden slats — a far more practical arrangement.

On many early beds, a little shelf can be found near the headboard which was intended as a support for a rushlight but, bedtime reading not having reached any degree of popularity, the feature soon fell into disuse.

The only other unique feature to be found on early beds was a small compartment near the pillow, a place of safekeeping for baubles and beads.

Many of these early oak beds are superbly carved and decorated.

At the start of Elizabeth I's reign, it was usually only the wealthiest people who wanted carved beds, but the fashion soon caught on and within twenty-five years they were accepted fairly widely by the more sober middle classes.

Needless to say, the fashionable set kept themselves one jump ahead of their more

*A Charles I oak tester bedstead, circa 1640, 4ft. 7½in. wide.*          **$12,250**

hidebound fellows by concentrating on inlay work of bog oak, boxwood, holly and sycamore, set in floral sprays and stars. Some extended their taste for decoration by adding painted panels and gilding, while others delighted in headboards emblazoned with highly colored coats of arms.

The first carving to be seen on beds was usually of an exaggerated form, with elaborate panels intersected by stiles with figures of goddesses and wild-eyed men. Later, the carving became more subdued and decorous, passing through simple, incised designs to the fielded panels.

Canopies became heavier and more massively elaborate with the molded panelling continuing underneath, and the deep molded friezes often intersected by corbels.

The thought of trying to get an undisturbed night's sleep with a few hundredweight of carved oak poised overhead is enough to perturb anyone, particularly if there are signs of wood beetle in the uprights . . . .

Seventeenth century householders evidently shared my qualms for, by the end of the century, these monstrous constructions began to fade from favour and drapes once more became the important feature.

This change of taste might well have been influenced to a large extent by the superb Italian beds which began to be imported into Britain at about this time.

Once again, with the woodwork being concealed behind drapery, frames become quite definitely plain and, indeed, the Italian manufacturers often spurned the use of wood altogether, making the frames from forged iron which was sometimes gilded.

By the time the 18th century had arrived, high ceilings had become fashionable and separate bedrooms were being built in new houses on the same floor as the major rooms.

As a result, state beds increased their height enormously, often reaching ceilings some eighteen to twenty feet above floor level. To make its presence felt, the top of a bed of that height had to be pretty elaborate and upper corners were enriched with ostrich feathers and imposing carved cornices.

Although most large houses boasted at least one of these massive beds to impress the more important visitors, most householders contented themselves with something a little more modest for regular nightly use.

Mahogany ousted oak and walnut for the posts at the foot of the bed and these, because they were once again visible from the outside, became much finer, with low relief carving. Panelled canopies once more returned to favor and some boasted fine friezes often further embellished with gadrooned borders.

*Heal and Son's mattress factory in the 1890s...*

Drapes were still to the fore at this time and Hepplewhite used them most effectively with the domed canopy.

Despite the numbers of beds made in this period, surprisingly few have remained, and this is a great shame, for they have a voluptuously romantic, Arabian Nights feel.

By the end of the century, beds had become much heavier again, with stout, deeply carved posts ornamented with leaves, pineapples and other symbols.

The typical, late 18th century bed is of mahogany, with a canopy and provision for drapes.

All these beds tend to look rather stark without their curtains, but when these are hung 'with enough material for many folds', as Sheraton suggested, they cannot fail to turn anyone on to turning in, even though the silks and damasks of an earlier age had, by this time, given way to muslin, chintz or linen.

Although, by the end of the 19th century, the four poster bed was struggling for survival, a few really exotic examples were produced in order to satisfy the cravings of those individuals who felt that bedtime was being stripped of romance and adventure — and had the money to pay for the indulgence of their fantasies.

Most of the beds produced early in the century, although not as splendid as their predecessors, still relied upon drapes for their allure. Some too were made in the Regency style, taking the form of a couch with scrolled head and foot boards, but even these were often set beneath tent-like canopies topped with gilded pineapples or crowns.

The introduction of metal decorations on furniture prompted a revival of the popularity of boulle-work — inlaid scroll patterns of brass and tortoiseshell — and some spectacular beds are decorated in this manner.

The early Victorian period saw the last of the really great, wooden four posters. After this time, firms such as Heal's made valiant efforts to prolong the style by producing a few elegant pieces but, in most households, there was no longer any room for them, bedrooms having become cluttered with wardrobes, washstands, commodes, dressing tables and chests of drawers and all the other appurtenances of civilised living.

The 19th century saw the Industrial Revolution in full swing and, iron being the metal of the age, a great many iron framed beds were produced. Although they suited the manufacturers, these creations found no favor with the designer Eastlake, for he is on record as having declared that the ornamental intersection resembled 'a friendly association of garden slugs'.

The salesmen, of course, loved the metal frames: they waxed quite lyrical about cleanliness and hygiene as though a wooden framed bed was an open invitation to disease.

*The magnificent bed at Osterley Park. (Cooper-Bridgeman)*

*A fine mahogany and giltwood bedstead at Temple Newsham House, circa 1765. (Cooper-Bridgeman)*

A few Parisian iron beds were made whose design features included masses of cast iron scrollwork and foliage but these, although very pretty, must have caused more than a few cracked heads for restless sleepers.

One of the most popular iron beds to have been produced was the tent bed, which had a mesh of springy steel laths to support the mattress in greater comfort.

Another name for this was the Officer's Bed, the design being such that you could pack the whole thing in minutes into a box four feet long by eleven inches wide.

The half tester first appeared towards the end of the 17th century, when the canopy extended just far enough over the bed to allow the curtains completely to enclose it without recourse to posts at the foot.

This style remained popular throughout the 18th century and reached its peak in the 19th century, when the tester, as a rule, allowed the curtains to veil only half the bed. Most were made of brass in the burgeoning British industrial capital of Birmingham, which had also become the center for metal bed manufacture.

The style of these beds varies enormously, and the brass tube may be of either round or square section set in an infinity of patterns. In some cases, the tester itself was fixed to the wall instead of the bedhead, particularly when it was intended to use the heavy, velvet drapes which rose to a brief popularity. Other, more exotic, versions were embellished with papier mache panels and rings of mother-of-pearl.

The 'Handsome mahogany Four-poster Bed' sold by Heal & Sons in 1853 for the princely sum of $18, had 'seven inch, octagon fluted pillars and a bold molded cornice with octagon corners' and it came complete with castors, rods, rings and a glossy coat of french polish (mattresses and linen optional).

If your great-grandfather was unable to afford that kind of money, there was a similar bed of japanned maple for as little as $5 and, for those with aspirations to nocturnal greatness, $70 would have secured a bed made of wood of a 'foreign walnut tree made to an elaborate and chaste design'.

Most of the beds which have survived from the early days are of the four poster variety — these having been long established as family heirlooms to be handed down and revered by succeeding generations.

With the advent of mass production methods in the 19th century, the vast reservoir of design ideas from earlier ages was tapped, just about every possible style and combination of styles making at least a brief appearance. During the last quarter of the century, the most popular revivals were those dating from the late 18th century and those reflecting the mysticism of the Orient.

**ANTHONY CURTIS**

# ANTIQUES
# REVIEW 1986

THE Lyle Official Antiques Review is compiled and published with completely fresh information annually, enabling you to begin each new year with an up-to-date knowledge of the current trends, together with the verified values of antiques of all descriptions.

We have endeavored to obtain a balance between the more expensive collector's items and those which, although not in their true sense antiques, are handled daily by the antiques trade.

The illustrations and prices in the following sections have been arranged to make it easy for the reader to assess the period and value of all items with speed.

You will find illustrations for almost every category of antique and curio, together with a corresponding price collated during the last twelve months, from the auction rooms and retail outlets of the major trading countries.

When dealing with the more popular trade pieces, in some instances, a calculation of an average price has been estimated from the varying accounts researched.

As regards prices, when 'one of a pair' is given in the description the price quoted is for a pair and so that we can make maximum use of the available space it is generally considered that one illustration is sufficient.

It will be noted that in some descriptions taken directly from sales catalogues originating from many different countries, terms such as bureau, secretary and davenport are used in a broader sense than is customary, but in all cases the term used is self explanatory.

Tobacco advertising sign, 'Red Indian', chromolithographed on thin cardboard, circa 1900, 28 x 22in. (Robt. W. Skinner Inc.) $275

A metal Kodak store sign, triangular with heavy metal bracket, 'Developing Printing Enlarging'. (Robt. W. Skinner Inc.) $85

Dr. Fitler's Rheumatic Syrup sign, circa 1880, 19½ x 13½in. (Robt. W. Skinner Inc.) $2,100

Early 20th century drug store Moxie sign, 23½ x 31¾in. (Robt. W. Skinner Inc.) $625

Duke's tobacco advertising sign, America, 18½in. wide. (Robt. W. Skinner Inc.) $225

Victorian House Mover's sign made of well-cut letters, foliage, birds etc., circa 1880. (Robt. W. Skinner Inc.) $400

Brooke Bond dividend Tea. (Street Jewellery) $37 £30

Viking Milk 'Latte Viking'. (Street Jewellery) $218

Hudson's Dry Soap, In Fine Powder. (Street Jewellery) $56

We Sell Sealed Shell. (Street Jewellery) $37

A 19th century roll down wall cigar advertisement, chromolithographed on canvas backed paper, 54 x 39½in. (Robt. W. Skinner Inc.) $140

Late 19th century Elgin watch advertising sign, entitled 'My Elgin's All Right', 22 x 15in. (Robt. W. Skinner Inc.) $150

'Buckeye' Farm Equipment sign, by The Winters Print & Litho Co., Springfield, Ohio', 1880-1890, 30 x 21¾in. (Robt. W. Skinner Inc.) $375

Pálethorpes 'Royal Cambridge' Sausages. (Street Jewellery) $93

Kodak glass and celluloid store sign, 37 x 15in., in black frame, circa 1910, with 'Kodaks' in 8in. gold recessed letter on black background. (Robt. W. Skinner Inc.) $475

Gossages' Dry Soap. (Street Jewellery) $93

National Benzole Mixture. (Street Jewellery) $93

Sun Insurance Office. (Street Jewellery) $125

Wincarnis 'The World's Greatest Wine Tonic'. (Street Jewellery) $562

Fry's Chocolate. (Street Jewellery) $187

'Coca Cola' advertising tip tray, oval, America, circa 1907. (Robt. W. Skinner Inc.)          $200

'Reliance' cigar display, manufactured by Nosch & Co., circa 1880, 17½in. high. (Robt. W. Skinner Inc.)   $1,300

The Spalding Co. Iron Advertising trade sign, the cast-iron pocket watch frame with zinc painted face, 22¼in. high, circa 1890. (Robt. W. Skinner Inc.)          $350

Lithographed advertisement for Egyptienne 'Straights' cigarettes, 31in. high. (Robt. W. Skinner Inc.) $110

We sell Lyon's 2d. Fruit Pies. (Street Jewellery)          $93

None Such Mince Meat sign, head of an Onondaga Indian chief, circa 1890, 28 x 20in. (Robt. W. Skinner Inc.)    $1,800

A metal Rose & Co. lithograph sign, and advertisement for 'Merchant Tailors', circa 1900, 26½in. high. (Robt. W. Skinner Inc.)          $325

'Schlitz Brewery' tin sign, circa 1915, 24in. diam. (Robt. W. Skinner Inc.)          $375

'White Rock' advertising tip tray, copy reads 'White Rock, The World's Best Table Water.' (Robt. W. Skinner Inc.)   $35

Large lithographed tin sign advertising Harvard Beer, circa 1910, 26⅜in. wide. (Robt. W. Skinner Inc.) $550

American 19th century sheet metal hatter's sign, 14in. high. (Robt. W. Skinner Inc.) $1,200

'Cafe' leaded glass window, in metal frame, circa 1900, 4ft.4in. high. (Robt. W. Skinner Inc.) $475

A shaving advertising sign, advertising 'Antiseptic Cup, Brush and Soap', circa 1910, 18¼ x 14in. (Robt. W. Skinner Inc.) $350

Player's Navy Cut Cigarettes. (Street Jewellery) $62

A metal 'El Roi-Tan' chromolithograph advertising sign, 24¼ x 20in. (Robt. W. Skinner Inc.) $100

Lithograph on tin, copyrighted by Paul Jones & Co., 1903, 28½ x 22¼in. (Robt. W. Skinner Inc.) $225

Late 19th century Clock Shop trade sign, iron and zinc painted, 23in. wide. (Robt. W. Skinner Inc.) $175

Tin advertising sign for 'Murphy Da-Cote Enamel', lithograph by H. D. Beach, Co., Ohio, circa 1925, 27 x 19in. (Robt. W. Skinner Inc.) $650

A late 16th century breast-plate of bulbous form, cut away at kidneys. (Wallis & Wallis)  $392

A composite suit of late 16th century cuirassier's half armor.  $1,562

A 17th century breast and bullet proof backplate, turned over borders and distinct medial ridge. (Wallis & Wallis)  $556

A 19th century red-lacquered kon-ito-odoshi nuinobe-do, with armor box. (Christie's)  $4,099

A Victorian Lt. Colonel's full dress uniform of The 2nd West York Artillery Volunteers. (Wallis & Wallis)  $607

A Victorian officer's uniform of The Yorkshire Hussars. (Wallis & Wallis)  $1,035

A 15th century Turkish breastplate, Krug, struck with the St. Irene arsenal mark. (Wallis & Wallis) $207

A French cuirassier's breast and backplate, both dated 1827. (Wallis & Wallis) $272

An articulated right-hand gauntlet, circa 1600, with flared cuff. (Wallis & Wallis) $76

A Georgian Grenadier Co. officer's short-tailed scarlet coatee of The East Norfolk Militia. (Wallis & Wallis) $256

A Victorian full armor and halberd, 19th century. $3,245

A Georgian officer's long-tailed scarlet coatee of The Royal Edinburgh Volunteers, circa 1805. (Wallis & Wallis) $492

# ARMS & ARMOR

A 19th century black lacquered kon-ito-sugake-odoshi
yokohagi-do, in a leather-
covered armor box.
(Christie's) $4,415

An 18th century Indo-Persian
body armor Char Aina of
4 plates. (Wallis & Wallis)
$133

A Lance-Corporal's khaki
service uniform of the
Rough Riders. (Wallis &
Wallis)          $319

A Victorian other rank's
full dress gray uniform
of The 13th Middlesex
(Queen's Westminster
Volunteer Rifles).
(Wallis & Wallis)
          $295

A Georgian officer's scarlet
short coatee of The 52nd
(Oxfordshire Light Infantry)
Regt., circa 1815. (Wallis &
Wallis)          $1,023

A Myochin suit of armor
dating from 1611. (Christie's)
$9,500

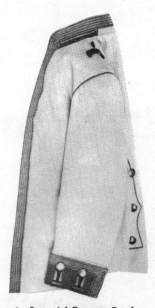

A Victorian suit of armor in the style of the 16th century, 67in. high. $5,896

A Victorian Squadron Sergeant Major's full dress part uniform of the Westmoreland & Cumberland Yeomanry. (Wallis & Wallis) $531

An Imperial German Cavalryman's parade uniform believed of the Garde du Corps. (Wallis & Wallis) $1,144

A complete Lt. Colonel's full dress uniform of The 15th (The King's) Hussars. $781

A pair of 18th century gold damascened Indian arm defences Bazu-Band, 12¾in., of solid shaped form. (Wallis & Wallis) $266

A cuirassier's three-quarter armor, circa 1640, the whole mounted on plastic dummy and wooden base. $7,370

A Nazi 2nd pattern Luftwaffe dagger, blade 10in., by Paul Weyersberg &
Co., wirebound plastic grip, plated pommel and crossguard, in its plate
sheath with two hanging rings. (Wallis & Wallis)          $100

A late 19th century Bavarian hunting knife with carved staghorn
handle, shallow diamond section blade 5¼in., steel crosspiece with
acorn finials and natural staghorn hilt. (Wallis & Wallis) $59

A 17th/18th century Moghul mutton fat jade khanjar with fine watered
steel double edged straight blade, the jade handle set with rubies in gold
mounts, 40.5cm. overall length. (Lawrence Fine Art)          $1,754

A mid 19th century Spanish plug bayonet, single edged straight blade
with spear point, blade 8½in., etched at forte 'FBCA Nl. De Toledo
Ano De 1843', in its fish skin covered wooden scabbard. (Wallis &
Wallis)          $174

A World War I knuckle trench knife, the single edged, curved, clipped
back blade 5¼in., etched Sutherland & Rhoden Sheffield, with one-
piece cast aluminium grip with finger holes, in its leather sheath.
(Wallis & Wallis)          $159

An 18th century Mahrattan double bladed dagger bichwa from
Tanjore, slender recurved double edged blade 8½in., with chiselled steel grip and pommel. (Wallis & Wallis)          $53

A Maine Gauche dagger, circa 1600, broad double edged blade 12in.,
with iron wirebound grip. (Wallis & Wallis)          $462

A Victorian heavy bladed Bowie knife, by George Butler & Co., straight spear pointed blade 7¾in., oval white metal crossguard and slab staghorn grip, in its blind tooled brown leather sheath. (Wallis & Wallis)$126

A wooden hilted version of the World War II pattern Commando dagger, tapering double edged blade 6¾in., in its brass tipped leather sheath. (Wallis & Wallis)                                    $81

A Victorian officer's staghorn hilt Skean Dhu of The 79th Highlanders, single edged spear blade 3½in., with scallop back edge. (Wallis & Wallis)                                    $118

A Georgian Naval officer's dirk, circa 1800, straight, double edged, tapering single fullered blade, 14in., with copper wirebound squared ivory hilt, in its leather sheath. (Wallis & Wallis)        $116

A Victorian romantic dagger, double edged spear pointed blade 5½in., the brass hilt heavily embossed with dolphin crossguard, in its brass sheath. (Wallis & Wallis)                              $108

A Swiss dagger, original blade of flattened diamond section, the angular gilt brass hilt with yewwood grip, the sheath cast and chased with the story of William Tell, overall length 16¼in., about 1570.
$40,898

An Italian Fascist Colonial police knife, double edged broad leaf-shaped blade 7½in., oval steel crosspiece, shaped black horn grips inset with oval brass cartouche. (Wallis & Wallis)            $139

A French M 1840 brass hilted sabre bayonet, recurving blade 20in. (Wallis & Wallis)                $118

A silver mounted Victorian dirk, Skean Dhu, single edged blade 4in., with scalloped back edge and natural staghorn tip shaped hilt with faceted Cairngorm set in beaded silver mount. (Wallis & Wallis)                $73

A large gold mounted Sumatran kris, wavy etched watered blade 15in., with scrolled top. Large one-piece carved ivory hilt, in its two-piece wooden scabbard. (Wallis & Wallis)                $406

An 18th century Moghul rock crystal khanjar, the slightly curved blade with inlaid decoration, the rock crystal handle carved in the form of a horse's head set with ruby eyes, 25.7cm. overall length.    (Lawrence Fine Art)                $669

A Victorian Scottish officer's dirk set of The Highland Light Infantry, scallop backed blade 11¼in., by Marshall & Aitken, Edinburgh, with corded black wood hilt and gilt thistle decorated mounts, with companion knife and fork. (Wallis & Wallis)                $830

A late Georgian Society dagger, shallow diamond section blade 5¼in., steel crosspiece with ball finials, bone hilt with fluted pommel, in its white metal mounted leather sheath. (Wallis & Wallis)    $151

A Georgian midshipman's dirk, diamond section blade 6½in., with turned ivory grip, in its copper gilt sheath. (Wallis & Wallis)$87

A World War I, 2nd pattern commando knife, double edged tapering blade 6¼in., by Wilkinson Sword, oval steel crossguard, diced brass hilt, in its leather sheath with brass chape. (Wallis & Wallis) $66

A World War I knuckleduster push dagger, spear blade 4½in., aluminium grip, stamped Robins Dudley, steel guard in its leather sheath with belt loop. (Wallis & Wallis)    $93

A Nazi Wehrmacht dress bayonet, by Robert Klaas, plated blade 9¾in., with diced black grips in its black painted metal scabbard. (Wallis & Wallis)    $87

A 17th/18th century Moghul jade khanjar with ribbed curved blade and with original red velvet sheath, 31cm., overall length. (Lawrence Fine Art)    $2,552

A Japanese dagger Hamidachi, blade 23.6cm., hira zukuri, itame hada, gunome hamon. Cord bound tsuka with shakudo fuchi kashira, in its black lacquered saya. (Wallis & Wallis)    $698

An early 18th century socket bayonet, broad, tapering double edged blade 17½in., plain socket, mounted with round wooden grip. (Wallis & Wallis)    $90

A Victorian pre 1881 Scottish officer's dirk set of The 78th Highlanders, scallop back edged blade 11in., in its patent leather covered wooden lined sheath, with companion knife and fork. (Wallis & Wallis)    $1,107

An officer's busby of The Alexandria, Princess of Wales's Own Yorkshire Hussars. (Wallis & Wallis) $471

A conical leather jingasa, lacquered to resemble a russet iron hachi, and a black lacquer jingasa. (Christie's) $724

A Prussian Guard Dragoon officer's pickelhaube, with leather and silk lining. (Wallis & Wallis)$750

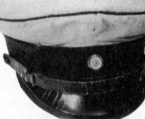

A cabasset, circa 1600, formed in one-piece, pear-stalk finial to crown, brass rosettes around base. (Wallis & Wallis) $159

An Imperial German officer's, Colonial Troops, tropical peaked cap with gray crown and blue cap band. (Wallis & Wallis)          $66

A Crimean period Russian black PL shako of The 29th Marines. (Wallis & Wallis) $405

A Prussian Guard Infantry-man Reservist's pickelhaube with brass mounts. (Wallis & Wallis)          $175

An officer's bell-top shako of The Uxbridge Yeomanry, circa 1831. (Wallis & Wallis) $1,107

A Victorian officer's helmet of The 7th (The Princess Royal's) Dragoon Guards. (Wallis & Wallis) $1,045

A Prussian trooper's helmet of The 2nd Cuirassier Regt., with gilt helmet plate and leather lining. (Wallis & Wallis)          $978

A Prussian Hussar officer's busby (Pelmutze), with gilt scroll helmet plate. (Wallis & Wallis)          $443

A Victorian officer's green cloth spiked helmet of The Durham Light Infantry. (Wallis & Wallis) $414

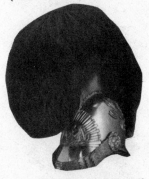

A Cuirassier's close helmet, circa 1600, two-piece skull with low comb and riveted border and hinged barred visor and peak. (Wallis & Wallis)          $665

An Edward VII officer's schapska of The 5th (Royal Irish) Lancers. (Wallis & Wallis)          $1,107

A Georgian officer's steel Roman type helmet of The Household Cavalry, circa 1820. (Wallis & Wallis)  $2,706

A Victorian officer's helmet of The Glasgow Yeomanry. (Wallis & Wallis)          $1,168

A kabuto with a thirty-two-plate russet-iron sujibachi fitted with copper gilt fuku-rin. (Christie's) $950

A trooper's lance cap of The City of London Imperial Yeomanry, Rough Riders, battle honors S. Africa 1900-02. (Wallis & Wallis)          $351

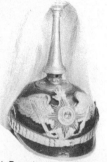

A Prussian Guard Infantry officer's pickelhaube, with gilt Garde eagle helmet plate. (Wallis & Wallis) $443

An Edward VII officer's lance cap of The 12th (Prince of Wales's Royal) Lancers with patent leather skull. (Wallis & Wallis) $1,012

A Victorian officer's blue cloth spiked helmet of The Volunteer Artillery. (Wallis & Wallis) $233

A Cuirassier's close helmet, circa 1620, two-piece skull, buff secured by sprung bottom catch. (Wallis & Wallis) $1,064

A 17th century russet-iron seven-plate hachi of Kara-kasa (Chinese hat) form, unsigned. (Christie's) $1,426

A Bavarian Infantry officer's pickelhaube, gilt helmet plate, fluted parade spike with black hair plume. (Wallis & Wallis) $371

A Prussian Infantryman's pickelhaube of The 91st Infantry Regiment, with leather lining. (Wallis & Wallis) $141

A late 16th century morion, brim with band of foliate decoration and roped edge. $2,044

An R.A.F. officer's full dress helmet, leather and fur skull and ostrich feather plume. (Wallis & Wallis) $164

A Victorian officer's blue cloth ball-topped helmet of The 5th Lancashire Artillery Vols. (Wallis & Wallis) $207

A Garde du Corps helmet, with tombak skull with German silver edging. (Wallis & Wallis) $1,783

A Victorian officer's helmet of The Hampshire Carabiniers with white metal skull and gilt mounts. (Wallis & Wallis) $283

A 19th century lacquered leather fire helmet with gilt metal lion comb. (D. M. Nesbit & Co.) $239

A late 16th century cabasset with brass plume holder. $1,258

A Prussian officer's pickelhaube of The 16th Dragoons, with leather backed brass chinscales. (Wallis & Wallis) $400

A Prussian other rank's helmet of The 6th Cuirassier Regt., with leather lining. (Wallis & Wallis) $572

An officer's straight-sided shako of a Victorian Yeomanry Regt., circa 1850. (Wallis & Wallis) $1,045

A Prussian Guard Infantryman's ersatz pickelhaube of black lacquered pressed felt, circa 1915. (Wallis & Wallis) $149

51

An Imperial Russian Artillery other rank's Kiva, circa 1880, contained in a leatherette hat box. (Wallis & Wallis) $1,090

A Cromwellian lobster tail helmet, the two-piece skull with suspension finial. (Wallis & Wallis) $556

A Royal Artillery Colonel's fur busby with white horse-hair plume, together with full-dress uniform. (Wallis & Wallis)      $185

A Bavarian Reservists' officer's spiked helmet with large gilt Royal Bavarian Arms helmet plate. (Military Antiques) $874

A brass 1843 pattern helmet of the 1st or The King's Dragoon Guards. (Wallis & Wallis)      $1,218

A Prussian General Staff officer's spiked helmet with large gilt Garde eagle helmet plate. (Military Antiques) $1,072

A Prussian Cuirassier officer's helmet with plated skull, gilt helmet plate and brass spike and mounts. (Wallis & Wallis) $1,090

A Prussian Foot Artillery NCOs ball-topped helmet with gilt eagle helmet plate. (Military Antiques) $247

A Victorian officer's gilt Albert pattern helmet of The 1st (King's) Dragoon Guards. (Wallis & Wallis) $1,044

A Cromwellian lobster tailed helmet, two-piece skull with medial ridge. Hinged peak with riveted borders and triple bar faceguard. (Wallis & Wallis)    $631

A Prussian officer's pickel-haube of The 1st Grenadiers, with patent skull, neckguard and peak. (Wallis & Wallis)    $586

An 1827 pattern Naval officer's cocked hat of black beaver, fan 10in., front 8½in. (Wallis & Wallis)    $436

A Bavarian officer's spiked helmet with large gilt Royal Bavarian Arms helmet plate. (Military Antiques)    $742

A late 19th century French officer's Kepi of a 'General De Brigade', in its original wooden box. (Wallis & Wallis)    $193

A Prussian Garde du Corps trooper's helmet, tombak skull with German silver edge mounts. (Wallis & Wallis)    $2,234

An officer's helmet of The Emperor's Bodyguard with large silvered parade eagle. (Military Antiques)    $3,025

A Baden Infantryman's ersatz (pressed tin) pickel-haube with brass spike and helmet plate. (Wallis & Wallis)    $114

An other rank's helmet of The Royal Horse Guards, with red horsehair plume, circa 1930. $597

A 16-bore officer's flintlock holster pistol, by D. Egg, 15in., barrel 9in., Tower proved, fullstocked with brass furniture. (Wallis & Wallis)          $475

A 6-shot .36in. Colt 1851 Navy single action percussion revolver ,13in., octagonal barrel 7½in., wooden grips with Maori style carving and iron backstrap. (Wallis & Wallis)          $931

A cannon barreled boxlock flintlock travelling pistol by E. Harris, circa 1785, 8in., turn off barrel 2¼in., Tower proved. (Wallis & Wallis)          $333

A 6-shot .44in. Russian Colt Bisley single action target revolver, 10½in., barrel 5½in., with molded hard rubber grips. (Wallis & Wallis)          $290

A 16-bore New Land pattern flintlock holster pistol, 15½in., barrel 9in., Tower proved. Fullstocked and regulation brass mounts. (Wallis & Wallis) $278

A 6-shot .36in. model 1851 third type Colt Navy single action percussion revolver, 13in., blued octagonal barrel 7½in. (Wallis & Wallis) $3,444

A 16-bore New Land pattern flintlock holster pistol, 15in., barrel 9in., Tower proved. Fullstocked, regulation stepped bolted lock. (Wallis & Wallis)
$290

A 5-shot 54-bore Tranter's patent double action percussion revolver, 12in., octagonal barrel 6in., Birmingham proved, engraved Wilkinson & Son. (Wallis & Wallis)      $455

A 20-bore nielloed silver mounted Cossack miquelet flintlock ball butted pistol, 17½in., barrel 11¾in.   (Wallis & Wallis) $514

A 13-bore Spanish miquelet flintlock belt pistol, 10½in., half octagonal barrel 6in., halfstocked, steel furniture and chequered grip. (Wallis & Wallis)      $417

A military wheellock pistol, octagonal barrel, wooden ramrod with steel tip, circa 1630, 21.3/8in.      $3,146

A 14-bore Austrian military percussion holster pistol, 16½in., barrel 9¾in., fullstocked, regulation brass mounts and muzzle band. (Wallis & Wallis)      $261

A .56in. Long Sea Service flintlock belt pistol, 19in., barrel 12in., Tower proved, with regulation brass mounts and brass tipped wooden ramrod. (Wallis & Wallis)          $707

A single shot 4 barreled flintlock holster pistol by Hunt, circa 1770, the barrels and furniture of light colored brass, 12½in., turn-off integral barrel unit 4½in. (Wallis & Wallis) $1,291

A composed 6-shot .36in. Colt London Navy 1851 single action percussion revolver, 13in., octagonal barrel 7½in., plated brass trigger guard and engraved backstrap. (Wallis & Wallis)                              $340

A late 18th century flintlock blunderbuss pistol, two-stage barrel belling at muzzle, breech struck with London proof marks and HM, signed H. Mortimer London, 14¼in.          $2,044

A 5-shot 54-bore Tranter's Patent 2nd model double trigger percussion revolver, 11½in., octagonal barrel 6½in., in its mahogany case. (Wallis & Wallis)                              $500

A 36-bore Belgian percussion target pistol, 16in., deeply rifled octagonal barrel 10in., Liege proved, halfstocked, adjustable set trigger and steel furniture. (Wallis & Wallis)                              $430

A 16-bore New Land pattern flintlock holster pistol, 15½in., browned barrel 9in., Tower proved. Full-stocked, regulation brass mounts and swivel ramrod. (Wallis & Wallis)                                    $569

A 6-shot 54-bore single action transitional reciprocating cylinder percussion revolver, 13in., octagonal barrel 6¼in. (Wallis & Wallis)                                    $472

A .56in. Sea Service flintlock belt pistol, 19in., barrel 12in., Tower proved, fullstocked regulation lock and brass mounts. (Wallis & Wallis)                                    $545

A double barreled Queen Anne style cannon barreled boxlock flintlock belt pistol with sliding pan cover by J. Rea, circa 1780, 8½in., turn-off barrels 2¼in., London proved. (Wallis & Wallis)            $1,230

A Joslyn percussion cap revolver, 5.7/8in. octagonal barrel, five-groove rifling, circa 1860, 12in. long.                                    $707

An 18-bore brass barreled flintlock Royal Mail coach pistol by Harding dated 1800, 15in., barrel 9in., engraved J. Harding. (Wallis & Wallis)                                    $861

57

A double barrel silver-mounted flintlock boxlock
pistol, breeches struck with London proof marks
and I G, circa 1760, 11¼in. long. $3,460

A 6-shot .36in. E. Whitney single action percussion Navy revolver, 13in., octagonal
barrel 7¾in., with plain walnut grips and
brass trigger guard. (Wallis & Wallis)
$204

An Austrian military flintlock holster pistol,
17in., barrel 10in., fullstocked, lock with
brass pan and regulation brass mounts.
(Wallis & Wallis)      $224

A 6-shot .44in. Starr double action percussion
revolver converted to central fire cartridge,
11½in., round barrel 5in., Continental proof
marks. (Wallis & Wallis)      $43

A mid 18th century silver-mounted rifled flintlock
holster pistol, blued two-stage barrel with muzzle
molding, signed Antoine Amain, 16¾in. long.
$1,022

A 12-shot .36in. Walch Navy single action percussion revolver, 12in., octagonal barrel 6in.,
patented 1858, with chequered two-piece grips
to angular butt. (Wallis & Wallis)   $725

A Dutch flintlock holster pistol, circular
barrel with top sighting rib of brass with
foresight, circa 1720, 20½in. $943

A 16-bore New Land pattern flintlock holster
pistol, 15½in., browned barrel 9in., Tower
proved. (Wallis & Wallis)      $922

A French percussion target pistol, 11in.,
screw-off octagonal barrel 3in., coil spring
propelled striker with side lugs, halfstocked
with fluted butt. (Wallis & Wallis)
                                  $279

A 16-bore New Land pattern flintlock holster
pistol, 15in., barrel 9in., Tower proved. Fullstocked, regulation brass mounts with swivel
ramrod. (Wallis & Wallis)        $239

A 5-shot Beaumont Adams patent double
action percussion revolver, 11½in., octagonal
barrel 5¼in., London proved. (Wallis & Wallis)
                                  $343

A Scottish flintlock pistol, three-stage barrel,
muzzle section slightly flared, lock plate signed T. Murdoch, circa 1760, 13¾in. long.
                                  $2,202

## POWDER FLASKS

# ARMS & ARMOR

A copper three-way powder flask, 4¼in., with hinged cavity for 12-bore balls. (Wallis & Wallis) $123

A 17th century powder horn, body of flattened cow horn, 11cm.     $1,474

A pistol sized copper powder flask 5in., with common brass top with blued spring and graduated nozzle. (Wallis & Wallis)     $55

Mid 19th century powder flask, translucent horn body, 7½in.     $95

A 17th century powder horn, body fashioned from section of antler, 12½in.     $589

A mid 19th century powder flask with measuring cup, 4¾in.     $80

An early 18th century Arab silver mounted powder flask Barutdan, 8in., of iron in coiled horn form. (Wallis & Wallis)     $72

A three-way embossed copper pistol sized powder flask 5in., with lacquered brass common top. (Wallis & Wallis)     $60

A 19th century Scottish dress powder flask with single suspension ring, 11in.     $324

# ARMS & ARMOR

A bag-shaped copper powder flask 5½in., the body stamped 'Sykes', with steel hanging ring. (Wallis & Wallis)     $55

A late 16th century South German powder flask of triangular form with incurved sides, 5.5/8in. high. $7,865

A gun sized copper powder flask 7¾in., with lacquered common brass top with blued spring. (Wallis & Wallis)     $65

An 18th century Persian priming powder flask, 5in. overall. $975

A 19th century powder flask, the bag-shaped body molded from bois durci(?), 5¼in.     $191

A gun-sized copper powder flask, 8¼in., nozzle graduated from 2¼ to 3 drams. (Wallis & Wallis) $91

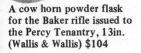

A cow horn powder flask for the Baker rifle issued to the Percy Tenantry, 13in. (Wallis & Wallis) $104

Late 16th/early 17th century powder horn with four small suspension rings, 23cm. $442

An early 19th century engraved powder horn, the body incised with a thistle encircling John Davis Royal Mail 1815, 12in. overall. $294

A Continental military flintlock doglock musketoon, circa 1740, 40in., barrel 25in., part octagonal part round and part of teardrop section, with standing rearsight. (Wallis & Wallis)      $292

A 28-bore percussion deer rifle built for a lady by Purdey, No. 1219, 44¾in., octagonal twist barrel 28in., shallow 12 groove rifling. (Wallis & Wallis)      $676

A late 18th century spring bayonet brass barrel flintlock blunderbuss, top flat signed H. W. Mortimer London, 31¼in.      $817

A brass barreled Irish flintlock blunderbuss with spring bayonet, 30¾in., half octagonal barrel 14½in., triangular bayonet 11½in., with roller bearing spring released by top thumb catch. (Wallis & Wallis)    $758

A .65in. Paget flintlock Yeomanry carbine, 31½in., barrel 16¼in., with Birmingham proofs, brass foresight and tall rearsight on barrel tang, the bolted lock with raised pan and roller on frizzen spring. (Wallis & Wallis)      $607

A double barreled 16-bore percussion sporting gun by George & John Deane, No. 516, 47in., browned damascus barrels 30in., engraved George & John Deane, on top rib, in its tooled pigskin lined close fitted brass bound mahogany case. (Wallis & Wallis)   $1,107

A .577in. two-band Enfield style Volunteer percussion rifle by J. Dickson & Son of Edinburgh, 50in., barrel 32½in., with ramp and ladder rearsight to 1100 yards. (Wallis & Wallis)                                        $731

A 20-bore percussion sporting rifle by Joseph Kuchenreuter converted from flintlock, 44in., octagonal barrel 29in., seven groove rifled and folding brass rearsight. (Wallis & Wallis)                                        $768

A 52-bore Westley Richards patent breech loading monkey tail, military style rifled percussion carbine, 41¼in., barrel 25in., Birmingham proved. (Wallis & Wallis)                                        $652

A .577in. two-band Enfield type Volunteer percussion rifle by E. Brooks, 49in., barrel 33in., Birmingham proved at 24-bore, ramp and ladder rearsight to 1100 yards. (Wallis & Wallis)                                        $465

A 28-bore tape primed Sharp's Patent breech loading percussion carbine, 39in., barrel 22in., with steel trigger guard. (Wallis & Wallis)                                        $264

A 10-bore India pattern Volunteer flintlock musket by Ketland, 54in., barrel 39in., Tower proved. Fullstocked, regulation brass mounts, steel ramrod and sling swivels. (Wallis & Wallis)                                        $678

# ARMS & ARMOR

An 18th century Persian miquelet flintlock gun, 42½in. octagonal barrel 28¾in., with chiselled ribs to swollen muzzle, fullstocked, with external mainspring. (Wallis & Wallis)          $266

A Moroccan snaphaunce gun Kabyle, 65in., barrel 50in., with traces of silver inlay at breech. Fullstocked, stock with fish tail butt, iron trigger guard, and fish tail butt cap. (Wallis & Wallis)          $305

A .65in. Elliott's pattern military flintlock carbine, 44in., barrel 28in., Tower proved, with regulation brass mounts, steel ramrod and saddle bar with lanyard ring. (Wallis & Wallis)   $872

A small brass barreled flintlock blunderbuss, circa 1675, three stage swamped barrel 13½in., the octagonal breech with raised band and sighting groove. (Wallis & Wallis)          $900

A 1796 pattern type British military 10-bore carbine, converted to percussion, 41½in., barrel 26in., Tower proved, with regulation brass mounts and full length open ramrod channel. (Wallis & Wallis)          $572

A .65in. Paget's pattern military flintlock carbine 32in., barrel 16in., proved with crowned MR, with regulation brass mounts, steel ramrod, saddle bar, sling swivels lanyard rings. (Wallis & Wallis)          $626

A 10-bore Brown Bess military flintlock musket 62½in., with 46in. barrel, Tower proved, complete with its triangular socket bayonet. (Wallis & Wallis)          $2,152

A 20-bore Bavarian percussion rifle built in the form of a wheellock 39½in., rifled octagonal barrel 26in., probably from an earlier weapon. (Wallis & Wallis)                              $472

A flintlock musketoon by I. Dafte, circa 1680, 36½in., swamped stepped barrel 22¼in., London proved on octagonal breech, with brass furniture. (Wallis & Wallis)                              $545

A 13-bore single barrel percussion sporting gun, 47in., half octagonal barrel 31in., halfstocked, foliate engraved lock and dolphin hammer. (Wallis & Wallis)                              $264

A late 17th century Continental wheellock sporting rifle, 43½in., octagonal barrel 31½in., with eight-groove rifling. Fullstocked, carved cheekpiece and engraved steel trigger guard. (Wallis & Wallis)                              $2,610

An Irish military style brass barreled flintlock blunderbuss, 30½in., half octagonal barrel 14¼in., with bell mouth. (Wallis & Wallis)                              $528

A .56in. flintlock birding gun by Wilson, circa 1760, with take-down barrel and extending butt, 53¼in., swamped barrel 41in., London proved. (Wallis & Wallis)                              $1,526

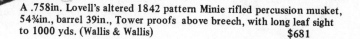

A .758in. Lovell's altered 1842 pattern Minie rifled percussion musket, 54¾in., barrel 39in., Tower proofs above breech, with long leaf sight to 1000 yds. (Wallis & Wallis)                              $681

An 1889 pattern Naval cutlass, straight, single edged blade 27½in., with black painted ribbed iron grip, in its leather scabbard. (Wallis & Wallis)                     $82

A 19th century wakizashi with kuroronuri scabbard, signed Goto Mitsuhisa, the blade 48.5cm. long. (Christie's)   $3,784

A Victorian Naval officer's sword, slightly curved blade 32in., by Galt & Co., Portsmouth, copper gilt hilt with folding side guard, and brass wirebound white fish skin covered grip, in its leather scabbard. (Wallis & Wallis)                     $118

An aikuchi wakizashi with a nashiji hilt and scabbard, the blade unsigned, Mino School, 16th century, 42.9cm. long. (Christie's)   $1,261

An early 17th century Northern European swept hilt rapier with long double-edged blade and single fuller, 52.5/8in. long.     $1,226

A Soviet Military shasqua, curved, single edged blade 31½in., brass mounted bird's head hilt with spiral wood grip, in its canvas covered wooden scabbard. (Wallis & Wallis) $123

A Victorian Cavalry officer's sword, circa 1880, of The 6th Dragoon Guards, slightly curved blade 34in., by Hawkes. (Wallis & Wallis)                     $412

An early 19th century Malayan sword klewang, broad, single edged blade 19¼in., swollen towards tip, with carved and polished one-piece black horn hilt. (Wallis & Wallis)          $65

A Georgian Tower Warder's sword, straight, plain double edged tapering blade 31½in., with copper gilt hilt with side shell guard and iron wirebound grip. (Wallis & Wallis)   $152

A mounted wakizashi with tamago-nuri scabbard, the blade signed Kuni Mizuta, 46.9cm. long. (Christie's)          $1,892

An early 18th century smallsword, hollow ground blade, the forte gilded and engraved with scrolls, punched Bradish Cutler Essex Bridge (?), with silver wirebound grip, 39in. long, and scabbard.          $471

A 19th century Moro sword barong, heavy single edged pointed blade 17½in., widest at center point with brass mounted wooden hilt bound with woven cords. (Wallis & Wallis)          $94

A Polish sword, circa 1800, broad very slightly curved single edged bi-fullered blade 30½in., fluted one-piece ebony grip and in its green leather covered scabbard with steel mounts. (Wallis & Wallis)          $418

A 19th century Chinese shortsword, tapered double edged blade 16in., of flattened diamond section with reeded wooden grip, in its tortoise-shell covered wooden sheath. (Wallis & Wallis)          $145

A Japanese sword katana, blade 85.1 cm., signed Ieyasu with two mekugi ana Midare hamon, itame hada, in its mother-of-pearl fleck lacquered saya. (Wallis & Wallis)                    $1,537

An 1821 pattern Heavy Cavalry officer's un-dress sword, slightly curved, pipe-back, clipped back blade 34in., with wirebound fish skin grip, in its steel mounted leather scabbard. (Wallis & Wallis)     $210

A Georgian Cavalry officer's sabre of The 10th Light Dragoons, circa 1790, curved, single edged blade 31½in., with steel hilt with flat knucklebow. (Wallis & Wallis)             $1,168

A European late 18th century Horseman's sword, plain, single edged curved blade 29½in., with brass half-basket hilt, pierced shell guard, fluted base and diced black ebony grips. (Wallis & Wallis)           $279

A presentation mameluke sword with curved single edged blade, made by Anders, Pall Mall, 38in. long, circa 1856, the scabbard of iron with heavy gilt brass furniture.                   $1,573

A French 1833 model Naval cutlass, slightly curved single edged blade 26½in., iron solid half basket guard and original grip. (Wallis & Wallis)                                       $97

A Georgian 1796 pattern E.I.C. Infantry officer's sword, straight single edged tapering blade 32in., by Osborn, with copper gilt hilt and simulated wirebound grip, in its black painted leather covered metal scabbard. (Wallis & Wallis)     $305

A Japanese sword wakizashi, blade 38.8cm., signed Kanemoto, gunome hamon, broad nie clusters and distinct mokume hada, in its red lacquered saya. (Wallis & Wallis)     $462

A Victorian Naval flag officer's sword, fitted with special pattern, straight square shanked blade, 30½in., by Henry Wilkinson, with copper gilt hilt and copper wirebound white fish skin covered grip. (Wallis & Wallis)     $212

A Victorian 1831 pattern general officer's mameluke sabre, curved clipped back blade 30½in., by Pulford & Co., London, with rounded grip secured with two rosettes, in its brass scabbard. (Wallis & Wallis)     $492

A Victorian 1821 pattern Rifle Corps officer's sword, slightly curved single edged blade 32in., by Moore & Co., in its steel scabbard. (Wallis & Wallis)     $125

A Japanese sword katana, blade 63.8cm., signed Hokinokami Fujiwara Hirotaka, broad gunome hamon with well defined Nie line, very tight itame hada. (Wallis & Wallis)     $1,599

# TSUBAS

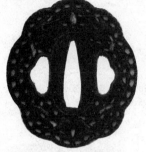

A Japanese pierced iron Nambam tsuba, 6.2cm., with gold nunome details. (Wallis & Wallis) $58

An 18th century circular iron tsuba with black patina, signed Echizen ju Kinai saku, 8.6cm. (Christie's) $832

An oval iron tsuba, 7.5cm., of mokko form chiselled with basket weave pattern. (Wallis & Wallis) $116

An iron jakushu tsuba of mokko form, 7.6cm.. (Wallis & Wallis) $92

A large Japanese pierced iron tsuba, 8.4cm., with flying geese inlaid with copper feet and a little gold nunome detail to wings. (Wallis & Wallis) $94

A 19th century oval Shibuichi tsuba, signed Unyensai Toshmitsu, 6.6cm. (Christie's) $330

A dark Shibuichi rounded-square tsuba, signed Hiromasa, mid 19th century, 6.7cm. (Christie's) $498

An irregular oval iron tsuba decorated in hikone-bori style, 7.3cm. (Christie's) $176

One of a pair of tsuba, Aizu Shoami School, 17th/18th century, 7.5cm. and 7.2cm. (Christie's) $332

A 17th century Mokkogata
iron tsuba, signed Izumi no
Kami Koike Naomasa,
7.5cm. (Christie's)$261

A fine Jakushu School iron
tsuba of squared form, 6cm.
(Wallis & Wallis)$168

An unsigned 19th century
oval Shibuichi tsuba,
6.4cm. (Christie's)
$141

A Mokkogata iron tsuba,
signed Yamashiro Kuniju
Umetada Mitsuyoshi,
8.4cm. (Christie's)
$297

A 19th century oval iron
tsuba, signed Choshu ju
Toyonobu saku (Okamoto
School), 7.9cm.(Christie's)
$330

An 18th century oval
shakudo-nanakoji tsuba,
unsigned, 7.1cm. (Christie's)
$261

A large iron mokko tsuba,
8.7cm., chiselled with a
laughing boy and dancing
frog beneath prunus. (Wallis
& Wallis)         $87

A Japanese iron Nara School
tsuba, 5.8cm. of irregular
form. (Wallis & Wallis)
$58

A large iron Kosukashi tsuba
of square form, 8.7cm., finely pierced in negative silhou-
ette. (Wallis & Wallis)
$209

A wooden painted Police truncheon, painted with crown, G.R., Manchester Town Arms and 'General Strike May 1926', with turned grip and leather wrist strap, 14½in. long. (Wallis & Wallis)     $32

A European, possibly German, 17th century fighting axe, broad blade with crescent shaped cutting edge, 8in. deep with forged socket mounted on an 18th century hardwood haft, length overall 38in.                    $162

An Edwardian camp axe used for the gralloch as well as small timber work and tent pegs, 15½in., crescent head 4½in. (Wallis & Wallis)          $93

A Partizan head, circa 1600, of plain form, raised central rib, small projecting side lugs, overall 23in. (Wallis & Wallis)     $138

A 19th century Indian scissors katar, 15in., hinged blades 7½in., with fold open when the grips are squeezed to reveal 6in. hidden central blade. (Wallis & Wallis)      $83

A Polish horseman's hammer, the head 16th century, the shaft later and some decoration added subsequently to the shaft, 21in. long, head 7¾in.                    $1,887

A 19th century Indian all steel axe zaghnal, 26in., heavy beak-shaped head with thickened tip surmounted by two brass tigers, on its steel haft with swollen grip finial and square spike to head. (Wallis & Wallis)                  $92

A Maori pointing staff Hani, 51in., carved overall with line and dentil decoration, including swirl patterns and mother-of-pearl eyes, the head carved as a stylized head with rudely pointing tongue. (Wallis & Wallis) $110

A 19th century Sudanese axe, 24¼in., on crescent head 6¾in., with trisula finial and bi-dent tip on its wooden haft covered with baby alligator skin retaining claws. (Wallis & Wallis) $92

A 19th century African Songe copper covered axe, 15¾in., iron head 4¾in. Haft entirely covered with sheet copper in relief. (Wallis & Wallis) $153

A 19th century Zulu rhino horn axe, 32½in., with shaped double edged steel head 11½in., on its 26½in. tapered rhinocerous horn haft with large swollen head. (Wallis & Wallis) $110

An early 19th century Indian all steel axe, crescent head 9¼in., with squared eye and shaped crest, steel haft and square section top spike. (Wallis & Wallis) $58

A Cogswell & Harrison thrust weapon of World War II design, triangular section blade 9½in.. Connected to a 'Gigli' wire, 24in. long, which may serve as a saw or garrotte, in its leather sheath. (Wallis & Wallis) $133

A Ken blade with itame-masame hada and medium suguba hotsure hamon of ko-nie, unsigned, 16th century, 27.1cm. long, in shirasaya. (Christie's) $551

# BAROMETERS

A Victorian stick barometer/thermometer by Chadburn Bros., Sheffield, 93cm. high. (H. Spencer & Sons) $272

A 19th century mahogany banjo barometer and thermometer, inscribed G. Selval. (H. Spencer & Sons) $310

Mid 19th century satinwood marine barometer by H. Hughes, London, 37in. high. $6,380

A barometer and thermometer with inset convex mirror and ivory turning handle. (Butler & Hatch Waterman) $359

A mahogany clock cum barometer, signed Willm. Terry London No. 285, 49in. high. $1,754

George III mahogany stick barometer, signed P. Caminada, Taunton, circa 1820, 38in. long. (Reeds Rains) $438

A Dutch inlaid mahogany triple tube barometer and clock, 51in. high. $1,595

Flame mahogany stick barometer by Worthington of London, 39in. long. (Ward & Partners) $1,178

# BAROMETERS

An early 19th century rosewood wheel barometer/timepiece, inscribed D. Gagioli & Son, 51in. high. $1,691

George III barometer/thermometer, by E. Wrench, London. (Michael Newman) $1,812

An early 19th century mahogany wheel barometer/timepiece, inscribed V. Zanetti, 50½in. high. $2,523

Late Georgian stick barometer by Roncketi, Manchester, 3ft.2in. high. (Capes, Dunn & Co.) $375

Early 19th century mahogany veneer barometer, France, 42in. high. (Robt. W. Skinner Inc.) $700

An old Admiral Fitzroy atmoscope barometer with 10in. circular face, 45in. high. (Vidler & Co.) $260

Early 19th century mahogany and satinwood inlaid stick barometer, 39in. high. (Stalker & Boos)$900

A Victorian mahogany banjo style wall barometer, face inscribed J. Amadio, 39in. high. (Stalker & Boos) $600

75

A large bronze incense burner in the form of a peach with a curled stalk, 23in. wide, Guangxu. $614

A bronze group of terriers, signed P. J. Mene, 8in. high. $1,316

Late Ming Dynasty gilt bronze censer with loop handles, 6.7/8in. wide. $2,587

A Ming Dynasty lacquered gilt bronze figure of a courtier, 16in. high. $1,131

Early 20th century Palmer Cox Brownie figural picture frame and framed lithograph on rococo base, 5¾in. high. (Robt. W. Skinner Inc.) $275

A large bronze head of Buddha, the face with rounded features, 22in. high, wood stand. $646

A Bergman cold-painted bronze group of an Arab trader and camel, Austrian, circa 1900, 6in. high. $702

A 17th/18th century splashed gilt bronze censer of oval section, 4¾in., with wood cover and stand. $1,697

Late 19th/early 20th century bronze Arctic bear and walrus, 7½in. long. (Robt. W. Skinner Inc.) $480

# BRONZE

A bronze figure of a naked woman, French, circa 1880, 33in. wide.  $1,734

A cold-painted bronze group of an Arab galloping on horseback, on a marble base, 7½in. high, Austrian, circa 1900. $760

Late 19th century bronze Egyptian Revival inkstand, supported on four lion-head hooved feet, 12¼in. long. (Robt. W. Skinner Inc.) $220

A bronze group of a little girl and her dog, signed A. G. Lanziroti, 20in. high, Italian, circa 1870, together with stand.  $3,465

A bronze statue of 'The Scout' by Prince Paul Troubetskoy, signed and dated 1911, 22in. high x 19in. wide. (Stalker & Boos) $4000

Late 17th century South German bronze figure of a lion, on a squared marble base, 9½in. high. $1,536

A Ming Dynasty gilt bronze figure of Buddha, seated in dhyanasana on a waisted lotus petal plinth, 9in. high. $808

An F. Preiss cold-painted bronze and ivory figure of 'The Archer', as a girl, 25.5cm. high. (H. Spencer & Sons)   $2,194

An 18th century large bronze vase with three lion mask handles, 25¾in. high. $1,212

# BRONZE

A bronze model of a seated rabbit, signed Tsunemitsu saku, Meiji period, 18.5cm. high. (Christie's)$661

Late 19th/early 20th century bronze figure of a hunter and his dog, by J. Heidepriem, Germany, 15.5/8in. high. (Robt. W. Skinner Inc.) $850

An 18th century parcel gilt bronze incense burner and cover, 8¼in. high. $646

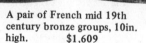

Mid 19th century bronze figure of Napoleon, after Canova, 27in. high. $1,389

A pair of French mid 19th century bronze groups, 10in. high. $1,609

A cold painted ivory and bronze figure of a mediaeval page, on onyx base, signed 'M. Munk, Vienna', circa 1900. $606

Bronze statue of a dancing nymph by Prof. Raffaelo Romanelli, the whole mounted on marble, 31in. high. (Stalker & Boos) $900

Late 19th/early 20th century bronze figure, La Source du Pactole , by E, Louis Picault, French, 30½in. high. (Robt. W. Skinner Inc.) $2,500

Late 19th century bronze oviform vase with trumpet-shaped neck, signed, 24.3cm. high. (Christie's) $315

# BRONZE

A 19th century French bronze sculpture of a standing man uncorking a bottle of wine, by Sarry, 25½in. high. (Stalker & Boos) $1,000

A bronze family of snipe by A. Dubucand, France, 10½in. long. (Robt. W. Skinner Inc.) $600

An F. Preiss cold-painted bronze, ivory and marble figure of 'Ecstacy', the whole raised upon a walnut stand, 128cm. high overall. (H. Spencer & Cons) $2,527

Pair of bronze figures of musician, by Claude M. Clodion, French School, 1738-1814, 14½in. high. (Robt. W. Skinner Inc.) $1,300

A 19th century heavily cast bronze broad oviform vase, decorated in niku-bori and takabori, 48cm. high. (Christie's) $788

A pair of bronze and gilt-bronze candlesticks of a man and a woman in 'Indian' costumes, 1ft.2in. high, circa 1860. $443

Late 19th century Oriental bronze and enamel eagle, Japan, 14in. high. (Robt. W. Skinner Inc.) $750

Russian bronze of a romantic couple, by Vasili Gratchev, 1880, 15½in. high. (Robt. W. Skinner Inc.) $1,700

An 18th century Sino-Tibetan gilt-bronze figure of Avalokitesvara seated, 8.9/16in. high. $7,438

Late 19th century bronze of a hunting dog, unsigned, the attached base stamped 'Susse Fres', 17in. high. (Robt. W. Skinner Inc.) $2,300

A bronze model of a tiger attacking a stag, signed Seiya, Meiji period, 28.3cm. long. (Christie's) $709

Bronze figure of a dromedary, inscribed Barye, 9½in. long. (Robt. W. Skinner Inc.) $475

A bronze of an altar boy, signed Delagrange, on square green marble base, 18¼in. high. (Robt. W. Skinner Inc.) $650

Late 19th century Russian bronze equestrian group, by E. Lanceray, 19½in. long. (Robt. W. Skinner Inc.) $3,750

An 18th century bronze figure of a Lohan, standing, his arms folded beneath a flowing robe, 5¾in. high. (Lawrence Fine Art) $158

A Tibetan gilt bronze figure of Gautama Buddha, sealed, 9in. high. (Lawrence Fine Art) $288

An Art Deco bronze and ivory figure group 'Friends' by D. Chiparus, signed, 41cm. high. (H. Spencer & Sons) $4,655

One of pair of 19th century ormolu perfume burners, 13½in. high, and fitted with sweetmeat bowls. (Capes, Dunn & Co.) $542

A bronze model of a monkey, signed Hidefuji, Meiji period, 25.6cm. high. (Christie's) $867

A bronze group of two tigers attacking an elephant, signed Seiya, Meiji period, 27cm. long. (Christie's) $394

A bronze model of an eagle, alighting on a wave-lashed rocky outcrop, 25in. high. (Lawrence Fine Art) $691

Japanese 20th century silver inlaid Oriental bronze urn, 14in. high. (Robt. W. Skinner Inc.) $750

Bronze figure of a pheasant, by Jules Moigniez, French, 20¾in. high. (Robt. W. Skinner Inc.) $1,850

A Lorenzl silvered bronze semi-draped female figure, on green onyx pedestal base, 11½in. high. (Capes, Dunn & Co.) $179

A Ming Dynasty gilt bronze figure of Guixing, 15¾in. high. $1,051

Late 19th century Russian bronze equestrian group, by E. Lanceray, 18in. long. (Robt. W. Skinner Inc.) $4,250

A Continental painted bronze figure of an Arab standing on a prayer rug, 10in. high. (Lawrence Fine Art) $245

A Mediterranean bronze
hawk, ribbed disc rests on
head of standing bird, 11in.
high. (Robt. W. Skinner Inc.)
$475

Pair of bronze gilt candelabra. (Brogden & Co.)
$403

Bronze female figure entitled
Truth by Bertram Mackennal.
(Bonham's) $13,800

A Chinese bronze crane,
19th century or earlier,
5ft.8in. high. (Woolley &
Wallis) $1,417

One of a pair of bronze
baluster vases, signed, 21¾in.
high. (Lawrence Fine Art)
$498

A bronze figure of Cupid
mounted on a white mar-
ble plinth, 12in. high.
(P. Wilson & Co.)
$235

A bronze, 'Le Fauconnier
Marocain', signed P. J. Mene,
French, 30in. high. (Robt. W.
Skinner Inc.) $2,600

Pair of French bronze figures
of Mercury and Venus, after
Bologna, 33.5in. high.
(Neales) $520

A gilt bronze and ivory group
of three young girls, signed
Chiparus, 6in. high. (Lawrence
Fine Art) $1,108

A French bronze figure of a young girl, on a Louis XVI style bronze plinth, 26in. high. (Lawrence Fine Art) $304

Pair of 19th century well patinated bronze groups. (Reeds Rains) $1,131

A patinated bronze of an ostrich, signed Jul. Hahnel, 21in. high. (Robt. W. Skinner Inc.) $125

A large bronze bacchanalian figure, signed F. Duret, 36in. high. (P. Wilson & Co.) $1,342

A pair of baluster-shaped bronze vases, signed Aug. Moxeau, 10in. high. (P. Wilson & Co.) $73

A 19th century European bronze satyr fountain, pale green patina, 20½in. high. (Robt. W. Skinner Inc.) $900

A bronze group, 'Charity', after Carrier, 41cm. high. (H. Spencer & Sons) $504

A bronze figure by Bertram Mackennal entitled Circe. (Bonham's) $15,360

One of a pair of Louis XVI gilt bronze andirons. $3,348

# BRONZE

A bronze figure of a thorough-bred stallion, signed by Isadore Bonheur, 49cm. high. (H. Spencer & Sons)     $990

A bronze group of a retriever by Philip Johann Hammeran, German, circa 1860, 8in. wide.     $152

A French parquetry ormolu and porcelain egroigneur, with a pair of lidded inkwells, 14in. wide, circa 1870.     $618

A large bronze Marli horse, after Coustou, on an ebonized plinth, 22in. high. (Lawrence Fine Art)     $586

Bronze statue of Zeus, signed Graefner Fec, mounted on a gray marble plinth, 23in. high. (P. Wilson & Co.) $823

A bronze of a bearded Galileo on an oval black marble base, 17in. high. (Anderson & Garland)     $650

A bronze hu of lozenge baluster shape, the rim lappet shaped, 15½in. high. (Lawrence Fine Art)     $415

Late 19th century patinated bronze of a Turk with a falcon, European, 16in. high. (Robt. W. Skinner Inc.)     $475

A bronze jardiniere of trefoil compressed globular form, signed, 14½in. diam. (Lawrence Fine Art)     $498

# BRONZE

Late 19th century Austrian bronze chicken on a dish, 7.1/8in. diam. (Robt. W. Skinner Inc.) $350

A bronze group of a fox pouncing on a duck, signed P. Hammeran, 9in. wide. $153

A bronze model of a tiger, its stripes inlaid with gold, malachite and carnelian, probably Ming Dynasty, 4¼in. long. (Lawrence Fine Art) $277

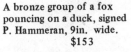

A bronze group of Chiron and Apollo, 17in. high. (Lawrence Fine Art) $805

Bronze of an Arab slave trader, indistinctly signed M. Fuch, 27¾in. high. $5,280

A 19th century French bronze figure of a stag with raised head by a tree trunk, inscribed P. J. Mene, 14½in. high. (Geering & Colyer) $992

Mid 19th century champleve tear-drop shaped vase, Japanese, 15in. high. (P. Wilson & Co.) $170

A 14th century French mediaeval bronze crucifix, 8in. high. (Robt. W. Skinner Inc.) $1,500

Late 19th century Oriental bronze vase with four raised owl faces, 9¼in. high. (Robt. W. Skinner Inc.) $325

A George II mahogany plate bucket with brass liner and loop handle, 1ft.1½in. high by 1ft. diam., circa 1755. $1,107

A George III mahogany peat bucket of cylindrical tapering form with two brass bands and handle, 15in. diam. (Lawrence Fine Art) $574

An early 19th century mahogany oval pail bound with brass, 33cm. wide. (H. Spencer & Sons) $339

A leather fire bucket, America, circa 1806, 13¼in. high. (Robt. W. Skinner Inc.) $2,100

A small oak butter tub with two plain brass bands, 8in. high. (Lawrence Fine Art) $134

One of a pair of mahogany wall buckets, each of D-shaped form, 1ft.5½in. high, circa 1800. $1,009

A George III mahogany and brass bound plate bucket with brass swing handle, 18in. high. (Dreweatt Watson & Barton) $524

A Victorian leather fire bucket, decorated with coat-of-arms. (D. M. Nesbit & Co.)$207

An early 19th century pail made up of bands of mahogany and fruitwood, brass bound, 29cm. diam. (H. Spencer & Sons) $587

Victorian mahogany tea caddy, 1840. (British Antique Exporters) $178

A wooden footwarmer, the cherry case with molded rims and wire bail handle, America, 1796, 9¼in. wide. (Robt. W. Skinner Inc.) $325

Small Victorian oak box with carved decoration, 1860. (British Antique Exporters) $38

A George III oval tea caddy, the lid centered by a leaf-cast silver handle, circa 1795, 5in. high. $3,203

Victorian oak double sided coal box, 1880. (British Antique Exporters) $43

Early 19th century melon-shaped tea caddy in stained beech with a stalk handle and iron lockplate, 5½in. high. $1,724

Victorian mahogany coal box with carved front, 1880. (British Antique Exporters) $71

Painted staved wooden cheese/butter box, possibly Shaker, circa 1830, 6½in. diam. (Robt. W. Skinner Inc.) $475

Victorian mahogany coal box, 1860. (British Antique Exporters) $71

A domed top rosewood ground box depicting Eridge Castle, 9.7/8in. wide. (Geering & Colyer) $159

Early 19th century decorative prisoner-of-war straw-work sewing case, 33cm. wide. $558

Early 19th century French prisoner-of-war bone dominoes casket. $1,276

One of a pair of Federal mahogany veneered knife boxes, probably England, circa 1810, 14¼in. high. (Robt. W. Skinner Inc.) $1,000

Early 19th century German stobwasser lacquered and painted snuff box, 4in. diam. (Capes, Dunn & Co.) $361

Late 19th century Japanese lacquered table top cabinet, 18¼in. wide. (Robt. W. Skinner Inc.) $475

A 19th century melon form burled wood caddy, 6½in. high. (Stalker & Boos) $400

'Day's Soap' wood box with label, box held 60 bars of soap, circa 1875, 16in. wide. (Robt. W. Skinner Inc.) $70

Chinese Peking enamelled three-tier covered box, 7in. high. (Stalker & Boos) $100

Mid 19th century rosewood, brass inlaid writing box, China, 19¾in. wide. (Robt. W. Skinner Inc.)$600

Late 19th century oak roll-top lap desk, America, 10½in. high, case 14 x 14in. (Robt. W. Skinner Inc.) $350

An English burr-walnut nautical writing box, 13½in. wide.          $430

A George III rolled paperwork tea caddy of elongated hexagonal shape, circa 1775, 7in. wide.$1,072

An 18th century melon fruitwood tea caddy, England, 6in. high. (Robt. W Skinner Inc.) $2,200

Early 19th century French prisoner-of-war bone dominoes casket, containing a set of double nines dominoes. $1,276

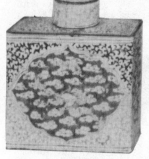

Late 19th century Komai rectangular cabinet, signed Nihon koku Kyoto ju Komai sei. (Christie's) $394

Chinese Peking, enamelled, covered tea caddy, with multi-colored dragon reserve panel decoration, 4½in. high. (Stalker & Boos) $195

Late Georgian mahogany tea caddy, sarcophagus shaped with ebony and boxwood cable inlay, 8¼in. wide. (Capes, Dunn & Co.) $58

A Spanish Gothic elaborately banded box, covered in red velvet, 26½in. wide. (Robt. W. Skinner Inc.) $900

A Georgian mahogany cheese cradle with carved acanthus leaf decoration. (Dee & Atkinson) $558

Late 18th century Scandinavian pine painted box with molded rectangular lid, 22in. wide. (Robt. W. Skinner Inc.) $500

A 19th century red lacquered leather box, China, with brass latch, 29in. wide. (Robt. W. Skinner Inc.) $375

A violin case by W. E. Hill & Sons, London, the satinwood case inlaid with stained fruitwood and mahogany stringing and boxwood parquetry. $8,791

A domed top rosewood ground box, depicting a ruined castle, 10½in. wide. (Geering & Colyer) $195

An 18th century set of surgeon's instruments, engraved Ambulance de S M. L'Empereur. (Christie's) $9,882

Early 18th century figured mahogany knife box with shaped front, 14½in. high. (P. Wilson & Co.) $353

A 19th century Indian coromandel games cabinet of waved rectangular shape, 17¼in. long. (Lawrence Fine Art) $242

A George III mahogany and boxwood strung rolled paper tea caddy, some of the glass panels cracked, 9in. wide. (Christie's) $118

A mahogany fly cabinet by Hardy Bros., Alnwick, containing four hundred flies, 46.5 x 34.5 x 22cm. (Lawrence Fine Art) $483

A George III mahogany tea caddy in the Chippendale style of ogee shape, 10½in. long. (Lawrence Fine Art) $321

A Georgian oak glove box, dated 1724, 13in. long. (Lawrence Fine Art) $187

A lacquer dressing table cabinet decorated in gilt, 14in. wide. (Lawrence Fine Art) $648

Mid 19th century tortoiseshell tea caddy, the interior with two-lidded compartments flanking a well, 12in. long. (Lawrence Fine Art) $217

A coaching casket, the main key operates a musical chime against unofficial intrusion, 16 x 10½ x 6in. (Wallis & Wallis) $545

A 19th century Japanese lacquer leaf-shaped box, 9½in. long. (Robt. W. Skinner Inc.) $1,600

A George III engraved ivory octagonal workbox, the sides with silvered metal carrying handles, 12in. wide. (Christie's) $224

A small Victorian brass-bound coromandel wood dressing case, circa 1870. $1,249

A 19th century papiermache cabinet with rising top enclosing compartments, 11 x 12½in. high. (Dreweatt Watson & Barton) $393

A Victorian dressing case with four glass boxes and seven jars, maker's mark WN London, 1863. $3,748

Late 19th century Japanese gold lacquered box, 4½in. long. (Robt. W. Skinner Inc.) $1,050

A black painted tin five division fly box containing approx. 250 gut-eyed salmon flies, 12in. wide. (Christie's) $508

Late 19th century/early 20th century walnut veneered rectangular cigar box with hinged lid, 8 x 11in. (P. Wilson & Co.) $198

Early 20th century lady's oak writing cabinet with folding writing slope. (P. Wilson & Co.) $281

An ivory and shibayama nest of boxes of rectangular shape, 10in. wide. (Lawrence Fine Art)      $1,247

An apothecary's chest, the mahogany case with recessed brass carrying handle, 10¾in. wide. (Lawrence Fine Art)      $771

A George III mahogany cutlery box, together with 71 pieces of cutlery. (Lawrence Fine Art)      $1,466

Early 19th century Regency papier-mache chinoiserie sarcophagus-shaped tea caddy, 7½in. high. (P. Wilson & Co.)      $103

An 18th century pear-shaped walnut tea caddy with hinged cover, 5½in. high. ((P. Wilson & Co.) $995

An ivory veneered Georgian tea caddy with a brass handle and tortoiseshell decoration. (Martel Maides & Le Pelley)      $930

A 19th century French, lobed oval, mother-of-pearl, gilt metal mounted casket fitted with three scent bottles. (Osmond Tricks) $390

Early 19th century American painted pine pipe box with single drawer and brass pull, 13¼in. high. (Robt. W. Skinner Inc.) $2,000

A George III mahogany sewing box with canted corners, 11in. long. (Lawrence Fine Art) $167

A 19th century ivory inlaid spice cabinet with eighteen drawers, India, 18in. high by 33in. wide. (Robt. W. Skinner Inc.) $1,000

A Regency sewing box covered in stamped red leather, with hinged cover, 11½in. wide. (Dreweatt Watson & Barton) $379

A George III mottled green stained pearwood tea caddy, as a gourd, with hinged cover, 13cm. high. (H. Spencer & Sons) $2,193

An Anglo-Indian ripple effect coromandel workbox with hinged lid, 17in. wide. (Reeds Rains) $283

A Georgian mahogany cutlery box of serpentine shape with brass handles, 9in. wide. (Lawrence Fine Art) $265

Late 18th century miniature chip carved chest with brass and iron strap mountings, Spain, 13½in. wide. (Robt. W. Skinner Inc.) $550

Early 20th century cloth and papier-mache Santa candy container, 11.1/8in. high. (Robt. W. Skinner Inc.) $210

A George III mahogany and scrolled paperwork tea caddy with hinged cover, dated 1789, 17.5cm. wide. (H. Spencer & Sons)$570

A Daylight Kodak, circa 1891, small and rare roll film camera for daylight loading, twenty-four exposures, 2¼ x 3¼in. (Robt. W. Skinner Inc.) $1,150

A tropical Ernemann Strut camera, 1920's, 3¾ x 5¾in., with Tessar 16.5cm. f4.5 lens No. 341760.. $404

No. 1 Kodak, serial 10607, circa 1889, factory loaded for one hundred exposures, 2½in. diam. (Robt. W. Skinner Inc.) $850

Cine-Kodak model A serial 01298 with motor drive unit. Eye and waist level finder, circa 1924, and instruction book. (Robt. W. Skinner Inc.) $175

Boston Camera Co. Hawkeye, 4 x 5in., 'Lunch Box Detective Camera'. (Robt. W. Skinner Inc.) $250

No. 6 folding Kodak Improved, circa 1893, B & L Universal lens in B & L Iris diaphragm shutter. (Robt. W. Skinner Inc.) $900

Kodak Colourburst 50 Instant camera, circa 1980, together with a Colourburst 100 Instant camera. (Robt. W. Skinner Inc.) $15

Eastman View No. 2, improved model of Century View and Empire State No. 2 with Scientific Lens Co. 6½ x 8½in. f16 wide angle lens. (Robt. W. Skinner Inc.) $250

Cine-Kodak serial 00908, circa 1923, original Kodak 16mm. projector, with eye level finder only. (Robt. W. Skinner Inc.) $225

Kodak Chevron 620 camera, with adaptor kit to convert Chevron to use 828 film, circa 1953. (Robt. W. Skinner Inc.)     $185

A Compass miniature camera, Swiss, circa 1937, with Kern CCL 35mm. f/3 lens.     $569

Kodak Retina Reflex S camera, type 034, circa 1959. (Robt. W. Skinner Inc.)     $65

No. 4-A Speed Kodak model A, serial 383, roll film camera for pictures 4¼ x 6½in., circa 1908. (Robt. W. Skinner Inc.)     $300

Burton's clinicamera, 3¼ x 4¼in., used by dentists, with instruction book, circa 1935. (Robt. W. Skinner Inc.)     $70

Boy Scout Kodak camera, case, instruction book, circa 1930. (Robt. W. Skinner Inc.)     $110

No. 3B Quick Focus Kodak model B, circa 1906. (Robt. W. Skinner Inc.)     $130

A Gandolfi field camera, English, circa 1970, with Kodak Ektar 12in. f4.5 in Universal Synchro shutter No. 5, 8 x 10in.     $569

Mid 19th century sliding-box wet-plate camera, with Petzval-type lens signed Lerebours et Secretan No. 8186, 6¼ x 4½in.     $657

An Erac bakelite pistol camera, English, circa 1931, fixed focus Meniscus lens, 18mm. square exposures on 20mm. roll film. $227

A reflex telephoto outfit made by Heinz Kilfitt Co. of Munich, for safari, sports and nature photography, circa 1950. (Robt. W. Skinner Inc.) $400

Girl Guide Kodak, with case, made for the Girl Guide Assoc., circa 1934. (Robt. W. Skinner Inc.) $240

A Stirn concealed vest camera, circa 1890, with conical lens for 6.4cm. diam. pictures.    $506

No. 3A Panoram Kodak, with Meniscus lens in revolving shutter for 3¼ x 10.3/8in. pictures, circa 1926. (Robt. W. Skinner Inc.) $175

Blair 4 x 5in. folding Hawkeye, with No. 2 Hemispherique Rapide lens in B & L diaphragm shutter, with fitted Blair roll holder. (Robt. W. Skinner Inc.) $200

Vanity Kodak, red V.P. Kodak series III camera in matching satin lined hard case, circa 1928. (Robt. W. Skinner Inc.) $160

Cine-Kodak K-100 Turbet, with Cine-Ektar 152mm. f4; 63mm. f2; 25mm. f1.4, and instruction book, circa 1958. (Robt. W. Skinner Inc.)    $192

Kodak Reflex 1A twin lens camera, f3.5 lens in Flash Kodamatic shutter, 620 film, circa 1947. (Robt. W. Skinner Inc.)    $70

A Regency ten-light chandelier with S-scroll arms, 4ft. by 2ft.10in., circa 1810. $5,775

An eight-light bronze chandelier cast after a design by Carlo Bugatti, circa 1910, 165cm. high. (Christie's) $1,632

A Sabino frosted glass chandelier, in three tiers, 1930's, 65cm. approx. maximum height. $1,206

A hammered copper lantern with tinted amber glass, by Gustav Stickley, circa 1912, 22in. high. (Robt. W. Skinner Inc.) $2,200

A cut glass ten-light chandelier, the saw-tooth corona hung with pendant drops, fitted for electricity, 38in. high. (Christie's) $3,663

A patinated wrought-iron and textured amber glass chandelier, attributed to Gustav Stickley, 28in. diam. (Robt. W. Skinner Inc.) $3,500

A 19th century ormolu and bronze eight-light hanging dish light, 34in. high. (Christie's) $1,270

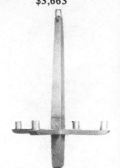

One of a pair of Dora Gordine four-branch chandeliers in hand-wrought tin of cruciform shape, inscribed 1932, 73cm. high. (Christie's) $2,041

A Georgian style glass chandelier, of six S-scroll ropetwist arms, 2ft.6in. diam. $2,310

# AMERICAN

A Tiffany pottery molded vase, New York, the mottled dark green and blue glaze on white ground, 7½in. diam., circa 1908. (Robt. W. Skinner Inc.) $600

A decorated Marblehead pottery pitcher of wide cylindrical form with angled handle, signed by A. Baggs, 6.1/8in. high, circa 1915. (Robt. W. Skinner Inc.) $1,400

A Grueby Art pottery vase, Mass., the matte green glaze initialled AVL, 5½in. high, circa 1905. (Robt. W. Skinner Inc.) $900

A decorated Marblehead vase of swollen cylindrical form tapering towards base, signed H.T., circa 1915, 5.3/8in. high. (Robt. W. Skinner Inc.) $350

A Marblehead pottery Art Deco vase, initialled AEB, circa 1930, 6in. diam. (Robt. W. Skinner Inc.) $90

A Grueby Art pottery molded vase/lamp base, circa 1905, 12¾in. high. (Robt. W. Skinner Inc.) $2,700

Late 19th century Chelsea Keramics Art Works pottery vase, Mass., 10½in. high. (Robt. W. Skinner Inc.) $1,800

A Grueby Art pottery vase of swollen cylindrical form tapering towards base, 11¾in. high, circa 1905. (Robt. W. Skinner Inc.) $3,700

A 20th century molded pottery 'steamboat' pitcher, cast after the original by George E. Ohr, 9in. high. (Robt. W. Skinner Inc.) $250

# CHINA

# AMERICAN

A Benington Parian teapot with domed cover, squirrel finial, 5in. high. (Robt. W. Skinner Inc.)  $350

A flint glaze enamel poodle with basket of fruit, Bennington, Vermont, 1849-58, 8½in. high. (Robt. W. Skinner Inc.)  $1,300

A Grueby Art pottery vase, Mass., with oatmeal glaze, 3.5/8in. high, circa 1905. (Robt. W. Skinner Inc.)  $300

Early 20th century blue Hampshire pottery vase, 3in. high. (Robt. W. Skinner Inc.)  $175

Saturday evening girl's pottery covered jar, Mass., circa 1914, 5¼in. high. (Robt. W. Skinner Inc.) $1,800

A Rookwood pottery vase with wide mouth, Ohio, circa 1882, 13½in. high. (Robt. W. Skinner Inc.)  $1,200

Rookwood pottery vase with sterling silver mesh, Ohio, 1893, 11¾in. high. (Robt. W. Skinner Inc.)  $1,500

A Newcomb College Art pottery pitcher, by Henrietta D. Bailey, circa 1919, 5¾in. high. (Robt. W. Skinner Inc.) $450

A Rookwood vellum vase, Ohio, style no. 1658B, initialled ETH, 1910, 14.7/8in. high. (Robt. W. Skinner Inc.)  $3,500

ARITA

One of a pair of 17th century Arita blue and white dishes, 35.7cm. diam. (Christie's) $1,024

A Japanese Arita porcelain two-handled bowl on a cast ormolu rococo base, 9in. diam. (Woolley & Wallis)    $676

Late 17th century Arita blue and white dish, base slightly cracked, 60.6cm. diam. (Christie's) $1,010

Late 17th century Arita blue and white octagonal bulbous bottle vase, 39.1cm. high. (Christie's) $7,128

Pair of late 17th century Arita blue and white oviform jars and shallow domed covers, approx. 19cm. high. (Christie's) $1,188

Late 19th century Arita baluster jar and high domed cover with seated karashishi finial, 64cm. high. (Christie's) $1,010

An Arita dish, painted in underglaze blue with fenced peonies enriched in iron red, green and gilt, 18in. diam. (Lawrence Fine Art) $129

A late 19th century Arita figure of a boy drummer, 7in. high.    $329

Late 17th century Arita blue and white dish, 40cm. diam. (Christie's) $346

A Belleek oval basket with cover of creamy lustrous glaze, 8in. diam. (Peter Wilson)      $366

A Belleek clover-shaped basket with woven three-strand base, 5in. diam. (Peter Wilson)      $231

A Belleek circular basket, the whole with a creamy lustrous glaze, circa 1891-1926, 8¾in. wide.      $2,587

One of a pair of Belleek flasks, circa 1863-91, 6in. high.      $862

A Belleek earthenware spirit flask for rum, 1863-91, printed dog and harp mark, 11¾in. high.      $739

One of a pair of Belleek ewers of waisted form, black printed marks, second period, 20cm. high. (Christie's)      $484

A Belleek standing figure of Hibernia, the whole unglazed with details picked out in iridescent glaze, 43.5cm. high. (Lawrence Fine Art)      $1,844

A Belleek, tinted, circular basket and cover, with four-strand base, circa 1891-1926, 8in. wide.      $1,724

One of a pair of Belleek vases modelled as conch shells supported on the backs of flying fish, 11.5cm. high. (Christie's)      $459

# BERLIN

One of twelve Berlin plates with pierced borders, blue sceptre, KPM and iron-red KPM marks, circa 1835, 24.5cm. diam. (Christie's) $885

A pair of Berlin porcelain male and female figures of grape harvesters in 18th century costumes, 8¾in. high. (Geering & Colyer) $682

One of twelve Berlin plates with pierced basketwork borders, circa 1780, 24cm. diam. (Christie's) $3,285

A mid 19th century KPM Berlin plaque of Albert, Prince Consort, 12 x 10¼in. $657

A Berlin lacquered faience green-ground vase, mock Chinese mark, Funcke's factory, circa 1720, 50cm. high. (Christie's) $821

A Berlin porcelain plaque, painted after Rembrandt with a portrait of his mother, impressed sceptre and KPM mark, circa 1880, 40 x 34.5cm. (Christie's) $665

One of a pair of KPM Berlin double-handled vases, circa 1880, 8¼in. high, red printed mark. $657

Pair of 19th century Berlin porcelain oviform pedestal vases and covers, 14in. high. (Edgar Horn) $585

One of a pair of KPM Berlin plaques, mid 19th century, 23cm. diam. $1,152

A Bow figure of a pedlar, in the white, 1755-56, some restoration, 6¾in. high.          $985

Pair of Bow figures allegorical of 'Freedom' and 'Matrimony', circa 1755-60, 7in. high.
$887

A figure of a bagpiper, probably Bow, early 1750's, 14.8cm. high.
$605

A Bow figure of a cook in white turban and apron, holding a plate with a ham and chicken, circa 1762, 16.5cm. high. (Christie's)
$665

A Bow bocage candelabrum group, circa 1765, crossed swords in underglaze blue, 10in. high.   $1,909

A Bow figure of a sports-man wearing a tricorn hat, circa 1752, 5¼in. high.
$308

A Bow figure of Neptune astride a dolphin, circa 1765, 19.5cm. high. (Christie's) $555

A Bow figure of a musician, circa 1765, anchor and dag-ger marks, 8¼in. high.
$763

A Bow figure of Cybele or Ceres, standing on high scrol-led base attended by a recum-bent lion, 9in. high.
$517

A Bow figure of a cat seated
on its haunches, circa 1756,
6.5cm. high. (Christie's)
$1,210

Pair of Bow figures of Jupiter
and Neptune, symbolising
Air and Water, circa 1755-60,
6¼in. high.     $591

Bow porcelain figure of a
tawny owl, circa 1760,
8¼in. high. $4,320

One of a pair of Bow sauceboats with fluted double-C
scroll handles, 22.5cm. wide.
(Lawrence Fine Art)
$1,372

A pair of Bow porcelain seated
figures of a monk and a nun
reading, 5.7/8in. high. (Geering
& Colyer)     $99

A Bow blue and white
sauceboat, circa 1760, 7in.
long.     $371

A Bow candlestick group,
personifying the Continents
of Asia and Africa, circa 1762,
6in. high.     $320

Pair of Bow figures of a shepherd
and shepherdess, circa 1765,
with anchor and dagger marks,
6in. high.     $677

A Bow candlestick group of
musicians, after Meissen
models by Kaendler, circa
1760-65, 8¾in. high.
$714

A Bristol christening mug of barrel form, circa 1775, painted X in blue, 10 in gilding, 3in. high.
$322

A Champion's Bristol figure of a classical female, circa 1773, 10in. high.
$774

A Bristol pottery mug with a column inscribed The Peace of Europe, 4.1/8in. high.
$179

A Bristol dessert basket of oval shape with pierced lattice sides, 1770-72, 8½in. over handles. $516

A Bristol sauceboat with foliate scroll handle, circa 1775, 7¼in. over handle.
$387

One of a pair of Bristol dessert dishes of diamond shape, circa 1775, 10in. long.
$645

A Bristol delft farmyard plate, painted with a bright yellow and blue cockerel, circa 1730, 22.5cm. diam. (Christie's)     $822

A Bristol pottery tankard inscribed The Peace of Amiens, 4¾in. high.
$105

A Bristol polychrome delft circular dish, 34cm. (Lawrence Fine Art) $297

# BRITISH

### CHINA

One of a pair of Bevington flower-encrusted vases with gilt scroll handles, modelled as oval baskets, blue cross and JB marks, circa 1860, 24cm. wide. (Christie's) $302

A Foley 'Pastello' earthenware vase of flattened globular shape, England, circa 1900, 16.5cm. high. (Christie's) $375

A large Wemyssware (Plichta) figure of a pig seated on its haunches, circa 1930, 43cm. long. (Christie's) $605

A Foley 'Intarsio' earthenware vase of ovoid shape with two handles, England, circa 1900, 26cm. high. (Christie's) $562

A pair of Samuel Alcock gilt busts of George IV and The Duke of York, circa 1830, 21.5cm. and 22.5cm. high. (Christie's) $665

A Pilkington's Royal Lancastrian vase of ovoid form, decorated by G. M. Forsyth, circa 1905, 29cm. high. (H. Spencer & Sons) $313

A Foley 'Intarsio' large vase and cover of baluster form, 40cm. high. (H. Spencer & Sons) $686

A Bilston patch box of circular form, circa 1775, 1¾in. diam., slight damage. $1,010

A Louis Wain model of a cat, printed and painted marks, 6¼in. high. (Christie's) $187

A circular muffin dish and cover, the base with red griffin mark, 23.5cm. diam. (Christie's) $532

A Birmingham Patriotic bonbonniere, the lid modelled in high relief with a recumbent lion, a yellow cloth between his jaws, on which lies a pink putto holding drumsticks and drum, circa 1765, 2¾in. wide. $1,047

A Parianware figure of a young girl wearing a bathing costume, 15in. high. (Reeds Rains) $98

A tall waisted coffee pot and cover, the base indistinctly inscribed, 25.5cm. high. (Christie's) $822

Bowl and pitcher with floral decoration, 1920. (British Antique Exporters) $80

An iridescent pottery vase with Art Nouveau pewter mounts and handles, 7in. high. (Capes, Dunn & Co.) $72

An L. N. Fowler ceramic phrenology bust, English, circa 1855, 11in. high. $1,391

A Shelley three-piece pottery nursery teaset, designed by Mabel Lucie Atwell, circa 1925, teapot 19.5cm. high, cream-jug 13cm. high and the sugar basin 10cm. high. (Christie's) $406

A Victorian decalomania vase and cover of inverted baluster form, 37cm. high. (H. Spencer & Sons) $587

# CHINA

Early 19th century Canton bowl decorated with picture panels of figures in garden and court room settings, 22in. diam. (P. Wilson & Co.) $968

A yellow-ground Canton enamel saucer dish, seal mark and period of Qianlong, 8.7/8in. $452

A Cantonese large porcelain punch bowl of flared circular form, 36cm. diam. (H. Spencer & Sons) $395

A Cantonese cylindrical vase with wooden stand, 18in. high. (Dee & Atkinson) $317

Pair of mid 19th century Canton famille rose baluster vases, mounted as oil lamps, 72cm. high. $1,123

A Cantonese vase with carved hardwood stand, 17in. high. (Dee & Atkinson) $243

One of a pair of Cantonese garden seats decorated with domestic scenes. (Worsfolds) $1,140

A baluster-shaped vase with two gilt figures of monkeys clasping fruit as handles, 13½in. high. (Butler & Hatch Waterman) $426

One of a pair of 19th century Canton garden seats of barrel shape of hexagonal outline, 49cm. high. (Lawrence Fine Art) $2,161

# CHINA

CANTON

A 19th century Canton porcelain bowl finely painted, gilded and enamelled, 11½in. diam. (Reeds Rains) $513

Late 19th century Canton bowl, 10in. diam. (P. Wilson & Co.) $144

A 19th century blue and white Canton porcelain reticulated basket with undertray, China, 10in. long. (Robt. W. Skinner Inc.) $600

A painted Canton famille rose vase with spade-shaped body, Jiaqing, 23½in. high. $1,501

Pair of Canton vases, 24in. high. (Dee & Atkinson) $762

A 19th century baluster shaped vase with hand-painted decoration and gilt handles, 23½in. high. (Butler & Hatch Waterman) $497

One of a pair of Canton hexagonal baluster jars and covers, 25in. high. $7,007

A Canton enamel fish tank decorated in famille rose enamels, 25.5in. (Woolley & Wallis) $1,298

One of a pair of 19th century Chinese vases, the handles in the form of flat kylins, 14in. high. (Banks & Silvers) $290

# CHINA

## CHELSEA

A Chelsea silver shaped oval dish painted in a bright palette, circa 1752, 24.5cm. wide. (Christie's) $3,367

A Chelsea decagonal teabowl and saucer, painted in iron-red and gilt, circa 1750. (Christie's) $2,177

One of a pair of Chelsea bough pots, each of fluted D section, circa 1756, 7in. high. $774

A Chelsea mug of baluster form, circa 1752-56, painted red anchor, 14cm. high. $1,478

One of a pair of Chelsea plates, iron-red anchor marks, circa 1755, 9in. diam. (Christie's) $770

A Chelsea figure of an ostler wearing a flowing white coat, black hat and black shoes, red anchor mark, circa 1755, 13cm. high. (Christie's) $5,806

A Chelsea plate, red anchor mark, circa 1755, 8¼in. diam. (Christie's) $660

A Chelsea-Derby porcelain figure of a shepherdess, circa 1765/70, 9¼in. high. (Geering & Colyer) $565

A Chelsea 'Hans Sloane' plate, circa 1754-55, red anchor mark and numeral 35, 23.5cm. diam. $1,848

A Chelsea-Derby teacup with entwined handle, and saucer, by James Bamford, circa 1775. (Neales) $493

A 'Girl in a Swing' gold-mounted scent bottle and stopper, 1751-54, 8.5cm. high. (Christie's) $1,572

One of a pair of Chelsea octagonal oblong dishes, red anchor period, circa 1750, 12½in. wide. (Christie's)$1,760

One of a pair of Chelsea-Derby custard cups and covers, interlaced A and anchor in gold, circa 1775, 3.1/8in. high. (Neales)        $609

A pair of Chelsea 'red anchor' figures, modelled as a peasant woman and a rustic youth, circa 1755, 7¼in. high.          $10,010

A Chelsea mug, the body painted with bouquets, circa 1752-56, 5½in. high.          $985

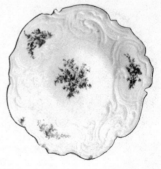

One of a pair of Chelsea artichoke tureens and covers, circa 1755, 16cm. high overall. (Christie's)          $19,354

A Chelsea gold mounted scent bottle modelled as the infant Bacchus giving Cupid a drink, circa 1765, the mounts circa 1830, 8.5cm. high. (Christie's)          $363

One of a pair of Chelsea 'red anchor' dishes, mid 1750's, 8¾in. diam.        $572

A Chinese Daoguang porcelain circular dish painted in green with the border painted in colors, 34cm. diam. (H. Spencer & Sons) $196

Mid 17th century blue and white wine-pot and cover of barrel shape, 17cm. high. (Christie's) $1,570

Early 17th century blue and white 'kraak' saucerdish, 34.5cm. diam. (Christie's) $1,239

Early 17th century blue and white garden seat of barrel shape, 40.5cm. high. (Christie's) $1,322

A 19th century Chinese circular fish bowl, painted in colored enamels, with two shi-shi blue glazed handles, 18in. diam. (Banks & Silvers) $1,667

A famille verte tall vase with liner, 17in. high. (Dee & Atkinson) $209

Mid 17th century blue and white shallow plate, encircled Xuande six-character mark, 19.6cm. diam. (Christie's) $4,959

Mid 17th century spherical unglazed pottery rice-wine jug, together with two similar, China, 10.5cm., 16.5cm. and 18cm. high. (Christie's) $172

Early 17th century blue and white 'kraak' saucerdish, 29cm. diam. (Christie's) $1,322

An 18th century Chinese porcelain circular charger, 38.5cm. diam. (H. Spencer & Sons)     $256

Mid 17th century blue and white globular hexagonal teapot and a cover, 12cm. high. (Christie's)
$1,322

One of a pair of Chinese octagonal-shaped 19th century famille rose wall plates, 9in. diam. (P. Wilson & Co.)     $38

Mid 17th century transitional blue and white cylindrical brushpot, 21.5cm. high. (Christie's)
$1,983

Mid 17th century blue and white urinal, the handle in form of a weasel biting in the cup-shaped mouth, 20cm. high. (Christie's)
$1,074

A 19th century majolica Chinese style garden seat in the form of a bundle of bamboo canes. (Bearnes)
$1,320

A 19th century Export porcelain Fitzhugh wash bowl, decorated in blue and gold, China, 16in. diam. (Robt. W. Skinner Inc.)     $750

Chinese export porcelain cider jug with intertwined twig handle, 11in. high. (Stalker & Boos)
$1,700

Mid 17th century blue and white shallow plate, encircled Xuande six-character mark, 19.6cm. diam. (Christie's) $1,983

A Clarice Cliff 'Blue Trees' fan-shaped vase with stepped flange handles, 33.8cm. diam. (Christie's) $270

A superb wall plaque by Clarice Cliff painted with a scene inspired by Diaghilev's costume design for The Ballet Russe. (Christie's) $10,000

Newport pottery Clarice Cliff 'applique' teapot and cover, 6in. high. (Reeds Rains)$582

A Clarice Cliff 'Sungay' single-handled 'Lotus' vase, circa 1930, 29.5cm. high. (Christie's) $675

A Clarice Cliff 'Night and Day' geometric shaped circular plate, circa 1930, 24.5cm. wide. (Christie's) $472

A Clarice Cliff 'Bizarre' 'Gayday' single-handled 'Lotus' jug, circa 1930, 29.7cm. high. (Christie's) $405

A Clarice Cliff 'Bizarre' vase, the ribbed body of ovoid shape with a broad neck, circa 1930, 25.5cm. high. (Christie's) $1,890

Part of a Clarice Cliff 'Fantasque' coffee service hand-painted in the 'Summer House' design, circa 1930, coffee pot 20.5cm. high. (Christie's) $1,012

A Clarice Cliff jar and cover, boldly painted in blue, purple, yellow, pink, gray and black, 24.5cm. high, 1930's. $497

A Coalport circular plate with swing handle signed with initials G.P., 9in. diam. (Anderson & Garland) $97

A Coalport tapered scent bottle with scroll handle, 5in. high, circa 1830. (Anderson & Garland)  $124

Part of a John Rose, Coalport, tea service of thirty-one pieces, circa 1810.  $1,971

A Coalport two-handled pot pourri vase and cover, the body of double gourd shape, circa 1835, 51cm. high. (Christie's) $605

Pair of Coalport 'Named View' vases and covers, each painted by E. O. Ball or P. Simpson, circa 1900, 14½in. high.  $431

A Coalport globular shaped pot pourri vase on three scroll feet, 6in. high. (Anderson & Garland) $91

One of a pair of Coalport vases, underglaze blue CD mark, 9¾in. high, circa 1830. (Anderson & Garland) $650

One of a pair of John Rose, Coalport, ice pails, covers and liners, circa 1805, 10¼in. $6,160

One of a pair of Coalport vases, painted with bouquets of flowers, 18.5cm. high. (Lawrence Fine Art) $171

# COPELAND

A Copeland table center-piece, two cherubs holding grapes supporting a center basket, 52cm. long. (Andrew Grant) $928

A Copeland Transvaal War tyg, circa 1900, 5¾in. high. $108

A Copeland & Garret figure of a recumbent spaniel, green printed mark, circa 1833-47, 7¾in. long. (Christie's) $1,540

A Copeland Parian bust of 'The Veiled Bride', made for the Crystal Palace Art Union, 14½in. high. $985

A large pair of Copeland vases, each painted by C. F. Hurten, signed, circa 1870, 19¾in. high. $3,225

A Copeland vase and cover, the ovoid body painted by L. Besche, signed, circa 1880, 15in. high. $1,612

A Copeland Parian group of 'The Sleep of Sorrow and the Dream of Joy', after the original sculpture by Rafaelle Monti, circa 1875, 18½in. high. $645

Late 19th century Copeland ironstone canted rectangular carving dish with gravy well, 21¼in. wide. (Dreweatt Watson & Barton) $177

A Copeland Parian bust of a young woman with flowing hair, 23in. high. (Outhwaite & Litherland) $650

A Davenport porcelain plate, the center circular panel painted with a view of 'Peak Tenerife', 23.5cm. diam, (H. Spencer & Sons) $218

A Davenport porcelain cabinet plate of shaped circular form, 24cm. diam. (H. Spencer & Sons)     $76

One of a pair of Davenport porcelain dessert plates, printed marks in brown. (H. Spencer & Sons) $261

A Davenport pottery Toby jug, impressed Davenport over an anchor and numbered 2, 24.5cm. high. (H. Spencer & Sons) $125

A Davenport porcelain garniture of three two-handled vases of baluster form, one 46.5cm. high, the other two 42cm. high. (H. Spencer & Sons) $3,270

A Davenport stone china ice pail, liner and cover. (H. Spencer & Sons) $632

A Davenport pottery plate of dished circular form, inscribed Longport over an anchor in red, 24cm. diam. (H. Spencer & Sons) $163

A Davenport porcelain bough pot with pierced gilt ring handles. (H. Spencer & Sons) $261

A Davenport porcelain plate of shaped circular form, printed mark in underglaze blue, 24cm. diam. (H. Spencer & Sons)     $76

A Davenport porcelain dish, the central oval panel painted with a view of 'The Bridge over the Peneus, at Larissa', 29cm. wide. (H. Spencer & Sons) $316

A Davenport porcelain trio of a coffee cup, tea cup and saucer, printed registration mark in underglaze blue. (H. Spencer & Sons) $56

One of a pair of Davenport porcelain dessert dishes, with printed marks in brown (H. Spencer & Sons) $261

A Davenport creamware bough pot and pierced cover with rustic molded handles. (H. Spencer & Sons) $403

A Davenport pottery Toby jug, seated wearing a black tricorn hat, 24.5cm. high. (H. Spencer & Sons) $141

A Davenport porcelain cup and saucer painted with cabbage roses in pink and gilt, together with coffee cup and plate. (H. Spencer & Sons)$119

A Davenport porcelain plate of shaped circular form, printed mark in underglaze blue, 23.5cm. diam. (H. Spencer & Sons)$109

A Davenport porcelain cup and saucer, standard printed mark in red. (H. Spencer & Sons) $41

A Davenport porcelain plate, the center panel painted with a view of 'Scarborough', 24cm. diam. (H. Spencer & Sons) $337

A Dedham pottery elephant charger, Mass., circa 1929, 12in. diam. (Robt. W. Skinner Inc.) $900

Early 20th century Dedham pottery cylindrical pitcher in grape pattern, 4½in. high. (Robt. W. Skinner Inc.) $700

Early 20th century Dedham pottery plate with Fairbanks house, 8½in. diam. (Robt. W. Skinner Inc.) $2,200

Late 19th century Dedham pottery vase with oxblood and black glaze, 7¼in. high. (Robt. W. Skinner Inc.) $1,200

Early 20th century Dedham pottery turkey trivet, 6in. diam. (Robt. W. Skinner Inc.) $400

Late 19th century Dedham pottery experimental drip vase, 6¼in. high. (Robt. W. Skinner Inc.) $500

Early 20th century Dedham pottery plate, stamped and dated 1931, 8¾in. diam. (Robt. W. Skinner Inc.) $1,600

An early 19th century Dedham pottery oak block pitcher, 5¾in. high. (Robt. W. Skinner Inc.) $900

A Dedham pottery round serving tray with rabbit pattern, signed by Maude Davenport, circa 1910, 13½in. diam. (Robt. W. Skinner Inc.) $1,308

119

# DELFT

Late 18th century Delft charger, probably Holland, with cobalt blue stylized floral decoration, 14in. diam. (Robt. W. Skinner Inc.) $400

A London delft blue and white inscribed and dated posset-pot and cover, 1691, 24cm. wide. (Christie's) $3,871

A London delft portrait charger, painted in blue, manganese and yellow, circa 1690, 35cm. diam. (Christie's)$2,661

An 18th century polychrome delft lion, Netherlands, 3.5/8in. long. (Robt. W. Skinner Inc.)$150

A blue and white delftware stem cup, dated 1717, 8cm. high.    $518

One of a pair of Dutch Delft leaf dishes, blue VH/3 marks probably for Hendrick van Hoorn at the Three Golden Ash Barrels, circa 1765, 21cm. wide. (Christie's) $3,285

A London delft blue and white Merryman plate, circa 1752, 20cm. diam. (Christie's)  $338

Late 18th century Dutch Delft fluted vase of octagonal baluster form and cover, 36cm. high, HL mark. (Lawrence Fine Art)    $78

An 18th century blue and white delft charger, signed '12' in underglaze blue on back, 13½in. diam. (Robt. W. Skinner Inc.) $350

Late 18th century blue and white Delft charger, signed P on back, Netherlands, 13½in. diam. (Robt. W. Skinner Inc.) $250

Late 18th century blue and white delft rabbit, 3¾in. long. (Robt. W. Skinner Inc.) $100

A Brislington delft Royalist portrait charger, circa 1680, 34cm. diam. (Christie's) $11,491

A 19th century polychrome Delft shield-shaped wall plaque, Netherlands, 22½in. high. (Robt. W. Skinner Inc.) $450

An English delftware puzzle jug, 6½in. high. $1,320

A Dutch Delft tobacco jar, the base with the mark of De Drie Klokken factory, 10½in. high, 18th century. $1,546

A 17th century English delft charger, painted in bright yellow, brown, green and blue, 32cm. (Lawrence Fine Art) $972

A delftware salt, probably Bristol, of circular section, circa 1730, 2¼in. high. $800

An octagonal London delftware Royal portrait dish, circa 1690, 8½in. across. $1,084

121

A De Morgan lustre vase, decorated in ruby lustre with fish swimming against pale amber waves, 15.6cm. high, 1888-97.    $482

A De Morgan lustre bowl, decorated by Fred Passenger, circa 1900, 19cm. diam. $425

A De Morgan vase, decorated by Joe Juster, 1880's, 31.2cm. high.$2,128

A De Morgan charger, decorated by Chas. Passenger, 1890's, 41.5cm. diam. $9,223

A De Morgan lustre vase, decorated by Fred Passenger, 1890's, 32.6cm. high. $1,135

A De Morgan plate, decorated by F. Farini, 1890, 22.8cm. diam.    $652

A De Morgan lustre vase, decorated by James Hersey, impressed Sand's End mark, painted initials and numbered 2227, 21.1cm. high, 1888-97. $425

A De Morgan lustre bowl, decorated by Fred Passenger, circa 1900, 19.2cm. diam. $312

A De Morgan vase decorated in shades of mauve, green, blue and turquoise with panels of flowers, 1890's, 15.6cm. high. $397

A Derby 'Pale Family' figure of a seated girl, circa 1756-58, 4¾in. high. $369

A Derby armorial shaped oval dish from The Duke of Hamilton service, circa 1790, 36.5cm. wide. (Christie's) $1,089

A Derby figure of a bagpiper, Wm. Duesbury & Co., circa 1768, 21cm. high. (Christie's) $423

Pair of Derby 'Mansion House Dwarfs', circa 1820, incised No. 227, 6¾in. high. $1,010

Late 18th century Derby figure of the actor David Garrick as Tancree, 9½in. high. (Woolley & Wallis) $660

Pair of Derby figures of Mars and Minerva, circa 1760, 6½in. high. $395

Late 18th century Derby figure of St. Philip, 10in. high (hands repaired). (Woolley & Wallis) $506

Pair of Derby figures emblematic of Spring and Summer, circa 1765, 5in. high. $517

A Derby figure of a gold-finch, circa 1775, 5½in. high. (Christie's) $660

A Royal Doulton china wall plaque, 'The Jester'. (Reeds Rains)$185

One of a pair of Doulton stoneware vases with globular bodies, by Eliza Simmance, 23cm. high, 1900's. $351

Doulton Lambeth stoneware cylindrical biscuit barrel with silver rim, swing handle and cover. (Reeds Rains)$216

A Doulton Lambeth stoneware jug by Florence Barlow, the cylindrical body incised with horses, 1874. 26cm. high.    $307

A Doulton stoneware jug and a pair of beakers with silver mounts, by Hannah Barlow, London 1878, the jug 24cm. high. (Lawrence Fine Art)     $634

A Royal Doulton polychrome glazed stoneware fountain figure designed by Gilbert Bayes, 1934, 105cm. high. (Christie's) $1,875

A Royal Doulton figurine, 'Butterfly', 6in. high. (Dee & Atkinson)          $333

Pair of Royal Doulton cylindrical vases painted by L. Johnson, 30cm. high. $701

A Royal Doulton figure 'Marietta', modelled as a young girl wearing fancy dress, 21cm. high, impressed date (19)33. $468

Large Doulton mask head jug, 'The Clown', red hair D5610, 6½in. high. ( Abridge Auctions ) $2,375

A Doulton Lambeth stonware lemonade jug by G. Tinworth with Hukin & Heath silver mount, London 1877, 9½in. high, and a matching beaker. (Reeds Rains) $270

A character jug, Field Marshall, the Rt. Hon. J. Smuts, 7in. high. (Outhwaite & Litherland) $1,276

A Royal Doulton 'George Robey' jug and cover, 1926, 9½in. high. $4,681

Six miniature Royal Doulton character jugs, the largest 1½in. high. (Reeds Rains) $393

A small Royal Doulton figure, 'Bluebird', 11.5cm. high, indistinct impressed date (19)28? $219

A Royal Doulton figure of 'The Old King' marked'A' on base, 10½in. high. (Reeds Rains) $33

A pair of Doulton stoneware vases, decorated by Hannah Barlow, 26cm. high. (H. Spencer & Sons)$460

Royal Doulton loving cup, one of a limited edition of 1000, signed Noke & Fenton, 10in. high. (Peter Wilson) $305

**DOULTON**

A metal mounted lidded
Doulton Lambeth jug,
decorated by H. Barlow,
dated 1881, 9in. high.
(P. Wilson & Co.)
$301

Royal Doulton figure group,
'Pride of Shires', HN2528,
circa 1930, 9¼in. high.
(P. Wilson & Co.)
$176

A Royal Doulton china
figure, 'Pickwick', HN
556, 7in. high. (Capes,
Dunn & Co.) $141

A Doulton Lambeth silicon
stoneware match holder
with silver rim, hallmarked
Chester 1893, 3in. diam.
(P. Wilson & Co.) $157

Royal Doulton figure,
'Spring Flowers', HN 1807,
designed by L. Harradine,
1937, 7¼in. high. (P. Wilson & Co.)   $207

A miniature Royal Doulton
character jug, 'Paddy', D
5926 designed by H. Fenton in 1938, 3½in. high.
(P. Wilson & Co.) $71

Royal Doulton group, 'Leda
and the Swan', HN 2826, designed and sculpted by R.
Jefferson, 2nd in the Myths
and Maidens series of five.
(P. Wilson & Co.)$805

One of a pair of Doulton
stoneware vases by Frank
Butler, 1890's, 17¼in.
high.·      $3,732

Royal Doulton figure,
'Roseanna', HN 1926, designed by L. Harradine,
1940, 8in. high. (P. Wilson
& Co.)      $183

A Royal Doulton figure, 'The Hinged Parasol', HN 1579 designed by L. Harradine in 1933, 6½in. high. (P. Wilson & Co.) $154

A Royal Doulton 'Chang' vase, by Chas. Noke and Harry Nixon, circa 1930, 7½in. high. (Capes, Dunn & Co.)     $1,248

A Royal Doulton pottery baluster vase decorated by Hannah Barlow, 12in. high. (Dacre, Son & Hartley)     $364

A Royal Doulton character jug, 'Mephistopheles', D5758 designed by C. J. Noke and H. Fenton in 1937, 3½in. high. (P. Wilson & Co.) $693

Royal Doulton figure 'Ts'u-Hsi Empress Dowager', designed and modelled by P. Davies from the Les Femmes Fatales series. (P. Wilson & Co.)     $390

A Royal Doulton 'Sung' vase, signed A. Eaton, 5¾in. high, printed Royal Doulton Flambe mark. (Capes, Dunn & Co.) $748

Royal Doulton jug, 'The Clown', D6322, designed by H. Fenton 1951, 6in. high. ( Abridge Auctions ) $900

A Royal Doulton Kingsware flagon, designed by Noke, circa 1905, 10in. high. (P. Wilson & Co.) $292

A Royal Doulton figure, 'The Skater', HN2117 designed by Margaret Davies in 1953, 7in. high. (P. Wilson & Co.)     $137

# DRESDEN

A Dresden group on oval base with gadrooned and gilt border, 24.5cm., crossed swords mark in underglaze blue. (Lawrence Fine Art) $549

Pair of Dresden candelabra, with branches for four lights, 50cm. high, crossed swords marks in underglaze blue. (Lawrence Fine Art) $1,178

One of a pair of Dresden 'Schneeballen' vases and covers of ogee form, 41cm. high. (Lawrence Fine Art) $201

A 19th century group of thirteen Dresden figures, the Monkey Band, 12cm. to 17cm., crossed swords marks in underglaze blue. (Lawrence Fine Art) $1,296

One of a pair of large Dresden vases, urn-shaped with double serpent handles, 47cm. high. (Lawrence Fine Art) $665

One of a pair of Dresden yellow-ground two-handled vases and covers, blue AR mark, circa 1880, 37cm. high. (Christie's) $507

Pair of Dresden standing figures, 23cm. and 20cm. high, crossed swords marks in underglaze blue. (Lawrence Fine Art) $343

A Dresden centerpiece on stand, the rococo shell scroll stem supporting an oval boat-shaped two-handled fruit bowl, 20½in. high. (Morphets) $1,094

One of a pair of late 19th century large Dutch blue and white vases and covers, 26in. high. (Woolley & Wallis) $924

Late 19th century Zsolnay Pecs pottery vase in the form of a Pre-Columbian vessel, 34cm. long. $239

A late 19th century Austrian Art Nouveau cream glazed porcelain figure, 30½in. high. (Edgar Horn) $286

An Austrian cold-painted pottery figure of an American colored gentleman. (Reeds Rains) $1,243

A large green porcelain centerpiece in three pieces of two shells supported by two cherubs. (Worsfolds) $60

A Rozenburg glazed earthenware vase, painted with flowering creeper and butterflies, circa 1900, 43cm. high. $382

A Rozenburg egg-shell porcelain vase, with cypher for 1899, 28cm. high. (Christie's) $1,000

A green procelain group of a viking in shell-shaped boat drawn by a swan. (Worsfolds) $81

One of a pair of Dutch decorated Bottger porcelain sake bottles, the porcelain circa 1720, 22cm. high. (Christie's) $1,516

# EUROPEAN

A Rozenburg pottery vase of flattened globular shape, the body hand-painted, circa 1910, 18cm. high. (Christie's)     $135

Peloton 'shredded coconut' plate, by Wilhelm Kralik, Bohemia, circa 1880, enamelled polychrome floral motif on a clear ground, 5½in. diam. (Robt. W. Skinner Inc.)  $80

An Art Deco ovoid stoneware vase, metallic brown/black against a natural ground, circa 1925, 33.5cm. high.          $382

# CHINA

A 19th century Danish porcelain bakebord, now as a table raised on cabriole supports, 83cm. long. (H. Spencer & Sons)       $4,469

A Royal Copenhagen stoneware figure of 'David and Goliath', modelled by Arno Malinowski, 68cm. high. (Christie's)  $1,080

A Longwy Atelier Primavera crackle-glaze moon-flask, 1920's, 29.5cm.high.          $216

One of a pair of Rotterdam models of shoes, in manganese and white, circa 1770, 16cm. long. (Christie's) $353

A glazed earthenware charger, designed by Vicke Lindstrand, 1950's, 45cm. diam.          $140

A Clement Massier art pottery vase, signed and bears impressed mark, 10in. high. (D. M. Nesbit & Co.)    $218

130

A famille rose foxhunting bowl, enamelled with two broad panels, circa 1780, 13in.     $1,115

A fish bowl, painted and enamelled with river scenes, 60cm. diam., Ch'ien Lung. (Lawrence Fine Art) $7,068

An oval dish, decorated in famille rose enamels, 31.5cm., Ch'ien Lung. (Lawrence Fine Art) $471

A Chinese famille rose charger. (Cooper Hirst) $541

One of a pair of mid 19th century Canton famille rose baluster vases, 22½in. high.     $929

A circular dish, enamelled in famille rose colors, 28.5cm., Ch'ien Lung. (Lawrence Fine Art) $360

19th century Chinese porcelain famille rose decorated garden seat of barrel form, 19in. high. (Stalker & Boos) $1,500

A mid 19th century yellow-ground famille rose goldfish bowl, molded and enamelled with the 'Hundred Antiques', 16in. diam. $600

One of a pair of famille rose vases, Qianlong, 11in. high.     $1,258

# FAMILLE VERTE

A Chinese famille verte
saucer dish, six-character
mark of Chenghua, but
Kangxi, 15½in. diam.
(Woolley & Wallis)
$1,419

A Chinese famille verte oval
censer/basin, Kangxi, 13¾in.
(Dreweatt Watson & Barton)
$1,548

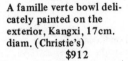

A famille verte bowl delicately painted on the
exterior, Kangxi, 17cm.
diam. (Christie's)
$912

A famille verte plate painted
in the center with a large
iron-red and gilt carp,
Kangxi, 21cm. diam.
(Christie's) $680

One of a pair of famille
verte garden seats with
panels depicting court
scenes, 19in. high.
(Outhwaite & Litherland)
$479

A famille verte saucer dish,
encircled Chenghua mark,
Kangxi, 34.5cm. diam.
(Christie's) $570

A Chinese famille verte
incense burner in the form
of a two storey house,
11in. wide. (Christie's)
$597

A famille verte oviform jar,
Kangxi, 19.5cm. high.
(Christie's) $1,134

A famille verte globular
teapot and cover, Kangxi,
20.5cm. wide. (Christie's)
$441

A Chantilly figure of a
seated Chinese girl with
nodding head, circa 1730,
20cm. wide. (Christie's)
$12,636

Pair of Tournai faience figures
of pug dogs, after the Meissen
models by J. J. Kandler, circa
1765, 15cm. high.(Christie's)
$11,372

A St. Cloud white teapot
and cover with flower finial,
circa 1720, 16.5cm. high.
(Christie's)          $253

A St. Cloud snuff box and
cover modelled as a Chin-
ese man, circa 1740, 5.5cm.
high. (Christie's)
$1,264

A small white Mennecy
baluster jug and cover
with hinged silver mount,
circa 1740, 11.5cm. high.
(Christie's)$1,769

A Mennecy hen snuff box
with silver gilt mount, mark
of Eloy Brichard, Paris,
1756-62, 5cm. wide.
(Christie's) $1,390

A Haviland Limoges porce-
lain fish vase, from a model
by Edouard Marcel Sandoz,
1920's, 23.5cm. high.
$510

A Vincennes small two-
handled bowl and cover,
circa 1753, 8cm. high.
(Christie's)  $1,895

Late 19th century French
enamel etui of tapering
form, the interior with gilt
metal fittings, 3¾in. long.
$258

# GERMAN

Late 19th century pair of large polychrome bisque figures, Germany, 22½in. high. (Robt. W. Skinner Inc.) $425

Pair of Hochst figures of children in fancy dress as a Sultan and Sultana, modelled by J. P. Melchior, circa 1770, 18 and 19.5cm. high. (Christie's) $16,427

One of a pair of Ludwigsburg rococo two-handled pot pourri vases and pierced covers, circa 1770, 28cm. high. (Christie's) $1,895

A Ludwigsburg group of a boar being attacked by three hounds, blue interlaced C mark, circa 1765, 17cm. long. (Christie's) $1,264

A German porcelain plaque painted with the Holy Family, after Vandyke, 32.5 x 27.5cm. (Lawrence Fine Art) $461

Early 20th century Royal Bayreuth poppy bowl and ladle, Germany, 7¾in. diam. (Robt. W. Skinner Inc.) $100

A German porcelain oviform bonbonniere with silver gilt mount, probably Furstenberg, circa 1770, 9cm. high. (Christie's) $569

A Frankenthal group of putti emblematic of Summer modelled by J. W. Lanz, circa 1756-59, 19.5cm. high. (Christie's) $379

Late 18th century German faience tankard, 16cm. high. (Christie's) $404

Early 18th century Nuremburg blue and white enghalskrug with hinged pewter cover and foot rim, 30cm. high. (Christie's) $1,011

Pair of Hochst figures of dancers, probably modelled by J. F. v. Luck, circa 1755, 18cm. high. (Christie's) $11,372

A Frankenthal coffee cup and saucer, with panels painted in puce camaieu, circa 1765. (Christie's) $821

A Nymphenburg putto emblematic of Autumn, modelled by F. A. Bustelli, incised D3, circa 1760, 9.5cm. high. (Christie's) $695

Mid 19th century Nymphenburg cabinet cup and saucer, painted with a view of Max Joseph Platz, Munich. (Lawrence Fine Art) $972

A Ludwigsburg figure of Mars, modelled by J. C. W. Beyer, circa 1765, 14cm. high. (Christie's) $569

Late 19th century German painted porcelain figure of a gentleman holding a goat, 8¾in. high. (Robt. W. Skinner Inc.) $50

Pair of 18th century North German rococo wall appliques of cartouche form, 59cm. high. (Christie's) $1,137

One of a pair of German porcelain four-light candelabra, blue cross marks, circa 1880, 38cm. high. (Christie's) $786

# GOLDSCHEIDER

A small Goldscheider head of a girl, modelled in full relief, circa 1920, 14cm. high.          $165

A Goldscheider-style figure of a nubian woman, 27in. high. (D. M. Nesbit & Co.) $283

A Goldscheider terracotta figure of a blackamoor, 23½in. high. (Graves, Son & Pilcher) $1,856

A Goldscheider earthenware wall mask, 1920's, 17cm. high.          $204

A Goldscheider pottery group of three North American colored boys, 23in. high. (Reeds Rains) $1,107

A Goldscheider porcelain head of a young woman with red lips and brown hair, 11½in. high. (Christie's)  $221

A Goldscheider pottery head of a woman wearing a blue curl pattern close fitting cap, her hand raised in front holding an apple, 9½in. high. (Capes, Dunn & Co.)$67

A large Goldscheider 'Butterfly Girl', after a model by Lorenzl, circa 1930, 48.5cm. high. $1,914

A Goldscheider earthenware head of a young woman, 1920's, 26.5cm. high.          $357

An impressed pottery
broad globular jar applied
with four loop handles,
Western Han Dynasty,
19.5cm. diam. (Christie's)
$570

An unglazed gray pottery
figure of a dog, Han
Dynasty, 16cm. long.
(Christie's) $784

A green-glazed red pottery
model of a pig sty in a
bowl, Han Dynasty, 24cm.
wide. (Christie's)
$2,280

A green-glazed red pottery
model of a granary, Han
Dynasty, 33.6cm. high.
(Christie's) $997

A small green-glazed pottery
model of a house, Han
Dynasty, 11.8cm. high.
(Christie's)    $712

A large green-glazed granary
jar molded with a natura-
listic ridged-roof, Han Dynasty, 48cm. high.
(Christie's) $2,851

A gray pottery figure of
a standing lady, Han
Dynasty, 30.5cm. high.
(Christie's) $1,211

A red-painted gray pottery
horse-head modelled with
flaring mouth and bulbous
eyes, Han Dynasty, 16cm.
wide. (Christie's)
$2,280

A green-glazed pottery vase
with large taotie and fixed
ring handles, Han Dynasty,
28cm. high. (Christie's)
$2,851

# IMARI

Late 19th century Japanese Imari porcelain bowl, 12in. diam., and another matching 9½in. diam. (Reeds Rains)          $378

.A late 17th century Imari jar and cover painted in inky underglaze blue, green, iron-red, black and gilding, 18¼in. high.          $786

An Imari bowl, the interior painted in a typical palette, 16in. diam. (Lawrence Fine Art)          $942

Late 17th/early 18th century Imari fluted baluster jar, 30.8cm. high. (Christie's)    $570

A pair of Imari figures of standing bijin, Genroku period, 39cm. high. (Christie's) $1,901

Late 17th/early 18th century Imari baluster jar painted in typical colors, 45cm. high. (Christie's)$1,261

An Imari dish painted with a brocaded band and a group of fenced peonies, 18in. diam. (Lawrence Fine Art)          $160

A 19th century Japanese Imari large vase of melon fluted semi ovoid form, 49cm. high. (H. Spencer & Sons)    $1,812

A Japanese Imari shallow bowl, 18in. diam. (Christie's)    $561

An Imari large deep compressed globular bowl, Genroku period, 41.2cm. diam. (Christie's) $2,365

One of a pair of late 17th/early 18th century Imari double-gourd vases and covers, 23.7cm. high. (Christie's) $788

An Imari bowl of U-shape with a flared rim, 8½in. (Lawrence Fine Art) $137

An Imari octagonal trumpet-shaped beaker vase painted in typical colors, 42.6cm. high. (Christie's) $625

One of a pair of Imari bottle vases and stoppers, 16in. high. (Lawrence Fine Art) $1,081

Late 19th century Imari jardiniere, Japan, 16in. diam. (Robt. W. Skinner Inc.) $2,700

Early 18th century Imari baluster vase, 51.3cm. high. (Christie's) $2,522

Late 17th/early 18th century Imari sake bottle, 18.2cm. high. (Christie's) $713

Late 17th/early 18th century Imari baluster jar painted in underglaze blue, iron-red, colors and gilt, 50.4cm. high. (Christie's) $1,782

# ITALIAN

A Capodimonte (Carlo III) white figure of Capitano Spavento from the Commedia dell'Arte, circa 1750, 14cm. high. (Christie's) $5,054

A Savona faience pottery plate depicting a seascape with Orpheus seated on a dolphin, 17in. (Locke & England) $161

Early 20th century Capodimonte Madonna and Child, marked with crowned N under base, 18.1/8in. high. (Robt. W. Skinner Inc.) $210

A Lenci earthenware box and cover, cover modelled with a dozing elf, dated 4.2.32, 21cm. $382

A Continental large white clay figure of an Italian boy, signed Mercadier, 96cm. high. (H. Spencer & Sons) $551

A Campania albarello of waisted cylindrical form, the reverse dated 1787 beneath the initials 'MF', 9½in. high. $423

Late 17th/early 18th century Caltagirone albarello of waisted cylindrical form, 10¼in. high. $814

A 16th century Urbino istoriato dish, 11½in. diam. (Robt. W. Skinner Inc.) $1,200

A large figure of a native girl, marked 'Lenci Torino Made in Italy', 1930's, 55.5cm. high. $510

# CHINA

# JAPANESE

A Kinkozan koro and cover of square quatrefoil globular form, signed, 7in. diam. (Lawrence Fine Art) $1,081

A Haniwa pottery model of a half-length figure of a warrior, circa 5th century A.D., 43.5cm. high. (Christie's) $1,544

A Kinkozan vase, the wide ovoid body enamelled and gilt with two wide panels, 12½in. high.
$1,144

Blown out Nippon porcelain vase of tapered bulbous form, Japan, circa 1900, 9¼in. high. (Robt. W. Skinner Inc.) $300

Late 19th century well-modelled Hirado blue and white group of five playful karashishi, 18.8cm. high. (Christie's) $570

A 19th century Kyoto ware calendar vase, inscribed Hoei kimoto tori ('A calendar for 1705'), 33.8cm. high. (Christie's) $1,663

A 17th century Japanese porcelain vase of semi-ovoid form, 29cm. high. (H. Spencer & Sons) $1,220

A Japanese tapered vase with rabbit head mounts, 36¾in. high. (Anderson & Garland) $783

Late 19th century Hirado blue and white oviform vase 26.2cm. high. (Christie's) $832

# JAPANESE

# CHINA

An Edo period pottery chaire of tapering high shouldered form, with a mottled opaque brown glaze, and ivory cover.
$343

Late 17th century Kakiemon water-dropper modelled as a mythical tortoise, 16.2cm. long. (Christie's)
$2,970

A Kinkozan dish of saucer shape painted with a scene of men and women at work.
$343

A fine pair of Kutani vases painted by Shoundo, late 19th century, 32cm. high.
$468

Late 17th century Kakiemon figure of a standing bijin, 36cm. high. (Christie's)
$10,692

A pair of Kyoto earthen-ware vases decorated in enamels and gilding, 7¾in. high.        $468

A Kinkozan earthenware vase, circa 1900, 24.5cm. high.
$605

A Japanese octagonal section jar decorated with eight of the Rakan of Sakyamuni, late 19th century.
$468

One of a pair of Oriental bulbous ware vases with covers, 14in. high. (Vidler & Co.)        $260

A Kangxi blue and white
vase and cover, 24.7in.
high, on early 19th cen-
tury rosewood veneered
stand. (Woolley & Wallis)
$1,109

A famille verte bowl, Kangxi,
30.5cm. diam. (Christie's)
$748

A Kangxi famille verte
winepot and cover in the
form of a cluster of bamboo.
$437

A pair of Kangxi blue and
white vases and covers,
painted with panels of figures in natural landscapes,
30.5cm. high. $312

An underglaze copper-red
pear-shaped vase with slender neck, Kangxi, 17cm.
high. (Christie's)
$1,890

A pair of Kangxi Buddhistic
lion joss stick holders,
20.5cm. high. $312

A Kangxi blue and white porcelain vase decorated with a
continuous scene of a sage and
his attendants, 18¼in. high.
$812

A Kangxi famille verte porcelain fishtank decorated
with four panels, 18in. diam.,
circa 1875.    $937

A blue and white baluster
vase with waisted neck,
Kangxi, 44cm. high.
(Christie's) $1,769

# KANGXI

A blue and white bowl painted on the exterior in vivid blue, encircled Chenghua six-character mark, Kangxi, 19.5cm. diam. (Christie's) $884

A peachbloom beehive-shaped water pot, Kangxi six-character mark and of the period, 12.7cm. wide. (Christie's) $1,260

One of a pair of green and aubergine dragon bowls, Kangxi six-character marks and of the period, 11.3cm. diam. (Christie's) $945

One of two blue and white baluster vases, Kangxi, 22.5cm. high, with wood covers. (Christie's) $1,020

A pair of famille verte figures of The Laughing Twins, Hehe Erxian, Kangxi, 27cm. high. (Christie's) $952

A blue and white yanyan vase, Kangxi, 46cm. high. (Christie's) $1,088

## KOREAN

A 12th century Korean celadon hexafoil cup and stand, Koryo Dynasty, the stand 15.5cm. diam. (Christie's) $2,566

A Korean celadon octagonal shallow bowl, Koryo Dynasty, 12cm. diam. (Christie's) $285

A Korean blue and white globular jar, late Choson Dynasty, 21cm. diam. (Christie's) $570

Japanese Kutani porcelain
bowl on bronze stand,
12½in. diam. (Stalker &
Boos) $1,000

A late 19th century Kutani
porcelain cat, 9½in. long.
$543

One of a pair of late 19th
century Kutani porcelain
covered jars, Japan, 13½in.
high. (Robt. W. Skinner Inc.)
$725

A Kutani shallow dish painted in iron red enriched in
gilt and black, six character
mark, 14½in. diam. (Law-
rence Fine Art) $201

A Kutani porcelain deep
bowl with aqua and yellow
figural decoration on aub-
ergine-ground, 13in. high.
(Stalker Gallery)
$1,800

One of a pair of Kutani
porcelain saucer dishes,
9½in. diam. (Stalker
Gallery) $125

One of a pair of late 19th
century Japanese Kutani porcelain vases, 38cm. high.
$1,062

Pair of Japanese Kutani
porcelain vases, ovoid
with trumpet necks, 10in.
high. (Capes, Dunn & Co.)
$146

Late 19th century Ao-
Kutani baluster vase with
short neck and wide rim,
54.3cm. high. (Christie's)
$1,426

A Bernard Leach St. Ives
stoneware bowl, 1950's,
22.6cm. diam. $425

An early Bernard Leach St.
Ives slipware bowl, 1920's,
17.7cm. diam. $212

A Bernard Leach stoneware
dish, decorated in a rust
and black tenmoku glaze,
1960's, 34cm. diam.
$2,128

A Bernard Leach stoneware
vase, 1960's, 15.4cm. high.
$113

A Bernard Leach ceramic
bead necklace, circa 1950,
46cm. long. $709

A Bernard Leach stoneware
vase, the tapered body of
rounded square section,
1960's, 19cm. high.
$425

A Bernard Leach stoneware
vase, circa 1960, 25.8cm.
high. $993

A Bernard Leach stoneware
bottle vase, circa 1970,
19.6cm. high. $638

A Bernard Leach stoneware
dish, 1950's, 34.3cm. diam.
$1,844

A William Reid Liverpool
blue and white sauceboat,
1755-60, 6¾in. wide.
$2,717

A Liverpool wall pocket of
spirally fluted cornucopia
shape, about 1750, 8in.
$231

A Liverpool Japan pattern
teapot and cover, enamel-
led and gilt with kiku mon,
circa 1770, 5in. high.
$967

Late 18th century Rev.
Andrew Eliot Liverpool
pitcher, 8¾in. high.
(Robt. W. Skinner Inc.)
$1,700

A Liverpool delft blue and
white slender baluster vase,
circa 1750, 14½in. high.
(Christie's) $1,870

An interesting Pennington's
Liverpool 'Thirsty Mask'
cream jug, circa 1770, 4in.
high.          $499

A Liverpool delftware plate,
painted in petit feu enamels
and gilding in Chinese Export
famille rose style, circa 1760-
70, 9½in. diam.  $387

A Liverpool transfer decorated mug, the cylindrical
body with strap handle,
circa 1800, 4.7/8in. high.
(Robt. W. Skinner Inc.)
$2,800

A Liverpool delft blue and
white armorial plate, circa
1750, 22.5cm. diam.
(Christie's)  $363

Pair of Longton Hall candlestick groups, circa 1756, emblematic of Spring and Autumn, 8¼in. high. $2,587

An early Longton Hall candlestick figure of Ceres, circa 1753-54, 11¾in. high. $392

A pair of Longton Hall figures of an Abbess and a Nun, each in white habit, circa 1755, 4.7/8in. high. (Christie's) $660

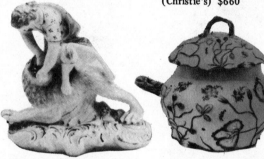

A Longton Hall circular melon tureen and cover, puce W mark, circa 1755, 11.5cm. high. (Christie's) $12,096

A Longton Hall group of Hercules and the Nemean Lion, circa 1755-56, 5¼in. high. $677

Rare Longton Hall tureen and cover of lobed circular shape, circa 1755, 12in. wide. £4,062

Pair of Longton Hall figures of an Abbess and a Novice, circa 1755-56, 5in. high. $837

A Longton Hall figure of Ceres, circa 1753-55, minor chips, 6¾in. high. $492

Pair of Longton Hall figures of a Gardener and Companion, circa 1755-60, 4¾ and 4¼in. high. $887

A Sunderland creamware
jug printed and enamelled
with a view of the cast-iron
bridge, Sunderland, 7½in.
high. (Woolley & Wallis)
$307

Sunderland lustre pottery
chamber pot with an
applied frog and cartoon
face in the interior. (Cooper
Hirst)        $384

Late 16th century Hispano
Moresque lustreware dish,
13½in. diam. (Robt. W.
Skinner Inc.)
$300

One of a pair of English
lustre jugs, circa 1820,
8in. high. (Christie's)
$550

A Staffordshire yellow-
ground lustre jug, transfer-
printed in black and en-
riched in colors, circa
1815, 7½in. high.
(Christie's)        $550

A Maw & Co. Ltd. ruby
lustre 'ship' ewer, designed
by Walter Crane, 1890's,
32cm. high. $3,121

A pearlware commemora-
tive jug, title 'Bonaparte,
Dethron'd, April 1st 1814',
circa 1814.        $187

A De Morgan lustre vase,
the bulbous body with
slender cylindrical neck,
1890's, 37.3cm. high.
$1,702

One of two Sunderland
lustre jugs, each inscribed
'Francis & Betsy Taylor',
circa 1845, 8¼ and 9¼in.
high.        $763

A Martinware stoneware flask entitled 'Water Baby', circa 1880. (Phillips) $3,360

A Martin Bros. stoneware bird group, 7½in. high. (Christie's) $2,280

A tall Martin Bros. bird with detachable head, signed and dated London and Southall 9, 1898, 13in. high. (Anderson & Garland) $6,630

A stoneware Martin Bros. bird tobacco jar and cover, dated 1903, 28cm. high. (Christie's) $4,354

A stoneware Martin Bros. grotesque double-face jug, dated 1903, 19cm. high. (Christie's) $1,496

A stoneware Martin Bros. bird tobacco jar and cover, dated 1903, 22.5cm. high. (Christie's) $2,449

A stoneware Martin Bros. gourd vase, circa 1900, 21cm. high. (Christie's) $216

A Martin Bros. stoneware flower vase with four trumpet-shaped necks, incised marks, 12½in. high. (Christie's) $198

A stoneware Martin Bros. jug in dark brown and blue glazes, circa 1900, 21cm. high. (Christie's) $136

Part of a Mason's ironstone dinner service of forty-eight pieces, circa 1830, pattern no. 103, diam. of dinner plate 10¼in. $1,971

Late 19th century Mason's octagonal baluster vase and cover with dolphin handles and knop, 25½in. high. (Dreweatt Watson & Barton) $799

One of a pair of Mason's ironstone soup tureens, covers and stands, circa 1825, 13in. $837

Part of a Mason's one hundred and seventeen piece ironstone dinner service, printed, painted and gilt with flowering plants and rocks in a fenced garden in Chinese famille rose style. (Lawrence Fine Art) $3,660

Part of a mid 19th century Mason's ironstone dessert service of nine pieces, plate 9in. diam. $616

A pair of Mason's ironstone baluster shaped octagonal vases with high domed covers, 20in. high. (Dreweatt Watson & Barton) $503

A Mason's bird of paradise pattern canted rectangular meat dish, circa 1850, 17in. long. (Dreweatt Watson & Barton) $148

151

# CHINA

## MEISSEN

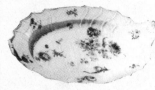

A Meissen oval shallow dish, with crossed swords mark. (Osmond Tricks) $302

A Meissen group of two swans and three cygnets, blue crossed swords and incised G 168 marks, circa 1880, 29cm. wide. (Christie's)    $386

A Meissen small oval tureen and cover, circa 1750, 28.5cm. (Lawrence Fine Art)    $1,455

A Marcolini Meissen group of four children on pedestals, 27.5cm., crossed swords and star mark in underglaze blue. (Lawrence Fine Art)    $594

One of a pair of 19th century Meissen porcelain cache pots, 4¼in. high. (Capes, Dunn & Co.)    $396

A Meissen group of a peasant woman, modelled by P. Reinicke, circa 1745, 15cm. high. (Christie's)    $1,137

A 19th century Meissen equestrian figure of a huntsman, 10¼in. high.    $277

A pair of 19th century Meissen porcelain male and female figures of grape harvesters in 18th century costume, 6¾in. high. (Geering & Colyer)    $682

A 19th century Meissen porcelain centerpiece, underglazed blue cross sword marks to base, 19in. high. (W. H. Lane & Son)    $1,040

An early Meissen, KPM, chinoiserie teapot and cover with Augsburg silver gilt mounts, painted by P. E. Schindler, circa 1725, 18cm. wide. (Christie's) $15,163

A Meissen figure of Venus seated in a shell- molded chariot, blue crossed swords marks, circa 1880, 16.5cm. wide. (Christie's) $749

A Meissen cockerel teapot and cover, modelled by J. J. Kaendler, circa 1740, 15.5cm. high. (Christie's) $2,022

A Meissen two- color pate-sur-pate ovoid vase and cover, circa 1900, 23cm. high. $797

A Meissen group of an Oriental musician and companion, modelled by J. J. Kaendler, circa 1745, 10.5cm. high. (Christie's) $1,643

A Meissen teapoy painted with flowers and insects, 11cm., crossed swords in underglaze blue. (Lawrence Fine Art) $434

A mid 18th century Meissen figure of a tinker, entirely in the white, 6½in. high. $572

A 19th century Meissen pagoda figure, after an original by J. J. Kaendler. (Woolley & Wallis) $1,118

A mid 18th century Meissen box with hinged lid modelled as a moss rose, 22in. diam. (Woolley & Wallis) $4,205

# METTLACH

German bisque half doll, incised marks suggest Mettlach production, circa 1910, 4in. tall. $397

Mettlach plaque, no. 2288, Germany, circa 1906, 17¼in. diam. (Robt. W. Skinner Inc.) $531

Early 20th century Mettlach pottery flagon, 16in. high. (Robt. W. Skinner Inc.) $281

A Mettlach tankard, Germany, 1898, of tapered cylindrical form with pewter cover, 7in. high. (Robt. W. Skinner Inc.) $350

Late 19th century Mettlach plaque, signed C. Warth, 16¾in. high. $187

German half litre painted pottery beerstein with decorative soft metal lid. $281

A Mettlach pottery vase with trumpet neck and drum-shaped body domed above and below, 12¼in. high. (Capes, Dunn & Co.) $96

A Mettlach plaque of a spring landscape, signed H. Cradl?, stamped Villeroy & Boch, 17½in. diam, Germany, 1910. (Robt. W. Skinner Inc.)$875

One of a pair of Mettlach vases with enamelled floral and pink polka dot decoration, circa 1889. (Robt. W. Skinner Inc.) $375

A 16th/17th century late Ming celadon qilin censer, 14.5cm. high. (Christie's) $1,283

Early 16th century Ming blue and white cylindrical censer, on three short lion-mask feet, 27.5cm. diam. (Christie's) $3,564

A large late Ming blue and white saucer dish, Jiajing six-character mark at the rim, 57cm. diam. (Christie's) $3,564

A Ming Dynasty pottery ridge tile, 14in. high, $1,099

A Ming Dynasty fahua garden seat of characteristic barrel shape, 13¾in. $1,374

A late Ming wucai double-gourd wall vase, 25.2cm. high. (Christie's) $883

A 15th century Ming blue and white baluster vase, 18.5cm. high. (Christie's) $1,140

A 15th/16th century Ming fahua oviform jar, 15cm. high. (Christie's) $1,710

A 14th/15th century blue and white vase with dragon-headed handles, 17.5cm. high. (Christie's) $712

# MINTON

Pair of Minton Japanese-style art pottery flask-shaped vases, each on four feet, circa 1871-75, 10in. high. (Geering & Colyer) $208

A 19th century Minton turquoise glazed 'faience' figure of a cat with blue-black eyes, 35cm. high. (H. Spencer & Sons)    $448

A Minton 'Majolica' teapot and cover, in the form of a crouching cockerel, 1872, 8in. wide.    $2,710

Minton Art Nouveau majolica bowl, date symbol for 1915, 16in. diam. (Barber's Fine Art)    $1,220

Pair of large Minton 'Majolica' blackamoors on stands, 1870, 70¾in. high overall.    $59,136

A Minton two-handled jar and cover, 1830-40, 30cm.    $461

A Minton 'Majolica' oyster stand, formed from four graduated tiers of oyster shells, 1869, 10in. high. $2,217

A Minton 'Secessionist' jardiniere and stand, with printed and impressed marks, circa 1910, 103.5cm. high. (Christie's)    $1,088

A Minton Parian group of Ariadne and the Panther on rectangular base, year cypher for 1867, 13.7in. high. (Woolley & Wallis) $390

A Minton majolica game tureen and cover, impressed mark and numeral 899, painter's mark 'R', circa 1880, 12½in. long. (Christie's) $550

A Minton jardiniere, circa 1880, impressed mark and shape number 2494, 12¾in. wide. $344

A white Minton group of two Amorini pulling a shell chariot. (Worsfolds) $135

A Minton ewer of tapering ovoid form with fluted neck and foot, by A. Boullemier, 11½in. high. (Neales) $464

One of a pair of Minton aesthetic movement pottery vases, the ovoid celadon ground painted in the Japanese manner, circa 1872, 10¼in. high. (Capes, Dunn & Co.) $317

A Minton majolica jug, as an iron bound barrel, date code for 1863, 38.5cm. high. (H. Spencer & Sons) $900

One of a pair of Minton terracotta circular plaques each painted by W. Mufsill, date code for 1877, 57.5cm. diam. $1,828

A Minton jardiniere in the Art Nouveau style. $792

One of a set of twelve Minton dessert plates, pattern no. G4266, circa 1885, 24cm. diam. (Christie's) $991

A Moorcroft pottery vase,
ovoid with inverse baluster
shaped neck, 12½in. high.
(Capes, Dunn & Co.)
$122

An early 20th century Wm.
Moorcroft 'Claremont' pat-.
tern bowl, 26cm. wide.
$542

A Moorcroft Florianware
vase of broad oviform
with garlic neck, printed
marks and inscribed W M
Des, 10½in. high.
(Christie's) $176

A large Moorcroft oviform
vase decorated with foliage
and fruit, 29cm. high.
(Andrew Grant)$567

A Moorcroft Florianware
vase of tapering oviform,
printed marks and inscribed
W M, 7in. high. (Christie's)
$221

A Moorcroft flattened
globular vase painted with
a fish, impressed marks,
signed in green, 12¼in.
high. (Christie's) $606

A Macintyre Moorcroft
pottery vase of inverted
baluster form, decorated
in the Art Nouveau style,
31cm. high. (H. Spencer &
Sons)      $470

A shallow Moorcroft bowl
painted with landscape design in the Autumnal shades
known as Eventide, circa
1928, 8½in. diam. (P. Wilson & Co.)    $110

A Moorcroft Florianware
blue jug with white Art
Nouveau design, 7¾in. high.
(Capes, Dunn & Co.)
$176

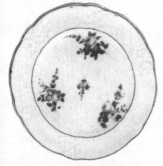

A London decorated Nant-
garw plate, circa 1817-22,
9¾in. diam.      $147

A fine Nantgarw plate decorated with blooms of carna-
tions, 24cm. diam., circa
1820.            $375

A Nantgarw plate, circa
1813-22, decorated in
London, 8½in. diam.
          $369

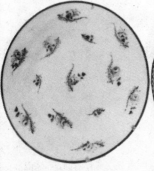

A Nantgarw plate painted
with pink rose-sprigs with
green leaves, circa 1817-22,
8.3/8in. diam.  $393

A London decorated Nantgarw
plate, painted with three exotic
birds in a landscape, circa 1820,
9¼in. diam.          $516

A London decorated Nantgarw
plate, circa 1817-22, impressed
mark, 8.3/8in. diam.
             $224

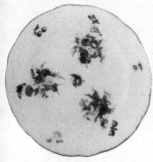

One of a pair of Nantgarw
plates, decorated in London
with butterflies, bouquets
and scattered sprigs of fruit
and flowers, circa 1813-22,
8.5/8in. diam.  $616

Nantgarw oval dish with shell-
molded rim handles, circa
1817-22, 14in. wide.
             $325

A Nantgarw plate, circa
1813-22, impressed
Nantgarw C.W., 9½in.
diam.      $677

A Newport pottery 'Bizarre' 'Fantasque' vase and internal stem-holder, 1920's, 24cm. wide.  $484

A Newport pottery 'Archaic' Bizarre vase, 1930's, impressed number 373, 17.75cm. high.  $851

A Newport pottery Bizarre vase with stepped flange handles, 1930's, 12cm. high.          $510

A Newport pottery Bizarre vase, deep inky blue at base, printed marks, 1930's, 36cm. high.  $1,135

A Newport pottery Bizarre charger, 1930's, stylized foliate design in blue, orange and green with blue border, 33.5cm. diam.
          $241

A 'bizarre' single-handled 'lotus' vase, 29.3cm. high. Newport, late 1930's.
          $468

A Newport pottery 'Bizarre' biscuit barrel and cover, 1930's, 15.5cm. high.
          $165

A Newport pottery 'Bizarre' 'Delicia' jar and cover, 1930's, 21cm. high.
          $510

A Newport pottery 'Bizarre' 'Fantasque' flower basket, 1930's, 37cm. high.
          $89

A Paris plate showing finely painted shells, Darte Factory, about 1820, 22.7cm. diam. $187

A Paris earthenware casket painted with a gallant and his lady, late 19th century. $562

A Paris plate painted in a bright palette with a bird, circa 1825, 23cm. diam. (Christie's) $312

One of a pair of mid 19th century Paris porcelain bough pots and covers, 9in. high. $972

Part of a 19th century Paris porcelain coffee set, green and gilt bordered with panels of hand-painted flowers, in Empire style. (Woolley & Wallis) $462

Late 19th century Paris porcelain teapot on matching burner, France, 8.5/8in. high. (Robt. W. Skinner Inc.) $120

Pair of Paris porcelain vases with dolphin handles, 21¼in. and 20¾in. high. (Graves Son & Pilcher) $1,218

A pair of Paris, Sevres style beakers, circa 1875. $312

One of a pair of Paris large vases, with spherical bodies and wide trumpet necks, 43.5cm. high. (Lawrence Fine Art) $172

# PILKINGTON

A Pilkington's Royal Lancastrian vase decorated by G. Forsyth, 1906, 19.2cm. high.                    $451

A Pilkington's Royal Lancastrian twin-handled vase decorated by Gordon Forsyth, 1908, 30.2cm. high.
$241

A Pilkington's double gourd lustre vase by Wm. S. Mycock, dated 1906.      $645

## PRATTWARE

A Prattware jug of slightly flattened baluster form with angular handle, circa 1780, 18.5cm. high. (Christie's) $306

A Prattware watchstand and a watch, circa 1810, top of clock restored, 8½in. high. $1,601

A Pratt oval plaque, modelled in bright colors in relief with The Vicar and Moses, Saturday Night, 13.5cm. high. (Lawrence Fine Art)      $235

A Pratt-type pearlware group, circa 1790, 15cm. high.
$1,187

A Pratt figure of a boy, after the model by Cyffle, on a square pedestal base, 17cm. high. (Lawrence Fine Art) $144

A plate with transfer decoration, 'The Truant', by F. & R. Pratt & Co., 9½in. diam. (P. Wilson & Co.) $91

A large Chinese famille rose punch bowl, Qianlong, 14¼in. diam. (Christie's) $978

An Export figure of a recumbent dog, Qianlong, 16cm. wide. (Christie's)$544

A green and yellow dragon bowl, Qianlong, six-character seal mark and of the period, 15.3cm. diam. (Christie's) $1,995

One of a pair of blue and white plates with shaped rims, Qianlong, 24cm. diam. (Christie's) $516

One of a pair of famille rose baluster vases of compressed hexagonal section, Qianlong, 29cm. high. (Christie's) $952

A Chinese famille rose dish, Qianlong, 22in. diam. (Christie's) $4,347

A Chinese famille rose tobacco leaf, shaped oval dish, 18¼in. wide, Qianlong. (Christie's) $5,217

An Export figure of a hound seated, Qianlong, 14.5cm. high. (Christie's) $1,769

A Qianlong 'Compagnie-des-Indes' marriage dish, 37.3cm. wide. $893

# ROYAL DUX

A Royal Dux porcelain figure of an Arab man, pink patch marks, 41cm. high. (H. Spencer & Sons) $151

A Royal Dux porcelain group of a lion, lioness and dead gazelle on rustic base, 19in. wide, no. 1600. (Dacre, Son & Hartley) $260

A Royal Dux figure of a young girl, naked, seated on a rock, 54cm. high. (Lawrence Fine Art) $432

Royal Dux figure of fisherman, with wife and child, pink triangle mark to base, 18in. high. (P. Wilson & Co.) $183

A fine pair of Royal Dux figures of a Shepherd and Shepherdess, 79cm. high. $1,562

A large Royal Dux figure of a peasant boy leaning on a wooden pitcher, 59cm. high. $468

Late 19th/early 20th century European Royal Dux nude female figure, 15¼in. high. (Robt. W. Skinner Inc.) $350

A Royal Dux porcelain figure group of a Dutch farm boy and girl, 30.5cm. high. (H. Spencer & Sons) $275

Royal Dux Art Deco part bisque figure of a nude girl, 10in. high. $156

A Royal Dux figure of a classically dressed young man holding a basket, 39cm. high.        $300

A fine Royal Dux group of a classical Grecian horseman with his charges, 43cm. high, circa 1900.        $625

A Royal Dux porcelain group 'The Blacksmith, his Wife and Child', 19in. high, no. 1944. (Dacre, Son & Hartley)        $520

A Royal Dux gilt porcelain figure of a girl bather seated on a rock, 19in. high. (Dacre, Son & Hartley)        $450

A large pair of Royal Dux porcelain figures of Huntsmen, pink patch marks, 69cm. high. (damaged). (H. Spencer & Sons)        $797

A Royal Dux porcelain standing figure of a maiden as a lamp, 82cm. high. (H. Spencer & Sons)        $691

A Royal Dux porcelain figure of an Arab woman, pink patch marks, 41cm. high. (H. Spencer & Sons)        $151

A Royal Dux figure group of two shire horses, red triangle mark applied to base, 36cm. high. (Osmond Tricks)        $264

A Royal Dux porcelain bottle vase with applied rustic handle, 44.5cm. high. (H. Spencer & Sons)        $244

# SATSUMA

# CHINA

A Satsuma type bowl of U-shape, signed, 4¼in. diam. (Lawrence Fine Art) $1,386

A Japanese Satsuma pottery baluster vase and cover, 50cm. high. (H. Spencer & Sons) $607

A Japanese Satsuma pottery dish painted in colors and gilt with children, 45cm. diam. (H. Spencer & Sons) $261

A 19th century Satsuma bowl, signed on the base Gyokushu, 15.5cm. diam. (Christie's) $617

A Satsuma style baluster vase, signed, on hardwood stand, 19in. high. (Lawrence Fine Art) $1,296

A 19th century Satsuma circular box and cover, signed on the base Hotoda zo, 15.1cm. diam. (Christie's) $427

A 19th century Satsuma cylindrical beaker vase with flaring rim, signed Fukyuen, 47.7cm. high. (Christie's) $1,010

Large Satsuma wall plate decorated with storks, flowers and foliage, 19in. diam. (Butler & Hatch Waterman) $348

Late 19th century Satsuma vase, Japan, with bulbous panelled body, 8¾in. high. (Robt. W. Skinner Inc.) $375

# CHINA

SATSUMA

A 19th century Satsuma pear-shaped vase decorated in iron-red enamels and gilt, 15.3cm. high. (Christie's) $356

Late 19th century Japanese Satsuma bowl, 4¾in. diam. (Robt. W. Skinner Inc.) $575

One of a pair of Satsuma type cylindrical vases, signed, 6in. high. (Lawrence Fine Art) $554

Late 19th century Satsuma cup and saucer, Japanese, 3½in. high. (Robt. W. Skinner Inc.) $150

A Satsuma pottery vase of cylindrical shape, 9in. high. (Capes, Dunn & Co.) $105

A 19th century satsuma bowl, of round shallow shape, signed on base, 6in. diam., Japan. (Robt. W. Skinner Inc.) $200

One of a pair of Satsuma baluster vases, 22in. high. (Dee & Atkinson) $165

A Satsuma large lidded jar, gilded figures on black ground, 13in. high. (Barber's Fine Art) $756

Late 19th century Satsuma vase, Japan, of tapered bulbous form with flaring rim, 11½in. high. (Robt. W. Skinner Inc.) $700

A First Empire Sevres porcelain two-handled cup and cover, 6½in. high. (Geering & Colyer)    $235

A Sevres pattern gilt metal mounted slender oviform vase and cover, signed A. Callot, circa 1880, 64cm. high. (Christie's)
$484

A Sevres bleu nouveau ground circular sugar bowl and cover with cherry finial, 12cm. high. (Christie's)    $1,264

A Sevres sucrier and stand with marble porphyry background, circa 1765-70. (Christie's) $1,390

A Sevres oval plaque painted with scene of 18th century rustic lovers, 9¾in. high. (Ward & Partners)
$260

A Sevres porcelain vase, decorated with a frieze of stylized deer, mottled brown and buff glass, 1931, 21.25cm. high.    $191

A Sevres coffee cup and cinquefoil saucer painted with flowerheads, the cup with date letter K for 1763. (Christie's) $1,074

A Sevres (hard paste) 'jewelled' egg cup, circa 1781-85, 4.25cm. high. (Christie's)  $948

One of a pair of Art Pottery vases, the ovoid body with turquoise ground, bears the mark M.P. Sevres in a circle of dots, 11in. high. (D. M. Nesbit & Co.) $130

# CHINA

One of a pair of late 19th century Sevres pattern bleu-celeste ground oviform vases and covers, 57cm. high. (Christie's) $1,451

A Sevres white biscuit figure of Pascal, after the model by Pajou, circa 1783, 32cm. high. (Christie's) $15,163

A Sevres verte pre coffee-cup and saucer, interlaced L marks in gray above the painter's mark of Claude Chas. Gerard, circa 1775. (Christie's)    $1,769

A Sevres pattern gilt metal mounted royal-blue ground two-handled vase, circa 1880, 44.5cm. high. (Christie's) $628

A Sevres two-handled ecuelle, cover and stand, blue interlaced L's enclosing date letter O for 1767, stand 20cm. diam. (Christie's)        $2,148

A Sevres bleu nouveau vase flacon a cordes and cover, circa 1770, 37cm. high. (Christie's) $25,272

A Sevres two-handled cup, cover and stand, circa 1760-65, the stand 19cm. diam. (Christie's) $6,950

A Sevres square tray painted in colors with a garland of flowers, the date letter G for 1759, 15cm. square. (Christie's) $1,011

One of a pair of Sevres pattern pink-ground oviform vases and covers, circa 1880, 43cm. high. (Christie's) $1,693

A Spode two-handled jar-diniere and stand, circa 1800, 10½in. wide. (Christie's) $1,400

One of a set of six Spode 'Japan' pattern plates, each decorated in underglaze blue, iron-red, green and gilding, circa 1825, 8in. diam. $451

One of a pair of Spode pas-tille burners and covers of flared form, circa 1820, 4¾in. high. $451

An early 19th century iron-stone baluster jar and cover, possibly Spode, 46cm. high. $547

Part of a Spode botanical yellow-ground dessert service, pattern no. 1569, circa 1795. (Christie's) $2,860

One of a pair of Spode beaded antique jars, early 19th century, 5½in. high. $500

A Spode trumpet shape vase, on short stem and circular base, 16cm. high, pattern 656 in red. (Lawrence Fine Art) $207

One of a pair of early 19th century famille rose cream-ware pottery plates, impres-sed Spode 16 pattern no. 3154, 10in. diam. (P. Wilson & Co.) $44

A Spode beaded New Shape Jar with gilt loop handles, circa 1810-20, 5in. high. $580

# CHINA

# STAFFORDSHIRE

A Staffordshire pearlware octagonal teapot and cover, the cover with swan finial, 15cm. high. (Lawrence Fine Art)    $69

A Rockingham cottage pastille burner and stand, lavender color with gilt details, 13cm. high. (Lawrence Fine Art)$302

One of a pair of 19th century Staffordshire greyhounds, Master McGrath and Pretender. (Bearnes)
$1,740

Pair of Rockingham figures of a young boy and a girl, inscribed no. 36, 4¾in. high. (Christie's)
$521

A Staffordshire figure of the boxer Tom Cribb, on an oval green-mound base. (Christie's)    $616

Pair of Staffordshire figural candleholders with gilt and multi-colored decoration, circa 1820, 8in. high. (Stalker & Boos)  $120

A Staffordshire portrait figure of William Palmer, the murderer, circa 1856, together with 'The Illustrated Life and Career of Wm. Palmer'.    $774

A Staffordshire model of Palmer's house, circa 1856.
$266

A Staffordshire portrait bust of Clive, his hair en queue, circa 1800, 24.5cm. high.(Christie's)
$665

# STAFFORDSHIRE

# CHINA

A Staffordshire teapot and cover, painted with flowers in pink and green, 15cm. high. (Lawrence Fine Art) $89

Large pair of Staffordshire seated King Charles spaniels, lustre decoration on off white, circa 1830, 15in. high. (Stalker & Boos) $125

A Staffordshire teapot with domed cover and high gallery, 14.5cm. high. (Lawrence Fine Art) $83

A Staffordshire Majolica jardiniere stand in the Art Nouveau style. $552

A Staffordshire toy tea service, creamware, painted with flowers in pink and green within pink line borders, comprising teapot, sugar basin, milk jug, five tea bowls and saucers. (Lawrence Fine Art) $302

One of a pair of Staffordshire porcelain figures of seated poodles, circa 1820, 5in. high. (Stalker & Boos) $150

An 18th century Staffordshire slipware dish, 27.5cm. diam. $922

A Staffordshire portrait bust of General Booth, circa 1900, 13in. high. (P. Wilson & Co.) $340

A 19th century Staffordshire oblong blue and white two-handled footbath, 18in. wide. (Dreweatt Watson & Barton) $473

A pair of Staffordshire porcelain miniature figures of poodles, 5cm. high, and a figure of a girl, 9cm. high. (Lawrence Fine Art) $244

A North Staffordshire loving cup, 8in. diam., inscribed 'The best is not too good for you 1698'. (Sworders) $8,640

A 19th century Staffordshire group depicting Wombwell's Menagerie. (Bonham's) $25,200

One of three Staffordshire figures of a youth, 14cm. high. (Lawrence Fine Art) $288

A Staffordshire group, The Tithe Pig, on a green base, 15cm. high. (Lawrence Fine Art) $249

A Staffordshire hen on nest with chicks, probably by T. Randall, circa 1820, 9in. long. (Robt. W. Skinner Inc.) $800

A Shorthose tea bowl and saucer, printed in colors with the Tea Party, together with another. (Lawrence Fine Art) $230

An early 19th century Walton-type Staffordshire figure of a doe and bocage. (Woolley & Wallis) $325

# STONEWARE

A salt-glazed stoneware two-handled dish, oval with ogee sides, 10½in. wide overall. (Capes, Dunn & Co.) $132

A four gallon crock, 'Whites Utica', cobalt blue floral wreath centering the date 1865. (Robt. W. Skinner Inc.) $450

A six gallon crock, by S. Hart, Fulton, cobalt blue lineal dog carrying a basket. (Robt. W. Skinner Inc.) $1,150

# CHINA

A Victorian stoneware garden gnome wearing a pointed red hat and green shorts, 2ft.3in. high. (Heathcote Ball) $300

Mid 19th century decorated three gallon stoneware jug, America. (Robt. W. Skinner Inc.) $100

A phosphatic splashed stoneware oviform jar with four double loop handles, Tang Dynasty, 29cm. high. (Christie's)$6,415

A two gallon milk pan, ovoid base, cobalt blue single flower. (Robt. W. Skinner Inc.) $80

A one gallon crock, by Whites, Utica, cobalt blue lineal bird on branch. (Robt. W. Skinner Inc.) $275

A salt-glazed stoneware three gallon crock, by Daniel Wetson and J. A. Gregg, N.Y., 1869-70, 9½in. high. $400

A Swansea cup and saucer
painted with full-blown pink
roses and green leaves, circa
1820.              $343

A Swansea inkstand and cover,
circa 1814-22, in the form of a
scallop shell, 3.7/8in.
                  $431

A Swansea plate painted by
Wm. Pollard, circa 1820-22,
8½in. diam.    $500

A Swansea armorial plate,
circa 1815-20, painted by
Henry Morris, 8½in. diam.
        $1,232

Part of a Swansea tea and
coffee service of twenty-seven-
pieces, circa 1814-22.
          $1,375

A Swansea 'Burdett-Coutts'
plate, circa 1814-22,
8.3/8in. diam.  $492

A Swansea plate, circa
1820, the center painted by
Wm. Pollard, 8¼in. diam.
        $616

Pair of Swansea vases, each of
elongated campana form,
circa 1815, 10in. high.
          $3,225

A Swansea pottery armorial
plate, decorated probably
by Thos. Pardoe, circa 1802-
10, 9.7/8in. diam.
              $554

A glazed pottery cup model-
led as a corpulent fish, Tang
Dynasty, 12cm. wide.
(Christie's) $4,276

An unglazed buff pottery
bust of a lady, Tang
Dynasty, 11.8cm. high.
(Christie's) $712

Tang pottery horse on
mahogany stand, China,
16½in. long. (Robt. W.
Skinner Inc.)
$2,000

A Sancai buff pottery
globular jar, Tang Dynasty,
16.8cm. high. (Christie's)
$3,991

Tang glazed pottery figure
of a lady, with stand, 10in.
high. (Robt. W. Skinner
Inc.) $600

A brown-glazed stoneware
pilgrim flask with thick
loop handles, Tang Dynasty,
24.5cm. high. (Christie's)
$14,256

A phosphatic splashed stoneware ewer with elephantine
dragon-head spout, Tang
Dynasty, 22cm. wide.
(Christie's) $17,107

A Sancai buff pottery figure
of a standing Bactrian camel,
Tang Dynasty, 57.2cm. high.
(Christie's) $9,979

A phosphatic splashed stoneware oviform jar with two
simple double loop handles,
late Tang Dynasty, 22.2cm.
high. (Christie's)
$3,706

# CHINA

A pair of Vienna slender oviform vases, covers and waisted circular plinths, signed Kreigsa, blue beehive marks, circa 1880, 113cm. high. (Christie's) $6,290

One of a pair of late 19th century Vienna circular plates, 12¾in. diam. (Reeds Rains) $196

Pair of Vienna gilt porcelain maidens in classical dress, signed Roesier, 16in. high. (Dacre, Son & Hartley) $425

A cased Vienna solitaire set, each piece painted with yellow birds, circa 1795, with original tooled red leather box. $1,224

Late 19th century Vienna green-ground oviform vase and cover, 37cm. high. (Christie's) $484

One of a pair of late 19th century Vienna vases and covers, 38cm. high. $1,080

A late 19th century Vienna porcelain two-handled vase of waisted inverted form, 38cm. high. (H. Spencer & Sons) $325

# WEDGWOOD

A Wedgwood Fairyland lustre bowl of octagonal shape, 1920's, 11¼in. wide.    $985

A Wedgwood pearlware nautilus shell compote and stand, impressed marks, iron-red pattern no. 7035, circa 1825, the stand 12¼in. wide. (Christie's)$605

A Wedgwood creamware diamond-shaped dish, painted by Emile Lessore with The Young Anglers, date code for 1862, 31.5cm. wide. (Christie's)    $434

One of a pair of large Wedgwood blue jasper dip pot pourri vases, covers and stands, late 19th century, 25½in. high overall.    $2,094

A Wedgwood Fairyland lustre plate, decorated with a panel of the 'Roc Centre', 1920's, 10¾in. diam.  $468

A Wedgwood & Bentley black basalt miniature bust of Aristophanes, circa 1775, 9.5cm. high. (Christie's)    $1,028

A Wedgwood 'Lahore' lustre vase and cover, 1920-29, 8¼in. high.  $2,464

A Wedgwood pearlware two-handled oval footbath, transfer-printed in blue with The Tower of London Pattern, circa 1840, 45cm. wide. (Christie's) $1,210

Early 19th century Wedgwood black and white jasper oviform vase and cover, 'impressed mark, 8¾in. high. (Christie's)    $990

One of a pair of Wedgwood majolica small dishes and a caneware jug, the dishes with pattern no. 2820K circa 1880, the jug early 19th century. (Christie's) $242

A Wedgwood creamware small diamond-shaped tray, impressed mark and letters, C, AVO, circa 1865, 6¼in. wide. (Christie's) $220

A Wedgwood & Bentley black basalt oval plaque molded in high relief with Boys as Musicians, circa 1775, 24.5cm. wide. (Christie's) $2,661

Mid 19th century Wedgwood three-color jasper two-handled vase and cover, 7¼in. high. (Christie's) $770

One of a pair of Wedgwood black basaltes sphinx candlesticks, circa 1800, 9¼in. high. $715

A Wedgwood & Bentley black basalt miniature bust of Ariadne, circa 1775, 10.5cm. high. (Christie's) $1,330

Late 19th century Wedgwood blue and white jasper two-handled urn-shaped vase and cover, 9¼in. high. (Christie's) $550

A Wedgwood blue and white jasper oval portrait medallion of Henry William, 2nd Earl of Uxbridge, modelled by Wm. Hackwood, circa 1830, 23cm. high. (Christie's) $6,653

One of a pair of Wedgwood lustre vases, gilt with dragons pursuing a flaming pearl among cloud scrolls, circa 1925, 21.5cm. high. (Christie's) $555

Early 19th century Wedgwood basalt bust of Mercury on stand, England, bust 14½in. high. (Robt. W. Skinner Inc.) $750

A Wedgwood Fairyland lustre 'Malfrey Pot and Cover', circa 1925, 9½in. high. $3,696

A Wedgwood Fairyland lustre flared vase, pattern no. Z4968, circa 1925, 23.5cm. high. (Christie's) $665

Tricolor jasperware footed urn with domed cover and knob finial, marked Wedgwood, possibly 'Dice' ware, circa 1820, 8½in. high. (Robt. W. Skinner Inc.) $1,200

A matched pair of Wedgwood black basalt library busts of Milton and Shakespeare, 36cm. and 37cm. high. (Lawrence Fine Art) $503

A Wedgwood black and white jasper vase, the body molded in white relief with Bacchanalian Triumph after the design by John Flaxman, 67cm. high. (Lawrence Fine Art) $1,944

A Wedgwood & Bentley black basalt circular inkwell, 6.4cm. (Lawrence Fine Art) $249

Early 19th century Wedgwood portland vase with loop handles, 10¼in. high. (Robt. W. Skinner Inc.) $750

Mid 19th century Wedgwood black basaltes vestal oil lamp and cover, 8¾in. high. (Christie's) $825

A Wedgwood/Whieldon
teapot and cover, with
crabstock handle, circa
1765, 6in. high.
$2,032

An 18th century Whieldon
pottery puzzle pipe splashed
with a brown glaze, 32cm.
long. (H. Spencer & Sons)
$518

A Whieldon figure of a
rabbit, circa 1750-60,
4½in. long.$4,435

A Whieldon cow creamer
and cover, circa 1760,
6½in. high. $1,601

A Whieldon group of lovers
embracing and seated on
rockwork, circa 1750, 12cm.
wide. (Christie's)
$9,677

A Whieldon type figure of
a horse, circa 1770, 7in.
long. (Christie's)
$3,300

A Whieldon figure of a lion,
glazed in cream and deep
green, its head with splashes
of brown and gray, circa
1750-60, 3in. wide.
$1,540

A Whieldon leaf dish, modelled with three overlapping
leaves, circa 1755, 7in. wide.
(Christie's)          $187

A Whieldon-type 'Dolphin'
sauceboat, circa 1770-75,
5.1/8in.          $308

181

# WILKINSON

A Wilkinson Ltd. 'Bizarre' 'Inspiration' charger, decorated with striped turquoise/blue glaze, 1930's, 39.5cm. diam. $331

A Wilkinson Ltd. 'Winston Churchill' Toby jug, designed by Clarice Cliff, circa 1940, 12in. high. $1,971

Two of a set of eleven Wilkinson Ltd. 'First World War' Toby jugs, 1914-18, each designed by Sir F. Carruthers Gould, 10¼ to 12in. high. $2,094

Part of a Wilkinson Ltd. dinner service, painted with a castle and trees in brown, orange and turquoise, 1930's. $382

A Wilkinson Ltd. 'Bizarre' jug, circa 1930, 29.5cm. high. $178

Wilkinson's pottery wall mask, by Clarice Cliff, 7in. high, printed factory marks. (Peter Wilson) $91

A Wilkinson Ltd. 'Fantasque' bowl, 1930's, 19.5cm. diam., together with an ashtray, 21cm. wide. $280

A large Wilkinson Ltd. 'Bizarre' wall mask, 1930's, 35.5cm. high. $357

A Ralph Wood figure of a
ram recumbent on mottled
green and ochre rockwork,
circa 1780, 18.5cm. wide.
(Christie's) $1,935

A Ralph Wood white por-
trait bust of Handel, circa
1785, 23cm. high.
(Christie's)   $434

A Ralph Wood figure of a
recumbent sheep, circa
1770, 7in. long.
(Christie's) $1,540

A Ralph Wood oval plaque
portrait of a woman, per-
haps Charlotte Corday,
circa 1780, 20cm. high.
(Christie's)    $665

Ralph Wood jug, modelled
by Jean Voysey, circa 1788,
25cm. high.   $531

A Ralph Wood oval plaque
of Patricia, circa 1775,
29cm. high. (Christie's)
$1,693

A Ralph Wood bust of
Milton, on a shaped rect-
angular socle, circa 1790,
22cm. high. (Christie's)
$484

A Ralph Wood figure of a
seated fox, circa 1780, 4in.
high. (Christie's)$625

A Ralph Wood triple spill
vase modelled as two
entwined dolphins, circa
1775, 20cm. high.
(Christie's) $1,330

A Worcester blue and white
sauceboat, mid 1760's,
7¾in. wide.          $364

A Worcester First Period
coffee cup and saucer,
painted in underglaze blue,
workmen's marks. (Law-
rence Fine Art)$263

First Period Worcester blue
and white relief molded
creamboat, 3in. high.
(Dreweatt Watson & Bar-
ton)          $162

Early 20th century Royal
Worcester pot pourri jar
and cover, the globular body
painted by J. Stinton, signed,
25.5cm. high.     $468

A pair of late 19th century
Royal Worcester white ground
wall pockets in the form of
conch shells, 10½in. high. (P.
Wilson & Co.)     $85

Royal Worcester vase and
cover signed James Stinton,
5in. high. (Reeds Rains)
          $193

A Worcester Japan pattern
dish, 1765-70, 23cm. diam.
          $572

A 20th century Royal Wor-
cester ewer, England, 15½in.
high. (Robt. W. Skinner Inc.)
          $650

A First Period Worcester
small plate with fluted border and gilt escalloped rim,
16cm. diam. (Lawrence
Fine Art)     $117

A Worcester First Period
sauceboat with shaped
edge, 17.2cm. wide. (Law-
rence Fine Art) $415

Part of a Royal Worcester
miniature tea service of four
pieces, the teapot and cover
3¼in. high. (Reeds Rains)
$353

A Worcester First Period
pickle dish, 8.8cm., small
workman's cross marks.
(Lawrence Fine Art)
$304

A Worcester First Period
cream jug, with sparrow-
beak spout, 9.5cm. square
seal mark. (Lawrence Fine
Art)            $388

A pair of Royal Worcester
female figures depicting
Autumn and Spring,
circa 1862-75, 11½ and
10½in. high. (Woolley &
Wallis)          $449

A Royal Worcester porcelain
beaker vase of waisted cylindrical form, painted by K.
Blake, 22cm. high. (H. Spencer & Sons)      $200

A First Period Worcester
saucer, crossed swords mark
and 9 in underglaze blue.
(Lawrence Fine Art)
$415

A Worcester blue and white
guglet painted with the
'Willow Bridge Fisherman's'
pattern, 22.5cm. high.
$1,430

A First Period Worcester
leaf-shaped dish with raised
ribs, 21.7cm. wide. (Law-
rence Fine Art) $388

A Worcester yellow-ground pleated oval sauceboat, circa 1765, 15cm. wide. (Christie's) $2,419

One of a pair of Worcester partridge tureens and covers, circa 1765, 14.5cm. wide. (Christie's) $1,935

A Worcester double-lipped two-handled sauceboat, the scroll handles with pugs' head terminals, circa 1755, 22cm. wide. (Christie's) $2,298

A Worcester fluted teabowl and saucer pencilled in black with two quail among shrubs, circa 1770. (Christie's) $1,572

A pair of Royal Worcester 'Ivory' figures of kneeling water-carriers, green printed marks, no. 637, date codes for 1910 and 1912, 25.5cm. high. (Christie's) $786

A Worcester mug of Lord Henry Thynne type painted with a river landscape, circa 1775, 12cm. high. (Christie's) $1,089

A Worcester blue and white mug with grooved loop handle, circa 1758, 8.5cm. high. (Christie's) $786

A Royal Worcester porcelain figure of The Violinist, printed mark in puce and numbered 1487, 52.5cm. high. (H. Spencer & Sons) $582

A Worcester blue and white small mug, painted with The Landslide Pattern, circa 1758, 6cm. high. (Christie's) $786

A Royal Worcester pot pourri bowl and cover. (Reeds Rains) $291

A Royal Worcester pot pourri vase in the form of a bird of prey, date code 1926, 9in. high. (P. Wilson & Co.) $242

A Royal Worcester figure group, originally one of a pair, modelled in the style of Kate Greenaway, 7in. high. (P. Wilson & Co.) $341

Pair of Royal Worcester porcelain figures of classical maidens, inscribed Hadley, 33.5cm. high. (H. Spencer & Sons) $470

A Graingers Worcester porcelain campana vase, 8in. high. (Dacre, Son & Hartley) $74

Pair of Royal Worcester porcelain figures of Middle Eastern musicians, printed marks in puce, 32.5cm. high. (H. Spencer & Sons) $537

A Worcester First Period tea bowl, fluted and painted with flower festoons. (Lawrence Fine Art) $102

A Royal Worcester porcelain figure of an Arab water carrier, printed mark in red, 25.5cm. high. (H. Spencer & Sons) $425

A Royal Worcester globular shaped vase, signed Stinton, with printed crown and circle mark, date code 1934, 3in. high. (P. Wilson & Co.) $154

# WORCESTER

One of two Worcester cups, 'The Willow Root', of flared beaker form, circa 1751-55.
$4,467

A Worcester Flight & Barr inkstand. (Bearnes)
$600

A Royal Worcester porcelain pot pourri vase, cover and liner, of baluster form, 25.5cm. high. (H. Spencer & Sons)    $350

A tankard of cylindrical form transfer printed in underglaze blue, unmarked but in the Worcester style, 5½in. high. (P. Wilson & Co.)
$176

A Royal Worcester vase with cover, painted by John Stinton, date code 1903, 16½in. high. (P. Wilson & Co.)    $880

One of a pair of ice pails, liners and covers, painted by P. Bradley, circa 1830. 33cm.    $12,056

A Royal Worcester vase painted and signed by Jas. Stinton, date code 1918, 5½in. high. (P. Wilson & Co.)    $154

A pair of Royal Worcester candle snuffers. (Worrall's)
$348

A Royal Worcester figure of Mr Pickwick, with printed crown and circle mark, date code 1897, 6½in. high. (P. Wilson & Co.)
$209

# BRACKET CLOCKS

THE most generally highly prized timepieces, acknowledged for their superb craftsmanship and design, are those known as bracket clocks — particularly those dating from the late seventeenth and early eighteenth centuries.

Although the technique of using a coiled spring instead of weights as a clock's driving force had been known since 1530, when it was used by Peter Henlein of Nuremburg, it was not until the introduction of the short bob pendulum by Fromanteel in 1658 that portable clocks really began to move. Earliest examples resembled truncated grandfather clocks, having square brass faces and plain ebony cases — though they sometimes had a little gilt enrichment. There is a glazed door at the rear, through which can be seen the finely engraved backplate, and a handle on the top enables the piece to be carried from room to room. All English bracket clocks run for at least eight days without rewinding, and nearly all early examples have a fusee movement. This, in the simplest terms, is a top-shaped brass contraption which houses the mainspring whose unwinding is controlled by means of gut, wire or something similar to a miniature bicycle chain coiled round the outside of the 'top'.

Continental clock movements — which can be recognized by the gear teeth set actually on the drum containing the mainspring — are not as sought-after as their English counterparts — whose drums are toothless.

The English movement can also be recognized by the positions of the winding holes in relation to each other and the axis of the hands: if the three points form almost a straight line — with no more than half an inch deviation — the chances are that the movement is English.

Late 19th century English ebonized quarter chiming bracket clock, 29in. high. (Christie's) $1,320

A George III mahogany striking bracket clock, the silvered dial signed James Wild London, 16in. high. (Christie's) $1,983

A large astronomical calendar clock, the corner of the 15½in. dial with a plaque signed John Naylor, 38in. high. $49,764

A walnut bracket clock, signed Robt. Allam, London, 47cm. high. (Christie's) $880

An early japanned bracket clock case containing a modern German clock, 15½in. high. $797

A George III mahogany striking bracket clock, the dial signed Francis Dorell London, 19in. high. (Christie's) $2,566

# BRACKET CLOCKS

A small early George III ebonized bracket clock, the dial signed Jno. Dwerrihouse, 16in. high. $1,914

An ebony veneered month bracket clock, the 8½in. dial signed Jonathan Puller, Londini Fecit, 14½in. high excluding later feet. $21,285

An Edwardian inlaid mahogany chiming bracket clock, circa 1900, 26in. high, with a mahogany bracket, 15in. high. $1,206

A mahogany bracket clock of pagoda form, the movement inscribed Robert Roskell & Son, Liverpool, 21in. high. (Outhwaite & Litherland) $436

A Regency walnut cased bracket clock with silvered dial, maker Raw Bros., London. (Morphets) $438

An ebonized gilt brass mounted quarter chiming bracket clock, signed Lambert & Co., London, 16½in. high. (Lawrence Fine Art) $1,464

A walnut chiming bracket clock, by Viner London, No. 2208, 22in. high, and a walnut bracket, 8in. high. $851

A George III bracket clock by Benjamin Dunkley, with brass dial, the mahogany case with brass carrying handles, 22in. high overall. (Dacre, Son & Hartley) $260

An ebonized chiming bracket clock, circa 1880, 25in. high, and a conforming bracket, 10½in. high. $1,064

A late Victorian ebonized chiming bracket clock, inscribed Thompson, Ashford, 24in., with later wall bracket.
$1,053

A mahogany chiming musical bracket clock, the 8in. dial signed John Taylor London, 24in. high.
$3,190

A George III mahogany striking bracket clock, the dial signed Thos. Wagstaffe London, 19in. high. (Christie's) $2,100

A bracket clock with eight-day striking movement, by Thompson, Ashford, 24in. high. (Vidler & Co.)
$310

A Regency mahogany and brass bound bracket clock by Handley & Moore, London, 17½in. high. (Capes, Dunn & Co.) $1,035

A small ebonized bracket clock, the 6in. dial signed Josiah Emery London, 14½in. high.
$4,785

A George III mahogany bracket clock with alarm, signed John Taylor, London, 54cm. high. (Christie's) $1,210

A small ebony veneered quarter-repeating bracket clock, the 6¼in. dial signed Joseph Knibb, London, 12in. high.
$18,447

A mid 18th century fruitwood case eight-day striking bracket clock, 20½in. high. (Woolley & Wallis)
$1,595

# BRACKET CLOCKS

A gilt brass mounted walnut quarter chiming bracket clock, 32¾in. high. (Lawrence Fine Art) $805

A small ebony-veneered quarter-repeating alarm bracket timepiece, the 6in. dial signed Jam: Cuff London, 13½in. high. $3,349

A rosewood bracket timepiece, signed Wm. Speakman, London, 20½in. high. (Lawrence Fine Art) $342

A large bracket clock with eight-day Continental movement chiming in eight gongs, 27in. high. (Anderson & Garland) $532

A mahogany bracket timepiece, signed Daniel Dickerson, Framlingham, 13in. high. (Lawrence Fine Art) $612

A small ebony veneered bracket clock, signed John Drew Londini Fecit, 14½in. high. (Lawrence Fine Art) $2,871

A mahogany bracket clock, signed Debois & Wheeler, Grays Inn Passage, 17¼in. high. (Lawrence Fine Art) $765

An ebonized wood bracket clock, by J. Lukavetzki Brunn, No. 174, 16in. high. (Robt. W. Skinner Inc.) $1,000

An ebonized quarter chiming bracket clock, signed on an inset plaque Danl. Catlin, Lynn, 20in. high. (Lawrence Fine Art) $1,064

An ebonized quarter repeating bracket clock, the 7in. dial signed J. Windmills London, 15½in. high.
$3,190

A mahogany bracket clock by Charles Frodsham, 24in. high, circa 1850. $574

An 18th century bracket clock in burr walnut case, with eight-day movement by Jos. Kirk, 16in. high. (Dreweatt Watson & Barton) $2,423

An ebony quarter striking bracket clock, the 7in. dial signed Wm. Speakman London, 14in. high.
$3,349

A small and very fine veneered ebony quarter repeating bracket clock, the 6in. dial signed Tho. Tompion Londini fecit, 12½in. high. $49,445

An ebonized quarter-repeating bracket clock, the backplate signed Nathaniel Hodges, 12½in. high.
$8,294

An ebony quarter-repeating bracket clock, the 7in. dial signed Henry Callowe, 15½in. high. $15,152

A George III mahogany bracket clock, dial signed Tomlin Royal Exchange London, 13in. high.
$2,233

A George III ebonized bracket clock, the 7in. dial signed Alexdr. Cumming London, 18½in. high.
$1,276

# CARRIAGE CLOCKS

**C**LOCKS intended for use whilst travelling — with their spring-driven movements — had been used to a small degree since the sixteenth century but they never really caught on until the French clockmakers began to produce them en masse early in the nineteenth century.

The original concept of the carriage clock as we know it was an English innovation, and it often incorporated such fancy and complex refinements as repeat and date mechanisms. There was sometimes even a dial indicating the phases of the moon.

Most of these clocks have silvered dials and are usually housed in ormolu cases, often embellished with corinthian columns on the front corners.

Carriage clocks made during the early nineteenth century usually had quite fine cast brass cases, with thick bevelled glass windows resting in grooves in the frame. The glass at the top was large; later it became much smaller and was let into a metal plate. Carrying handles are usually round on these early 19th century clocks, tapering toward the ends and, because there is often a repeat button on the top front edge, the handles usually fold backwards only.

The alarm is pretty obvious, having its own small dial with arabic numerals and a single hand situated at the bottom of the face. The driving mechanism for the alarm is the small brass barrel situated about three quarters of the way up the clock and to one side.

A strike mechanism is indicated, by two large brass barrels with toothed ends which sit side by side at or near the bottom of the works.

A French porcelain panelled 'bamboo' carriage clock, 7in. high.(Lawrence Fine Art) $1,996

A grande sonnerie alarm carriage clock, dial signed Le Roy & Fils Pals., 5¾in. high.$1,595

A grande sonnerie carriage clock, the base plate with the stamp of A. Brocot, 5¾in. high.$1,435

A French brass grande sonnerie carriage alarm clock, 7¼in. high. (Lawrence Fine Art) $452

A brass carriage timepiece, the movement with cylinder escapement, 6¼in. high. (Lawrence Fine Art) $252

A lacquered brass one-piece striking carriage clock, the backplate stamped Hy. Marc Paris, 5½in. high. (Christie's) $525

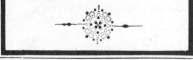

A miniature French gilt brass carriage timepiece, with the trade stamp of Henri Jacot, 3¾in. high. (Lawrence Fine Art) $306

A late 19th century French carriage clock in gilt 'bamboo' chinoiserie case, inscribed John Bennett, Paris, 8in. high. (Dreweatt Watson & Barton)       $1,637

A gilt metal striking carriage clock, the dial with concave ivory Arabic chapter, the case with stamp of Drocourt, 6¾in. high. (Christie's) $816

A small minute-repeating mantel or travelling timepiece signed Cole London, 3¾in. high. $957

A silver calendar carriage clock, the silver dial with gold Breguet hands, the backplate signed Jump, 6¼in. high. $27,115

A porcelain mounted carriage clock, the repeating lever movement stamped Maurice et Cie, 5½in. high. $1,276

A French brass carriage clock, the movement with lever escapement, 6in. high. (Lawrence Fine Art) $385

A gilt metal porcelain mounted carriage clock with lever platform, the case with stamp of Japy Freres, 9½in. high. (Christie's)       $3,616

A small carriage timepiece, the 1in. dial signed Payne London, 3in. high. $1,435

## CARRIAGE CLOCKS

A grande sonnerie carriage clock, the base with the stamp of Henri Jacot, 7in. high.  $1,435

A lacquered brass striking carriage clock with enamel dial with engine-turned gilt mask, gorge case, stamp of Drocourt, 5¾in. high. (Christie's)  $816

A gilt metal striking miniature carriage clock with enamel dial, 3¼in. high. (Christie's)  $933

A gilt metal striking one-piece carriage clock, the backplate stamped in an oval Hy. Marc Paris, 6¾in. high. (Christie's)  $816

A champleve enamelled brass carriage clock with cut compensated balance to lever platform, 7in. high. (Christie's) $2,916

A gilt metal one-piece grande sonnerie carriage clock with bridge to helical spring of 'jewelled' lever platform, probably Franche Comte, 5½in. high. (Christie's)  $1,283

A silvered and parcel gilt grande sonnerie calendar carriage clock, 7¼in. high. (Christie's)  $2,333

A porcelain mounted alarm carriage clock, the repeating lever movement with gong striking, 6¼in. high.  $1,754

A brass striking carriage clock, enamel dial inscribed Le Roy & Fils 57 New Bond Street Made in France, 5½in. high. (Christie's)   $443

An early multi-piece gilt carriage clock by **Paul Garnier**, 5¾in. high. (Christie's) $2,799

A silvered brass oval miniature carriage clock, the case with stamp of A. Margaine, 8cm. high. (Christie's) $309

A lacquered brass striking carriage clock, the ivorine dial with gilt mask, cannelee riche case, stamped for Henri Jacot, 6in. high. (Christie's) $525

A gilt metal striking carriage clock with silvered lever platform, the gilt chapter ring signed Le Roy Paris, 6¼in. high. (Christie's) $525

A gilt metal striking carriage clock with dial signed Lucien Paris, 6¼in. high. (Christie's) $642

A gilt metal striking carriage clock with enamel dial, 5¼in. high. (Christie's) $933

A gilt metal grande sonnerie carriage clock with strike/ repeat on gongs with selection lever in the base, 6¼in. high. (Christie's) $1,516

A gilt metal grande sonnerie carriage clock with enamel dial, case with stamp of Henri Jacot, 7in. high. (Christie's)$1,925

A lacquered brass grande sonnerie giant carriage clock, 8¼in. high. (Christie's) $1,516

# CLOCK SETS

A popular nineteenth century interior decor innovation was the 'garniture de cheminee'. The designs and quality of these sets is as diverse as that of clocks alone, there being variously shaped and ornamented timepieces. Side ornaments generally took the shape of urns, figures or candelabra. Many sport porcelain panels and faces of blue, green or pink ground with floral decoration by Sevres or Limoges, and have urn shaped finials. As regards the clocks, a plain white porcelain face with a glazed door often indicates an early nineteenth century piece. Later clocks, without doors, were designed to sit on velvet covered bases beneath glass domes.

The early nineteenth century clocks usually have a locking plate movement – one in which the strike mechanism is independent of the timing mechanism. This is indicated by a large wheel, often situated on the back plate which has notches of different lengths cut into the outer rim; short for one, longer for two and so on up to twelve.

Later clocks have a rack and snail movement, which means that the strike mechanism is incorporated with the other works. This is indicated by a step ladder arrangement built into the wheel which drives the hour hand.

An ormolu and porcelain garniture, circa 1870, clock 15½in. high, the pair of candelabra, 14in. high.            $1,000

A Mexican onyx and champleve enamel four-glass clock garniture, circa 1900, the clock 20in. high, the urns, 14in. high. $812

A champleve enamel Mexican onyx and gilt metal garniture, circa 1900, the clock 13½in. high, the pair of urns 11in. high.
$1,000

An ormolu mounted Imari porcelain clock vase garniture, the circular enamel face indistinctly signed, 20in. high. (Christie's)     $2,025

A gilt spelter and porcelain composed garniture, the clock 22in. high, circa 1880, the pair of 'Sevres' covered urns, circa 1860, 15½in. high.          $1,000

A gilt metal and cloisonne enamel clock set in the Gothic style, the dial signed W. Angus Paris, 17 Lord Street, Liverpool, 20½in. high, the candelabra 17¼in. high. (Christie's)          $1,620

A 19th century French ormolu clock set, 20in. high. (Graves, Son & Pilcher)          $1,680

Late 19th century French black marble and bronze clock garniture, height of clock 21in., height of statues 18½in. (Robt. W. Skinner Inc.)          $850

A gilt bronze and champleve enamel clock garniture, the clock 14in. high, the urns 12½in. high.          $1,021

A French gilt brass clock garniture, the two train movement with Brocot type suspension, signed Rollin a Paris, 21in. high. (Lawrence Fine Art)          $1,530

# LANTERN CLOCKS

THE first truly domestic time-pieces were called lantern clocks. Proper old lantern clocks run for thirty hours and only have an hour hand – the minute hand was not introduced until about 1690 – but this is not to say that a clock with only one hand dates necessarily from the 17th century, for the smaller, local clock-makers continued to turn out the less complicated, one-handed timepieces for a further hundred years.

Earliest examples either stood on a bracket or were equipped with an iron ring at the back. This allowed the clock to be hung on a nail driven into the wall and it was levelled and steadied by means of spikes at the base.

Many of the early lantern clocks had a weight supported on a rope. This was found to be an unsatisfactory arrangement, since the rope often frayed, spreading fluff from the worn parts around the works of the clock, and then snapped, so the ropes were often replaced with chains.

During the 19th century, these clocks began to be mass-produced, particularly in Birmingham, and, although these have similar cases to the earlier ones, they are fitted with fusee movements and short internal pendulums. These can easily be identified from the front by the winding holes – the others have weights, not springs.

Others, even later – are fitted with a small, eight-day French carriage clock movement which can be seen clinging to the back of the face with the winding key sticking out of the back.

Wing alarm lantern clock, circa 1700, 15½in. high. $1,875

Early 19th century alarm clock with silvered square dial, inscribed Samuel Taylor. (Capes, Dunn & Co.) $161

A silver and gilt inlaid striking Japanese lantern clock, 19th century, 250mm. high. $2,838

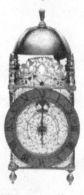

Late 17th century lantern clock in posted frame, 14in. high, restored. $2,000

An Italian brass and iron lantern clock, probably circa 1700, 35cm. high. (Christie's) $3,750

A brass lantern clock for the Turkish market, signed John Ellis, London, 36cm. high. (Christie's) $660

A lantern clock with a 6½in. dial engraved with a ring of tulips, 15in. high. $702

A wing lantern clock, the 6in. dial signed John Ebsworth at ye (sign of the crossed keys) in Lothbury Londini Fecit, 15½in. high, with a wood bracket. $2,838

Late 17th century lantern clock, 5¾in. dial signed Henry Jones in ye Temple, 15½in. high. $2,000

A lantern clock, the broad chapter ring signed Thatcher Cranbrook, 13½in. high. $1,986

An early lantern clock, the 7in. dial signed Thomas Knifton at the (crossed keys) Lothbury Fecit, 12in. high. $2,552

A brass lantern clock by Edward Clement, circa 1791, with single hand, (no pendulum or weight), 13¼in. high. (Robt. W. Skinner Inc.) $1,100

A brass lantern clock, circa 1880, the dial with leaf-engraved central reserve signed Goldsmiths & Silversmiths Co., London, 16½in. high. $964

Late 17th century Swiss clock with shaped rectangular iron dial, 40cm. high. (Christie's) $1,875

A late 17th/early 18th century brass lantern clock, 38cm. tall, complete with 18th century oak wall bracket. (Andrew Grant) $1,155

## LONGCASE CLOCKS

**D**URING the last quarter of the eighteenth century, manufacturers turned their attentions to quantity rather than quality, making such economies as the use of white painted wood or iron faces after 1790.

At first, faces were eight to nine inches square, of brass, with flowers and scrolls engraved in their centers. These increased to about ten inches square by the sixteen eighties, when the wider cases were introduced. From the beginning of the eighteenth century, faces were usually twelve inches square, or larger following the introduction of the arch.

This was in widespread use by 1720 and, on early examples, was often less than a semicircle.

The silvered brass chapter ring with its engraved roman numerals grew along with the face, and the inner rim was marked with quarter and half hour divisions. The elaborate hour hand reached to the interior of the chapter ring, while the plainer minute hand — if the clock had one — reached to the outer rim.

The earliest spandrels were of cupids' heads between curved wings. Later this became elaborate scrollwork which, by 1700, incorporated a female mask.

Dates of this sort are only general guides, of course, and by no means infallible, but they can be very useful in establishing an approximate date of birth — or at least ruling out a falsely early date. For instance, the fleur-de-lys, used to mark the half hours, was seldom employed after the 1740s — the same decade in which larger arabic numerals replaced the roman as minute markers. After 1750, an engraved brass or silvered face without a chapter ring was often used, and from 1775, a cast brass or enamelled copper face was introduced.

A late 18th century inlaid mahogany longcase clock, inscribed Wenham, Deerham, 231cm. high. (H. Spencer & Sons) $2,108

An early 19th century oak and mahogany crossbanded and inlaid longcase clock, circa 1810, 92in. high. (Reeds Rains) $464

Westminster chime grandmother clock, no pendulum, 1920. (British Antique Exporters) $90

A walnut month going equation longcase clock, signed Geo. Graham, London, 240cm. high. (Christie's) $77,000

A George III Scottish mahogany longcase clock, dial signed John Peatt Crieff, 6ft. 10in. high.
$2,392

George III mahogany cased longcase clock by John Lloyd of London. (Phillips)
$4,320

An Edwardian inlaid mahogany longcase clock with eight day movement. (H. Spencer & Sons)
$1,116

A 19th century mahogany longcase clock in the 18th century Gothic style, 215cm. high. (H. Spencer & Sons)
$2,193

A late George III longcase clock in mahogany case with eight-day three-train movement, 95½in. high. (Dreweatt Watson & Barton)
$1,834

An olivewood longcase clock, dial signed Joseph Knibb, 6ft.4in. high.
$28,710

A George III mahogany longcase clock, arch inscribed Thos. Conley, Whitby. (H. Spencer & Sons)
$868

George II figured walnut longcase clock, by J. Marsh, London, 97in. high overall. (Reeds Rains)
$3,479

# LONGCASE CLOCKS

A late 18th century longcase clock by C. Horwood of Bristol, 235cm. high. (Osmond Tricks) $2,358

A 17th century walnut marquetry longcase clock, inscribed Thos. Taylor in Holborn, London, 85in. high. $6,853

A walnut longcase clock, signed A. Dunlop, London, 8ft.10in. high. (Lawrence Fine Art) $2,153

An early 19th century Irish mahogany longcase clock, dial signed Edwd. Smith, 6ft.6in. high. $1,595

An oak longcase clock, signed Thos. Brown, Birmingham, 6ft.11½in. high. (Lawrence Fine Art) $1,052

A longcase clock in mahogany, the dial inscribed Parke, 90in. high. (Outhwaite & Litherland) $1,890

A mahogany longcase clock, signed Andrew Evans, Stockport, 8ft.6in. high. (Lawrence Fine Art) $877

A brass-faced grandfather clock in oak case, by Thos. Collier, circa 1830. (Ward & Partners) $1,950

An Edwardian inlaid mahogany longcase clock with eight-day movement. (H. Spencer & Sons) $496

A Hepplewhite mahogany inlaid tall case clock, by Wm. Bancroft, Scarborough, circa 1810, 98in. high. (Robt. W. Skinner Inc.) $2,750

An early 19th century mahogany longcase clock, engraved Martin Hall. (H. Spencer & Sons) $696

A carved oak longcase clock, signed Peter Nichols, Newport, 7ft.5½in. high. (Lawrence Fine Art) $733

A marquetry longcase clock, signed on the chapter ring Windmills, London, 7ft.1½in. high. (Lawrence Fine Art)$6,380

A walnut miniature longcase clock in the George III style, 152cm. high. (H. Spencer & Sons) $1,186

An 18th century longcase clock, inscribed JN Greaves, Newcastle, 89in. high. (Anderson & Garland) $2,210

A mahogany longcase clock with eight-day movement rack striking, 7ft. 2½in. high. (Lawrence Fine Art) $685

A late 17th century green lacquered longcase clock, 97in. high. (Anderson & Garland) $2,352

A figured mahogany longcase striking regulator, signed Whistler, 6ft.7in. high. (Lawrence Fine Art) $2,928

An inlaid mahogany longcase clock, signed Peter Walker, London, 7ft.8in. high. (Lawrence Fine Art) $2,262

A George III oak longcase clock, inscribed Thornton, Lutterworth. (H. Spencer & Sons) $464

An 18th century walnut cased clock by Jno. Baylis of Bromyard. (Aldridges) $1,920

An 18th century walnut and mahogany longcase clock by Bronne, Liverpool. (H. Spencer & Sons) $1,032

An Austrian beechwood longcase clock painted to simulate mahogany, circa 1900, 207.9cm. high. (Christie's) $680

George III oak and mahogany crossbanded longcase clock , circa 1785, 7ft.4in. high. (Capes, Dunn & Co.) $914

A carved oak long-
case clock, with 3
weights, key and
winder, circa 1880,
98in. high.
$2,871

A late 18th century
George III maho-
gany longcase clock,
inscribed Robert
Hood, London, 94in.
high. $9,838

A Louis XV design
longcased clock
by Gilbert, Bel-
fast. (Russell
Baldwin & Bright)
$3,750

An early 19th cen-
tury mahogany long-
case clock with brass
dial and eight-day
movement. (P. Wil-
son & Co.)
$2,620

A George III long-
case clock, the
dial inscribed Jno.
Williams, London,
90¾in. high. (Drew-
eatt Watson & Bar-
ton) $1,703

A large boulle bracket clock
and pedestal, inlaid with
cut brass on a tortoiseshell
ground, 92in. high. overall.
(Banks & Silvers)
$3,697

A Federal pine grain
painted tall case
clock, by S. Hoadley,
Conn., circa 1830,
86in. high. (Robt. W.
Skinner Inc.)
$13,000

Thirty-hour alarm
longcase clock, dial
by Wm. Kipling, in
a walnut marquetry
case in Dutch style.
(P. Wilson & Co.)
$1,189

An Edwardian painted satinwood longcase clock, the chapter ring signed Wm. Eastwood, 8ft.2in. high. (Christie's) $2,100

A late Georgian mahogany longcase clock, the brass dial signed Samuel Shepley, Stockport, 8ft. high. (Christie's) $3,033

A walnut longcase clock, the 12in. dial signed Wm. Threlkeld London, 8ft.8in. high. $4,785

A Georgian mahogany longcase clock, the dial inscribed J. Leroux, Charing Cross, 86in. high. (Christie's) $2,737

Queen Anne style mahogany tall case clock, James Wady, Rhode Island, circa 1750, 84in. high. (Robt. W. Skinner Inc.) $14,500

A mahogany longcase regulator, the Franklin type dial signed Vulliamy Pall Mall London, 5ft.11in. high. (Christie's) $8,748

A pine polychrome decorated tail case clock, Connecticut, circa 1830, 85in. high. (Robt. W. Skinner Inc.) $5,200

A late 19th century German walnut polyphon musical disc clock. (Warren & Wignall) $4,875

## MANTEL CLOCKS

AS a basic rule French mantel clocks are nearly all decoration while English models are nearly all clock.

Early French makers to look for are Lepine, Janvier, Amand, Lepaute and Thuret, who started to use a great deal of elaborate scrollwork at the end of the seventeenth century. If you find a clock by any of these makers you have certainly found a clock. Things to look for are a verge escapement — which is loosely indicated by a horizontally turning crown wheel with sharp teeth just above the pendulum — a painted face or porcelain numerals and a winding hole placed in the face where you least expect it. Pendulums should be pear shaped bobs on brass rods.

By the 19th century, everyone decided they wanted one of these flashy French clocks to add an air of opulence to the lounge. Consequently, manufacturers began doing a spot of overtime.

The word that really matters in any description is 'ormolu' — that is, it is made of a hard metal, such as brass, which is rough cast before being chiselled and engraved by hand and, finally, coated with a thin amalgam of gold and mercury.

Cheaper nineteenth century mass produced clocks have a similar appearance — at first glance — but they are made of spelter. This is a soft metal which is simply cast and gilded. Clocks with decoration of this kind should sell for about a quarter of the price of the ormolu pieces. The infallible test is to scratch the underside of the clock; if the gold colour comes away to reveal gray metal, it's spelter, if brass is revealed it is ormolu. Another test is to tap the case sharply with a coin. If the sound is sharp and pingy, you have hard metal; if it is a dull thud, you have soft.

A mid 19th century French mantel clock with eight-day movement, 21in. high. (Dacre, Son & Hartley) $2,852

A white marble and ormolu portico clock, circa 1830, the white enamel annular dial signed LeRoy a Paris, 19½in. high. $957

A Swiss automaton mantel clock, 9in. high.(Christie's) $1,866

A small Restoration ormolu mantel clock in Louis XV style, the enamel dial signed S. Devaulx Palais Royal 124, 11in. high. $612

A gilt metal desk timepiece of long duration and in the manner of Thos. Cole, 7½in. high. $1,276

A Continental gilt metal candle alarm with florally engraved plinth case, 5in. high. (Christie's) $700

# MANTEL CLOCKS

A cast iron blinking eye timepiece, 'Sambo', America, circa 1860, 16in. high. (Robt. W. Skinner Inc.) $1,200

Late 19th century nickel plated paperweight timepiece, by New Haven Clock Co., 7½in. high. (Robt. W. Skinner Inc.) $130

A gilt metal timepiece, The Plato Clock, circa 1903, 6in. high. (Robt. W. Skinner Inc.) $55

An Empire bronze and gilt-bronze mantel clock, circa 1815, 31½in. high. $1,435

Late 19th century Faberge gold mounted and jewelled nephrite miniature timepiece, 5.5cm. $4,789

Art Deco hardstone and cloisonne enamel desk clock, with 13J Swiss movement, 4.1/8in. high. (Robt. W. Skinner Inc.) $925

A cast iron and mother-of-pearl shelf clock by Terry & Andrews, with painted dial, circa 1855, 15¾in. high. (Robt. W. Skinner Inc.) $150

Early 19th century boulle mantel timepiece, the movement signed Barrauds & Lund, 10½in. high. $925

An ormolu pendule d'Officier with grande sonnerie and alarm, 8¼in. high. $3,987

A gilt bronze mantel clock, the dial with silvered chapter ring, 18½in. high, circa 1850.    $606

Swinging doll timepiece, by Ansonia Clock Co., circa 1890, 8in. high. (Robt. W. Skinner Inc.) $500

A silver and rosewood travelling or mantel clock, 6¼in. high.    $638

A Federal mahogany shelf clock, by Reuben Tower, Massa., 1836, 34½in. high. (Robt. W. Skinner Inc.) $7,500

Mid 18th century Turkish hexagonal brass cased table clock, 150mm.    $3,030

A Federal mahogany inlaid shelf timepiece, by A. Whitcombe, Massa., circa 1790, 13½in. high. (Robt. W. Skinner Inc.) $18,000

A cast iron front mantel clock, polychrome painted, America, circa 1890, 11¾in. high. (Robt. W. Skinner Inc.) $80

Early 20th century gray marble and glass Art Deco mantel clock, France, 11in. high. (Robt. W. Skinner Inc.)    $310

Cast iron mantel clock with painted dial and eight-day time and strike movement, America, circa 1860, 20in. high. (Robt. W. Skinner Inc.)    $275

# MANTEL CLOCKS

## CLOCKS & WATCHES

A French gilt brass mounted boulle bracket clock, signed Leroy a Paris, 18in. high, excluding bracket. (Lawrence Fine Art)    $1,038

A French porcelain mounted gilt brass mantel clock, with the trade stamp of Miroy Freres, 14½in. high. (Lawrence Fine Art)    $252

An iron weight-driven alarm chamber timepiece in the Gothic manner, 22in. high.    $2,552

A French free standing bronze spelter sculptural clock, with the trade stamp of S. Marti, 48½in. high. (Lawrence Fine Art)    $879

Late 19th century French classical Revival brass and glass mantel clock, 14½in. high. (Robt. W. Skinner Inc.)    $325

A George III quarter striking musical automaton clock, backplate signed T. H. Barrell London, 22in. high.    $3,509

A carved wood Art Nouveau mantel clock, by the Chelsea Clock Co., Boston, circa 1920, 18¼in. high. (Robt. W. Skinner Inc.)    $550

Champleve and brass mantel clock, France, circa 1900, 8in. high. (Robt. W. Skinner Inc.)    $750

Bobbing doll timepiece, by Ansonia Clock Co., circa 1890, the bisque figure suspended from a spring under movement. (Robt. W. Skinner Inc.)    $775

Mid 19th century ormolu
mounted bracket clock,
France, backplate engraved
'Fiault Paris, Reparee par
Bourdin', 45in. high. (Robt.
W. Skinner Inc.)
$1,700

A French black marble and
porphyry perpetual calen-
dar mantel clock, signed
Francis Glading, 15¼in.
high. (Lawrence Fine Art)
$1,264

A Louis XV-style ebonized
and ormolu mounted bracket
clock with fusee movement,
3ft.11in. overall. (Capes,
Dunn & Co.)　$206

Swinging doll timepiece, by
Ansonia Clock Co., circa
1890, 12in. high. (Robt. W.
Skinner Inc.) $600

An Art Deco style circular
pink mirror glass electric
mantel clock. (Fox & Sons)
$222

Late Victorian oak
and gilded brass min-
iature longcase clock,
dial signed Monk,
Bolton, circa 1890,
18in. high. (Reeds
Rains)　$232

Late 19th century bronze
and ormolu figural mantel
clock, France, 28½in. high.
(Robt. W. Skinner Inc.)
$1,600

A Louis XIV French ormolu
mounted boulle bracket clock,
signed Gribelin a Paris, 49½in.
high. (Lawrence Fine Art)
$2,662

A Victorian eight-day calendar clock by B. Jacobs, Hull,
15¾in. wide. (Woolley &
Wallis)　$520

# MANTEL CLOCKS

An ebonized balloon bracket clock, signed J. Leroux, London, 18¾in. high. (Lawrence Fine Art)        $771

A 19th century black onyx mantel clock with bronze figural mountings, France, 21¼in. long. (Robt. W. Skinner Inc.) $325

A George III gilt-metal mantel clock with a 3¼in. dial by Ellicott, 11¾in. high.        $1,595

Early 20th century green onyx glass and brass mantel clock, by Ansonia Clock Co., Conn., 11in. high. (Robt. W. Skinner Inc.)    $300

Late 19th century circular silver mounted hardstone desk clock by Fabergé, St. Petersburg, 12.3cm. $1,654

Federal mahogany pillar and scroll clock, by Eli & Samuel Terry, Conn., circa 1825, 28½in. high. (Robt. W. Skinner Inc.) $650

A walnut mantel clock, the movement of the Black Forest type with wooden plates, 17in. high. (Lawrence Fine Art) $452

A French gilt brass and jewelled porcelain mounted mantel clock, with the trade stamp of Japy Freres, 16¾in. high. (Lawrence Fine Art) $532

A French four glass and gilt brass mantel clock, the two-train movement with Brocot suspension, 14¼in. high. (Lawrence Fine Art) $532

A late 19th century French timepiece with 3½in. plain glass dial, 9½in. high. $446

Early 20th century marble base mantel clock, probably French, dial marked Bigelow & Kennard, Boston, 12½in. high. (Robt. W. Skinner Inc.) $650

An early 19th century Black Forest clockmaker timepiece, movement signed J. T. Wilson Stamford, 15in. high. $1,036

A French four glass and brass mantel clock, the movement with Brocot type escapement, stamped H. P. & Co., 13¾in. high. (Lawrence Fine Art) $479

Mid 19th century French ormolu and marble figural mantel clock, signed Carandas, A Versailles, 18½in. high. (Robt. W. Skinner Inc.) $425

Late 19th century Champleve, glass and brass mantel clock, France, 10¾in. high. (Robt. W. Skinner Inc.) $650

An eight-day time and strike clock with J. Pradier bronze, 11in. long. (Robt. W. Skinner Inc.)$800

An opalescent glass clock frame by R. Lalique, 4.3in. high. (Woolley & Wallis) $667

A carved mahogany mantel clock, by Marsh, Gilbert & Co., Conn., circa 1825, 37in. high. (Robt. W. Skinner Inc.) $750

# MANTEL CLOCKS

A walnut double dial calendar shelf clock, by Seth Thomas Clock Co., 32in. high. (Robt. W. Skinner Inc.) $1,500

A gilt bronze and porcelain mantel clock, signed Leroy Freres a Paris, circa 1879, 10½in. high. $638

Double steeple mahogany wagon spring shelf clock, by Birge & Fuller, Conn., circa 1846, 26in. high. (Robt. W. Skinner Inc.) $1,400

An Empire carved mahogany shelf clock, by M. Leavenworth & Son, Conn., 30in. high. (Robt. W. Skinner Inc.) $1,500

A Louis Philippe gilt bronze mantel clock with eight-day striking movement and a glass dome, 16½in. high. (Woolley & Wallis) $467

Empire triple decker mantel clock, by Birge, Mallory & Co., circa 1840, 36in. high. (Robt. W. Skinner Inc.) $550

Empire carved mahogany mirror clock by Munger & Benedict, New York, circa 1830, 39½in. high. (Robt. W. Skinner Inc.) $1,500

An ormolu and marble mantel clock, French, 12in. high, circa 1860. $1,039

Late 19th century oak double dial calendar shelf clock, by Waterbury Clock Co., 24in. high. (Robt. W. Skinner Inc.) $550

216

Late 19th century silver plated mantel clock, by Leroy & Fils, Paris, 14. 3/8in. high. (Robt. W. Skinner Inc.)$250

An ebonized wood and gilt bronze bracket clock by Winterhalder & Hoffmeir, 27¼in. high, circa 1880. $574

Late 19th century ebonized wood miniature tall clock, by G. Hubbell & Son, 24in. high. (Robt. W. Skinner Inc.)     $1,100

A rosewood shelf clock, attributed to Atkins Clock Mfg. Co., Conn., circa 1855, 18¾in. high. (Robt. W. Skinner Inc.) $1,300

A late Victorian novelty clock in the form of a ship, the pendulum surmounted by a figure of a helmsman at the wheel. (H. Spencer & Sons)     $928

A Federal mahogany pillar and scroll clock, by Seth Thomas, circa 1820, 30in. high. (Robt. W. Skinner Inc.) $1,000

An Empire mahogany and mahogany veneer shelf clock, by Hotchkiss & Benedict, N.Y., circa 1830, 38in. high. (Robt. W. Skinner Inc.) $1,000

Late 19th century bronze and marble mantel clock, 23½in. high. (Robt. W. Skinner Inc.) $400

A late 19th century oak double dial calendar shelf clock, by Waterbury Clock Co., 29in. high. (Robt. W. Skinner Inc.) $500

# SKELETON CLOCKS

**I**T is a widely held belief that skeleton clocks — almost all of which were made during the 19th century — were the work of apprentices, made during their final year of study and so designed that examiners could observe the working and workmanship of each part with a minimum of effort.

While this might well have been the practice from which the style originated, its popularity throughout the Victorian period necessitated the masters' involvement in their manufacture. English models are of fret-cut brass, with silvered brass chapter rings, and are usually to be found on wooden bases beneath glass domes — for they are naturally prone to dust damage.

Some strike the hour with a single 'ping' on the bell at the top. This action is cunningly contrived by means of a pin on the minute hand wheel which, approaching the hour, lifts the hammer and lets it drop as the hour passes. Very rare examples have full striking mechanisms or even chimes.

Another variety is the French skeleton clock. This is usually much smaller, having solid front and back plates — often engraved on later examples — and enamelled chapter rings.

Late 19th century brass skeleton clock with fusee movement, England, 16in. high. (Robt. W. Skinner Inc.) $650

A skeleton clock, the silvered dial signed John Carr Swaffham, 9½in. high. $1,116

A 19th century brass skeleton clock of Gothic design, 12in. high. (Capes, Dunn & Co.) $335

A 19th century pierced brass repeating cathedral skeleton clock with glass dome. (Andrew Grant) $1,339

A skeleton clock with an annular silvered chapter ring and pierced hands, the plaque signed Litherland Davies & Co., 17½in. high. $3,828

A Brighton Pavilion skeleton clock with pierced silvered chapter ring, 16½in. high. $3,263

# WALL CLOCKS

ALTHOUGH wall clocks of a sort had been in existence for quite some time, it was not until Pitt imposed a tax on clocks, in 1797, that the impetus was given for the manufacture of large wall clocks which could be hung in public places for all to see. This is why many large wall clocks are still known today as Act of Parliament Clocks. The earliest of these rather resembled a big headed grandfather clock chopped off at the knees and are often as much as 5ft. high.

By the arrival of the Regency period, wall clocks had reduced in size to about eighteen inches in width, many veneered in rosewood with brass scroll inlay. The larger, Victorian, wall clocks are referred to as Vienna regulaters and have a mahogany case and an elaborate pendulum. You will most probably find one driven by means of a spring, but those employing weights are better quality as a rule.

Among the most plentiful are those made by a certain Mr. Chauncey Jerome, of Connecticut, who began mass producing wall clocks with glazed fronts and pretty painted scenes on the lower half.

Chauncey made them so cheaply though, that, when he sent a shipload to Britain, his valuation seemed so low that H.M.'s Customs men decided he was just trying to avoid paying the proper tax. Calling his bluff, or so they thought, they bought the entire cargo for Her Majesty's Government.

Chauncey immediately loaded a couple more ships to the gunwales with his cheap clocks in the hope that the Customs men would repeat their generous gesture — they did not.

Late 19th century pressed wood advertising timepiece, by Baird Adv. Clock Co., 31in. long. (Robt. W. Skinner Inc.) $1,400

Victorian oak wall clock with pendulum, 1890. (British Antique Exporters) $112

Victorian oak hanging wall clock with pendulum, 1900. (British Antique Exporters) $101

A lacquered tavern timepiece, with 25in. cream painted wooden dial, the case inscribed J. Bartholomew, 57in. high. $3,894

An Act of Parliament timepiece, signed beneath the dial Thomas Fenton, London. (Lawrence Fine Art) $865

Victorian Vienna wall clock with pendulum, 1880. (British Antique Exporters) $277

# WALL CLOCKS

A 19th century wall clock contained in an oak case with brass dial, 43in. high. (Anderson & Garland) $627

A George II giltwood cartel clock, signed James Smyth, London, circa 1750, 30in. high. (Stalker & Boos) $2,250

A Federal mahogany lyre timepiece, Henry Allen Hinckley, Massa., circa 1825, 38in. high. (Robt. W. Skinner Inc.) $2,000

A walnut regulator wall clock, by E. Howard & Co., Boston, circa 1875, 43in. high. (Robt. W. Skinner Inc.) $3,400

A late 17th century Italian day and night clock, signed Jean Baptiste Gonnon a Milan, 20 x 23½in. (Lawrence Fine Art) $3,061

Rosewood veneer wall regulator, by Seth Thomas, Conn., circa 1860, 31¼in. long. (Robt. W. Skinner Inc.) $550

A walnut calendar timepiece, by New Haven Clock Co., circa 1900, 32in. long. (Robt. W. Skinner Inc.) $450

A multi-dial longcase laboratory timepiece, by T. Wright, case 6ft.9in. high. (Lawrence Fine Art) $1,397

Jolly Tar wall timepiece, manufactured by Baird Clock Co., New York, 30½in. high. (Robt. W. Skinner Inc.) $1,150

A George III giltwood cartel timepiece with single fusee movement, 35in. high. $693

Boston Beer Co. wall timepiece, manufactured by the New Haven Clock Co., circa 1900, 14in. diam. (Robt. W. Skinner Inc.) $550

An oak double dial calendar clock, by Waterbury Clock Co., circa 1900, 29in. long. (Robt. W. Skinner Inc.) $1,100

A wall clock in carved mahogany case. (Butler & Hatch Waterman) $130

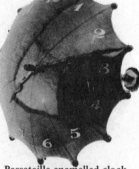

Bassetaille enamelled clock, open blue umbrella incorporating 24ct. gold leaf numerals on dome, 3½in. diam., France, circa 1900. (Robt. W. Skinner Inc.) $450

A figured mahogany trunk dial wall timepiece, the 15in. silvered dial signed Charles Fox, 57½in. long. (Lawrence Fine Art) $825

A grain-painted astronomical calendar clock, by Gabs Patent Welch Spring & Co., circa 1880, 30½in. long. (Robt. W. Skinner Inc.) $3,400

An eight-day striking and chiming longcase clock movement inscribed John Fletcher. (Capes, Dunn & Co.) $258

Late 19th century 'Coca Cola' walnut regulator timepiece, by Gilbert Clock Co., 30in. long. (Robt. W. Skinner Inc.) $325

# WALL CLOCKS

A mid 19th century wall clock contained in a walnut case, all enclosed by a black and gilt painted glass panel door, 40in. high. (Anderson & Garland)
$537

A Black Forest wall clock, circa 1840, the 11in. molded wood dial with alarm disc, 15½in. high.
$370

A 19th century gilt cartel clock by Mynuel, Paris. (Dee & Atkinson)
$1,599

A mahogany wall timepiece, Elnathan Taber, Massa., circa 1825, 34.7/8in. long. (Robt. W. Skinner Inc.)
$8,000

A Georgian mahogany wall dial clock, the dial signed Robt. Mawley London, 13½in. diam. (Christie's)
$1,050

A Vienna walnut regulator wall clock. (R. K. Lucas & Son)        $420

A Federal presentation mahogany banjo timepiece, by A. Willard, circa 1820, 40½in. high. (Robt. W. Skinner Inc.)
$2,200

A small Black Forest wall clock, circa 1850, the 6cm. enamel dial mounted on a repousse brass surround, 4¾in. high.     $737

A 19th century French Dore bronze cartel clock, 27in. high. (Stalker & Boos)     $1,700

# WATCHES

IT was primarily the need for navigation aboard ship which gave the impetus for the development of accurate timepieces in the 18th century, for although single handed watches had been in use for over a hundred years, they were of little use without a minute hand.

As with many new developments a number of notable English and French watchmakers came to the fore and if you are lucky enough to find a watch by Tompion, Mudge, Quare, Graham, Frodsham, Ellicot, Barraud, Leroux or Breguet, you will have a prize indeed.

Notable makers from this century are Rolex, Piquet, Cartier and Movado.

These days, collecting watches by makers of note can be an expensive business but there are a multitude of silver cased watches from the 19th century which can form the basis of a fascinating collection.

A Continental 14 kt. gold cased keywind pocket watch, the circular gilt dial with gilt Roman numerals. (H. Spencer & Sons)   $246

A silver pair cased verge watch No. 656 by Andrew Dunlop of London, 56mm. diam., circa 1700.   $1,595

An 18 kt. gold half hunting cased keyless lever watch, hallmarked Birmingham 1910, 50mm. (Lawrence Fine Art)   $465

A 14 kt. gold combined watch/lighter, the case engine-turned overall, 46mm. high. $638

A mid 16th century spherical gilt metal French watch case, 52mm. diam.   $1,467

A 9 kt. gold Prince Imperial watch, 1932, by Rolex, length overall 41mm.   $1,021

Early 19th century gold
floral enamel quarter
repeating cylinder watch
with center seconds,
65mm. diam. (Christie's)
$46,200

A small enamelled gold
verge watch, Swiss, circa
1800, 30mm. diam.
(Christie's) $165

Late 19th century enamelled
silver openface lever watch
with center seconds, for the
Chinese market, 39mm.
diam. (Christie's)
$462

An enamelled gold cylinder
watch, signed F. delynne a
Paris, no. 206, 40mm.diam.
(Christie's) $11,000

A quadruple case verge
watch for the Turkish market, signed Edw. Prior,
London, 70mm. diam.
(Christie's)$3,850

A Swiss gold and enamel
keyless lever watch, the
dial signed Hartog, 48mm.
diam. (Christie's)
$1,400

A silver triple cased verge
watch for the Turkish
market, the movement
signed Isaac Rogers Lon-
don 18925, 72mm. diam.
(Christie's) $1,516

A gold pair case verge
watch set with rubies, signed Jos. Martineau Sen.,
London, 53mm. diam.
(Christie's)
$13,200

A gold and enamel bridge-
cock verge watch signed
Guex A Paris, 52mm. diam.
(Christie's)    $2,216

A Swiss gold and enamel cylinder watch, the movement signed Mottu, Geneve, 34mm. diam. (Christie's) $758

A chased gold hunter cased minute repeating lever watch with automaton, signed Paul Matthey-Doret, Locle, 58mm. diam. (Christie's) $4,400

A French gold and enamel verge watch, the bridge-cock movement signed Le Febure A Paris No. 792, 36mm. diam. (Christie's) $525

A gold quarter-repeating automaton watch, 55mm. diam., circa 1820. $4,466

A gold openface chronograph with register, signed Patek Philippe & Co., Geneve, 44mm. diam. (Christie's) $2,640

A Swiss repousse gold quarter repeating bridge-cock verge watch signed Terrot & Thuillier Geneve 5889, 49mm. diam. (Christie's) $1,575

A Swiss gold and enamel bridge-cock verge watch signed Alliez Bachelard & Terond Fils N. 61141, 45mm. diam. (Christie's) $816

An enamelled gold hunter cased watch, Swiss, circa 1910, 52mm. diam. (Christie's) $2,860

A gold repousse pair cased verge watch signed Wm. Addis London 1812, 48mm. diam. (Christie's) $1,283

# WATCHES

A gold hunting cased minute-repeating keyless lever watch No. 1720 by S. J. Rood & Co. of London, hallmarked 1889, 53mm. diam.
$2,871

A gold open face Masonic watch, signed Dudley Watch Co., Lancaster Pa., no. 597. (Christie's)
$1,430

An 18kt.gold quarter repeating pocket watch, keyless, with white enamel dial plate with black Roman numerals. (H. Spencer & Sons)    $492

A gold hunter cased quarter repeating watch with concealed erotic automaton, Swiss, circa 1890, 50mm. diam. (Christie's)
$2,640

An 18kt.gold half hunter keyless lever gentleman's pocket watch. (Reeds Rains)
$496

A gold verge watch by Andre Hessen of Paris, 52mm. diam., circa 1790. $1,307

A yellow metal keyless cylinder fob watch or miniature clock in the form of a Lancashire style longcase clock, 46mm. high. (Christie's)
$642

Audemars Piguet No. 154003, gold hexagonal cased skeleton keyless lever watch, 50mm. diam.
$2,711

A gentleman's 18kt.gold half hunter cased keyless pocket watch, inscribed C. R. Pleasance, Sheffield. (H. Spencer & Sons)      $196

A gold hunter cased minute repeating watch, signed L. C. Grandjean, Locle, 53mm. diam. (Christie's)
$1,650

A small oval gilt metal verge watch, signed N. Vallin, length including pendant 53mm.
$3,445

A gold hunter cased minute repeating chronograph with perpetual calendar and moon phases, signed H. Redard & Son, Geneva, 51mm. diam. (Christie's)
$7,700

Mid 19th century lady's 18kt.gold open face pocket watch, Berthoud, Paris. (Robt. W. Skinner Inc.)     $600

A gold hunter cased split-second chronograph with register, the dial signed Jules Renaud, 45mm. diam. (Christie's)
$825

An 18kt.gold half-hunter cased quarter repeating pocket watch, inscribed A. Bach, London 182'. (H. Spencer & Sons)
$988

A Swiss gold and enamel open-faced keywind watch, signed Milleret & Tissot a Geneve, 34mm. (Lawrence Fine Art)
$532

A Swiss eight-day silver combined watch and lighter, 1928, 100mm. high.
$612

Late 18th century gilt-metal pair cased striking cylinder chaise watch No. 213 by Marriott of London, 132mm. diam.     $3,509

# CLOCKS & WATCHES

## WRIST WATCHES

A 9 karat gold Prince wrist-watch by Rolex, 20 x 41mm., Glasgow 1934.
$1,754

An 18 karat white gold and diamond wristwatch by Rolex, with a Prima movement, 20 x 45mm., Glasgow 1926.
$1,084

An gentleman's Swiss 18kt. gold cased calendar wrist watch by Leonidas. (H. Spencer & Sons)
$598

A white gold wristwatch, signed Patek Philippe, Geneva, with nickel 18-jewel cal. 23-300 movement. (Christie's)
$1,430

An 18 kt.gold and enamel wristwatch, 1924, by the Welsam Watch Co., length overall 35mm.$332

A gold wristwatch with center seconds, signed Rolex Oyster Perpetual. (Christie's) $1,320

A gold Cartier wristwatch, the movement signed E. W. & Co. Inc., length overall 30mm.
$3,180

An 18kt.gold perpetual calendar wristwatch, 1950/52, by Patek Philippe, no. 967642, 34mm. diam.
$11,484

An 18kt.gold wristwatch, by Patek Philippe, no. 834704, length overall 36mm.    $2,169

# WRIST WATCHES

An 18 kt. two-color gold
Rolex Prince, 1930, no.
70864, length overall
41mm.  $3,573

A 14 kt. gold gentleman's
wristlet watch by Rolex
with perpetual chronometer
movement. (Reeds Rains)
$1,041

A gold wristwatch, signed
Agassiz Watch Co., dial
signed Tiffany & Co., in
an 18 kt. gold case.
(Christie's) $825

A gold wristwatch, signed
Audemars Piguet, with
18 kt. gold bracelet, signed
Tiffany & Co. (Christie's)
$880

A gold wrist chronograph
with register, signed C. H.
Meylan Watch Co., the
silvered dial signed Marcus
& Cie. (Christie's)
$1,430

A two-color gold wrist-
watch with box and certificate, signed Rolex, Prince,
no. 77625. (Christie's)
$3,300

A gold wristwatch with
center seconds, signed
Patek Philippe, Geneva,
with 14 kt. rose gold
bracelet. (Christie's)
$1,100

A gold wristwatch chrono-
graph with perpetual calendar and moon phases, sig-
ned Patek Philippe & Co.,
Geneve, circa 1946-50.
(Christie's)
$22,000

A gold wristwatch, signed
Piaget, with nickel 18-
jewel lever movement and
18 kt. gold buckle to leather strap. (Christie's)
$715

# CLOCKS & WATCHES

## WRIST WATCHES

A gentleman's 14 kt. gold wristwatch, LeCoultre, 17J, complete with a leather strap. (Robt. W. Skinner Inc.) $400

A 9 kt. white and yellow striped gold Rolex Prince, 1931, length overall 41mm. $3,318

An 18 karat white and yellow gold Prince wristwatch by Rolex, 25 x 43mm., Glasgow 1929.     $4,785

A thin gold wristwatch, signed Audemars Piguet, with nickel 20-jewel lever movement. (Christie's) $660

A Cartier 18 kt. gold wristwatch, the movement by the European Watch Co., length overall 26mm. $2,042

A lady's platinum diamond and seed pearl wristwatch, signed Verger, Paris. (Christie's) $2,420

A gold wristwatch by Jaeger Le Coultre, circa 1930. $2,233

An 18 karat tri-color Prince wristwatch by Montre Royale, 27mm. wide, London 1976. $1,595

An 18kt. gold gentleman's wristwatch, Patek Philippe, Geneve, 15J. (Robt. W. Skinner Inc.) $1,200

# CLOISONNE

Chinese cloisonne baluster-shaped vase with long trumpet neck, 17½in. high. (Reeds Rains) $391

One of a pair of 19th century cloisonne enamel figures of zebras. $67,200

One of a pair of cloisonne enamel vases of ovoid shape, each with a midnight blue ground, 9¾in. high. (Lawrence Fine Art) $317

Pair of Oriental cloisonne rouleau-shape vases with everted rims, 12½in. high. (Capes, Dunn & Co.) $158

A Chinese cloisonne incense burner in the form of a wig stand, 12in. high. (Reeds Rains) $337

Pair of mightnight-blue ground cloisonne enamel vases of square baluster shape, 14½in. high. (Lawrence Fine Art) $637

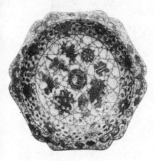

A cloisonne enamel dish 7.1/8in., Wanli. $743

One of a pair of cloisonne vases, circa 1900, 7.1/8in. high. $858

Late 19th century cloisonne enamel round plaque, 12in. diam. (Robt. W. Skinner Inc.) $350

An Imperial cloisonne enamel compressed globular bowl, the base with Qianlong four-character mark, 75cm. diam. (Christie's) $9,694

Late Qing Dynasty cloisonne enamel and gilt bronze double moon-flask, formed as two circular flattened bottles conjoined, 36cm. high. (Christie's) $1,710

A 16th/17th century Ming cloisonne enamel deep bowl with widely everted rim, 27.5cm. diam. (Christie's) $2,280

Late 19th century cloisonne enamel chocolate pot with loop handle, Japan, 7in. high. (Robt. W. Skinner Inc.) $200

A cloisonne enamel dish, the blue ground decorated with a quail, 18in. diam. (Lawrence Fine Art) $144

A Japanese cloisonne vase with lozenge-shaped body, 9¼in. high. (Capes, Dunn & Co.) $201

A cloisonne enamel and gilt bronze pear-shaped bottle, incised Qianlong five-character mark, 14cm. high. (Christie's) $498

Late 18th/19th century pair of cloisonne enamel red-ground tall rectangular panels, 64.5 x 32cm. (Christie's) $4,276

A Namikawa cloisonne enamel slender baluster vase and domed cover, circa 1900, 11.5cm. high. (Christie's) $4,277

# CLOISONNE

One of a pair of cloisonne
enamel oviform jars and
domed covers, circa 1800,
16cm. high. (Christie's)
$356

A small cloisonne enamel
and gilt bronze circular
box and cover, Qianlong
five-character mark, 6.5cm.
diam. (Christie's)
$213

Late 19th century cloisonne
enamel on copper vase,
Japan, 6¼in. high. (Robt. W.
Skinner Inc.)        $75

One of a pair of Ando
cloisonne enamel slender
oviform vases, late Meiji
period, 30.3cm. high.
(Christie's)$4,099

A cloisonne enamel koro decorated with silver wire.
$5,112

An Elkington & Co. clois-
onne vase, dated 1875,
32cm. high. $638

Late 19th century cloisonne
circular dish decorated in
colors on a pale blue ground,
59.2cm. diam.(Christie's)
$891

Late 19th century cloisonne
vase of baluster form, Japan,
23in. high. (Robt. W. Skinner Inc.)        $150

Late 19th century cloisonne
opaque enamel on copper
plate, Japan, 12in. diam.
(Robt. W. Skinner Inc.)
$150

233

# COPPER & BRASS

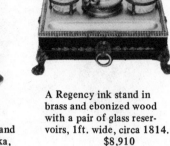

A swivel mounted brass cannon, trunnions stamped Montrose 1831, mounted on a painted wooden block, 16 x 8 x 7 1/8in.
$629

An enamelled cast iron and brass lavabo, by F. Dutka, Wien, 30in. high. (Robt. W. Skinner Inc.) $200

A Regency ink stand in brass and ebonized wood with a pair of glass reservoirs, 1ft. wide, circa 1814.
$8,910

Late 15th century North German or Flemish brass candlestick on spool-shaped foot, 12¾in. high.
$2,552

Pair of mid 18th century brass table candlesticks, probably French, 7¼in. high.        $558

One of a pair of 19th century stamped brass Italian renaissance design candelabra, 15¾in. high. (Robt. W. Skinner Inc.)$150

An early 19th century plated on copper two-handled urn of bulbous shape, 16¼in. high. (Geering & Colyer)
$464

One of a pair of brass pricket candlesticks with spirally-turned shafts, inscribed 1703, 17in. high. (Christie's)
$724

A Tibetan gilt copper figure of Buddha, seated in dhyanasana, sealed, 8in. high. (Lawrence Fine Art) $230

A French brass and steel harness maker's plough gauge, the steel blade with a turned wood handle, 6in. wide. (Lawrence Fine Art)          $77

Two straps hung with eight brasses of various patterns. (Lawrence Fine Art)
$123

An 18th century model cannon, brass barrel with muzzle molding,  mounted on stepped wooden wheeled carriage, 17in.          $755

One of a pair of 19th century brass Sabbath candelabra, 49cm. high.
$1,815

Pair of cast brass newel post finials in the form of lions seated guardant on octagonal bases, 14½in. high. (Reeds Rains) $251

A 16th century German brass candlestick , 10½in. high.          $1,595

Early 18th century pair of brass candlesticks with bell-shaped feet, 9½in. high.
$350

A 16th century European brass alms dish, depicting Adam and Eve in the Garden of Eden, 15¾in. diam. (Robt. W. Skinner Inc.)
$300

Pair of mid 18th century brass table candlesticks, the lobed circular bases rising to mushroom-knopped stems, 8in. high.
$350

A cast iron and brass fire basket with serpentine brass front, approx. 42 x 37in. high. (Lawrence Fine Art) $870

One of a pair of 18th century Georgian brass candlesticks with knop stems, 7½in. high. (Lawrence Fine Art) $399

Copper kettle with a porcelain handle. (Brogden & Co.) $66

An 18th century Dutch brass wine cooler on stand. (Phillips) $4,080

Pair of 18th century cast brass candlesticks of twisted baluster form, 11in. high, France. (Robt. W. Skinner Inc.) $425

A Regency brass tea urn with raised and pierced lid, 13in. high. (Christie's) $167

A 17th century brass candlestick with drip pan and wide spreading circular base, 9½in. (Russell Baldwin & Bright) $1,750

A hammered copper wall plaque, by Gustav Stickley, circa 1905, 20in. diam. (Robt. W. Skinner Inc.) $3,100

Mid 19th century European cast brass ornate Victorian ewer, 32½in. high. (Robt. W. Skinner Inc.) $300

A pair of George III brass candlesticks with slender knop and baluster stems, 8¾in. high. (Lawrence Fine Art)    $55

Copper helmet-shaped coal scuttle. (Brogden & Co.)    $69

A pair of brass office candlesticks with spiral twist turned stems and urn finials, 16in. high. (Woolley & Wallis)    $547

A 17th century brass candlestick engraved 'For the use of ye Company of Joyners and Carpenters', dated 1690, 9in. high. (Gorringes)    $7,920

An oval milk canister, the hinged lid with brass name plate 'Mrs Hawkes'. (P. Wilson & Co.)    $49

A 19th century brass goffer stand with lead loaded base, 9in. high. (P. Wilson & Co.)    $110

A Georgian spherical body copper samovar with knopped cover and twin ring handles. (Edgar Horn)    $129

Pair of late 19th century brass candlesticks with wax pans, 8½in. high. (P. Wilson & Co.)    $131

A hammered copper wall plaque, by Gustav Stickley, circa 1905, 15in. diam. (Robt. W. Skinner Inc.)    $4,600

A large 16th/17th century brass Nuremburg alms dish, the rim stamped with flower heads, 21in. (Dreweatt Watson & Barton) $593

Log box with pressed brass decoration, 1880. (British Antique Exporters) $58

An early 17th century English brass warming pan, dated 1613, 12in. diam., the wood handle a later replacement. $212

Victorian firescreen of polished copper, 1880. (British Antique Exporters) $51

A copper and brass 'Bell Resonator' ear trumpet, English, mid 19th century, 6in. long. $227

A WMF brass standing table mirror, circa 1900, 40cm. high. (Christie's) $434

One of a pair of 18th/19th century brass wall sconces, dated 1750, 17¾in. high. $312

A William and Mary brass table candlestand with a pair of scroll arms, 8in. wide. $1,606

Victorian brass preserving pan with fixed handle, 1850. (British Antique Exporters) $63

A Steiner Motschmann-type bisque doll, France, circa 1860, with fixed glass eyes, 12¾in. high. (Robt. W. Skinner Inc.)     $1,700

Lenci doll in provincial costume, circa 1930, 19in. high. (Robt. W. Skinner Inc.) $300

A musical jester doll which bangs its cymbals and plays a tune when its tummy is pressed. (Christie's) $720

Bisque headed bebe, marked 1907, with sticker printed Bebe Jumeau, 24in. high. (Christie's)     $864

An Izannah Walker doll with brushed hair and painted boots, circa 1873, 17in. high. (Robt. W. Skinner Inc.) $5,500

German bisque headed doll with original blue knitted frock and hat, 13in. high. (Christie's)     $816

A Simonne bisque shoulder-headed fashion doll, French, circa 1870, 17½in. high. $2,415

Lenci girl, dressed in cerise felt dress, hat and shoes, 1930's, 16in. high. (Robt. W. Skinner Inc.) $70

A bisque shoulder headed fashion doll, possibly by Bru, French, circa 1880, 12in. high.  $1,188

American plastic character doll, by Terri Lee, circa 1965, 16in. high. (Theriault's)     $225

A 'walking/crying' Bru Jeune R bisque doll, French, circa 1895, 24½in. high, in original Bebe Bru Marchant No. 9 box.
$4,752

A Jumeau bisque doll with real auburn hair wig, French, circa 1880, 20½in. high.
$1,900

French bisque child doll, marked Mon Cheri, by Lanternier Et Cie, circa 1915, 18in. high. (Theriault's)
$400

Set of lithographed paper dolls on heavy cardboard, depicting Hansel and Gretel, printed in Germany, circa 1890, 7½in. high. (Theriault's)
$35

A Bahr & Proschild bisque doll, impressed B & P 320.12 de, in white broderie-anglaise dress, German, circa 1885, 21in. high.
$1,425

A shoulder-waxed-composition doll, German, circa 1880, 16in. high, right arm loose.     $174

A waxed shoulder-composition doll, circa 1880, 21½in. high, slight cracking to face.     $316

German all bisque character doll of Kewpie, Rose O'Neill's fantasy creature, circa 1910, 11in. high. (Theriault's)
$400

An early shoulder-papier-mache doll in original clothes, French, circa 1840, 11½in. high. $554

German bisque character doll with composition bent limb baby body, by Kley & Hahn, circa 1915, 13in. high. (Theriault's) $550

American wooden character doll, by Schoenhut of Philadelphia, circa 1911, 16in. high. (Theriault's) $600

A Kammer & Reinhardt/ Simon & Halbig bisque character doll, impressed 121 42, German, circa 1910, 17in. high. $665

Two dolls, one impressed with a clover leaf 5, the other W.D. 5, with fixed brown glass paperweight eyes, German, circa 1900, 13½in. high. $1,267

American cloth character doll, produced by Izannah Walker of Rhode Island, circa 1860, 26in. high. (Theriault's) $1,400

German bisque child doll wearing an original Shaker costume, by Armand Marseille, circa 1925, 16in. high. (Theriault's) $300

German bisque character baby doll, by Kley & Hahn, circa 1915, 17in. high. (Theriault's) $825

A Simon & Halbig bisque doll impressed 1079, with jointed wood and composition body, German, circa 1890, 28in., together with a pair of kid doll's gloves. $792

Simon & Halbig version of the Gibson Girl, circa 1900, 25in. high. (Theriault's) $900

French walking doll by Jules N. Steiner, circa 1880, 15in. high. (Theriault's) $800

Simon & Halbig bisque child doll with clockwork mechanism, circa 1890, 22in. high. (Theriault's) $900

A 19th century papier-mache doll, circa 1850, 7½in. high. (Theriault's)$275

Pair of French bisque shell dolls, probably by F. Gaultier, circa 1875, 10½in. high. (Theriault's) $2,000

German celluloid character doll, wearing original outfit, marked Kecsa, 16in. high. (Theriault's) $175

American carved wooden swivel headed doll by Joel Ellis, circa 1878, 13in. high. (Theriault's) $1,000

A 19th century porcelain doll with slight pink tinted complexion, 14in. high. (Theriault's) $200

English cloth character doll with velvet head, probably Chad Valley, circa 1935, 20in. high. (Theriault's)$225

# DOLLS

Japanese bisque character doll, with French type composition and wooden jointed body, circa 1910, 13in. high. (Theriault's) $325

Italian cloth character Lenci doll, by Madame di Scavini, circa 1930, 19in. high. (Theriault's) $250

French bisque child doll, by E. Denamur, circa 1885, 11in. high. (Theriault's) $850

A large shoulder-papier-mache doll with kid body and wooden lower limbs, German, circa 1830, 24in. high. $950

Set of four articulated paper dolls, circa 1890, each 9in. high. (Theriault's) $100

A shoulder-waxed-composition doll with blonde mohair plaited wig, German, circa 1880, 18in. high. $443

German bisque character doll, the wooden ball-jointed body with 'walker' mechanism, circa 1910, 27in. high. (Theriault's) $1,100

Simon & Halbig bisque character doll, wooden ball-jointed body with adult modelling, circa 1900, 27in. high. (Theriault's) $14,000

French bisque child doll with blonde human hair wig, marked 137, 14in. high. (Theriault's) $1,000

An early Kathe Kruse cloth doll with swivel joints at hips, German, circa 1911, 17in. high. $1,346

Steiner bisque head girl doll with five-piece composition body, Paris, circa 1890, 9in. high. (Robt. W. Skinner Inc.) $600

A black bisque doll impressed 34-24, with jointed wood and composition body in original pink dress, probably French, circa 1910, 14¼in. high. $1,900

A Biedermeier shoulder-papier-mache doll with painted face, circa 1825, 10½in. high. $475

Four German all bisque character dolls, depicting characters from 'Our Gang', 2in. to 3½in. high, together with a book, 1929. (Theriault's) $150

French bisque child doll, by Jules N. Steiner, circa 1885, 14in. high. (Theriault's) $1,800

German bisque character doll with five-piece papier mache body, by Armand Marseille, circa 1925, 7in. high. (Theriault's) $400

An autoperipatetikos cloth-headed doll, stamped Patented July 1862: also Europe 20 Dec. 1862, American, circa 1862, 9in. high. $506

A swivel-head shoulder-bisque doll, with kid body, French, circa 1860, 13in. high, together with a cream chintz bag, circa 1880. $1,188

# DOLLS

Italian cloth character doll, Lenci, by Madame di Scavini, circa 1925, 21in. high. (Theriault's)    $400

A large Lencidschango Oriental cloth doll, 23in. high, circa 1925, together with a late 19th century Chinese silk tunic.    $633

Italian Lenci cloth character doll, by Madame di Scavini, circa 1925, 17in. high. (Theriault's)    $450

French bisque character doll, SFBJ, circa 1915, 12in. high. (Theriault's)    $3,200

Pair of cloth character dolls, made by Norah Wellings, England, circa 1930, each 11in. high. (Theriault's)    $350

French cloth character doll, by Poupees Gerbs, circa 1924, 28in. high. (Theriault's)    $250

A china-headed doll, the cardboard and stuffed body with squeaker and china lower limbs, German, circa 1860, 15in. high. $1,267

A bisque headed Pulchinelle puppet, impressed 2, French, circa 1870, 24in. high.    $1,742

A George I wooden doll, the gesso-covered head with finely painted blushed cheeks, English, circa 1725, 16in. high. $17,424

245

English cloth character doll, by Dean's Rag Book Co. Ltd., of Lupino Lane, 13in. high. (Theriault's) $300

American plaster character Buddha-like figure, by Rose O'Neill, 5½in. high. (Theriault's) $45

German all bisque miniature doll with blue glass eyes, by Kestner, circa 1900, 5in. high. (Theriault's) $300

A Kammer & Reinhardt/ Simon & Halbig bisque character doll impressed 126 24, German, circa 1910, 11in. high. $380

Trio, German all bisque miniatures, by Gebruder Heubach, circa 1900, each about 5in. high. (Theriault's) $725

American composition character doll of Pinocchio made by Ideal Novelty & Toy Co., circa 1935, 12in. high. (Theriault's) $200

A shoulder-bisque doll with fixed blue glass eyes, German, circa 1890, 17in. high. $380

German bisque character doll, by Armand Marseille, circa 1920, 24in. high. (Theriault's) $625

A Simon & Halbig bisque doll, impressed 1079, in original crocheted underclothes, German, circa 1890, 13in. high. $475

German all bisque minia-
ture doll, probably by
Kestner, made for Strobel
& Wilken, circa 1900, 8in.
high. (Theriault's)
$200

American carved wooden doll and
animal, 'Milkmaid and Cow', by
Schoenhut of Philadelphia, each
8in. (Theriault's)      $600

American composition
character doll of Shirley
Temple, circa 1935, 13in.
high. (Theriault's)
$400

Italian Lenci cloth charac-
ter doll, by Madame di
Scavini, 13in. high.
(Theriault's) $200

Pair of German all bisque
novelty dolls, possibly by
Gebruder Heubach, circa
1900, 4in. high. (Theri-
ault's)      $250

A large shoulder-china doll
with kid body in original
dress, German, circa 1860,
20in. high.      $253

A poured shoulder-wax
doll with fixed blue glass
eyes, English, circa 1880,
18½in. high.  $506

A George II wooden doll
with blonde real hair nailed-
on wig, English, circa 1750,
16in. high. $15,840

American wooden charac-
ter doll with intaglio
brown eyes, by Schoen-
hut of Philadelphia, circa
1911, 15in. high. (Theri-
ault's)      $350

A large German enamel
table snuff box, circa 1762,
5in. wide.    $1,103

Late 18th century Bilston
enamel bonbonniere model-
led as an apple, 1¼in. high.
(Christie's)    $475

Late 18th century Staffordshire oblong, enamel writing
set case, 2.5/8in. long.
(Christie's)  $1,304

A Louis XVI two-colored
gold and enamel aide-
memoire, Paris 1776, 3¼in.
high. (Christie's)
$850

A 19th century champleve
opaque enamel on copper
vase, China, 17¼in. high.
(Robt. W. Skinner Inc.)
$175

An enamelled silver vesta
case, S. Mordan & Co.,
London, 1885, 1½in. high.
$527

A Birmingham rectangular
white enamel snuff box
with engraved gilt metal
mounts, circa 1765, 2¾in.
long. (Christie's)
$283

A Birmingham enamel
scent bottle of rococo
flask form on oblong base,
circa 1760, 3½in. high.
(Christie's)    $567

A Birmingham rectangular
enamel snuff box with
waisted sides, circa 1765,
3¼in. long. (Christie's)
$453

# ENAMEL

An oval Battersea enamel patch box with a puce field, 1½in. wide. (P. Wilson & Co.)  $55

A 17th century Limoges polychrome enamel bowl, from the Laudin workshops, 12.4cm. across. $283

A Swiss gold and enamel snuff box formed as a butterfly, by Remond, Lamy & Cie, Geneva, circa 1800, 3½in. long. (Christie's)  $5,670

A Victorian enamelled silver vesta case, S. Mordan & Co., London, 1891, 2¼in. high.  $527

An enamelled silver cigarette case, maker's mark A/Bros, Birmingham, 1907, 3½in. wide.  $1,129

Champleve opaque enamel on copper vase, China, possibly 18th century, 14.3/8in. high. (Robt. W. Skinner Inc.) $225

A German enamel snuff box, circa 1757, 3¼in. wide.  $815

A German silver gilt mounted white enamel etui, circa 1765, some of the contents with later Dutch control marks, 4in. high.(Christie's)  $737

A Swiss circular gold and enamel box, the cover painted with Homer, Minerva and the personification of Vanity, circa 1820, 3in. diam. (Christie's)  $2,268

Mid 18th century French mother-of-pearl fan, the sticks pierced and carved with three rocaille cartouches, 11.3/8in. long. $903

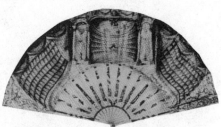

A documentary fan, Italian, circa 1795, 10.3/8in. long. $1,317

An ivory fan, possibly English, the shaped sticks pierced and painted with red and blue interlaced ribbons, circa 1760, 10.5/8in. long. $326

An 18th century Italian painted fan with a view of St. Peter and the Vatican. (Bonham's) $288

A late 19th century lace trimmed gauze fan, signed J. Patte, having floral gilt and silvered decorated mother-of-pearl sticks. (Geering & Colyer) $101

Mid 18th century European framed fan, gouache on skin, on foiled pearl sticks, guard length 11¾in. (Robt. W. Skinner Inc.) $350

A Duvelleroy diamond-set blonde tortoiseshell fan, circa 1900, 13¾in. long, in original red leather case. $2,006

Mid 18th century Jacobite fan, probably English, the mottled sticks and guards of stained red ivory, 10¼in. long. $978

A 19th century Chinese Export black and gilt
lacquer fan, in fitted lacquer case, 12.7in. wide.
(Woolley & Wallis)                    $220

An ivory fan with pierced and foiled sticks,
French, circa 1780, 10.7/8in. long.
                                    $602

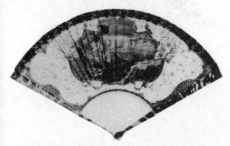

European early 18th century varnished and
painted ivory brise fan with plain tortoiseshell
guards, guard length 8¼in. (Robt. W. Skinner
Inc.)                               $575

A mother-of-pearl fan, the sticks and guards
pierced, carved and engraved, circa 1870, 11in.
long.                               $351

Mid 18th century German ivory fan, the leaf
painted with the Continence of Scipio in the
manner of Pietro da Cortona, 11in. long.
                                    $903

A gem-set ivory brise fan, Vienna, circa 1905,
7¾in. long.                         $305

An ivory brise fan, the finely pierced sticks
decorated with carved vignettes, circa 1780,
9¾in. long.                         $376

A folding fan, gouache on paper, pearl sticks
with gold foil decoration, French, circa 1770,
guard length 10½in. (Robt. W. Skinner Inc.)
                                    $125

THE earliest beds, of a form that would be recognized and accepted today, date from the 16th century — in Britain, anyway. Before that time the most important feature of the rich man's bed was the drapery, often of velvet or silk intricately embroidered with hunting or hawking scenes, which was suspended from the ceiling by means of rings.

This drapery would enclose a simply constructed oak framework of such crude design and make that it was rarely considered worth taking when the family moved house. The framework was usually made with holes drilled through ends and sides, a length of rope being threaded through the holes to form an open-mesh base on which would be supported a rush-work pallet and a couple of feather mattresses. Coverings would include sheets, often of silk, blankets and an embroidered bedspread probably trimmed with fur.

The poor man's bed was more often than not a heap of leaves or straw laid in a shallow box — and the most important feature as far as he was concerned was whether or not the leaves were dry.

Up and coming families, rich enough to afford large coffers, would sleep on these, the lids made a little more hospitable by means of straw palliasses.

Once the idea of beds caught on, however, the family bed soon became the most important item of furniture in the household, great sums of money being expended on its purchase. One of the best extant examples of this is the Great Bed of Ware, made in 1595, which was a massive ten feet eight inches wide.

A 19th century Chinese parcel gilt and maroon-painted bridal bed, 58½in. wide. (Christie's) $8,100

A Robert Thompson 'Mouseman' oak bed, signed with a carved mouse, 152.2cm. wide. (Christie's) $924

Late 19th century Eastlake influence walnut bed, America, 58½in. wide. (Robt. W. Skinner Inc.) $550

Late 19th century Victorian
brass bed, America, 87in. wide.
(Robt. W. Skinner Inc.)
$1,800

A Charles I oak tester bedstead, circa 1640, 4ft.7½in.
wide.　　$12,210

A Gustav Stickley oak bed,
designed by Harvey Ellis,
59½in. wide. (Robt. W.
Skinner Inc.)
$20,000

A 17th century oak four-
poster bed with canopy,
53in. wide, 75in. long
overall. (Butler & Hatch
Waterman)
$1,595

A 19th century French carved and gilded bed, circa
1860, 6ft. wide.
$7,233

Mahogany and inlaid bed,
4ft.6in. wide, circa 1900.
(British Antique Exporters)
$187

Federal tiger maple tall post
bed, New England, circa
1830, 54in. wide, 72in. long.
(Robt. W. Skinner Inc.)
$1,600

Pair of Gustav Stickley oak
twin beds, 40in. wide.
(Robt. W. Skinner Inc.)
$3,000

An Elizabethan oak tester
bed with box-spring mat-
tress, 7ft. wide overall, circa
1580-1603.
$30,932

# BOOKCASES

MOST early bookcases were designed by architects and made to fit a particular wall as the house was built. Fortunately for us, furniture designers such as Chippendale, Hepplewhite and the Adams', designed bookcases in sections in order that they might be moved into and out of houses.

Chippendale was among the first designers to build bookcases as separate units and it is clear that the architectural feeling of existing designs had some influence on the manner in which his were styled.

There were any number of open bookshelves designed at the end of the 18th century and such is their practicality that they have remained popular ever since.

The Georgian variety, elegantly tall and narrow with nicely graduated shelves are made of mahogany, rosewood or satinwood, often japanned black or green and decorated with painted scenes or brass inlay. Some have cupboards or drawers in the base and they are supported on a variety of feet: bracket, scroll, claw, turned or with a shaped apron.

The revolving bookcase is the ideal piece of furniture for the idle bibliophile or for the family which lacks the wall space necessary for the more conventional methods of book display and storage.

Made in significant quantities between 1880 and 1920, many were given as free gifts by fast talking sales representatives, who offered them as inducements to potential purchasers of the innumerable home educator or encyclopaedia volumes which were in vogue at the time.

A 20th century mahogany breakfront floor standing bookcase, 84 x 48in. high. (P. Wilson & Co.)
$594

One of a pair of Victorian mahogany glazed bookcases, 63cm. wide. (Chelsea Auction Galleries)
$582

A late Georgian bookcase/cupboard, 4ft. wide. (J. R. Bridgford & Sons)
$1,351

A George III mahogany bookcase, the upper part of two 16-panel astragal glazed doors, 61in. wide. (Boardman)
$2,782

Three section leaded glass Globe Wernicke, 1900 (British Antique Exporters)
$211

Late Victorian mahogany library bookcase with ogee molded cornice, 3ft.6in. wide. (Capes, Dunn & Co.)
$684

# FURNITURE

## BOOKCASES

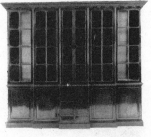

A George IV mahogany breakfront bookcase, circa 1825, 7ft.8in. wide. $3,533

An oak revolving bookcase from the Tabard Inn, Carlyle 77in. high. (Anderson & Garland) $858

A large mahogany library bookcase of double breakfront form, 9ft.9in. wide, circa 1880. $4,232

A George IV mahogany cabinet bookcase with ebonized strung borders, 4ft.9in. wide, circa 1825. $2,852

A George IV mahogany breakfront bookcase, inlaid with brass medallions, 8ft.4in. wide, circa 1825. $4,974

A large mid 19th century mahogany breakfront bookcase, 9ft.3in. wide. (Anderson & Garland) $2,600

An early 19th century mahogany breakfront bookcase, 9ft.5in. wide. $8,870

A George II mahogany and crossbanded mahogany cabinet bookcase, circa 1740, 3ft.9in. wide. $2,926

A late Victorian mahogany breakfront bookcase, the bookshelves enclosed by glazed tracery doors, 8ft. 2in. wide. (Woolley & Wallis) $5,160

## BOOKCASES

A George III satinwood bookcase on later turned feet, circa 1790, 2ft.4in. wide. $5,726

A Victorian mahogany breakfront bookcase, the upper part with four glazed doors, 124in. wide. (Morphets) $12,969

One of a pair of French Empire mahogany open bookcases, circa 1810, 1ft.10½in. wide. $2,326

A George III mahogany breakfront bookcase, with a fitted writing drawer, 7ft.11in. wide, circa 1800. $4,242

A George III-style mahogany bookcase in two parts, 3ft. 7in. wide. $1,016

A large George III mahogany breakfront secretaire library bookcase, 9ft.5in. wide, circa 1800. $8,250

A mahogany breakfront library bookcase with four glazed doors, 7ft.3in. wide, circa 1840. $3,744

A late Regency mahogany bookcase cupboard with two glazed doors, on four metal hairy paw feet, 53½in. wide. (Lawrence Fine Art) $893

One of a pair of Regency mahogany and crossbanded open bookcases, 2ft.7½in. wide, circa 1810. $1,463

# BUREAUX

THE writing desk was born in the monasteries of the Middle Ages, originally as a small, Gothic style oak box with a sloping lid hinged at the back like old fashioned school desk tops.

As time passed and men of letters increased their output, the writing box grew and was made a permanent fixture in the copying rooms of the monasteries, being built upon a stand, usually high enough to be used by a man standing or seated on a high stool.

Later, the hinges of the lid were moved from the back to the front, allowing the lid to fall forward on supports and form a writing platform in the open position. The practice on the Continent was to cover this area with a "burel" or russet cloth, probably named from the latin *burrus* (red), the colour of the dye used in its manufacture. It is doubtless from here that we gain the word bureau, though the connotations of the word have changed somewhat since it was first coined.

The bureau remained little more than a box on a stand until the close of the 17th century when it was married to a chest of drawers for obvious practical reasons. From that time onward, there have been few changes in the design beyond relatively small stylistic alterations which were reflections of the changing tastes of the fashionable rather than modifications dictated by practical usage.

Late George II mahogany bureau on ogee front supports, 43in. wide. (Reeds Rains)
$1,155

Queen Anne burr mulberry bureau with sloping fall-front, 23½in. wide. (Reeds Rains)　$6,118

Late 19th century Louis XV-style ormolu and walnut veneer lady's desk, Paine Furniture Co., Boston, 31½in. wide. (Robt. W. Skinner Inc.)
$3,100

A Georgian mahogany bureau with fall-front, the drawers with brass drop handles. (Worsfolds)
$2,616

Mid 19th century barrel roll desk with four ogee drawers, 57in. wide. (Robt. W. Skinner Inc.)
$2,400

A lady's inlaid walnut writing desk, the super-structure with a pair of glazed cupboards, 2ft. 10½in. wide.
$1,442

# BUREAUX

A Queen Anne maple slant lid desk, New England, circa 1760, 36in. wide. (Robt. W. Skinner Inc.) $2,200

A 19th century Chippendale-style mahogany block front desk, America, 40in. wide. (Robt. W. Skinner Inc.) $1,500

A Chippendale birch slant lid desk, Massa., circa 1780, 39in. wide. (Robt. W. Skinner Inc.) $2,100

A Queen Anne walnut and crossbanded bureau, 3ft.2in. wide, circa 1710. $1,828

Victorian carved mahogany fall-front desk, America, circa 1900, 42½in. wide. (Robt. W. Skinner Inc.) $700

A Georgian oak bureau with a fitted interior, on later bracket feet, 39½in. wide. (Lawrence Fine Art) $925

Late 18th century George III walnut veneer slant lid desk, 35½in. wide. (Robt. W. Skinner Inc.) $1,900

A William and Mary walnut bureau inlaid with oval panels and spandrels of burr wood, 36½in. wide. (Lawrence Fine Art) $4,620

Mid 18th century German rococo walnut veneered secretary, 38½in. wide. (Robt. W. Skinner Inc.) $2,500

A George I walnut bureau in two parts, the interior with twenty drawers, pigeon holes and a well, 57in. wide. (Dreweatt Watson & Barton) $11,890

Chippendale mahogany slant lid desk with original brass hardware, Massa., circa 1780. (Robt. W. Skinner Inc.) $3,300

A George III mahogany slope-front bureau with fitted interior outlined in boxwood, 114cm. wide. (Osmond Tricks) $982

A Dutch 18th century walnut bureau, on carved claw and ball feet, 4ft.2½in. wide. (Geering & Colyer) $2,030

A mahogany bureau with fitted interior and brass snake handles, 38in. wide. (Dee & Atkinson) $739

A George II oak bureau with fall-front, on shaped bracket feet, circa 1730, 3ft. wide. $2,442

An early 18th century Queen Anne walnut bureau in cross-banded wood, 2ft.6in. wide. $4,118

Late 18th century George III painted satinwood bureau, re-veneered and painted in the 19th century, 2ft.8in. wide. $3,637

A Tuscan walnut bureau, constructed from a 16th century cupboard, 3ft.3in. wide.          $1,058

## BUREAUX

A Louis XV-style kingwood bureau de dame, 2ft.2in. wide, circa 1890. $709

A late 17th century Italian walnut bureau, inlaid with finely etched ivory, 46in. wide. (Banks & Silvers) $6,815

A Chippendale mahogany serpentine desk, Mass., circa 1780, 41½in. wide. (Robt. W. Skinner Inc.) $5,000

A George III satinwood bureau with kingwood banding and later satinwood medallions, circa 1790, 102cm. wide. $1,093

An early Georgian oak bureau, having a fall-front, revealing stepped and fitted interior, 36in. wide. (Locke & England) $975

A 19th century mahogany inlaid bureau with fall-flap on ogee bracket feet, 42in. wide. (Lawrence Fine Art) $1,610

An oak drop-front desk, by Gustav Stickley, circa 1912, 32in. wide. (Robt. W. Skinner Inc.) $900

A George I walnut, crossbanded and herringbone inlaid bureau with brass drop handles, 36in. wide. (Dacre, Son & Hartley) $4,092

A Louis XV-style kingwood and inlaid bombe-shaped bureau de dame with ormolu galleried top, 27½in. wide. (Dacre, Son & Hartley) $472

Mid 19th century mahogany writing desk on stand, the top with fall-front and fitted interior, 44in. wide. (P. Wilson & Co.)      $572

Mid 18th century walnut bureau with shaped well interior, 37½in. wide. (P. Wilson & Co.) $935

A Sheraton period faded mahogany roll-top pedestal desk fitted with brass swan-neck handles, 3ft. 10in. wide. (Woolley & Wallis) $2,565

An 18th century oak bureau with ivory escutcheons, on bracket feet, 40in. wide. (Coles, Knapp & Kennedy) $902

A Biedermeier period mahogany bureau with a convex shaped fall-front, 40½in. wide. (Reeds Rains) $645

A German walnut and cross-banded bureau, the fall-front revealing a stepped and fitted interior, 3ft.3½in. wide, circa 1710.      $3,300

A 19th century George I-style walnut veneered bureau with slope fall-front, 73cm. wide. (H. Spencer & Sons) $960

William and Mary pine fall-front desk, Mass., circa 1730, 36¼in. wide. (Robt. W. Skinner Inc.) $12,000

A George III mahogany bureau with gilt metal drop handles and key escutcheons, 81cm. wide. (H. Spencer & Sons) $3,842

# BUREAU BOOKCASES

THE introduction, at the end of the 17th century, of higher ceilings encouraged the development of taller items of furniture and one of the most successful adaptations of existing designs to the new fashion was the bureau bookcase which entailed quite simply the placing of a cabinet on top of the already popular sloping front bureau.

The earliest Queen Anne bureau cabinets had panelled doors to the upper section, often containing Vauxhall mirror glass, which enclosed a multitude of small drawers and pigeon holes.

Since bureau bookcase carcasses tend to be very similar, the pattern made by the glazing bars is a good aid to establishing the date of a piece. Unfortunately, however, it is not infallible, since many of the designs were used throughout the different periods.

Broadly, however, in the late 17th century, the glazing was of plain rectangles secured with putty behind substantial, half round moldings. In the 1740's, the glass was mounted in a wavy frame and the establishment of mahogany soon after meant that, by the 1750's, the glazing bars could be finer and more decorative — usually forming 13 divisions or shaped in the fashion of Gothic church windows.

At the end of the 18th century, Hepplewhite introduced diamond glazing and also flowing curves and polygonal shapes, often enriched with foliate designs, in the glazing of his furniture. Sheraton too, used similar forms, often enhanced by their superimpositions on pleated silks.

Most reproductions of this period are of plain mahogany enhanced with a boxwood string inlay and a conch shell in the center of the bureau flap.

An Edwardian inlaid mahogany bureau bookcase, 3ft. wide. (J. R. Bridgford & Sons)   $700

Early 18th century walnut bureau bookcase enclosed by a pair of glazed doors, 3ft.4in. wide. (Elliott & Green)   $4,620

A George III mahogany bureau bookcase, 36in. wide. (Reeds Rains)   $4,070

An early 20th century mahogany bureau bookcase, 3ft.6in. wide. (J. R. Bridgford & Sons)   $904

An 18th century Dutch marquetry bureau cabinet, the upper glazed section, enclosing shelves, 3ft.6in. wide. (Russell Baldwin & Bright)   $3,741

A Georgian mahogany bureau bookcase with double panel doors, 42in. wide. (Dee & Atkinson)   $1,845

# FURNITURE

# BUREAU BOOKCASES

A Queen Anne black-japanned bureau cabinet, 3ft.4in. wide, circa 1710.
$49,500

A late Victorian mahogany bureau bookcase in Sheraton Revival-style, on bracket feet, 30in. wide. (Woolley & Wallis)
$1,715

A Georgian rosewood veneered and mahogany bureau bookcase, 90in. high. (Anderson & Garland)
$1,957

A Queen Anne-style walnut bureau bookcase, circa 1900, 3ft. wide.
$1,644

A George III mahogany bureau bookcase with astragal glazed doors, 124cm. wide, circa 1770. $1,673

An Edwardian inlaid mahogany bureau bookcase with astragal glazed doors, 39in. wide. (Reeds Rains)
$567

A George II oak bureau bookcase, the fall-front with concealed well, drawers, pigeon holes and central cupboard, 39in. wide. (Locke & England)
$1,798

A 19th century mahogany cylinder bureau cabinet in the Georgian style, 128cm. wide. (H. Spencer & Sons)
$1,935

A George III mahogany bureau bookcase, fitted with brass handles, 90in. high. (Anderson & Garland)
$5,330

A George III mahogany
and crossbanded bureau
bookcase, circa 1790,
3ft.1in. wide.
$2,260

A George III mahogany
bureau bookcase with a
later broken arched pedi-
ment, 42in. wide. (Law-
rence Fine Art)
$3,801

A Georgian mahogany bur-
eau bookcase, the two
glazed doors with curved
astragals, 39in. wide. (Lawrence Fine Art)
$3,757

A Dutch marquetry and
mahogany bureau bookcase
in three sections, circa 1760,
3ft.9in. wide.
$12,581

A George II mahogany
bureau cabinet with original
brass ring handles, 42in.
wide. (Dreweatt Watson &
Barton)     $4,716

A Chinese padoukwood
bureau cabinet, the pair of
doors each with a mirrored
glass painting, circa 1780,
3ft.8in. wide.
$47,850

A walnut bureau cabinet
on bun feet, 3ft.4½in. wide,
circa 1700.  $8,580

A Queen Anne walnut bureau-
bookcase with fall-front, circa
1710, 36in. wide. (Neales)
$9,280

Late 18th century George
III oak bureau-bookcase,
3ft.1in. wide.
$2,116

# CABINETS

CABINETS, as pieces of furniture, saw their British beginnings in the 17th century, when designed basically for either specialized storage or display. They were introduced by craftsmen imported from the continent.

It was during the 18th and 19th centuries, however, that cabinets began to achieve a certain importance when they served to meet the needs of a nation obsessed with learning. Everybody it would seem, began to collect things; coins, shells, fossils, ores, mineral samples, china — and what was the point of amassing vast collections of these wonders without having the means of displaying them for the enjoyment of family and admiring friends?

Cabinets, then, became indispensable, and although most of the earlier examples were imported from Europe, a few were actually made in Britain. Even these, however, were usually made by foreign craftsmen working in British factories and they were commonly attributed to other European countries despite the fact that they were physically made here.

Handles can be a useful pointer to the age of a piece of furniture, though not, I hasten to add, infallible, for they were continually swapped around or replaced.

Earliest handles were brass drop loops which were held on to the backplates with brass or iron wire or, after 1700, by the heads of nutted bolts. The heavier brass loop handles began to be used in 1735, and each bolt head is mounted on a separate backplate.

Pierced backplates date from about 1720 and continued to be used, with the addition of ornamental key escutcheons, until about 1750, when sunken escutcheons began to be used.

Victorian 'Gothic' oak side cabinet with fleur de lys finials, 37in. wide.(Reeds Rains) $478

A 19th century marble-topped and boulle inlaid serpentine-fronted cabinet, 43in. wide. (W. H. Lane & Son) $780

A French breakfront side cabinet with a rouge marble top and on cabriole legs, 3ft. wide. (Woolley & Wallis) $2,052

Hoosier kitchen cabinet with metal fittings, 1920. (British Antique Exporters) $123

Victorian oak four-drawer filing cabinet, 1880. (British Antique Exporters) $337

Late 19th century Regency-style mahogany demi-lune cabinet, 34in. wide. (Robt. W. Skinner Inc.)$500

Late 19th century Dutch marquetry breakfront cabinet, walnut, fruitwood and other veneers, 59in. wide. (Robt. W. Skinner Inc.) $1,800

An early 19th century rosewood breakfront side cabinet with green marble top, 5ft.9in. wide. $1,742

A French kingwood and ormolu molded demi-lune hanging display cabinet, circa 1850, 3ft. wide. $1,609

One of a pair of George III mahogany small writing cabinets, 3ft.1½in. wide, circa 1800. $41,250

A Charles II japanned cabinet on stand, circa 1670, 3ft.9in. wide. $5,775

A late Victorian ebonized side cabinet in the Arts & Crafts style, 93cm. wide. (H. Spencer & Sons) $731

Renaissance Revival rosewood and ebonized wood music cabinet, 35½in. wide. (Robt. W. Skinner Inc.) $750

A George IV breakfront side cabinet in mahogany-stained wood, 4ft.4in. wide, circa 1820. $4,455

A 19th century Chinese cinnabar lacquer cabinet, fitted with various shelves, 15¾in. wide. (Stalker & Boos) $450

# FURFNITURE

A George IV rosewood side cabinet of inverted breakfront form, circa 1825, 5ft. 8in. wide.     $1,346

A George-style black and gilt lacquered cabinet in the chinoiserie manner, 3ft. wide. (Geering & Colyer)     $1,113

A George III mahogany collector's cabinet containing a collection of shells, circa 1780, 2ft. wide.     $2,138

A lacquered stacking double cabinet on stand, each pair of doors and the sides painted in polychrome on gilt, 2ft.9in. wide. $1,325

A George III mahogany and kingwood crossbanded secretaire cabinet, circa 1790, 3ft.1in. wide.     $4,389

A Brainerd & Armstrong Co. spool cabinet with twelve glass front drawers over one oak drawer, circa 1900, 37in. high. (Robt. W. Skinner Inc.)     $475

A Victorian walnut and ormolu mounted breakfront cabinet, 6ft.3in. wide, circa 1860.  $3,218

An ebonized and pietra dura mounted side cabinet, stamped 'Edwards & Roberts', circa 1860, 2ft.11in. wide.     $2,194

Renaissance Revival burl veneer and ebonized wood sideboard cabinet, America, circa 1865, 53in. wide. (Robt. W. Skinner Inc.)     $1,500

# CABINETS
## FURNITURE

A French 18th century walnut cabinet with drawers, 25in. wide. (Robt. W. Skinner Inc.)     $700

Victorian oak three section filing cabinet, 1880. (British Antique Exporters)     $191

A 17th century ormolu mounted tortoiseshell and ebony cabinet on stand, probably Flemish. (W. H. Lane & Son) $3,640

An Edwardian rosewood cabinet with boxwood stringing and fine inlays, 3ft.8in. wide. (Vidler & Co.)     $532

A French kingwood cabinet with rouge marble top on cabriole supports, 58in. wide. (D. M. Nesbit & Co.)     $392

A Japanese lacquer cabinet on William and Mary stand with chased gilt metal clasps, 37in. wide. (Lawrence Fine Art)     $39,600

Edwardian oak fall-front desk cabinet, 1910. (British Antique Exporters)     $112

Shannon filing cabinet, 1880. (British Antique Exporters) $583

Victorian oak triple filing cabinet with key, 1880. (British Antique Exporters)     $456

# CANTERBURYS

**O**RIGINALLY designed to hold sheet music, this particular item could just as well have been called the Archbishop since, according to Sheraton, it was named after the Archbishop of Canterbury, who was among the first to place an order for one. Most of the original, late 18th century, varieties were rectangular in shape and were made with a drawer in the base, doubtless for the storage of less popular pieces of music. Castors enabled them to be pushed beneath the piano and the two or three partitions in the upper section were usually dipped in the middle to allow easy removal of the sheets of music.

Regency canterburys are of mahogany or rosewood; the later Victorian examples are generally of burr walnut with flamboyantly fretted partitions or barley twist supports.

Late 19th century satinwood music canterbury, the X-shaped divisions centered by stylized leafage, 20in. (Lawrence Fine Art) $1,391

An early Victorian rosewood canterbury on turned feet with brass cup castors. (Biddle & Webb)$570

A Regency rosewood canterbury, the four divisions with stick splats, 1ft.7½in. wide, circa 1810. $760

A Victorian walnut music canterbury on pierced lyre-shaped end supports, circa 1850, 2ft. wide. $965

A Victorian burr walnut and rosewood canterbury whatnot, 2ft.3in. wide. (Capes Dunn & Co.) $664

A French-style mahogany standing canterbury with lyre supports, 36cm. high. (Chelsea Auction Galleries) $299

# CRADLES

THE earliest cradles were simply made from hollowed out sections of tree, the natural shape of the wood being ideally suited to rocking. Others were slightly grander, being made in the form of a box suspended between X supports. This method of construction allowed the cradle to be rocked while raising it clear of the damp floor.

At first they were panelled, box-like structures with turned finials at the corners and mounted on rockers. At the end of the 16th century, the end and sides at the head of the cradle were extended to offer protection against draughts, and this development naturally evolved into a hood which was sometimes hinged to swing back out of the way.

The basic style of the 17th century cradle lasted throughout the following century, often with a curved hood, and even into the 19th century when it often bore Gothic decoration. By far the most important development, however, was the return of the swinging cot which made a brief appearance early in the century before really coming into its own after Sheraton and Hepplewhite had honored it with their attentions.

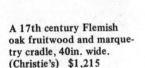

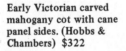

A 17th century Flemish oak fruitwood and marquetry cradle, 40in. wide. (Christie's)  $1,215

Early Victorian carved mahogany cot with cane panel sides. (Hobbs & Chambers) $322

A Queen Anne oak cradle with fielded panelled construction, 3ft.3in. long, circa 1705.  $562

A Regency mahogany frame caned side baby's cot with hood, swinging on brass brackets, 3ft.5in. (Woolley & Wallis)          $387

An Edwardian oak baby's cot with bobbin uprights, 100cm. wide. (Chelsea Auction Galleries) $139

A Victorian mahogany cradle with swan neck head on turned supports. (Butler & Hatch Waterman) $999

## DINING CHAIRS

THE Hepplewhite style is renowned for its flowing curves, shield, oval and heart-shaped backs and straight lines broken by carved or painted wheat ears and corn husks, all of which Hepplewhite adapted from the work of Robert Adam, the distinguished architect/designer and published in his famous guide: *The Cabinet Maker and Upholsterer.*

Another distinctive Hepplewhite design incorporated the three feathers crest of the Prince of Wales in the backs of chairs and he also favored finishing chairs with japanned decoration of various ground painted with floral garlands, corn husks and medallions.

Though his designs have much in common with those of Hepplewhite, Thomas Sheraton (1751-1806), a drawing master from Stockton on Tees, much preferred straight lines to the curves favored by Hepplewhite, his chairs achieving their feminine delicacy with their fine turning and slender frames.

Sheraton served his apprenticeship as a cabinet maker but he never actually manufactured furniture himself, concentrating on creating designs which he published in his *Cabinet Maker's and Upholsterer's Drawing Book (1791-1794).*

Thomas Chippendale designed and made furniture for the wealthy in his premises in St. Martin's Lane, London, establishing styles of his own rather than copying and adapting those of others. Like Sheraton and Hepplewhite, Chippendale published his designs, which were used by cabinet makers throughout the country, with the result that a considerable number of "Chippendale" chairs were produced in a variety of qualities and a medley of styles.

Victorian oak chair on turned legs, 1880. (British Antique Exporters)     $26

One of a set of six Victorian mahogany chairs on turned legs, 1870. (British Antique Exporters)     $188

One of a set of four Victorian stick back kitchen chairs, 1860. (British Antique Exporters)     $137

One of four oak Art Nouveau chairs, 1910. (British Antique Exporters)     $106

One of a set of six 20th century dining chairs. (British Antique Exporters)     $70

An Anglo-Portuguese walnut dragon chair, 1760. (British Antique Exporters)$650

271

# DINING CHAIRS

One of a set of six Austrian cherrywood chairs with balloon backs, circa 1840, distressed.  $2,560

One from a set of six Victorian carved mahogany chairs, with buttoned seats, circa 1850.        $1,115

One of a set of eight late 18th/early 19th century George III carved beechwood side chairs. (Robt. W. Skinner Inc.)
$6,750

One of a set of seven Regency mahogany dining chairs including an armchair, circa 1820.    $2,217

One of a pair of Federal shield back mahogany side chairs, Massa., circa 1800. (Robt. W. Skinner Inc.)
$8,000

One of a set of four George I walnut dining chairs, the curved backs with vase-shaped splats. (Lawrence Fine Art) $1,595

One of a pair of Queen Anne or early George I mahogany side chairs with urn-shaped backs. (Stalker & Boos)
$2,200

One of a set of six George III mahogany dining chairs, circa 1805.  $1,709

One of a set of four walnut chairs in the manner of Daniel Marot, circa 1700.
$6,600

One of a set of six Victorian mahogany chairs with balloon backs, circa 1855. $1,243

One of a set of six early 19th century French provincial ashwood dining chairs. $3,174

One of a set of six 19th century mahogany dining chairs with circular backs and seats, probably Continental. (Lawrence Fine Art) $845

One of a set of five late George II mahogany chairs, circa 1760. $2,534

One of a pair of Queen Anne walnut chairs, circa 1710. $4,620

One of a set of six George III mahogany dining chairs with leaf carved crest rails. (Dreweatt Watson & Barton) $2,610

One of a set of six Regency simulated rosewood dining chairs, circa 1810. $3,484

One of a pair of George II mahogany hall chairs with heart-shaped back, circa 1750. $1,188

One of a set of six Regency mahogany dining chairs, the concave toprails inlaid with brass stringing, circa 1820. $4,395

# DINING CHAIRS

One of a set of six mahogany dining chairs in the Georgian style. (Lawrence Fine Art) $1,694

Chippendale carved mahogany side chair with urn-shaped back splat, circa 1760. (Stalker & Boos) $1,000

One of a set of four William IV rosewood dining chairs with solid cresting rails. (Lawrence Fine Art) $1,148

One of a set of eleven late Regency period faded rosewood side chairs on front turned waisted fluted legs. (Woolley & Wallis) $4,257

One of a pair of mid 18th century mahogany hall chairs with lyre-shaped backs. (Woolley & Wallis) $3,540

One of a set of four 19th century Chippendale-style carved mahogany dining chairs. (Robt. W. Skinner Inc.) $1,500

George II carved and parcel gilt walnut side chair on claw and ball feet, circa 1750. (Robt. W. Skinner Inc.) $550

One of a pair of George II walnut chairs with tassel-hung scroll toprails, circa 1740. $6,600

One of a pair of cherry Queen Anne side chairs, New England, circa 1740. (Robt. W. Skinner Inc.) $1,900

One of a set of six Regency-style inlaid mahogany side chairs, circa 1880. (Robt. W. Skinner Inc.)
$1,400

George II mahogany side chair with reticulated urn-shaped back splat, circa 1765. (Stalker & Boos)
$450

One of a set of four Sheraton mahogany side chairs with leather upholstered seats. (Stalker & Boos)
$1,200

An early 18th century Yorkshire Mortuary chair. (Dacre, Son & Hartley)
$572

One of a set of eight George I style gilt-gesso side chairs on cabriole legs with acanthus-leaf carved feet. $2,197

One of a set of four George II mahogany dining chairs on claw and ball feet. (Dreweatt Watson & Barton)
$3,108

One of a harlequin set of six George III oak and elm spindle-back chairs, circa 1800.     $1,501

One of a set of six mahogany Country made Chippendale-style dining chairs, seats upholstered in floral chintz. (Outhwaite & Litherland)$3,375

One from a set of four George III-style satinwood painted chairs, circa 1890.
$744

Queen Anne maple side chair with a rush seat, New England, circa 1770. (Robt. W. Skinner Inc.) $2,600

One of a set of six late 18th/ early 19th century Hepplewhite provincial mahogany side chairs. (Robt. W. Skinner Inc.)     $2,500

One of six Victorian mahogany dining chairs on turned and fluted front legs. (P. Wilson & Co.) $707

One of a set of eight post-Regency mahogany dining chairs with drop-in seats, circa 1830. (Neales) $2,144

One of a set of five Chippendale mahogany side chairs and one English Chippendale mahogany side chair, America, circa 1780. (Robt. W. Skinner Inc.)     $4,800

Early 18th century William and Mary red painted maple side chair, New Hampshire. (Robt. W. Skinner Inc.) $650

One of a set of six 19th century walnut chairs with spring upholstered seats. (Lawrence Fine Art) $908

Queen Anne mahogany side chair with claw and ball feet, Rhode Island, circa 1750. (Robt. W. Skinner Inc.)     $18,000

One of a set of Georgian mahogany dining chairs with pierced vase-shaped splat backs. (Anderson & Garland) $3,915

# FURNITURE

One of a set of nine George V mahogany dining chairs with over-stuffed seats. (H. Spencer & Sons) $2,318

One of a set of eight late George II walnut dining chairs with shaped cresting rails. (Lawrence Fine Art)    $21,653

A carved oak Yorkshire chair with acorn drop finials to the carved rail. (Butler & Hatch Waterman)    $326

A 17th century oak Lancashire chair with arched cresting rail, 44½in. high. (W. H. Lane & Son) $196

A 19th century walnut hall chair, the oval back panel carved with a whippet, scrolls and grotesque masks. (Vidler & Co.) $182

One of a set of eight William IV mahogany frame balloon back single dining chairs. (Edgar Horn) $1,662

One of a set of six George III-style mahogany frame hoop-back dining chairs. (Edgar Horn)    $1,117

One of a set of six 19th century Lancashire spindle back dining chairs. (Reeds Rains) $1,037

One of a set of six early 20th century George I style mahogany dining chairs with hoop backs. (Neales) $1,286

# EASY CHAIRS

WING chairs have been made since the 17th century, this being one of the few designs to have remained virtually unchanged since its conception, only the legs changing shape according to the dictates of fashion.

The Queen Anne wing chairs had high cabriole legs canted from the corners which demanded extra stretchers for strength. The legs were later straightened and squared off with the inside edges chamfered, before the Georgian influence saw a return of the cabriole legs, but shorter this time and terminating in ball and claw feet.

The armchair by Thomas Chippendale is one of the best chairs ever made. Beautifully constructed to a superbly elegant design, it is strong, graceful and comfortable; a truly classic example of everything a chair should be.

The strong rectangle of the back is softened by the flow of the humped top rail and the arm supports, molded and richly carved with feathers, terminate in cabochon ornament above the graceful acanthus carved cabriole legs with claw and ball feet.

The mid Victorian period abounds with furniture showing the exaggerated curves and floral and leaf carving which clearly reflect the Louis XV rococo influence and beautifully designed chairs of this period simply cry out to be sat in.

Earlier examples had filled-in arms and rather plain frames of mahogany or rosewood but, within a few short years, they developed open arms and grandly flamboyant lines.

Walnut, being easier to carve, was widely used for the later chairs in this style and backs, arms, front rails and knees were adorned with welters of leaves, roses and bunches of grapes of superb quality.

One of a set of four George II carved mahogany chairs, circa 1750. $8,250

A prie dieu chair in rosewood, the back panel and seat in gros point. (Butler & Hatch Waterman) $148

A Victorian walnut nursing or lady's chair. (Brogden & Co.) $123

Part of a bergere suite with dual-caning and turquoise dralon upholstery, the couch 6ft. wide. $1,258

A tall back, slat sided rocker with leather spring cushion by Gustav Stickley, 41½in. high. (Robt. W. Skinner Inc.) $550

One of a set of fourteen late George I mahogany side chairs, including two with arms. (Lawrence Fine Art) $134,640

# FURNITURE

## EASY CHAIRS

Victorian mahogany parlor chair on turned legs, 1860. (British Antique Exporters)     $98

One of a pair of Charles II design heavily carved dining chairs. (Worsfolds) $290

Regency period bergere chair with cane panels within a carved and fluted mahogany frame. ((Hy. Duke & Son) $1,560

Fine Victorian walnut spoon-back chair, 1850. (British Antique Exporters) $685

A George II mahogany library armchair with cabriole legs on leaf-carved scroll feet, circa 1755. $4,455

Victorian walnut, tapestry parlor chair, 1875. (British Antique Exporters) $437

One of a set of four 19th century carved mahogany elbow chairs with turned and fluted legs. (Dacre, Son & Hartley) $1,209

An early Victorian walnut framed cabriole leg easy chair. (Biddle & Webb) $816

A 15th century English oak choir stall, 27in. wide. (W. H. Lane & Son) $861

279

A George III mahogany
scroll armchair on cabriole
legs, circa 1770.
$1,582

One of a set of eight George
III giltwood armchairs with
molded cartouche-shaped
backs, circa 1780.
$5,940

A George III mahogany
elbow chair with arched
upholstered back, elbow
rests and seat. (Lawrence
Fine Art)   $3,168

A mid Victorian carved
walnut elbow chair with
flower carved and molded
frame. (Dacre, Son & Hartley)      $708

A Gustav Stickley oak office
chair with leather back and
seat, circa 1907, 36in. high.
(Robt. W. Skinner Inc.)
$3,000

Part of a Renaissance Revival
inlaid and ebonized wood parlor suite, America, circa
1865. (Robt. W. Skinner Inc.)
$875

A George II walnut wing
armchair, circa 1730.
$3,174

Chippendale mahogany loll-
ing chair, attributed to J.
Short, Mass., circa 1780.
(Robt. W. Skinner Inc.)
$7,000

Early 18th century Queen
Anne walnut upholstered
wing chair with drop-in
cushion, England. (Robt.
W. Skinner Inc.)
$2,300

# FURNITURE

A Louis XVI beechwood fauteuil with cartouche-shaped back and seat frame carved with marguerites. (Woolley & Wallis) $873

A low seat chair with stuffed over seat in handworked wool tapestry. (Butler & Hatch Waterman)$111

One of a pair of George III painted beech open armchairs with oval backs. (Dreweatt Watson & Barton) $9,432

A Victorian walnut scroll armchair, with padded arms, circa 1870. $572

A slat sided armchair with cushion seat, by L. & J. G. Stickley, circa 1912. (Robt. W. Skinner Inc.) $1,000

A framed low chair with carved walnut legs, upholstered in tapestry with button-back. (Brogden & Co.) $264

A late George II mahogany library armchair with serpentine back, circa 1750. $6,270

One of a pair of lady's and gentleman's Victorian mahogany armchairs, upholstered in rose and silver floral cloth. (Reeds Rains) $1,231

A George I walnut wing armchair, upholstered in gros and petit-point woolwork. $3,418

## EASY CHAIRS

A child's Lancashire spindle-back wing open arm rocking chair with rush seat. (Capes, Dunn & Co.)    $218

Cast iron dentist's chair with red plum upholstery and and brass paw feet. (Christie's)    $312

Victorian mahogany parlor armchair, circa 1870. (British Antique Exporters)    $562

Victorian mahogany parlor armchair, circa 1860. (British Antique Exporters)    $562

A pair of early 19th century Louis XVI-style giltwood fauteuils with adjoining foot stool forming a duchesse. (Andrew Grant)    $990

A mid 19th century mahogany show wood frame armchair, the legs fitted with brass castors. (Edgar Horn)    $456

One of two late 19th century occasional chairs with walnut frames. (P. Wilson & Co.)    $288

A French bergere duchesse with carved scrolling decoration and cane work panels, 82in. long. (Anderson & Garland)    $1,090

American bentwood rocking chair, 1900. (British Antique Exporters)$178

## ELBOW CHAIRS

POSSIBLY the greatest problem confronting a designer of chairs has always been that of creating a style robust enough to survive while retaining a degree of elegance.

Very few designers achieved this happy blend, most coming down on the side of strong practicality and a few, such as Sheraton and Hepplewhite, concentrating on a fashionable delicacy at the expense of strength. Chippendale was the man who came closest to combining the two elements and it is this which has made chairs based on his designs among the most popular ever made.

Beside the elegance of his designs, Hepplewhite is to be remembered for the explicit instructions given in his book regarding the materials to be used for the purpose of covering his chairs: for japanned chairs with cane seats, cushions covered in linen; for dining chairs, horse hair material which may be either plain or striped; for upholstered chairs, red or blue morocco leather tied with silk tassels.

While most surviving Sheraton chairs are made of mahogany, they can also be found in satinwood, painted white or gold or even japanned.

The delicacy of his design demands that a fine fabric be used to cover the upholstery, green silk or satin being generally considered the most suitable.

More suited to the parlor than the dining room, his chairs must be treated with the utmost delicacy for, not being a manufacturer himself, Sheraton concerned himself more with the aesthetics of design than with the practicalities of use.

Victorian pub chair with saddle seat, 1870. (British Antique Exporters) $108

Victorian elm elbow chair with 'H' stretcher, 1860. (British Antique Exporters) $97

An 18th century mahogany framed elbow chair with pierced splat back and drop-in seat. (Elliott & Green) $1,320

An 18th century Chinese padoukwood open arm elbow chair with cane seat. (Geering & Colyer) $1,984

A George II walnut elbow chair with shaped uprights and lift-out seat. (Lawrence Fine Art) $1,504

A child's kidney-shaped back armchair in hardwood, circa 1850. (P. Wilson & Co.) $176

# ELBOW CHAIRS

## FURNITURE

One of a set of four walnut Italian neo-classical armchairs with rush seats. (Robt. W. Skinner Inc.) $600

Late 18th century oak and walnut settle chair, probably England, 29in. wide. (Robt. W. Skinner Inc.) $1,300

One of a pair of Adam style shield-back open armchairs in satin birch. (Osmond Tricks) $1,048

One of a pair of Chinese Chippendale style mahogany open arm elbow chairs with drop-in seats. (Geering & Colyer) $3,668

A George II walnut carved armchair with C-shaped back, circa 1750. $1,172

A mahogany frame open arm elbow library chair in the early Georgian manner by Howard & Sons. (Geering & Colyer) $1,146

One of a pair of Chippendale mahogany open armchairs, circa 1775. (Stalker & Boos) $2,750

Late 18th century bowback Windsor armchair, New England. (Robt. W. Skinner Inc.) $4,600

One from a set of six Regency mahogany chairs with brass inlaid toprails, circa 1810. $3,575

One of a set of seven Regency beechwood chairs including a pair of armchairs, circa 1810.        $1,139

One from a set of twelve George III-style mahogany chairs, modern.
$1,644

A late 18th century Continental elm chair with padded serpentine seat. (Dreweatt Watson & Barton)   $609

An early 17th century James I oak armchair.
$2,442

One of a set of seven brass-mounted stained beech chairs including an armchair, circa 1805.   $3,011

A Charles I oak box-base armchair, circa 1640, 1ft.10in. wide.
$1,383

One of a set of eight George III mahogany dining chairs, with leather-covered drop-in seats, circa 1800.
$5,860

One of a set of four Italian walnut armchairs in Renaissance style, with leather covered seats.
$2,442

One of a set of six Regency mahogany dining chairs, including an armchair, circa 1820.  $1,425

# ELBOW CHAIRS

A Windsor ash, maple and pine continuous braceback armchair, stamped W. Dewitt, circa 1770. (Robt. W. Skinner Inc.)    $2,200

One of a set of eight Mainwaring mahogany dining chairs with pillar backs and tapestry seats. (Worsfolds)    $1,197

A tub armchair by Rennie Mackintosh for the Ingram Street Tea Rooms in Glasgow. (Christie's & Edmiston's)    $4,350

One of a set of eight mahogany dining chairs in the Chippendale manner with wide serpentine seats. (Banks & Silvers)    $5,655

An Eastlake walnut armchair, by G. Hunzinger, New York City, circa 1876. (Robt. W. Skinner Inc.)    $1,150

One of a pair of George II mahogany chairs, in the manner of T. Chippendale, with wide studded seats. (Banks & Silvers)    $2,175

A 19th century shield-back hand-painted satinwood open armchair. (W. H. Lane & Son)    $467

A Windsor fanback braceback armchair with shaped saddle seat, New England, circa 1770. (Robt. W. Skinner Inc.)    $1,700

A 19th century stag's antler elbow chair supported on deer feet. (John H. Raby & Son)    $810

An oak wainscot armchair. (Worsfolds) $1,573

A cherry armchair with shaped crest rail above vase splat, New England, circa 1780. (Robt. W. Skinner Inc.)     $1,900

A child's early Georgian-style walnut open armchair with tapestry drop-in seat. (Capes, Dunn & Co.) $381

Dutch mahogany 'birds and foliage' inlaid elbow chair with front hoof feet and silk damask seat. (Chelsea Auction Galleries) $1,064

One of a set of seven George IV carved mahogany rail-back chairs, circa 1825. $1,568

One of a set of eight Chippendale-style mahogany dining chairs. (Reeds Rains) $1,860

One of six 18th century matching yewwood and elm spindle-back Windsor chairs. (Andrew Grant)
$3,525

Victorian oak carving chair with padded back, 1850. (British Antique Exporters) $200

American rocking chair, 1880. (British Antique Exporters)   $163

A mid 19th century mahogany marquetry armchair with scroll arms. (P. Wilson & Co.)    $418

A yew and elm Windsor elbow chair, with crinoline stretcher. (Butler & Hatch Waterman)    $543

A 20th century mahogany armchair in the Hepplewhite-style with wheat-ears. (P. Wilson & Co.)    $110

One of a set of twelve Regency-style mahogany chairs, modern.    $1,118

One of three Sheraton period cream and gilt painted open arm elbow chairs with upholstered seats. (Geering & Colyer)    $3,844

A Victorian oak elbow chair with square panelled back and stuff over seat. (Vidler & Co.)    $208

One of a set of eight Chippendale period mahogany dining chairs. (William H. Brown)    $6,120

William and Mary banister back armchair, New England, circa 1740, 45½in. high. (Robt. W. Skinner Inc.)    $3,300

Georgian mahogany elbow commode chair, no crock, floral tapestry on lift-out seat. (Barber's Fine Art)    $111

# CHESTS
## OF DRAWERS

THROUGHOUT the transitional period from coffer to chest of drawers, there were a great many variations on the basic theme but, eventually, a practical and attractive formula emerged about 1670. Not slow to respond to the demand, cabinet makers produced vast quantities of chests of drawers, employing, as a rule, the familiar native wood, oak, for the purpose.

The architectural geometric moldings proved popular as decoration and these were glued and bradded in position — a practice which continues to the present day.

As taste developed, there arose a need for more sophisticated chests in more exotic woods such as figured walnut, which was put on to an oak or pine carcass.

The use of veneers made the manufacture of molded drawer fronts impractical and, consequently, more emphasis was placed on the figuring of the veneers as a decorative feature. The oyster design was particularly popular and results from careful cutting of the veneer from a tree bough. This is glued vertically on to the drawer front, the figuring being meticulously matched, and it is crossbanded on the edges, often with an intermediate herringbone inlay.

The drawers are now found to slide on the horizontal partitions which separate them and they are finely dovetailed, where earlier they were more crudely jointed or even nailed together.

Walnut continued as the most favored wood for chests of drawers until the middle of the 18th century, when it gave way to Spanish mahogany.

Chippendale cherry tall chest with original brass pulls, New England, circa 1770, 38in. wide. (Robt. W. Skinner Inc.)
$4,300

An early Victorian faded mahogany Wellington chest, the drawers with ebony knob handles, 24in. wide. (Woolley & Wallis)
$1,045

A Lombard small walnut chest inlaid with ivory, 1ft. 8½in. wide, circa 1700.
$937

Victorian mahogany round cornered chest of drawers, 1860. (British Antique Exporters)
$151

Georgian oak chest of drawers with brass loop handles, 1790. (British Antique Exporters)
$371

A tulipwood veneered chest of six drawers, in the French manner, with Sevres type floral plaques, 2ft.6in. wide.
$1,229

## CHESTS OF DRAWERS

Federal cherry bureau, probably Penn., circa 1800, 40in. wide. (Robt. W. Skinner Inc.)   $2,700

A George I walnut and crossbanded chest on later bracket feet, 3ft.6in. wide, circa 1715.   $893

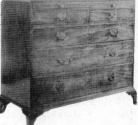

A George III mahogany bachelor's chest with mahogany crossbanding, 4ft.1½in. wide. (Capes, Dunn & Co.)   $472

One of a pair of 19th century sycamore chests of drawers of pale color, 37½in. wide. (Lawrence Fine Art)   $17,424

An early George III small mahogany chest of four graduated drawers surmounted by a slide, 30in. wide. (Lawrence Fine Art)   $7,920

A Victorian teak and brass mounted military chest in two parts, 3ft.1in. wide, circa 1890.   $665

A George III mahogany serpentine fronted chest, 3ft. 7in. wide, circa 1780.   $2,009

Early 18th century German maplewood chest, 35½in. wide. (Christie's)   $1,367

George III inlaid mahogany serpentine chest with brass drop handles, 3ft. wide. (Capes, Dunn & Co.)   $3,197

Chippendale mahogany
serpentine bureau with
original plate brass pulls,
Mass., circa 1770, 30¾in.
wide. (Robt. W. Skinner
Inc.)    $20,000

A Charles II walnut chest,
of two short and three long
drawers, 3ft.3in. wide, circa
1680.         $1,091

A Chippendale mahogany
serpentine bureau, pro-
bably Mass., circa 1770,
35½in. wide. (Robt. W.
Skinner Inc.)
        $3,250

A George IV mahogany small
bow-front chest with rosewood crossbanded top, 2ft.
4in. wide, circa 1825.
        $1,455

Victorian mahogany round
cornered chest of drawers,
1860. (British Antique
Exporters)    $351

A Jacobean oak chest of
four alternate shallow and
deep drawers with brass
handles, 3ft.1in. wide.
(Capes, Dunn & Co.)
        $889

George I walnut and herringbone crossbanded bachelor's
chest with baize lined folding top, 30in. wide. (Reeds
Rains)    $2,926

A William and Mary walnut
chest with ebonized stringing with oval plaque to top,
39in. wide. (R. H. Ellis &
Sons)         $1,193

A George II mahogany
chest with rounded rect-
angular crossbanded top,
30in. wide. (Dacre, Son &
Hartley) $1,625

# FURNITURE

## CHESTS OF DRAWERS

Chippendale mahogany serpentine bureau on ogee bracket base, Mass., circa 1760, 38in. wide. (Robt. W. Skinner Inc.) $7,500

A Dutch marquetry chest in the Empire style, 21in. wide. (Outhwaite & Litherland) $1,820

A Queen Anne yew venee- red chest with original brass plate handles and escutcheons, 38½in. wide. (Banks & Silvers) $2,247

A mahogany chest of drawers on square bracket feet, 3ft.10in. wide. (Brog- den & Co.) $319

An 18th century Anglo- Dutch corner dressing chest veneered on oak, 35¾in. wide. (Lawrence Fine Art) $1,089

A George III bow-fronted mahogany chest of two short and two long drawers, 35½in. wide. (Coles, Knapp & Kennedy) $463

A George III walnut cross- banded chest with brass handles, 31in. wide. (Anderson & Garland) $4,389

Chippendale tiger maple blanket chest, New England, circa 1780, 36in. wide. (Robt. W. Skinner Inc.) $1,400

A mahogany chest fitted with four drawers on bracket feet, 91cm. wide. (Andrew Grant) $770

A George III mahogany serpentine-fronted chest, circa 1770, 3ft.1in. wide. $9,609

A Louis XV influence chest, the whole painted to simulate grained veneer, Italy, 48½in. long. (Robt. W. Skinner Inc.) $750

A George II mahogany chest on shaped bracket feet, circa 1750, 3ft.1½in. wide. $686

A Federal mahogany and bird's-eye maple veneer chest of drawers on four turned legs, circa 1795, 40in. wide. (Robt. W. Skinner Inc.) $2,200

An early 18th century inlaid walnut chest of drawers with brass oval drop handles, 35½in. wide. (Elliott & Green) $4,840

A George II Cuban mahogany chest of drawers with original brass furniture, 33in. wide. (D. M. Nesbit & Co.) $2,562

A George III mahogany and satinwood crossbanded bow-front chest, circa 1800, 3ft. 5¾in. wide. $549

A George II mahogany chest of drawers with brass swan neck handles, 2ft.9in. wide. (Edgar Horn) $1,289

A George II walnut and crossbanded chest of drawers with serpentine front, 2ft.3½in. wide. $18,018

# CHESTS OF DRAWERS

Fine Victorian mahogany bow-front barlety-twist supported chest of drawers, 1855. (British Antique Exporters) $436

A George III oak straight front chest crossbanded in mahogany, 102cm. wide. (Osmond Tricks) $470

Georgian mahogany chest of drawers, 1800. (British Antique Exporters) $498

Round cornered Victorian mahogany secretaire chest of drawers, 1860. (British Antique Exporters) $953

Edwardian walnut serpentine chest of drawers, 1910. (British Antique Exporters) $181

Round cornered Victorian mahogany chest of drawers, 1860. (British Antique Exporters) $381

Georgian walnut chest of drawers, 1780. (British Antique Exporters) $890

A Georgian mahogany chest of drawers with ivory shield escutcheons and brass bail handles, 2ft.10in. wide. (Edgar Horn) $916

Victorian mahogany military chest, 1840. (British Antique Exporters) $1,012

# CHESTS ON CHESTS

IN the early 18th century, the tall-boy, or chest on a chest, began to replace the chest on a stand and, by about 1725, had virtually superceded it.

Tallboys are made in two parts; the upper chest being slightly narrower than the lower and, although they are inclined to be bulky, this is often minimised visually by means of canted and fluted corners.

Early examples were veneered in finely grained burr walnut and often sport a sunburst decoration of box-wood and holly at the base, which usually has the fashionable bracket feet.

As an added bonus, buyers of these superb pieces of furniture often get a secret drawer in the frieze as well as the brushing slide fitted above the oak lined drawers in the lower section.

Despite the obvious difficulty in reaching the top drawers and the competition from wardrobes and clothes presses, tallboys were made in vast quantities throughout the second half of the 18th century. So common were they, in fact, that George Smith, in his Household Furniture observed that the tallboy was an article ". . . of such general use that it does not stand in need of a description".

As a rule, tallboys were made of mahogany and ranged in quality from rather plain, monolithic but functional pieces to magnificent, cathedral-like specimens with elaborate cornices, fluted pillars flanking the upper drawers, low relief carving on the frieze and fine ogee feet.

Their popularity lasted until about 1820 when the linen press, with cupboard doors to the upper section, proved to be more practical.

Victorian mahogany bow-front chest on chest, 1860. (British Antique Exporters) $1,145

Fine Georgian mahogany bow-front chest on chest, 1780. (British Antique Exporters) $1,657

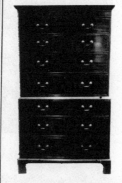

Georgian mahogany chest on chest, 1790. (British Antique Exporters) $1,597

A George III mahogany tallboy, 46in. wide. (Christie's) $2,246

A mahogany tallboy with brass snake-drop handles and escutcheons. (Dee & Atkinson) $825

Chippendale maple tall chest on bracket base, New England, circa 1770, 36in. wide. (Robt. W. Skinner Inc.) $2,800

## CHESTS-ON-CHESTS

A George III mahogany tallboy on bracket feet, 38in. wide. (Lawrence Fine Art) $1,512

An 18th century Continental mahogany chest-on-chest, 43in. wide. (Robt. W. Skinner Inc.)    $2,750

A Chippendale tiger maple chest-on-chest, New England, circa 1780, 39in. wide. (Robt. W. Skinner Inc.)     $7,750

A George III mahogany chest-on-chest, 3ft.7½in. wide, circa 1765.    $1,389

A George III mahogany chest-on-chest, circa 1760, 3ft.8½in. wide.          $1,859

A George III-style mahogany chest-on-chest, 3ft. 10in. wide.    $892

A George I walnut secretaire tallboy, circa 1720, 3ft. 6in. wide.   $8,580

A Georgian mahogany tallboy with brass swan neck handles, on bracket feet, 42in. wide. (Butler & Hatch Waterman)          $1,240

A George III mahogany chest-on-chest, circa 1760, 3ft.8in. wide.          $2,541

A George III mahogany bow-front chest-on-chest, 3ft.7in. wide, circa 1800. $833

A Queen Anne walnut tall-boy with a molded cornice, with shaped apron and later high bracket feet, 40½in. wide. (Lawrence Fine Art) $1,742

Chippendale cherry chest-on-chest, New England, circa 1770, 38in. wide. (Robt. W. Skinner Inc.) $3,250

A George I walnut secretaire tallboy on shaped bracket feet, circa 1720, 3ft.5½in. wide. $11,550

A George III mahogany secretaire chest-on-chest, 3ft.7½in. wide, circa 1760. $1,636

A William and Mary oyster-veneered walnut chest-on-chest, 43½in. wide. (Christie's) $4,505

A George III mahogany chest-on-chest, circa 1770, 3ft.6in. wide. $1,409

A George III mahogany serpentine front tallboy chest on ogee bracket feet, 4ft. overall. (Woolley & Wallis) $6,345

A George III mahogany chest-on-chest, 3ft.3in. wide, circa 1760. $1,358

## CHESTS ON STANDS

TOWARDS the end of the 17th century, many chests were raised on stands; often with an extra drawer in the lower section. The reason for this may have been to create a sense of fit proportion between furniture and the high ceilinged rooms of the period, or it may have reflected the stiff backed deportment which was considered proper at that time, raising furniture to a height at which the operative parts could be reached without stooping or bending in an unfashionable manner.

Legs of stands were either turned or barley twist, and were braced with shaped stretchers ending in bun feet.

There were a few pieces made of oak but most, if we are to judge by the survivors, were made of pine with walnut veneer and oak lined drawers. Some sport fine arabesque marquetry decoration, their tops having an oval design in the center and triangular corner pieces. There are half round moldings between drawers which, with the ovolo lip on the top of the stand, are characteristic of pieces of this period.

It is not uncommon to find later bases under these pieces for, although they were generally pretty well made, when full they were inclined to be just that bit too heavy for the rather delicate stands on which they originally stood.

Although of delicate constitution, the chest on a stand continued to be made in the early part of the 18th century but, instead of the barley twist legs with shaped stretchers, we find that the later pieces have flowing cabriole legs with ball and claw feet and acanthus leaf decoration on the knees.

A George I walnut small chest on stand, 1ft.11in. wide, circa 1715.
$8,712

Queen Anne maple bonnet top highboy, New England, circa 1760, 38in. wide. (Robt. W. Skinner Inc.)     $4,000

A floral marquetry William and Mary veneered chest of drawers, 3ft.4in. wide. (Woolley & Wallis)
$7,410

A George II walnut chest on stand on later cabriole supports, 40in. wide. (Lawrence Fine Art)
$2,376

A George II walnut tallboy with a cavetto cornice, 40in. wide. (Lawrence Fine Art)
$2,444

A Queen Anne walnut chest on stand with an ogee cornice above a cushion drawer, 39in. wide. (Lawrence Fine Art)     $2,684

# FURNITURE

# CHESTS ON STANDS

A mid-Georgian breakfront secretaire cabinet, possibly Irish, 63in. wide.(Christie's) $6,739

An oak chest of two long drawers raised on a stand having six barley-twist legs, 3ft.2in. wide. (Vidler & Co.) $421

An inlaid miniature mahogany chest of three drawers with brass drop handles. (Worsfolds)     $457

A George I walnut and herringbone crossbanded chest-on-stand, 40in. wide. (Christie's)  $3,931

An early 18th century walnut chest on stand, the base with one long drawer, 3ft.2in. wide. (Capes, Dunn & Co.) $599

A walnut serpentine chest on stand with four graduated drawers with brass handles, 30in. wide. (Butler & Hatch Waterman) $411

A Queen Anne-style walnut chest on stand, 67in. tall. (Warren & Wignall) $1,330

A 17th century William and Mary walnut highboy with burled walnut veneers, 35in. wide. (Robt. W. Skinner Inc.)   $1,550

Queen Anne tiger maple highboy on cabriole legs, Massa., circa 1740, 69in. high. (Robt. W. Skinner Inc.) $16,000

299

# CHIFFONIERS

THIS delightful piece first put in an appearance around 1800 when it achieved instant popularity.

It was designed, possibly as an alternative for the large sideboards of the period, or as a replacement for the commode, whose flowing lines and profuse decoration were not to the taste of the leaders of Regency fashion.

Whatever its parentage, the chiffonier was made, often in pairs, with a glass fronted cabinet in the lower part and, usually, shelves above, which were frequently constructed with lyre or fine scroll shaped supports.

Earlier pieces were made usually of rosewood and, occasionally, of satinwood, while those of later manufacture were of either of those woods and mahogany.

Victorian mahogany mirr-
ored back chiffonier, 1860.
(British Antique Exporters)
$621

Victorian mahogany two-
door mirrored back chiff-
oner with key, 1860.
(British Antique Exporters)
$245

Victorian mahogany two-
door chiffonier, 1860.
(British Antique Exporters)
$445

A William IV rosewood
chiffonier with raised mirror
back with open tier, circa
1835, 2ft.6in. wide.
$1,190

A George IV mahogany
chiffonier, circa 1825,
3ft.10in. wide.$629

Early 19th century maho-
gany chiffonier, the base
with a pair of pleated silk
panel doors, 2ft.9in. wide.
$2,279

# COMMODES & POT CUPBOARDS

**C**OMMODES made an appearance in Britain as early as the 16th century, when Henry VIII possessed one. It was covered in black velvet, garnished with ribbons and fringes and studded with over 2,000 gilt nails. Seat and arms were covered in white fustian filled with down and it came complete with lock and key, which Henry kept about his person to prevent illicit use.

Britain, however, was for a long time sadly lacking in examples of the plumber's art for, as late as the sixteenth century, it was deemed sufficient to retire a mere "bowshot away". The closing years of that century saw a single ray of enlightenment. In 1596 Sir John Harrington of Keleton — near Bath, appropriately — invented the valve closet with flushing cistern.

An early 19th century Dutch parquetry walnut bedside cupboard with galleried top, 19.5in. wide. (Woolley & Wallis)     $802

Victorian cylindrical mahogany pot cupboard with marble top.
$125

A Georgian Chippendale-style mahogany commode with tambour front, 20in. wide. (Locke & England)
$487

A George III mahogany tray-top bedside commode, 1ft.9in. wide, circa 1790.
$437

A Christopher Dresser ebonized bedside cabinet with brass drop loop handle, and fitted interior, 36.4cm. wide. (Christie's)
$4,898

Late 18th century mahogany bedside cupboard with tray-top and pull-out commode below, 20½in. wide. (Elliott & Green)
$682

# COMMODE CHESTS

THE name commode was first used in France, where it served to describe diverse pieces of furniture. Some took the form of a heavy table with drawers below, while others resembled sarcophagus-shaped coffers with lids, but the most widely accepted use of the term refers to those elaborate and ornate chests of drawers destined for the drawing room.

Most early French commodes had their basic rectangularity softened by subtle curves in the rococo manner – a popular style from the accession of Louis XV in 1715. Good examples are often beautifully inlaid with birds, garlands of flowers and musical instruments beside having superb ormolu mounts and handles made by such masters as Cressent, Gouthiere and Caffieris.

Just after the mid century, a number of commodes were made to blend with the Chinese style rooms which had become fashionable, and decorated panels were imported – portraying domestic scenes – for inclusion in their manufacture.

By the 1780s, many commodes appeared with fine decoration after the styles of Angelica Kaufmann and Pergolisi – often painted in the form of cupids set in ovals surrounded by painted flowers and scrolls. Another style, particularly favored by Adam, was that of a white ground on which were colored urns set amid wreaths and surrounded by friezes of gilt molding. Toward the end of the century, however, the commode slipped somewhat from its former importance in fashionable drawing rooms and the quality took a predictably downward turn.

Early in the 19th century, commodes lost their flamboyance altogether, returning to a rectangular form and resembling more the chiffonier.

Late 18th/early 19th century Louis XV provincial parquetry commode on cabriole legs, 56½in. wide. (Robt. W. Skinner Inc.) $600

Mid 18th century provincial walnut commode with waved rectangular molded top, 48in. wide. (Christie's) $7,425

A mid 19th century commode with four drawers and lion paw feet, 100cm. wide. (Chelsea Auction Galleries) $670

A Louis XV-style kingwood and rosewood bombe commode, circa 1900, 4ft.5in. wide.          $594

Late 17th/early 18th century Louis XIV harewood and mahogany commode, 51¼in. long. (Robt. W. Skinner Inc.) $3,000

A late 18th century mahogany and inlaid commode chest, probably Dutch, 3ft.10½in. wide. (Geering & Colyer) $4,464

A Louis XV-style rosewood, kingwood and marquetry inlaid serpentine front commode chest, 2ft.11¼in. wide. (Geering & Colyer) $870

A rococo Revival marble top commode, America, circa 1860, 16in. wide. (Robt. W. Skinner Inc.) $125

An ormolu mounted kingwood and fruitwood commode of Louis XVI-style, 34¾in. wide. (Christie's) $2,700

One of a pair of George III kingwood commodes in the French style, 50in. wide. (Lawrence Fine Art) $142,560

A bow-fronted commode chest in satinwood, the drawers with marquetry inlay in colored woods, 51in. wide. (Butler & Hatch Waterman) $682

A Dutch mahogany bombe commode with gilt-metal handles, 3ft.3in. wide, circa 1770. $1,227

COMMODE CHESTS

A Regency French provin-
cial walnut commode with
mask handles, 50½in. wide.
(Christie's) $6,114

A Louis XV marquetry com-
mode of serpentine shape
with a gray veined Carrara
marble top, 56in. wide.
(Lawrence Fine Art)
$20,592

A George III mahogany
serpentine-fronted commode,
circa 1770, 4ft. wide.
$6,435

Late 19th century Louis XV
style kingwood parquetry
commode of bombe-shape,
38½in. wide. (Lawrence
Fine Art)   $2,549

Louis XVI marquetry two-
drawer chest, 20in. wide.
(Robt. W. Skinner Inc.)
$450

A Dutch oak, ebony and
satinwood inlaid breakfront
commode, 34in. wide.
(Christie's)      $868

A French serpentine fronted
commode chest with marble
top, 37in. wide. (Butler &
Hatch Waterman)
$1,207

One of a pair of South German walnut and crossban-
ded commodes, circa 1720,
2ft.1in. wide.$4,646

A Louis XV-style bombe
front Dutch commode with
a white marble slab top,
22in. wide. (Outhwaite &
Litherland)$3,780

304

# CORNER CUPBOARDS

**B**ROADLY speaking, there are three basic types of corner cupboards and, of these, the earliest was the hanging variety. This was followed, in early Georgian days, by the free standing corner cupboard or cupboard-on-stand and, later and less successfully, by the low-level standing cupboard.

The earliest examples of hanging corner cupboards to be found are usually japanned in the Oriental style.

By the mid 18th century, as architectural styling of furniture became popular, many corner cabinets sported fine pediments whose details reflected the fashionable variations of the period.

Broken-arch pediments were featured on many of the more sophisticated pieces — often in the swan-neck style with a center entablature — but hanging corner cabinets were largely neglected by the major designers at this time.

Most of the antique corner cupboards found today date from the last quarter of the eighteenth century — the period during which the greatest number were produced, and those of the best quality made.

Bow-fronted models were popular, made of mahogany, with double doors about twelve inches across.

Decoration was usually kept to a minimum, most of the good pieces relying on the figuring of the wood, but some were embellished with satinwood stringing or an inlaid conch shell motif on the door.

Broken pediments continued to be used to some extent, together with dentil cornices and pear-drop moldings, while lattice work can also be found on some of the chamfered sides.

Victorian pine full length corner cupboard, 1860. (British Antique Exporters) $465

Pine corner cupboard, New England, 48in. wide, circa 1780. (Robt. W. Skinner Inc.) $2,100

Pine corner cupboard, New England, 85in. high, circa 1800. (Robt. W. Skinner Inc.) $2,200

Country Chippendale barrel back cupboard, Rhode Island, circa 1770, 46in. wide. (Robt. W. Skinner Inc.) $2,500

Early Victorian pine corner cupboard, 1840. (British Antique Exporters) $673

Georgian pine corner cupboard with key, 1850. (British Antique Exporters) $633

An 18th century standing
oak corner cupboard in
two parts, 48in. wide.
(Lawrence Fine Art)
$2,541

A George III lacquered bow-
front corner cupboard,
23½in. wide. (Lawrence
Fine Art)     $484

Late 18th century double
oak corner cupboard with
flat front and four panel
doors, 30in. wide. (P.
Wilson & Co.)
$1,735

Early 19th century oak and
mahogany inlaid bow-front
corner cupboard. (P. Wilson
& Co.)     $610

George III mahogany bow-
fronted hanging corner cupboard, 3ft.2in. high. (Capes,
Dunn & Co.)     $580

An early 20th century bow-
front corner hanging cupboard
in figured mahogany, 40in.
wide. (P. Wilson & Co.)
$445

A small satinwood serpen-
tine fronted corner vitrine,
the single door part glazed,
circa 1900, 27 x 40in. (P.
Wilson & Co.) $962

Painted pine corner cup-
board on turned bulbous
feet, New England, circa
1800, 51in. wide. (Robt.
W. Skinner Inc.)
$2,900

A late 18th century Dutch
mahogany standing corner
cupboard, 98in. high.
(Anderson & Garland)
$2,990

A Dutch walnut standing corner cabinet with a domed cornice, 4ft.3in. wide, circa 1740.          $3,364

An Edwardian mahogany and inlaid standing corner cabinet, circa 1910, 2ft.4in. wide.          $1,029

A George II Cuban mahogany bow-front corner cupboard with original brass fret escutcheons and 'H' hinges, 28in. wide. (Woolley & Wallis)          $731

A 19th century Swiss painted pine cabinet inscribed Johannes Muller, Anno 1834, 33in. wide. (Dreweatt Watson & Barton)          $2,358

One of a pair of gilt metal mounted and marble topped satinwood corner cabinets, circa 1870, 3ft. 10in. high. $3,360

A flame mahogany bow-front corner cupboard with molded cornice. (Ward & Partners)          $780

A Federal pine carved corner cupboard, circa 1815, 48in. wide. (Robt. W. Skinner Inc.)     $2,300

A George III mahogany and boxwood line inlaid standing corner cupboard, 44in. wide. (Dreweatt Watson & Barton) $1,310

A bow-fronted crossbanded corner cupboard. (Taylors)          $299

# COURT CUPBOARDS

IN days of old one of the great status symbols was the size of the family dresser or court cupboard. The king's would stretch from floor to ceiling while those of lesser men would have been correspondingly smaller.

As the 17th century wore on, they tended to become much wider than their height and their decoration grew progressively plainer. Although still produced in country districts, cupboards of this type were being ousted from fashionable dining rooms by the more sophisticated walnut or lacquered furniture.

Apart from oak, these may be found to be made of walnut, though the interior is usually still of oak, and vary from being quite plain to sporting exotic carving.

It was a nice custom at the time to give one of these as a wedding present and many will be found bearing the initials of the happy pair and the date of their nuptials.

A 17th century oak court cupboard, 6ft. wide. (Warren & Wignall) $1,197

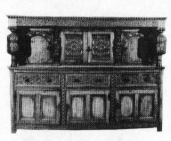

A Tudor-style carved oak court cupboard, possibly late 17th century, England, 92½in. wide. (Robt. W. Skinner Inc.) $1,750

Early 18th century oak court cupboard, the doors with ivory escutcheons, 56in. wide. (Robt. W. Skinner Inc.) $1,300

A Georgian Welsh oak duo-darn, the cornice with two acorn shape pendant finials, 51in. wide. (Lawrence Fine Art) $1,187

A 17th century carved oak court cupboard with molded cornice, 5ft.2in. wide. (Capes, Dunn & Co.) $896

A 17th century oak court cupboard with original brass hinges and escutcheons. (Locke & England) $1,625

# CREDENZAS

ALTHOUGH I have heard these items classed as anything from sideboards to chiffoniers, most dealers refer to them as credenzas. The word is Italian and applies to a long, low cabinet with up to four doors, a style which first made its appearance in this form during the last quarter of the 18th century.

They are quite large but have the virtue of combining the functions of various pieces of furniture, being suitable for displaying both china and silver while providing a covered storage area for less worthy pieces.

Many are veneered in burr walnut with ormolu mounts on the pilasters and have a small amount of inlay in the center door. Another decorative style used on French credenzas made by various firms is that known as Boulle. This is the inlay of interlocking pieces of brass and tortoiseshell, introduced by Andre Charles Boulle back in the late 17th century.

An Arts & Crafts period inlaid walnut credenza, 6ft.6in. wide. (J. R. Bridgford & Sons) $1,121

A mid 19th century red boulle breakfront credenza with ebonized top, 6ft.5in. wide. (Woolley & Wallis)$922

Victorian ebonized and walnut crossbanded credenza. (Reeds Rains) $967

A Victorian slight breakfront credenza in burr walnut with satinwood floral scroll inlay and stringing, 182cm. wide. (Osmond Tricks) $1,134

A gilt mounted walnut credenza. (Brogden & Co.) $1,072

A Victorian walnut credenza, the central cupboard enclosed by a pair of mirror panelled doors, 188cm. wide. (H. Spencer & Sons)$1,041

Mid 19th century Renaissance Revival rosewood credenza, America, 56in. long. (Robt. W. Skinner Inc.)     $1,200

Victorian rosewood marble top and mirrored back credenza, 1840. (British Antique Exporters) $626

A walnut credenza, the center cupboard doors inset with Sevres panels flanked by two domed glass fronted cupboards. (Worsfolds)     $2,025

# CUPBOARDS

CUPBOARDS tended to become plainer as their development progressed with hardly any ornamentation beyond the turned pediments below the frieze which, occasionally, had a wisp of foliated scroll carving.

The cupboard doors in the lower section are usually divided into an arrangement of one horizontal and two vertical panels, which is typical of 17th century furniture, and the doors on the upper section are fielded.

Totally genuine pieces should be open to the floor inside the bottom cupboard, which should contain a single shelf.

Early English furniture was usually made of oak, this being the tried and tested native hardwood but, by the end of the 17th century, the more refined tastes of the fashionable town dwellers demanded furniture of more exotic woods such as walnut.

The supply of walnut was met mainly from Europe but, in 1709 an extremely hard winter killed off most of the trees and the French, perturbed by the depleted state of their stocks, placed an embargo on the export of walnut in 1720.

About 1730, as a result of public pressure, the import duty on Spanish mahogany was lifted and designers were able seriously to turn their attention to exploiting the possibilities of this wood, which is extremely strong and hard.

As trade was developing and the demand increasing for finer detail, such as astragal glazed doors for example, importers turned their eyes towards Jamaica and the West Indies from where the fine grained Cuban mahogany was obtained and so great was the demand that in 1753 alone, over half a million cubic feet were imported.

Late 17th/18th century French provincial oak bonnetiere, 41in. wide. (Lawrence Fine Art) $738

A painted pine cupboard supported by bracket feet, Conn. River Valley, circa 1800, 54in. wide. (Robt. W. Skinner Inc.) $950

A pine slant-back cupboard, New England, circa 1800, 49in. wide. (Robt. W. Skinner Inc.) $4,600

Victorian walnut linen press, 1875. (British Antique Exporters) $855

An 18th century oak bonnetiere, probably Austrian, 29in. wide. (Lawrence Fine Art) $1,476

A late Gothic oak hutch cupboard or aumbry, 3ft. 6in. wide. $3,907

Georgian mahogany linen press, 1800. (British Antique Exporters) $731

Walnut cabinet with panelled cupboard doors, 1920. (British Antique Exporters) $333

Georgian pine linen press, 1800. (British Antique Exporters)    $735

Late 18th century housekeeper's cupboard, oak mahogany banded, 83in. wide. (P. Wilson & Co.) $3,685

Early 19th century Scandinavian painted cupboard with scalloped base, 43in. wide. (Robt. W. Skinner Inc.) $800

An 18th century oak cupboard having a molded cornice and double doors with shaped and fielded panels, 22in. wide. (Outhwaite & Litherland)  $1,105

Georgian pine housekeeper's cupboard, 1790. (British Antique Exporters) $850

A late 18th century housekeeper's cupboard in oak mahogany crossbanded, 6ft. 6in. wide. (P. Wilson & Co.) $1,637

Georgian pine housekeeper's press, 1790. (British Antique Exporters) $650

A Queen Anne burr walnut press cupboard, 5ft. wide, circa 1710. $10,395

A 19th century marquetry meuble d'appui in Louis XV style in kingwood and rosewood, 30½in. wide. (Lawrence Fine Art) $1,955

A Charles II large chest in oak and walnut veneered with snakewood and ebony, in three sections, 50in. wide. (Lawrence Fine Art) $3,509

An early 16th century Gothic oak hutch cupboard or aumbry, 3ft.4½in. wide. $7,651

Late 17th/early 18th century oak tack cupboard/settee with shoe foot trestle base, 73½in. high. (Robt. W. Skinner Inc.) $1,100

A Charles II style oak press cupboard , circa 1860, 4ft. 11½in. wide. $1,716

Late 17th century Flemish oak cupboard on later bun feet, 46½in. wide. (Lawrence Fine Art) $1,955

A 17th century oak cupboard of rectangular form with plank top, 114cm. wide. (H. Spencer & Sons) $992

Pine stepback cupboard, New England, circa 1820, 65½in. high. (Robt. W. Skinner Inc.) $2,000

A mid 17th century Charles I oak cupboard, with later trestle feet, 4ft.6½in. wide. $2,767

A 17th/18th century Italian pine and marquetry cupboard inlaid in walnut and sycamore, 30in. wide. (Lawrence Fine Art) $1,257

A 17th century Swiss or Bavarian German oak enclosed cupboard-base table, 4ft.9in. long. $7,163

Greco-Roman Revival mahogany linen press in two sections, Massa., circa 1810, 54in. wide. (Robt. W. Skinner Inc.) $3,000

An oak food cupboard in Medieval style, constructed in the 19th century, using 16th century panels, 4ft.5in. wide. $11,070

A Flemish 17th century oak standing cupboard, 2ft.4½in. wide. $2,116

A mid 18th century mahogany press cupboard with dentil cornice, 3ft.8in. wide. $1,130

A 19th century Dutch marquetry kas, walnut, fruitwood and other stained veneers, 78in. wide. (Robt. W. Skinner Inc.) $2,300

A Flemish carved oak press cupboard with mask carved terminals, 4ft.10in. wide, circa 1620. $1,053

# DAVENPORTS

THIS is a very delightful little desk which originated during the final years of the 18th century.

Primarily a lady's desk, it is one of those rare pieces in which the virtues of practicality and elegance are beautifully combined to produce a comfortable yet compact piece of functional furniture.

Earlier davenports were usually made of rosewood or satinwood and were boxlike in structure apart from the sloping top which would either pull forward or swivel to the side in order to make room for the writer's lower limbs. They stand on bun, small turned or, occasionally, bracket feet and better examples sport a fine brass gallery to stop pens and small objects from falling down the back.

While most examples are about two feet wide, it is well worth looking for the smaller ones (about 15 inches to 18 inches wide), for these can fetch twice as much as the larger models even though they usually have only a cupboard at the side instead of drawers.

It was during the William IV period that the davenport gained its name and its popularity.

The story goes that one Captain Davenport placed an order for one of these writing desks with Gillows of Lancaster, a well-known firm of cabinet makers at the time. Known during its manufacture as "the Davenport order", the first desk was completed and the name stuck, being applied to all subsequent orders for a desk of this particular style.

Davenports were, at the middle of the 19th century, at the height of their popularity and at peak quality for, although they remained in vogue to a certain extent for the remainder of the century, the standard of workmanship employed in their construction declined steadily.

Georgian walnut davenport with carved decoration, 1880. (British Antique Exporters. $542

A Victorian burr walnut davenport with hinged writing slope, 2ft.9in. wide, circa 1850. $625

A mid 19th century walnut piano-top davenport with a lift-up lid, 21½in. wide. (Outhwaite & Litherland) $1,282

A 19th century Oriental carved, lacquered and gilt davenport desk, China, 28¾in. wide. (Robt. W. Skinner Inc.) $1,600

A Victorian inlaid walnut davenport with maple lined interior and raised stationery compartment. (Morphets) $467

A Victorian rosewood harlequin davenport, circa 1850, 1ft.11½in. wide. $1,536

A Victorian burr walnut davenport with a rear hinged stationery compartment, 1ft.11in. wide, circa 1850. $750

A Georgian mahogany davenport on bun feet with sliding top and writing slides. (Barber's Fine Art) $1,562

A Victorian figured mahogany davenport with shaped front supports. (Sandoe Luce Panes) $1,200

Late 19th century lacquer davenport with Oriental figure decoration, 21in. wide. (Coles, Knapp & Kennedy) $268

A William IV mahogany sliding top davenport with four drawers. (Boardman) $845

A William IV rosewood davenport with a gallery and a lined writing slope, 2ft. wide, circa 1830. $937

A Victorian figured walnut davenport with serpentine front with hinged sloping writing surface, 54cm. wide. (H. Spencer & Sons) $620

A Victorian burr walnut and ebonized harlequin davenport, 1ft.11in. wide, circa 1870. $1,909

Regency rosewood davenport on squat turned feet, 20in. wide. (Warner Sheppard & Wade) $2,128

# DISPLAY CABINETS

IN the early 18th century, Oriental porcelain and Delftware became extremely popular and a need arose for suitably fine cabinets with glazed upper sections in which to display it to its full advantage.

Early styles had straight cornices and doors glazed in half round moldings, the whole supported on turned legs with stretchers. As taste developed, however, heavy architectural styles in the manner of William Kent became popular, often displaying dentil cornices, and broken-arch pediments, with fielded panelled doors below the glazed section.

It was not long before the heavy, architecturally styled cabinets were recognised as being inappropriate for the display of delicate china and porcelain. They were quickly relegated to the libraries of the nation for the storage of books, their places being taken in fashionable drawing rooms by far more graceful display cabinets.

Never slow to turn an imported fashion to their advantage, designers such as Chippendale helped to perpetuate the taste for things Oriental by producing fine Chinese-influenced styles incorporating some incredibly delicate fretwork.

Dutch marquetry was another popular decorative style consisting of naturalistic birds and flowers executed in shaped reserves. Shading of the leaves and flowers was, during the first half of the 18th century, achieved by dipping the veneered shapes part way into hot sand but this later gave way to a method of engraving the shading on to the actual surface of the finished marquetry pattern.

An Arts & Crafts oak display cabinet with painted panel to the railed upstand, 107cm. wide. (Osmond Tricks) $577

Edwardian domed top oak cabinet, 1910. (British Antique Exporters) $91

A Victorian walnut side cabinet with gilt metal mounts, 41in. wide. (Lawrence Fine Art) $1,327

An 18th century walnut display cabinet, the base with two short and three long drawers, 43in. wide. (Boardman) $2,247

An Edwardian mahogany breakfront display cabinet, 197cm. wide. (Osmond Tricks) $898

A late Victorian satinwood inlaid demi-lune display cabinet on stand, 2ft.8in. wide, circa 1890. $1,901

A 19th century satinwood vitrine with an astragal glazed door, 75cm. wide. (Osmond Tricks) $1,915

An ebony veneered side cabinet with ivory inlay, after a design by Christopher Dresser, circa 1870. $3,480

A Chippendale-style mahogany display cabinet on stand on ball and claw feet, 6ft.10in. x 3ft.4in. wide. (Russell Baldwin & Bright) $1,225

Late 19th century French-style mahogany vitrine, D-shaped with cast brass mountings, 29in. wide. (Robt. W. Skinner Inc.) $750

A French inlaid mahogany display cabinet with reverse breakfront marble top, 61½in. wide. (D. M. Nesbit & Co.) $1,580

An Edwardian inlaid mahogany display cabinet, satinwood inlay to front, 38½in. wide. (Barber's Fine Art) $1,116

A Dutch walnut veneered floral marquetry inlaid cabinet, on front bun and side bracket feet, 5ft.7in. wide. (Woolley & Wallis) $2,970

A 19th century boulle bijouterie table lined in red plush velvet, 31 x 19½in. (Morphets) $456

A mahogany display cabinet with glazed doors and velvet covered shelving. (Worsfolds) $324

## DISPLAY CABINETS

A Louis XV-style mahogany and ormolu mounted vitrine, in the manner of Vernis Martin, circa 1900, 2ft.10in. wide.
$1,543

A Japanese hardwood display cabinet with asymmetrical arrangement of shelves, cupboard and drawers, 4ft. 11½in. wide. $1,001

A 19th century French vitrine of double serpentine outline, 34in. wide. (Morphets) $1,917

An Edwardian mahogany display cabinet with a pair of Gothic doors enclosing four shelves, 109cm. wide. (Osmond Tricks)$957

A 19th century French display table. (Cooper Hirst) $1,040

Hepplewhite mahogany china cabinet in two parts, circa 1790, 50½in. wide. (Stalker & Boos) $2,200

An Edwardian mahogany and inlaid display cabinet, 4ft.6in. wide, circa 1910. $1,940

An Edwardian inlaid mahogany display cabinet with leaded glass bow-front door, 48in. wide. (Morphets) $432

A mahogany display cabinet of Chinese Chippendale design enclosed by astragal glazed doors, 44in. wide. (Morphets) $777

# FURNITURE

# DISPLAY CABINETS

An Edwardian satinwood bow-front display cabinet of Sheraton influence, 42in. wide. (Morphets)
$1,179

A French small vitrine in kingwood with ormolu mounts of serpentine outline with rouge marbled top, 27in. wide. (Lawrence Fine Art)        $698

A Victorian walnut breakfront display cabinet with central glazed panel, by Johnstone & Jeanes, 48in. wide. (Reeds Rains)
$1,354

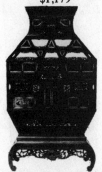

An Eastern carved hardwood display cabinet, 130cm. wide. (H. Spencer & Sons)
$2,440

Mid 19th century rectangular rosewood Empire style display cabinet, with glazed top. (P. Wilson & Co.)
$1,126

A French transitional-style mahogany and ormolu mounted demi-lune vitrine, circa 1890, 2ft.4in. wide.
$1,609

A French mahogany and satinwood marquetry bow-front vitrine, 2ft.4in. wide, circa 1900.    $859

An Edwardian inlaid mahogany display cabinet with a pair of astragal glazed doors, 164cm. wide. (H. Spencer & Sons)        $1,315

A mahogany Art Nouveau display cabinet, the mirrored top with open canopy, 48in. long. (Outhwaite & Litherland)        $1,130

319

# DISPLAY CABINETS

A 19th century French rosewood vitrine with gilt metal mounts, 35in. wide. (Lawrence Fine Art) $1,397

A boulle secretaire display cabinet with egg and dart cornice, 3ft.8in. wide. $2,884

One of a pair of early George III chinoiserie japanned display cabinets on stands, 3ft. 2in. wide, circa 1760. $68,992

A bow-fronted painted satinwood display cabinet, the cornice with a pair of urn finials, 3ft.6in. wide. $3,135

An Art Nouveau oak vitrine with glazed cupboard, 62.3cm. wide, circa 1900. (Christie's) $1,632

Early 20th century Edwardian bow-fronted painted satinwood display cabinet, 4ft.8in. wide. $2,696

An Edwardian mahogany display cabinet inlaid with satinwood stringing, circa 1910, 2ft.3in. wide. $640

A mahogany breakfront display cabinet, in Chinese Chippendale style, circa 1910, 5ft.9in. wide. $4,891

Early 19th century Colonial calamander display cabinet on shaped bracket feet, 57in. wide. (Christie's) $5,400

# DRESSERS

THE name "dresser" could possibly derive from the fact that its sole original function was to provide a surface on which the food could be dressed before serving, completion of this stage of culinary activity being signalled to ravenous diners by the beating of a drum.

In order to simplify their work and cut costs, cabinet makers of the late 17th century often neglected to produce elaborately turned legs for their products, making do with wavy shapes cut from flat boards instead.

It has been recorded that a few mediaeval cupboard-type dressers had a form of shelving above them but it was not until the beginning of the 18th century that the idea really caught on and became a fully developed, everyday reality.

Another popular innovation in the early 18th century was the inclusion of a row of small spice drawers set in front of the backboard along the top.

Most early dressers with shelves had no backboards to them, these often being added later in the century.

One of the reasons for shelves — apart from the obvious one that people were using more cooking utensils than hitherto — was to display the English Delftware which served most families as a substitute for the expensive Chinese porcelain displayed in the homes of people of wealth.

By the mid 18th century dressers had been ousted from fashionable dining rooms by large side tables or sideboards made of mahogany, the faithful old dressers being relegated to the kitchens or the servants' quarters.

In rural districts, however, dressers continued to hold pride of place in the parlors of farmhouses, positions they richly deserved.

An oak dresser with drawers having brass drop handles, 70in. wide. (Dee & Atkinson) $1,397

A Georgian oak dresser, the top crossbanded with mahogany, 191cm. wide. (H. Spencer & Sons) $2,091

An 18th century crossbanded oak dresser base. (J. R. Bridgford & Sons) $2,825

George III oak dresser with mahogany crossbanding. (Reeds Rains) $2,728

# DRESSERS

An 18th century oak dresser with brass handles, the back fitted with five spice drawers, 64in. wide. (Morphets) $2,664

A George II oak dresser with pine platform base, 5ft.0½in. wide, circa 1750. $1,828

An oak Welsh dresser with five mahogany crossbanded drawers with brass handles, 70in. wide. (Dee & Atkinson) $1,107

An 18th century small oak dresser, 54in. wide. (Lawrence Fine Art) $2,057

Victorian pine Welsh dresser, 1840. (British Antique Exporters) $555

An oak dresser with brass swan neck handles, backplates and escutcheons, 72½in. long. (Outhwaite & Litherland) $1,950

A Flemish-style ebonized oak dresser commemorating a 1789 wedding. (Worsfolds) $1,596

A Georgian oak dresser, the shelves with shaped cornice, 70½in. wide. (Lawrence Fine Art) $3,352

A reproduction oak and mahogany crossbanded Welsh dresser, the drawers with brass loop handles, 5ft.3in. wide. (Capes, Dunn & Co.) $981

An early Georgian small oak and yewwood low dresser, 54in. wide. (Lawrence Fine Art)     $2,095

An English oak chest with hinged top opening to deep well, circa 1790, 61½in. long. (Robt. W. Skinner Inc.)     $1,200

A 17th century oak small dresser, the top having thumb mold edge, 4ft.9in. wide. (Capes, Dunn & Co.)     $495

Victorian pine Welsh dresser, 1860. (British Antique Exporters)     $415

A Georgian high oak dresser with an ogee cornice above open shelves, 57in. wide. (Lawrence Fine Art)     $2,549

A mid 18th century Swansea Valley oak dresser, 6ft. wide. (Edgar Horn)     $3,276

An early 19th century mahogany and oak dresser with brass handles, 66in. long. (Outhwaite & Litherland)     $1,362

A late Georgian oak high dresser with backed shelves above the base, 68½in. wide. (Lawrence Fine Art)     $1,386

A mid 18th century-style oak Welsh dresser with brass drop handles, 71in. long. (Dacre, Son & Hartley)     $2,028

# DUMB WAITERS

DUMB-WAITERS were extremely fashionable during the final quarter of the 18th century and throughout the Regency period, although there is evidence that they were available as early as 1727, when Lord Bristol purchased one from a cabinet maker named Robert Leigh.

It was Sheraton, with a turn of phrase as elegant as one of his own chairlegs, who described the dumb-waiter as "a useful piece of furniture to serve in some respects the place of a waiter, whence it is so named".

Generally consisting of three or four graduated shelves revolving around a central column, dumb-waiters were usually made with a tripod base terminating in feet whose style varied with the transient fashions of the period. The shelves, largest at the bottom, were sometimes made from single pieces of wood and sometimes constructed with flaps.

A late George III mahogany two-tier dumbwaiter, 2ft. 8½in. high, circa 1810. $1,058

A George III mahogany dumb waiter, the turned baluster shaft fitted with three circular graduated tiers, 24in. wide. (Christie's) $954

A George III mahogany three-tier dumb waiter with outswept tripod legs, 43in. high. (Anderson & Garland) $975

A Georgian mahogany two-tier dumb waiter on tripod base.(Jacobs & Hunt) $1,454

A George II mahogany three-tier dumb waiter on tripod base, 3ft.6½in. high, circa 1750. $1,125

A George III mahogany two-tier dumb waiter on tripod support, 2ft.1½in. diam., circa 1760. $687

# KNEEHOLE DESKS

KNEEHOLE desks were originally designed for use as dressing tables and are basically, chests of drawers with recesses cut to accommodate the knees of persons seated before the mirror which stood on top.

It soon became apparent, however, that they made ideal writing tables and they stayed as dual purpose pieces of furniture until the latter half of the 18th century.

A particularly fine example comes from the William and Mary period and is made of walnut with ebony arabesque marquetry panels. These are inlays of floral and geometric scrolls, usually found within a simple, rectangular frame. This desk rests upon small bun feet typical of the period and has a recessed cupboard with a small drawer in the apron above. The drawers are made of oak and have dust boards fitted between them.

Although the kneehole desk with a center cupboard was still popular in the mid 18th century, the style developed somewhat to incorporate two pedestals, each having three or four drawers, surmounted by a flat table top which itself contained two or three drawers.

At first these were made as single units, often double sided to stand in the center of a room, and soon became extremely popular in libraries. They were, however, rather large and cumbersome in this form and later models were made in three sections to facilitate removal and installation.

Pedestal desks date from about 1750 until the end of the 19th century and the difficulty in pricing them stems from the fact that the style changed hardly at all during that time.

Victorian oak twin pedestal cylinder desk, 1860. (British Antique Exporters)          $583

An Edwardian satinwood, crossbanded, boxwood and ebony line inlaid kidney-shaped writing table, 48in. wide. (Dreweatt Watson & Barton)          $1,048

Victorian oak roll-top desk, 1880. (British Antique Exporters)          $480

A George III-style mahogany bow front kneehole writing table, made-up, with gilt-tooled leather inset, 4ft.1in. wide.          $434

# FURNITURE

## KNEEHOLE DESKS

Edwardian kidney-shaped inlaid mahogany kneehole desk with tooled leather inset top, 49in. wide. (Reeds Rains)
$1,022

A Victorian burr walnut pedestal desk, the inset top above three frieze drawers, 4ft.3in. wide, circa 1860.
$1,828

Victorian oak twin pedestal cylinder desk, 1860. (British Antique Exporters)
$730

A mahogany small kneehole desk in the Georgian style, 31½in. wide. (Lawrence Fine Art) $1,543

An early Georgian walnut kneehole desk with brass drop handles, 75cm. wide. (H. Spencer & Sons)
$2,337

An early George III mahogany kneehole dressing table on bracket feet, 35½ x 30½in. high. (Lawrence Fine Art) $3,247

A George I walnut kneehole desk on later bracket feet, 31½in. wide. (Lawrence Fine Art) $4,470

A small mahogany kneehole secretaire desk, 29½in. wide. (Lawrence Fine Art)
$2,415

A Chippendale period mahogany kneehole dressing table with molded top, on bracket feet. (Woolley & Wallis)
$1,239

A mahogany pedestal desk with cylinder front enclosing green tooled leather inset, 4ft. wide. (Vidler & Co.) $843

A walnut kneehole desk with eight oak lined cross-banded drawers, 39in. wide. (Dee & Atkinson) $1,232

A George III mahogany knee-hole desk with gilt tooled green leather inset top. (Dreweatt Watson & Barton) $986

An early 18th century Queen Anne walnut kneehole writing table on bracket feet, 2ft.6in. wide. $6,652

An 18th century walnut veneer kneehole desk. (R. R. Leonard & Son) $19,698

A George I black and gold lacquer kneehole desk on bracket feet, 32¾in. wide. (Woolley & Wallis) $5,900

An early George III maho-gany kneehole desk with brass handles, 33½in. wide. (Anderson & Garland) $2,405

A George I walnut veneered kneehole desk/writing chest with herringbone line inlay, 35in. wide. (Woolley & Wallis) $3,045

A late Georgian small maho-gany kneehole desk, 35in. wide. (Lawrence Fine Art) $1,744

# LOWBOYS

**A**LTHOUGH many more sophisticated dressing tables were constructed during the 18th century, the lowboy remained extremely popular — probably a sign of its great versatility as a piece of furniture.

The normal construction was an arrangement of three drawers disposed around a kneehole, though I have seen examples having an additional pair of drawers, or one long, single drawer, set immediately below the top.

The most expensive examples are those made of mahogany or walnut, with bold cabriole legs, often enhanced with shells on the knees, but their country cousins of elm or oak are much more reasonably priced. The latter usually have straight, square legs chamfered on their inside edges or rounded legs with pad feet.

The lowboy was often set against the wall below one of the new Vauxhall plate glass mirrors, which were about eighteen inches high and set in plain molded frames.

Edwardian mahogany lowboy dressing table, 1910. (British Antique Exporters)$373

A Queen Anne cherry lowboy on four cabriole legs, 35½in. wide, circa 1740. (Robt. W. Skinner Inc.) $20,000

George I walnut veneer lowboy raised on cabriole legs, circa 1720, 30in. wide. (Stalker & Boos) $4,000

A Queen Anne walnut side table with three drawers and cabriole legs, 2ft.6in. wide, circa 1715. $5,913

A Queen Anne walnut lowboy raised on four fruitwood cabriole supports, 27½in. wide. (Lawrence Fine Art) $4,026

A George III oak and walnut lowboy fitted with brass handles, 30in. wide. (Anderson & Garland)$2,194

# SCREENS

SCREENS have been in widespread use since at least the fifteenth century, for warding off draughts, for protecting sensitive complexions from the fire's heat or for privacy.

Hardly surprising, perhaps, the quality of screens' manufacture has varied but little from those early days, and the materials used are still very much the same too; from simple buckram, wickerwork, wood and needlework to extravagant finishes for royalty, including gold lace and silk. During the reign of Charles II, some fine examples, having up to twelve folds, and decorated with superb lacquer work were imported from the East. Today, of course, one of these would cost many thousands of pounds.

By the William and Mary period, small screens fitted with sliding panels of polished wood or embroidery had become popular and these developed into the cheval screens of the 18th century. Small pole screens also put in an appearance at this time, though these became more numerous as the eighteenth century gave way to the nineteenth.

A 19th century Chinese two-part red lacquer screen, 71in. high, panels 24in. wide. (Robt. W. Skinner Inc.)$800

Late 17th/early 18th century six-fold Japanese screen, painting on paper with silk brocade border, each panel 22in. wide. (Robt. W. Skinner Inc.)   $3,500

Late 19th century Japanese lacquer ivory and mother-of-pearl inlaid two-fold screen, each fold 74 x 34in. (Capes, Dunn & Co.)   $374

Four-fold Oriental lacquer, mother-of-pearl and stone inlaid screen, each panel 17½in. wide. (Robt. W. Skinner Inc.)   $750

Victorian leaded light fire-screen, 1875. (British Antique Exporters)
$126

A three-sectioned oak screen, by Gustav Stickley, circa 1913, each panel 21½in. wide, 66in. high. (Robt. W. Skinner Inc.) $6,000

An oil on canvas fireboard, possibly New Hampshire, circa 1835, 38in. high, 43in. wide. (Robt. W. Skinner Inc.) $1,300

A Chippendale period mahogany pole screen with acorn finial. (Geering & Colyer) $390

Victorian oak barley twist firescreen, 1880. (British Antique Exporters) $25

An eight-fold gold-ground coromandel screen decorated in polychrome, each fold 7ft. high, 1ft.4in. wide. $1,617

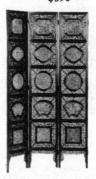

Late 19th century six-fold carved screen in hardwood with panels of light wood, each fold 7ft.2½in. high, 1ft.5in. wide. $4,293

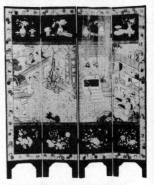

Early 20th century Chinese four-part coromandel screen, black lacquer still life panels, 72in. high, panels 16in. wide. (Robt. W. Skinner Inc.) $700

A mid 19th century Chinese hardwood and mother-of-pearl inlaid firescreen, 2ft. high. $518

An early Victorian satinwood four-fold draught screen, the panels enclosing thirteen 19th century Sporting and Coaching prints after H. Hall, J. F. Herring, C. C. Henderson and others, 78in. high. (Christie's) $1,071

A mid 19th century rosewood and brass combined pole screen, wine and games table with adjustable top. (P. Wilson & Co.) $655

# SECRETAIRES

THE name escritoire (or, scritoire as it was originally) was applied to the piece of furniture produced towards the end of the 17th century in answer to the demand for a cabinet with a falling front; prior to this time, all larger pieces had been equipped with double doors.

Although this design has been used ever since with only minor variations, it has never achieved the overwhelming popularity attained by some of the other writing cabinets and desks. The upper level, revealed by dropping the front, contains a multitude of drawers with pigeon holes above. The drop front, in the lowered position, is usually supported by a pair of brass jointed stays.

A secretaire chest is, basically, a chest of drawers whose deep fitted top drawer has a fall front which pulls forward to allow a sizable writing area with room below for the knees.

Having been made from the last quarter of the 18th century until the present day, they are to be found in an extremely wide range of styles, qualities and prices.

When buying such a chest it is wise to bear in mind the similarity between it and a chest of drawers — you might well be buying an old chest of drawers which has undergone a modern conversion job!

Look carefully at the sides of the secretaire and the depth of the top drawer; the sides need to be thicker and stronger for a secretaire than an ordinary drawer, therefore a conversion will show if the sides appear to be of newer wood than those of the other drawers. The depth of the top drawer should be the largest in the chest and marks will show on the side of the carcass if the supports have been altered to achieve this.

Mid 19th century burl walnut desk curio, France, 37½in. wide. (Robt. W. Skinner Inc.)$1,000

A mid 18th century Continental inlaid secretaire chest of various woods, 40½in. wide. (Dacre, Son & Hartley)$1,178

Late 18th century floral marquetry secretary, Holland, 48in. wide. (Robt. W. Skinner Inc.) $1,900

Mid 19th century Renaissance Revival fall-front desk, America, 45in. wide. (Robt. W. Skinner Inc.) $800

An Empire mahogany secretaire a abattant, the stepped top with secret drawer, 48½in. wide. (Reeds Rains) $836

A George III cedar secretaire bookcase, 47in. wide. (Christie's) $1,404

# SECRETAIRES

Federal mahogany plantation secretary desk, Southern States, circa 1810, 45in. wide. (Robt. W. Skinner Inc.) $3,000

A George III mahogany secretaire chest, the writing drawer enclosing a fitted interior, circa 1770, 2ft. 10in. wide. $1,172

An early 19th century Continental mahogany secretaire a abattant with a fall front, 38in. wide. (Lawrence Fine Art) $1,078

A 16th century Spanish vargueno, the interior has seventeen ivory and gilt molded drawers, 38in. long. (Robt. W. Skinner Inc.) $2,000

A Georgian mahogany brass bound military chest, the upper section with secretaire drawer, 109cm. wide. (H. Spencer & Sons) $1,117

A Chinese side cabinet with fitted drawer and cupboard above. (Ward & Partners) $1,300

An Edwardian mahogany cylinder desk with two glazed doors above a cylinder front, 30in. wide. (Lawrence Fine Art) $2,153

A Louis XV-style walnut and crossbanded harlequin secretaire commode, 2ft.4in. wide, circa 1860. $2,009

A Victorian walnut secretaire Wellington chest, 2ft. wide. (Vidler & Co.) $1,066

A Queen Anne walnut secretaire with a molded cornice above a cushion frieze drawer, 40½in. wide. (Lawrence Fine Art)    $4,752

A Regency mahogany secretaire chest, stamped Edwards & Roberts, 46½in. wide. (Banks & Silvers)    $1,450

A George III mahogany secretaire press with Gothic cornice and fitted trays to upper section, 48in. wide. (Locke & England)    $3,000

A Victorian teak military secretaire chest in two sections with inset brass corners and handles, 41¾in. wide. (Woolley & Wallis)    $1,014

A Dutch marquetry secretaire a abattant with inlaid interior. (Mallams)    $2,280

A Biedermeier figured mahogany secretaire chest on bracket feet, 3ft.6in. wide. (Capes, Dunn & Co.)    $567

A George I walnut secretaire cabinet, the upper part with eight drawers and adjustable shelves, 47in. wide. (Dreweatt Watson & Barton)    $4,930

A Federal mahogany tambour secretary, circa 1795, 40in. wide. (Robt. W. Skinner Inc.)    $4,000

A Louis Phillipe kingwood veneered small secretaire a abattant with a marble top, 26in. wide. (Woolley & Wallis)    $1,215

# SECRETAIRE BOOKCASES

NOT unnaturally, secretaire bookcases were developed at about the same time as bureau bookcases and were dictated by the same fashionable taste.

A useful, though not absolutely reliable guide to dating a piece is to look closely at the interior fitting of the secretaire drawer; generally speaking, the better the quality the earlier the date. It is often disappointing to find that, among the late 19th century reproductions of earlier furniture, the rule was, "what the eye doesn't see, the heart doesn't grieve" — finely finished exterior surfaces concealing a considerable amount of scrimping on the small drawers and pigeon holes in the fitted compartments of secretaires and bureaux.

Attention should also be centered on the oak lined drawers as a guide to date of manufacture, for it was in about 1770 that a constructional change occurred.

Until this time, the drawer bottoms were made with the grain of the wood running front to back but, from this time onward, the grain will be found to run from side to side, the bottom often being made of two separate pieces of wood supported by a central bearer.

The secretaire bookcase, dating from 1820, is more reasonably priced than most at the moment, though it, and pieces like it, seem to be increasing in value from week to week.

It still has the basic shape of an 18th century piece but the classical pediment with its scroll ends is typical of the Regency period as is the delicate carving on the curved pilasters.

Pieces of this kind are made of mahogany or rosewood, the latter being the most expensive, and they always present an attractive and well finished appearance from the outside.

A George III mahogany secretaire bookcase with a later added cornice, 50½in. wide. (Lawrence Fine Art) $2,933

A George III mahogany secretaire bookcase, 97cm. wide, circa 1790. $1,673

Chippendale secretary bookcase in two parts, raised on bracket feet, circa 1800, 15½in. wide. (Stalker & Boos) $3,750

A late Georgian mahogany secretaire bookcase, the drawer stamped Kentluck & Kent's London, 45in. wide. (Lawrence Fine Art) $5,099

A 19th century mahogany secretaire bookcase with two glazed doors with curved astragals, 47in. wide. (Lawrence Fine Art) $2,601

A late George III mahogany secretaire cabinet, 100cm. wide. (H. Spencer & Sons) $1,220

A George III mahogany and crossbanded secretaire bookcase, 2ft.8in. wide, circa 1800. $950

A large 19th century mahogany breakfront bookcase with secretaire drawer, 94in. wide. (Anderson & Garland) $7,182

A George III mahogany secretaire bookcase, circa 1800, 3ft. wide. $3,364

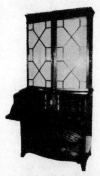

An early 19th century Georgian mahogany secretaire bookcase with three long drawers, 4ft.8in. wide. (Farrant & Wightman) $2,664

A late Georgian mahogany breakfront secretaire library bookcase with bow-wings, 157in. wide. (Lawrence Fine Art) $15,048

A 19th century secretaire bookcase with a stepped cornice, dated 1792, 47in. wide. (Anderson & Garland) $3,640

A German mahogany secretaire bookcase, circa 1850, 3ft.7in. wide. $1,148

A large 19th century mahogany breakfront secretaire bookcase, 8ft.4in. high. (Anderson & Garland) $3,900

An early 19th century mahogany secretaire bookcase, 42in. wide. (Dreweatt Watson & Barton) $2,960

# SECRETAIRE BOOKCASES

A George III mahogany secretaire bookcase with two thirteen pane glazed doors, 44in. wide. (Lawrence Fine Art) $2,692

French late 19th century ebonized and ormolu mounted boullework secretary, 43¼in. wide. (Robt. W. Skinner Inc.) $1,900

An Edwardian mahogany inlaid secretaire bookcase with two glazed doors enclosing shelves, 28in. wide. (Lawrence Fine Art) $1,914

A George III mahogany secretaire bookcase, circa 1790, 3ft.4in. wide. $4,774

A George III-style mahogany and satinwood breakfront bookcase, circa 1910, bearing trade label of 'Warings, Liverpool', 4ft.2in. wide. $1,975.

Late 18th/early 19th century Hepplewhite mahogany and mahogany veneer secretary, England, 33½in. wide. (Robt. W. Skinner Inc.) $3,300

A Victorian walnut secretary, the lower desk section with roll-top, 44½in. wide. (Robt. W. Skinner Inc.) $2,500

A secretaire bookcase believed to have been made by Joseph Rowan, 4ft. 11½in. wide, circa 1872. $8,400

A late George III mahogany secretaire bookcase with brass handles, 39in. wide. (Dreweatt Watson & Barton) $3,144

## SETTEES & COUCHES

SETTLE, settee, sofa, chaise longue or daybed — they are all basically alike yet each has its exclusive character and shape and its exclusive place in the scheme of things. A settle is a wooden bench having both back and arms; a settee is a settle with an upholstered seat, arms and back. A sofa is a more luxuriously upholstered settee; a couch, a luxurious sofa, although more suitable for reclining than sitting on. A chaise longue is a daybed with the addition of an armrest.

There are a number of Regency couches, all of which are influenced by the styles of Egypt, Rome or early Greece.

It was Sheraton in his *Cabinet Dictionary* who first introduced a couch of this style to England and its scroll ends and lion's paw feet made it one of the most elegant fashions to have been seen at that time. Inevitably, the style became popular and exerted considerable influence, not only on the furniture of the period but on the whole conduct of domestic life in that it seemed to embody the spirit of gracious living.

Until the decline of the Regency period, the upholsterer played a very minor role in the production of home furnishings and was really not in the same league as the cabinet maker, his work consisting mainly of hanging curtains and tapestries and lining walls with material.

Around the 1840s, however, there was a small, bloodless revolution within the furniture factories, the upholsterer rising to hitherto unheard of heights in his craft, virtually dictating the shape and style of chairs and settees and leaving the cabinet maker only the responsibility for making relatively simple frames of birch or ash.

An oak settle with slats and spring cushion seat, by Gustav Stickley, circa 1907, 79in. long. (Robt. W. Skinner Inc.) $6,700

A Queen Anne style three-seat, high back settee with loose cushions. (Dee & Atkinson) $715

A Regency ebonized and gilt painted settee, on turned and tapered supports, 82in. wide. (Christie's) $912

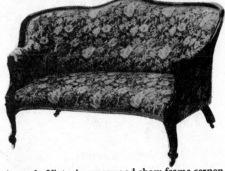

An early Victorian rosewood show frame serpentine-shaped back settee, 5ft.5in. long. (Wooley & Wallis) $880

Victorian mahogany framed chaise longue with carved backboard, in cut dralon. (Farrant & Wightman)   $619

Late 19th century American fancy wicker chaise longue, with rolled crest over latticework back, 74in. wide. (Robt. W. Skinner Inc.)   $350

Federal mahogany inlaid sofa, New England, circa 1810, 74in. wide. (Robt. W. Skinner Inc.)   $2,400

A Regency simulated rosewood and upholstered small scroll-end settee with gilt metal mounts, circa 1810, 4ft.6in. wide.   $3,511

A 1930's Knole three-seater settee, re-upholstered in rose velvet, with fringed and braided decoration. (Butler & Hatch Waterman)   $870

A 17th century box-seated settle in oak, richly carved, the back is divided into four panels and the front into six panels. (Butler & Hatch Waterman)   $1,486

A mid 19th century buttoned-back walnut settee, upholstered in ribbed velvet. (Locke & England)   $1,240

Classical Revival carved mahogany sofa with arched padded back, America, 1835, 84in. long. (Robt. W. Skinner Inc.)   $600

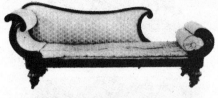

A Greco-Roman Revival carved mahogany couch, probably Boston, circa 1820, 84½in. long. (Robt. W. Skinner Inc.)    $425

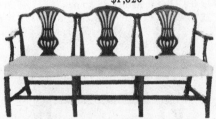

A Regency period cane seated sofa in rosewood. (William H. Brown)
$1,620

A pair of chaises longues by De Sede fashioned as a pair of giant boxing gloves. (Christie's)    $7,800

Late 18th/early 19th century George III walnut three-back settee, England, 76¾in. wide. (Robt. W. Skinner Inc.)
$1,700

An oak hall settle with leather covered spring cushion seat, by Gustav Stickley, 56in. wide. (Robt. W. Skinner Inc.)
$2,100

Part of a late Victorian walnut suite, the settee with a serpentine seat on dwarf cabriole supports, with a lady's open arm easy chair. (H. Spencer & Sons)    $1,143

A Victorian carved walnut and button-upholstered settee, covered in rose-pink dralon, 6ft.5in. wide, circa 1850.    $1,463

A 19th century neo-Baroque scroll-arm sofa with button upholstered arms and back, 256cm. wide. (Osmond Tricks) $314

A George II-style walnut settee with wavy top rail. (Reeds Rains)     $2,046

A Moorish carved hardwood settle all over inlaid with geometric motifs in mother-of-pearl, raised on bun feet. (H. Spencer & Sons)     $587

An Edwardian rosewood and ivory inlaid two-seat settee with peacock fan back, upholstered in green damask. (Dee & Atkinson)     $675

An early Victorian rosewood frame chaise longue with a serpentine side seat, 5ft.4in. long. (Woolley & Wallis)     $516

Early 20th century bentwood settee, Austria, the serpentine crest over three oval caned panels, 44in. long. (Robt. W. Skinner Inc.)     $700

Late 19th century Queen Anne-style child's tea bench, walnut and walnut veneer, 32½in. wide. (Robt. W. Skinner Inc.)     $950

A panelled prairie settle with spring cushion seat, by L. & L. G. Stickley, circa 1912, 29in. deep. (Robt. W. Skinner Inc.)  $9,000

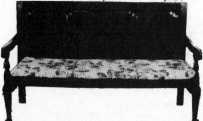

A mid Georgian oak and mahogany cross-banded settle on cabriole supports and pad feet, 72in. wide. (Christie's)     $451

# SIDEBOARDS

M OST pieces of furniture have clearly traceable roots planted firmly in the distant past. Not so the sideboard. In the form we know it today this particular item first appeared on the scene in or around 1770.

Prior to that time, certainly, there were sideboards (Chaucer — and who could argue with his evidence? — mentions a 'sytte borde') but these were no more than side tables, sometimes marble topped, which contained neither drawers nor cupboards.

The introduction of a sideboard as a piece of furniture designed for storage came about for one main reason; the hard drinking habits of 18th century Englishmen established a need for a convenient hidey hole in which to keep large quantities of drink close by the dining table. Robert Adam is on record as having said 'The English, accustomed by habit, or induced by the nature of the climate, indulge more largely in the enjoyment of the bottle than the French."

It is thought that Robert Adam was the first to couple the drawerless side table with a pair of pedestals, one to either end, often placing knife boxes on the top.

Although Shearer, on the other hand, usually takes the credit for joining the three sections together, as illustrated in his Guide of 1788, there are records of Messrs. Gillows informing one of their customers in 1779 that " . . . we make a new sort of sideboard table now, with drawers, etc., in a genteel style, to hold bottles . . ."

Chippendale, Sheraton and Hepplewhite, too, are all contenders for the title "Father of the Modern Sideboard".

An oak sideboard, by Gustav Stickley, 1907, 66in. wide. (Robt. W. Skinner Inc.) $850

A Sheraton mahogany inlaid breakfront sideboard with cellarette drawer and cupboard, 82in. wide. (Dee & Atkinson) $1,905

Victorian mahogany six-drawer North Country sideboard, 1860. (British Antique Exporters) $680

A George III mahogany breakfront sideboard with brass drop handles, 153cm. wide. (H. Spencer & Sons)$1,483

# SIDEBOARDS

An oak sideboard with plate rack by Gustav Stickley, circa 1904, 69½in. wide. (Robt. W. Skinner Inc.) $3,300

Large Jacobean-style oak sideboard by Maples & Co., on compressed bun feet, 7ft.6in. wide. (Capes, Dunn & Co.) $387

A George III period mahogany and line inlaid breakfront sideboard, 4ft.11in. wide. (Geering & Colyer) $2,175

A George III mahogany serpentine sideboard with double arched brass rail to the back, 30¾in. wide. (Lawrence Fine Art) $2,415

A Renaissance Revival walnut sideboard with white marble top, America, circa 1865, 78in. wide. (Robt. W. Skinner Inc.) $900

A Regency mahogany sweepfront sideboard with two central drawers, 54in. wide. (Lawrence Fine Art) $1,397

A Limbert mirrored oak sideboard, Michigan, circa 1910, 54in. wide. (Robt. W. Skinner Inc.) $700

A George III mahogany serpentine-fronted sideboard, decorated with inlaid ebony and boxwood stringing, 66in. wide. (Anderson & Garland) $3,640

Late 19th century rococo Revival marble top walnut server, probably England, 59½in. long. (Robt. W. Skinner Inc.) $700

A William IV mahogany pedestal sideboard with stylized scroll back on bracket feet, 85in. long. (Lawrence Fine Art) $556

A Regency mahogany bow-fronted sideboard with raised back, 48in. wide. (Reeds Rains) $704

A Hepplewhite period mahogany bow-front sideboard with a central drawer, 3ft.8in. wide. (Woolley & Wallis) $2,530

An oak sideboard with plate rack and slightly arched apron, by L. & J. G. Stickley, 54in. wide. (Robt. W. Skinner Inc.) $500

A late Georgian mahogany bow-fronted sideboard with satinwood crossbanding, 58in. wide. (Locke & England) $2,000

Late Victorian Arts & Crafts pollard oak and ebonized sideboard, 7ft.6in. x 7ft.3in. high. (Capes, Dunn & Co.) $309

Late 19th century Sheraton-style bowfront sideboard in mahogany with white stringing and edging overall, 36in. wide. (P. Wilson & Co.) $1,021

A Victorian carved mahogany sideboard with central drawer flanked by two cupboards. (Worsfolds) $545

Small George III mahogany bow-fronted sideboard, 36in. wide. (Barber's Fine Art) $496

# FURNITURE

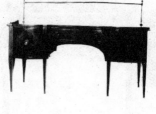

20th century oak sideboard with cupboards. (British Antique Exporters)
$30

George III mahogany and crossbanded sideboard with raised brass rail. (Reeds Rains)    $2,065

Victorian mahogany four-door sideboard, 1850. (British Antique Exporters)
$1,191

A George III mahogany sweep-front sideboard fitted with two central drawers flanked by a cupboard and deep drawer, 72in. wide. (Lawrence Fine Art)    $2,549

Victorian walnut mirrored back sideboard, 1875. (British Antique Exporters)
$386

A Sheraton period mahogany bow-front sideboard, decorated with inlaid satinwood crossbanding, 5ft. wide. (Anderson & Garland)    $5,059

Twin pedestal Victorian mahogany mirrored back sideboard, 1860. (British Antique Exporters)
$552

A George III mahogany swell-front sideboard with ebony string and disc inlay, 4ft.6in. wide. (Capes, Dunn & Co.)    $1,308

Victorian mahogany and mirrored back three-door sideboard, 1860. (British Antique Exporters)
$746

# STANDS

SUCH was the ingenuity of past craftsmen and designers that there is a purpose built stand for just about everything from whips to cricket bats.

The 17th century ancestor of the anglepoise lamp was the candlestand. Its purpose was to supplement the general lighting, and the ordinary style was made of walnut or elm and consisted of a plain or spiral turned shaft supported on three or four plain scrolled feet.

At the turn of the 18th century a vase shape was introduced at the top of the pillar. This was often as much as a foot across and elaborately decorated with acanthus.

There were a number of delicate little stands made during the second half of the 18th century for the purpose of supporting books or music. The earliest of these resemble the mahogany tables which were popular at the time, having vase-shaped stems and tripod bases but with the addition of ratchets beneath their tops which permitted adjustment of the surface angle.

Ince and Mayhew improved the design by adding candle branches either side of the top and Sheraton (anything you can do . . .) made his stands adjustable for height by means of a rod through the centre column which was clamped or released by the turn of a thumb screw.

The Victorian walnut duet music stand is particularly good with its turned central column and carved cabriole legs. These stands often have intricate fretwork tops, and the lyre design may give way elsewhere to a series of scrolls or leaf patterns.

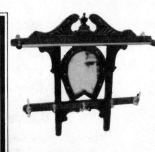

Victorian mahogany hanging hat rack, 1900. (British Antique Exporters)$75

Victorian walnut hall stand with two trays, 1880. (British Antique Exporters) $246

Victorian walnut hallstand with two trays and Wedgwood tiled back, 1875. (British Antique Exporters) $401

Victorian mahogany butler's tray on stand, 1860. (British Antique Exporters) $193

Barley twist oak trolley with tray, 1900. (British Antique Exporters) $45

A circular Chinese carved hardwood urn stand, the top inset with grey marble, 16in. diam. (Edgar Horn) $362

## STANDS

A Regency mahogany jardiniere, urn-shaped with leaf-shaped slatted sides, 1ft.9in. high. (Capes, Dunn & Co.) $542

One of a pair of large Corinthian wood and metal columns on square bases, 48in. high. (Butler & Hatch Waterman) $283

A spinning wheel with bobbin turned spokes. (Butler & Hatch Waterman) $239

Chippendale mahogany candlestand, New England, circa 1780, 28½in. high. (Robt. W. Skinner Inc.) $1,000

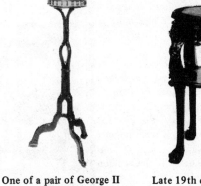

One of a pair of George II mahogany torcheres, 3ft. 4in. high, 11in. diam., circa 1755. $4,455

Late 19th century Oriental teakwood marble top stand, 19½in. high. (Robt. W. Skinner Inc.) $225

A Louis XV-style kingwood and floral marquetry jardiniere, 2ft.1in. high, circa 1870 $1,178

A Regency mahogany reading stand, inlaid with ebonized stringing, circa 1810, 1ft.8in. wide. $644

Federal birch two drawer stand on four square tapering legs, 29½in. high, circa 1800. (Robt. W. Skinner Inc.) $950

A Regency mahogany adjustable music stand with fitted candleslides, 18in. high. (Locke & England) $1,170

An early 19th century mahogany adjustable map reading/buffet stand, 3ft. (Woolley & Wallis)        $609

One of a pair of William and Mary marquetry candlestands, on later turned columns, 39in. high. (Lawrence Fine Art) $3,484

A Regency mahogany stand table with crossbanded octagonal snap-top adjustable for height, 1ft.3in. x 1ft.1in. (Capes, Dunn & Co.) $695

Pair of Italian torcheres, one in the form of a caryatid and the other as Atlantes.        (Worsfolds) $262

A mahogany tripod stand of Chippendale design with circular snap-top and claw and ball feet. (Capes, Dunn & Co.)        $1,807

Hepplewhite mahogany dressing stand, X stretchered, circa 1800. (Stalker & Boos) $550

Late 19th century Oriental teakwood marble top stand, China, 32in. high. (Robt. W. Skinner Inc.) $400

Regency rosewood teapoy. (Reeds Rains)$2,204

# STANDS

FURNITURE

Victorian mahogany and inlaid pedestal, 1870. (British Antique Exporters) $393

An early 19th century metamorphic set of mahogany folding library steps, 36in. high extended. (Boardman) $599

Victorian oak stickstand with brass plaque, circa 1900. (British Antique Exporters) $113

A Regency mahogany and crossbanded ebony boxwood strung teapoy with brass lion paw feet, 15in. wide. (Christie's) $351

Brass bound lap desk on stand, 1880. (British Antique Exporters) $187

A Regency mahogany and satinwood crossbanded rectangular teapoy with canted angles, 12in. wide. (Christie's) $673

Victorian brass tray on stand, 1880. (British Antique Exporters) $81

One of a pair of 19th century Sheraton-style candlestands with octagonal revolving trays, 44in. high. (Barber's Fine Art) $440

Victorian mahogany hall stand with two trays, 1870. (British Antique Exporters) $175

# STOOLS

NOWADAYS stools tend to be classed very definitely with the also-rans in the domestic furniture popularity stakes — a sad fall from the Middle Ages when they were an essential part of the social equipment of every household.

At court the sovereign alone sat on a chair — raised on a dias to ensure that no head was higher than his — while stools were provided for the wives of Princes, Dukes and important Court officials. The menfolk, it seems, simply stood around nattering.

In the middle class houses, the head of the house always occupied a chair, as did invited guests, while lesser males and women of the household had to be content with stools — those of the men being slightly higher than the ladies. It is difficult to be sure whether this difference in the heights of ladies' and gents' stools had a social significance.

By the late 16th century most households could boast the acquisition of at least a couple of chairs. Stools were still, however, by far the most widely used form of seating, though wall benches, settles and coffers made comfortable with cushions were rising fast in popularity.

The stool regained a certain renewed popularity towards the end of the 18th century, taking on new shapes as it developed, including that of the double stool.

All the leading designers of the period produced at least a few ideas, though many of these displayed a startling dissimilarity between their illustrations in the trade catalogues and the actual pieces of furniture as seen on the showroom floor.

Victorian mahogany stool with cross stretchers, 1860. (British Antique Exporters) $72

A George III mahogany and upholstered serpentine-fronted window seat, circa 1790, 107cm. wide. $3,217

A Classical Revival mahogany and rosewood stool, on four square flaring legs, top 22 x 15in. (Robt. W. Skinner Inc.) $800

A William and Mary style walnut long stool with old needlework seat, 41in. long. (Coles, Knapp & Kennedy) $488

A 20th century early Georgian-style walnut dressing stool with four cabriole legs. (P. Wilson & Co.) $297

One of a pair of neo-classical carved wood benches in the manner of Thos. Hope, 3ft. long. (Woolley & Wallis) $17,670

An oak piano bench with cut-out handles, by Gustav Stickley, circa 1907, 36in. wide. (Robt. W. Skinner Inc.) $1,100

A Jacobean oak stool with rising top. (Locke & England) $1,091

A mahogany stool with padded rectangular top on triple-ring turned legs joined by foliate clasps, 19in. wide. (Christie's) $744

A Jacobean oak stool with carved and turned supports. $2,400

A William and Mary black and parcel gilt stool with four S-scroll legs, 20in. diam. (Lawrence Fine Art) $9,820

A leather topped footstool, by Gustav Stickley, 20¼in. wide. (Robt. W. Skinner Inc.) $750

A Dutch 18th century style mahogany marquetry stool on claw and ball feet, 21in. wide. (Anderson & Garland) $492

A George III-style window seat of Chippendale design, upholstered in hide with brass studding. (Bracketts) $533

A large rectangular Victorian walnut stool with molded cabriole legs, 30 x 25in. (P. Wilson & Co.) $445

A Hepplewhite period stool, with upholstered serpentine seat, on mahogany legs. (Geering & Colyer) $384

A 17th century oak oblong stool on baluster supports, 1ft.6in. wide. (Capes, Dunn & Co.) $250

One of a pair of George I needlework covered walnut stools, 1ft.7½in. wide, circa 1715. $23,408

An Elizabethan joint stool, circa 1580, made of inlaid padoukwood. $4,800

Classical Revival mahogany stool, possibly New York, circa 1825, 21in. wide. (Robt. W. Skinner Inc.) $250

A mid 16th century Tuscan carved walnut prie dieu, 2ft. 3in. wide. $2,279

A Georgian rosewood stool with a floral tapestry covered seat, 22½in. wide. (Anderson & Garland) $975

# SUITES

SETS of furniture which have stayed together over the years, be they from the bedroom or the parlor, will always command a premium well in excess of the sum of the individual articles.

Matching beds, dressing table, wardrobe and chests are always keenly sought but by far the most popular are the parlor suites. A set of four dining chairs together with two easy chairs and a chaise longue from any period will fetch good money but deep buttoned examples from about 1850 with rosewood or walnut frames will always achieve sums in excess of four figures.

Of particular interest are those suites which include a set of six or more dining chairs especially if their frames sport carving on the top rail and knees or if they are enhanced with ormolu embelishments.

Part of an Edwardian Art Nouveau mahogany inlaid seven-piece suite, comprising a two-seat settee, two tub chairs and four single chairs. (Dee & Atkinson)                                    $800

Part of an Edwardian inlaid part-upholstered drawingroom suite comprising settee, two armchairs and four singles with green velvet upholstery. (P. Wilson & Co.)                              $1,067

Renaissance Revival walnut and walnut veneer bedroom set, the bed converts into twin beds, label 'Daniels, Harrison & Son Mfrs. of Furniture', 1864, headboard 82in. wide. (Robt. W. Skinner Inc.) $3,700

Part of a seven-piece wicker parlor set by Heywood Bros., Mass., comprising a settee, two armchairs, platform rocker, lady's rocker, side chair and occasional table. (Robt. W. Skinner Inc.) $2,000

Early 20th century group of carved bear furniture of Swiss origin. (Chelsea Auction Galleries) $3,302

Part of a 19th century giltwood salon suite of seven pieces, consisting of a canape, 61in. wide, two fauteuils and four single chairs. (Anderson & Garland) $2,860

A three-piece Victorian walnut framed suite, composed of a lady's and gent's armchair and single ended sofa, all covered in green dralon and buttoned. (P. Wilson & Co.)                    $1,703

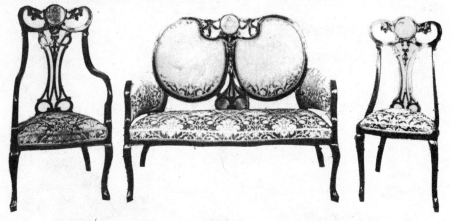

Part of an Edwardian mahogany seven-piece drawingroom suite, comprising two-seater couch, a pair of elbow chairs and four single chairs, upholstered in beige floral brocade and standing on cabriole legs. (Edgar Horn)
$1,248

Part of an ornate seven-piece Victorian walnut parlor suite, 1870. (British Antique Exporters)                    $1,141

# CARD & TEA TABLES

AS the design of card tables progressed, tops tended to become square in shape, but with circular projections on the corners which were dished to hold candlesticks and which also had oval wells for money and chips.

The legs became progressively bolder, the earlier spade and club feet giving way to lions' paws or ball and claw designs. In about 1720, mahogany superceded walnut as the most widely used wood in the construction of gaming tables, though, occasionally, more exotic woods, such as laburnum, were used.

Prior to this time, carving had generally been rather limited — perhaps a shell motif on the knee — but with the introduction of the harder mahogany, more intricate designs, such as lion masks, were added and hairy lions' paw feet employed, accounting for the denomination "lion period" often being applied to early Georgian furniture.

By the 1770s, gambling had reached such a peak that King George III felt it necessary to forbid the playing of cards in any of the Royal Palaces and Horace Walpole, that indefatigable commentator on the fashions of his time, is reported to have remarked that the gaming at Almacks, where young blades were losing as much as £15,000 in a night, was ". . . worthy of the decline of the Empire".

Although the Prince of Wales, who was later Prince Regent and finally King George IV, extolled the virtues of games of cards, it would appear that the popularity of the pastime had waned somewhat, for 19th century cabinet makers were producing far fewer card tables than their predecessors.

A George III satinwood card table with kingwood crossbandings edged with stringing, 37¾in. wide. (Lawrence Fine Art) $4,051

A Regency rosewood crossbanded and brass inlaid D-shaped card table, 35in. wide. (Dreweatt Watson & Barton) $769

A George III mahogany and crossbanded demi-lune card table, 3ft. wide, circa 1790. $907

## CARD & TEA TABLES

A Federal mahogany inlaid card table, D-shaped front with serpentine sides, America, circa 1795, 17in. wide. (Robt. W. Skinner Inc.) $2,900

A 19th century walnut card table of serpentine shape with fold-over top, 2ft.9in. wide. (Vidler & Co.) $468

A Louis XV-style kingwood and inlaid rosewood card table, circa 1900, 2ft.7in. wide. $2,079

A Regency rosewood card table with fold-over top on squared baluster column, 3ft. wide. (Russell Baldwin & Bright) $1,573

A George I mahogany games table, the double hinged lobed top enclosing a backgammon board, 34in. wide. (Christie's) $2,176

Regency rosewood card table with baize-lined turnover top, 3ft. wide. (Warner Sheppard & Wade) $505

A Victorian burr walnut fold-over card table of serpentine outline, 34in. wide. (Morphets) $651

A William IV rosewood card table with fold-over top, 91cm. wide. (H. Spencer & Sons) $444

A 19th century French boulle serpentine fold-over card table, 35in. wide. (Morphets) $570

A Regency mahogany tea table with ebonized stringing, 3ft. wide, circa 1810. $797

A Victorian burr walnut serpentine fold-over top card table, baize lined, 3ft. wide. (Edgar Horn) $761

A Federal mahogany and mahogany veneer card table, circa 1815, 37in. wide. (Robt. W. Skinner Inc.) $2,100

A Regency inlaid rosewood fold-over top games table with parquetry border decoration, 35½in. long. (Outhwaite & Litherland) $2,016

A mahogany gaming table with shaped foliate inlay top and carved Chippendale legs, 34½in. long. (Robt. W. Skinner Inc.) $1,000

A Regency mahogany folding swivel-top card table with brass claw castors. (D. M. Nesbit & Co.) $436

A George II mahogany card table with baize-lined interior, 31in. wide. (Lawrence Fine Art) $2,287

Late 18th/early 19th century Dutch rosewood and marquetry card table with folding top, 32½in. wide. (Andrew Grant)$564

A Sheraton period mahogany fold-over top demilune card table with rosewood crossbanding. (Edgar Horn) $705

## CARD & TEA TABLES

An early Georgian rectangular fold-over games table with concertina-action. (Outhwaite & Litherland) $4,725

A George III mahogany and crossbanded rectangular card table with lined folding top, 35¾in. wide. (Dreweatt Watson & Barton) $725

A George III satinwood, crossbanded and painted D-shaped card table with fold-over top, 39in. wide. (Dacre, Son & Hartley) $3,900

A George I-style walnut and crossbanded card table with fold-over top, circa 1920. 3ft. wide. $1,430

Federal mahogany and mahogany veneer card table, Mass., circa 1820, 36in. wide. (Robt. W. Skinner Inc.) $900

A late 18th century mahogany D-shaped tea table on reeded sabre legs, 3ft. (Woolley & Wallis) $896

A Regency brass-inlaid rosewood card table, 3ft. wide. circa 1810. $976

One of a pair of Edwardian satinwood card tables in the George III style, 47in. and 46in. wide. (Lawrence Fine Art) $11,088

One of a pair of Regency satinwood and rosewood card tables, 2ft.5in. high by 2ft.11in. wide, circa 1815. $4,950

One of a pair of Regency mahogany fold-over games tables, with brass feet and castors, 36in. wide. (Dee & Atkinson)  $3,117

George III mahogany fold-top games table with serpentine top, circa 1770, 33in. wide. (Stalker & Boos)  $2,000

A Regency rosewood and coromandel banded card table with gilt metal mounts, circa 1815, 3ft.0½in. wide.  $950

A walnut card table, the hinged top enclosing a panel of needlework in gros and petit point, 34½in. wide. (Christie's)  $2,091

Federal mahogany, mahogany veneer, card table, the shaped top with half serpentine ends, 36in. wide, New England, circa 1815. (Robt. W. Skinner Inc.)  $1,100

A George III satinwood card table, circa 1785, 2ft.11½in. wide.  $2,851

A George II mahogany chinoiserie 'concertina-action' card table, circa 1750, 2ft. 11½in. wide. $1,504

One of a pair of George IV Anglo-Indian rosewood card tables, 3ft. wide, circa 1830.  $14,850

Late 18th century George II walnut games table, 34in. wide. (Robt. W. Skinner Inc.)  $3,000

# CONSOLE TABLES

CONSOLE tables are so named for the console, or bracket, which is used to support them against the wall in the absence of back legs.

Perhaps surprisingly, their development came later than that of most other tables for they did not appear until the early 18th century, when house interiors became more sophisticated, with furniture being designed to blend into the entire decorative scheme. It was not, in fact, until about 1730 that eagle console tables achieved real popularity following their appearance in the court of Louis XIV where, as a rule, they were placed beneath a pier glass and sported superbly figured tops of Italian marble.

On the original tables, the marble tops were regarded as being by far the most important features (console tables were described as "marble slab frames" in early inventories) and they were carefully selected for fine grain and exquisite color gradation and harmony from such notable suppliers as Signor Domenico de Angualis. The Victorians having rather less flamboyant tastes, tended to go more for plain white tops in preference to the pinks and greens of the earlier examples and were inclined to build up the rococo ornamentation with gesso instead of producing the fine, gilded carving of the original period.

A parcel gilt rosewood console table, circa 1840, with a marble top, 4ft.5in. wide. $1,066

One of a pair of rosewood and painted console tables, in the manner of Thos. Hope, 1ft.11in. wide, circa 1805. $11,088

An early George II giltwood pier table, in the manner of Wm. Kent, 3ft.3¼in. wide, circa 1730. $9,240

George II mahogany demi-lune lift-top console table on cabriole legs, circa 1750, 29½ x 14¾ x 29in. high. (Stalker & Boos) $1,400

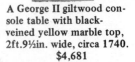

A George II giltwood console table with black-veined yellow marble top, 2ft.9½in. wide, circa 1740. $4,681

One of a pair of Victorian French-style walnut and kingwood banded console tables, circa 1860, 3ft.5in. wide. $1,430

# DINING TABLES

LOO tables are named for the three to five handed variant of whist which became a fashionable craze during the mid 19th century. The circular top and central pillar design of these tables made them the ideal surface on which to play loo; allowing the players to distribute themselves evenly and comfortably without anyone being perched uncomfortably on a corner with lower limbs cramped against a table leg.

Usually made of mahogany or rosewood, they have turned or reeded central columns on a platform base with either bun, claw or lion's paw feet.

During the Victorian period, the style of these tables became more elaborate and the erstwhile plain center columns and feet more decorative. Tables of this period are nicely made with superbly carved bases and beautifully figured walnut tops which have a most useful tip up action operated by two screws placed underneath, making it possible for them to be stood out of the way when not in use.

As the loo table developed, the top became more of an oval shape and the lower section was made rather more elaborate than hitherto. The single, central pillar was enlarged into a cage of four columns and the rather plain splayed legs were often embellished with an amount of low relief carving.

The Gothic revival of the 1850s, following A.W.N. Pugin's exhibits at the Great Exhibition, brought about a resurgence for old English carved oak.

The feeling conveyed by furniture typical of this period is that of the solidity of the British Empire; patriotically made of English oak in a monumental style which seemed destined to last for ever.

Regency rosewood center pedestal dining table, 1830. (British Antique Exporters) $766

An early 19th century figured mahogany octagonal pedestal tip table with brass castors, 42in. (Dee & Atkinson) $861

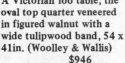

A Victorian loo table, the oval top quarter veneered in figured walnut with a wide tulipwood band, 54 x 41in. (Woolley & Wallis) $946

A Regency circular breakfast table in rosewood with a beaded edge, 52in. diam. (Outhwaite & Litherland) $8,066

A 19th century exhibition center table, the top within a chequered ivory and ebony surround, 45in. diam. (Boardman) $6,420

Victorian mahogany loo table on platform base, 1880. (British Antique Exporters) $226

A late George III period mahogany rectangular top breakfast table, with brass terminals and castors, 3ft. 10½in. wide. (Geering & Colyer) $2,730

An early Victorian rosewood breakfast table, the circular top with beaded edge, 145cm. diam. (H. Spencer & Sons) $2,580

A William IV mahogany circular patent extending dining table, 4ft.11in. diam., extending to 6ft.5½in. or 8ft.1in.　$41,602

A Killarney yewwood pedestal table inlaid with satinwood stringing, circa 1840, 5ft. wide. $1,726

An early 19th century drum library table, the top inset with a panel of gilt tooled red leather, circa 1820, 90cm. diam. (Osmond Tricks) $1,928

Mid Victorian burr walnut breakfast table with fine floral inlay, 3ft.10½in. diam. (W. H. Lane & Son) $840

A Regency rosewood and crossbanded circular pedestal table, inlaid with brass stringing, circa 1810, 3ft. 11½in. diam. $1,389

A George III mahogany oval tilt-top pedestal table, circa 1800, 4ft.5in. wide. $1,054

A George IV mahogany and rosewood crossbanded pedestal table, 4ft.2in. diam., circa 1825.　$1,118

A Victorian walnut marble top table, America, circa 1870, top 44 x 28in. (Robt. W. Skinner Inc.) $850

A Regency brass-inlaid rosewood center table with circular top, 4ft. diam., circa 1820.          $4,950

William IV rosewood pedestal dining table with circular tilt-top, 50in. diam. (Reeds Rains)          $1,244

A George III satinwood-crossbanded mahogany breakfast table, circa 1800, 3ft.6in. wide.
          $1,457

A Victorian circular snap-top burr walnut veneered breakfast table, with cabriole legs, 4ft.6in. diam. (Woolley & Wallis)
          $984

An early 19th century German circular rosewood dining table, circa 1830, 3ft.6in. diam.
          $4,521

A George III satinwood crossbanded mahogany breakfast table, 4ft.8in. wide, circa 1790.
          $4,884

A Regency breakfast table, the rectangular top in 'plum pudding' mahogany, 61 x 48½in. extended. (Lawrence Fine Art) $11,880

A George III mahogany octagonal tip-up breakfast table, 42½in. wide. (Dreweatt Watson & Barton)
          $1,361

## DINING TABLES

A Regency satinwood octagonal library table (with re-veneered top). (Warren & Wignall) $4,655

A Regency mahogany breakfast table on splayed quadrapartite base, 58in. wide. (Christie's) $2,106

A William IV coromandelveneered center table, 5ft. 0½in. by 4ft.2in., circa 1830. $6,600

A late George III mahogany breakfast table, the rounded rectangular top with yewwood crossbanding, 40 x 58½in. (Lawrence Fine Art) $1,397

A late Georgian mahogany breakfast table on a turned pillar on four fluted supports, 41¾ x 66in. (Lawrence Fine Art) $1,117

A Regency rosewood tip-up top center table decorated with an inlaid brass band, 50in. diam. (Anderson & Garland) $985

A Victorian drum library table, the revolving top with inset leather panel, 48in. diam. (Lawrence Fine Art) $977

A 19th century boulle inlaid center table, the oval top of double serpentine form, 57 x 36in. (W. H. Lane & Son) $556

A George III mahogany satinwood crossbanded and boxwood lined drum table, 46in. diam. (Christie's) $1,684

A George IV rosewood dining table of circular form, 137cm. diam. (H. Spencer & Sons) $1,891

A late Regency mahogany breakfast table with tip-up top, 47in. diam. (Lawrence Fine Art) $1,476

A William IV circular top dining table dividing in the center to allow four additional insert leaves, 4ft. x 8ft. (Locke & England) $2,145

## DRESSING TABLES

LARGE dressing tables complete with mirrors were, if we are to judge from the design catalogues, made in profusion throughout the eighteenth century and some, Chippendale's in particular, were very fine indeed.

Designers of the period vied with each other to see who could cram in the greatest number of ingenious little fitments, each designer claiming every innovation as his own and decrying all others for having pinched his ideas. Sheraton, in particular, was fascinated by the challenge and his design became more and more complex as he progressively widened the scope of his ideas until, toward the end, it would seem that he was attempting to develop the ultimate, all-purpose item of furniture. One of his later creations was a superbly eccentric construction incorporating hinged and swing mirrors, numerous drawers, a washbasin, compartments for jewelry, writing materials and cosmetics, not to mention the commode.

By far the most popular dressing tables to come from the second half of the eighteenth century were described by Shearer as 'dressing stands'. These were usually of quite small size, standing on fine, elegant legs and fitted with hinged box lids.

During the Victorian period, there were a few small dressing tables but, as a rule, the Victorians preferred them rather more solidly proportioned. The Edwardians, on the other hand, seem to have taken to them with a little more enthusiasm and produced a number in the styles of the late eighteenth century, but with a few Victorian rococo embellishments thrown in for good measure.

Edwardian mahogany and inlaid dressing table, 1910. (British Antique Exporters) $125

Victorian oak two-tier dressing table with triple mirror, 1900. (British Antique Exporters) $335

A gilt bronze mounted walnut dressing table, with a bevelled oval mirror, 5ft. 1in. wide. $1,442

Victorian mahogany Duchess dressing table with matching marble top washstand, 1870. (British Antique Exporters) $817

Victorian pine dressing table, 1880. (British Antique Exporters) $356

Early 19th century Empire crotched walnut dressing table, France, 28in. wide. (Robt. W. Skinner Inc.) $650

# FURNITURE

A George III mahogany bow-
fronted kneehole dressing
table with satinwood strung
borders, 3ft.1in. wide, circa
1790.          $1,901

A Napoleon III boulle and
ebonized table a ouvrage
with ormolu mounts, circa
1850, 2ft.3in. wide.
                          $886

A George III mahogany and
boxwood lined dressing table
with rectangular sliding mirror plate, 43in. wide.
(Christie's)          $729

An Edwardian Sheraton
Revival inlaid satinwood,
bowfronted kneehole dres-
sing table, 51in. wide.
(Reeds Rains)$432

A late 19th century lady's
ebonized and boulle dressing table, 62cm. wide. (H.
Spencer & Sons)
                          $387

A classical Revival mahogany
bureau with mirror on scroll
supports, New England, circa
1825, 37in. wide. (Robt. W.
Skinner Inc.)  $1,700

A George III satinwood
dressing table edged with
stringing, raised on six
square tapering support,
32¾in. wide. (Lawrence
Fine Art) $2,851

A Federal painted dressing
table, New England, circa
1795, 36in. wide. (Robt.
W. Skinner Inc.)$700

A George III mahogany and
satinwood gentleman's
dressing table, circa 1790,
3ft.3in. wide.$3,803

A George III mahogany bowfront dressing table, 3ft. wide, circa 1790. $1,463

A rococo Revival rosewood bureau with carved leafy scroll crest with centering baroque cartouche, America, 44½in. wide. (Robt. W. Skinner Inc.) $700

A 20th century mahogany Sheraton-style dressing table with serpentine front, 49in. wide. (P. Wilson & Co.) $638

A Louis XV kingwood poudreuse, the hinged central section with mirror, 29¼in. wide. (Dacre, Son & Hartley) $796

A George IV mahogany dressing table with oblong swing mirror, 48in. wide. (Reeds Rains) $660

A mirrored dressing table with circle pulls, by Gustav Stickley. (Robt. W. Skinner Inc.) $1,400

A George III mahogany, gentleman's enclosed dressing table, 30in. wide. (Lawrence Fine Art) $701

Mid 19th century rococo Revival marble top Princess bureau, America, 54½in. wide. (Robt. W. Skinner Inc.) $1,050

A George III oak kneehole dressing/writing table fitted with three drawers, 77cm. wide. (Osmond Tricks) $262

# DROP-LEAF TABLES

FROM about 1750 until the end of the 18th century, furniture designers strove to break away from traditional styles in the attempt to create something completely different and this period saw a multitude of legs, flaps and movements built into tables which extended, opened, hinged, turned and folded up in order to achieve the maximum possible surface area in the smallest practicable space.

One of the simpler designs to emerge from this orgy of inventiveness was the envelope table — obviously so called from the triangular shape of the flap — which has all the attributes of a good Georgian table, being made of nicely grained mahogany and having cabriole legs and pad feet.

Another form of drop-leaf table has rectangular flaps which sometimes reach almost to the ground. Though essentially country made and of simple design, with straight, square legs chamfered on the inside edge, units of this kind were often used to form part of the large extending tables so popular throughout the 18th century — often with D-shaped tables fastened on to the ends.

Made from about 1850 and continuing in popularity until the end of the 19th century, Sutherland tables were manufactured in a variety of woods; earlier examples are usually of rosewood and burr walnut, later ones employing walnut or mahogany.

This little table, named after Queen Victoria's Mistress of the Robes, Harriet the Duchess of Sutherland who died in 1868, is ideal for the smaller dining room for it will seat six when fully open yet, closed, will stand quite comfortably out of the way.

An Edwardian inlaid mahogany Sutherland table. (Butler & Hatch Waterman) $210

Late 19th century walnut Sutherland table with half round drop leaves, 39 x 34in. (P. Wilson & Co.)                    $340

A Victorian burr-walnut Sutherland table on turned cheval frame, 2ft.9in. x 3ft.3in. fully extended. (Russell Baldwin & Bright) $696

A Chippendale maple dining
table, New England, circa
1760, 43in. wide. (Robt. W.
Skinner Inc.) $375

A late Regency mahogany
Pembroke table with brass
foliate scroll paw feet, 48in.
long extended. (Lawrence
Fine Art)      $838

A Queen Anne tiger maple
and maple dining table,
New England, circa 1760,
41½in. wide. (Robt. W.
Skinner Inc.)
       $3,000

Queen Anne maple dining
table, New England, circa
1760, 41½in. long. (Robt.
W. Skinner Inc.)
       $3,800

A George IV mahogany
rectangular drop-leaf pedestal breakfast table, circa
1825, 2ft.10in. wide.
       $400

A Queen Anne maple dining
table, with rectangular drop-
leaf top, 45in. long, circa
1760. (Robt. W. Skinner Inc.)
       $1,800

Federal mahogany drop-
leaf dining table, America,
circa 1795, 46 x 96in.
(Robt. W. Skinner Inc.)
       $2,000

A late George III triangular
drop-leaf table, circa 1790,
3ft.10in. open. $982

A George III mahogany
Wake table, circa 1780, 5ft.
11in. long.    $1,001

A Chippendale mahogany dining table, Newport, circa 1770, 48in. wide. (Robt. W. Skinner Inc.) $15,000

A George II oval faded red walnut drop-leaf dining table on cabriole legs and pad feet, 4ft.6in. wide, circa 1740.     $1,170

An 18th century mahogany round drop-leaf table with four dog legs and pad feet, 42in. diam. (P. Wilson & Co.)     $488

A Chippendale maple tea table, New England, circa 1780, 28in. wide. (Robt. W. Skinner Inc.) $1,600

A Regency mahogany Pembroke table with brass claw feet and unusual ball castors, 36 x 43in. extended. (Lawrence Fine Art) $1,028

Queen Anne maple dining table, New England, circa 1760, 37in. wide. (Robt. W. Skinner Inc.) $4,750

A Queen Anne maple tea table, New England, circa 1750, 29¼in. wide. (Robt. W. Skinner Inc.) $1,000

George II mahogany drop-leaf table raised on cabriole legs, circa 1750, 42in. wide. (Stalker & Boos) $1,900

A George II triangular mahogany table with curved flaps. (Phillips & Jolly) $2,760

# GATELEG TABLES

THE gateleg table has remained one of the most popular styles ever since its introduction during the 17th century, even those being made today having the same basic design and movement as the originals.

Usually made of oak, though occasionally of more exotic woods such as yew or walnut, the majority of gateleg tables have tops of round or oval shape and the legs are braced with stretchers which, like the main frame, are cut to take the pivoting "gate" leg. (Larger tables are constructed with two gatelegs on each side).

Although these tables have been made since the 17th century, the vast majority date from the late 19th and early 20th centuries.

As a rule, prices reflect top size and, when the length of the closed table is greater than four feet, they really begin to soar into large figures.

The cabriole leg is so called from its likeness in shape to the leg of an animal (it's derived from the French word meaning "goat's leap") and implicit in the meaning is the suggestion of a free, dancing movement which would obviously be destroyed if stretchers were employed.

The change from gateleg to gate tables was a direct result of the switch in fashion towards cabriole legs and, once free of encumbering stretchers, the table's movement could be simplified in that two of the actual legs could now be swung out to support the flaps. This cleaned up the lines of the leg section by allowing the omission of the two extra "gatelegs" whose four additional verticals made the underside of the closed table look somehow impenetrable.

A late 17th century oak gateleg table, 48 x 58in. (P. Wilson & Co.)    $1,506

An oak gateleg table, constructed from a 17th century refectory table, 5ft.7½in. open.
$2,930

Late 17th/early 18th century red walnut gateleg table with oval top, 3ft.11in. wide.
$2,145

An early 18th century oak oval gateleg dining table, raised on turned supports. (Osmond Tricks)      $2,205

A large George II red walnut oval twin flap top dining table, covered in dark varnish, 5ft.8in. x 6ft.2in. (Woolley & Wallis)      $5,060

An oak gateleg dining table, the oval twin flap top on turned baluster supports, 82in. wide, open. (Christie's)      $421

A 17th century yewwood gateleg dining table, 57in. wide, open. (Christie's) $4,505

An early 18th century oak gateleg table with oval top and drawer, 56in. extended. (Lawrence Fine Art)      $1,386

A William and Mary oak gateleg table with oval top, fitted with two drawers, 41 x 40in. (Lawrence Fine Art)      $628

A William and Mary cherry and pine gateleg table, New England, circa 1730, 42in. long. (Robt. W. Skinner Inc.)      $3,000

An oak two-flap gateleg table on barley sugar twist supports, 4ft. x 4ft.9in. (Bracketts)      $736

# LARGE TABLES

NAMED after the monastic dining rooms in which they were originally used, refectory tables are based upon a very old design.

The name is now given to virtually any long table with legs on the outside edge although it originally applied only to those having six or more legs joined by stretchers at ground level.

Widely used until the end of the Jacobean period (1603-1688), refectory tables dwindled in popularity after that time, though they have been made in small numbers ever since.

The design of tables changed at the beginning of the 19th century from the rectangular and D-ended styles to tables which were either round or sectional.

The latter were extremely practical tables for, besides allowing ample leg room, they could by the simple addition of more units be extended at will from four seaters to a length more suited to a banquet.

Bases had plain or turned columns with three or four splayed legs which were either plain or reeded, terminating in brass castors.

Another large table is the Victorian extending dining table which being heavy and massive, most people instinctively associate with the Victorian period. This type of table, usually made of mahogany, though sometimes of oak, extended by means of a worm screw operated by a handle in the centre and allowed the addition of one or two extra leaves. Occasionally the centre leaf was equipped with dropdown legs as a means of providing extra stability when the table was fully extended.

An oak framed full size snooker table with inch and threequarter five slate bed, together with electric light canopy, table cover and a set of snooker balls. (P. Wilson & Co.)
$2,928

An oval dining table, the frieze inlaid with stringing, on brass castors, 43½ x 55in. (Lawrence Fine Art)     $1,676

George II Cuban mahogany swing leg dining table, the oval top opening to 5ft. (Hobbs & Chambers)     $2,834

A Regency rectangular extending dining table, 57in. wide, the architectural leaf cabinet containing five additional leaves, circa 1820. (Neales)     $7,440

A late 17th/early 18th century solid walnut center refectory table with two-plank top, 30¼ x 77½in. (Lawrence Fine Art) $4,118

A William IV mahogany two-pillar dining table with an additional leaf, 104in. extended. (Lawrence Fine Art) $2,233

A Regency mahogany two-pillar dining table with brass terminals and castors, 4ft.4in. x 6ft.1in. (Capes, Dunn & Co.) $10,286

A William IV mahogany 'D' end extending dining table, circa 1835, 9ft.11in. long. $3,657

A George IV extending mahogany dining table, raised on ten turned and reeded tapering supports, 182¼in. extended. (Lawrence Fine Art) $8,236

A George IV mahogany extending patent dining table, possibly by T. Wilson, 7ft. 10½in. open, circa 1825. $4,950

Early 19th century large three-pillar mahogany dining table, 14ft.9½in. extended. $12,870

A large 19th century circular mahogany library table, 7ft. diam. (Anderson & Garland) $8,580

An early 17th century Dutch oak table, 7ft.
long.                              $5,209

A Regency mahogany and crossbanded dining table, with telescopic action and one
leaf, 4ft.6in. x 6ft. fully extended.
                                   $1,834

A late Regency mahogany two-pillar dining
table, the rounded top with fluted edge,
46 x 116in. extended. (Lawrence Fine Art)
                                   $9,504

A Regency mahogany triple-pedestal 'D' end
dining table, circa 1810, 5ft. x 9ft.11in.
                                   $8,351

Shaker pine and butternut dining table, New
England, circa 1800, 82¼in. wide. (Robt. W.
Skinner Inc.)          $7,000

A James I-design oak refectory table, 7ft.
10in. long.            $877

A Regency mahogany three-pillar dining
table with rounded ends and two loose
leaves, 155½in. extended. (Dreweatt
Watson & Barton)       $8,990

A Regency mahogany twin-pedestal 'D'
end dining table, circa 1810, 8ft.3in.
fully extended.        $9,070

## LARGE TABLES

A 17th century oak refectory table with
two-plank top raised on four rising baluster supports, 107 x 31in. (Lawrence Fine
Art)                                    $2,925

A George III mahogany D-end dining table,
9ft.6in. including leaf insertion, circa 1790.
                                        $14,437

Early 20th century William and Mary-style
trestle foot table, by Wallace Nutting,
Mass., 60in. wide. (Robt. W. Skinner Inc.)
                                        $800

A 17th century and later oak refectory
table with rectangular top, 119in. long.
(Christie's)                            $2,896

A George III mahogany three-pillar dining
table with D-shaped ends, 53½ x 145in.
(Dreweatt Watson & Barton)
                                        $13,100

Late 17th century oak refectory table with
four-plank top, 108 x 33½in. (Lawrence
Fine Art)                               $3,489

A George III mahogany extending dining
table with fourteen square tapering legs,
47 x 110½in. extended. (Lawrence Fine
Art)                                    $4,470

An oak director's table with trestle base,
by Gustav Stickley, 96½in. long. (Robt.
W. Skinner Inc.)                        $11,000

# OCCASIONAL TABLES

THERE are a wealth of occasional tables made for every conceivable function, but it is often the material and decoration which gives an added attraction.

Following the discovery of mineral springs at Tunbridge Wells by Lord North in the early part of the 17th century, a tourist industry grew and, of the many objects produced to meet the demand for souvenirs, articles inlaid with woods of various colors proved most popular.

Earliest forms of Tunbridge ware were of geometric patterns, similar to parquetry, but this quickly developed into representations of landscapes, buildings and scenic views, generally contained within fine borders. Unlike parquetry, however, Tunbridge ware was made from thin strips of wood glued together and then fret-cut into the thin layers which were veneered on to a variety of objects from small boxes to table tops.

On large surfaces, a cube pattern proved very popular, the various visible surfaces of the cubes being suggested by clever selection of natural woods — dyeing of wood being considered infra dig.

Originally a product of the East, papier mache made its European appearance in Paris. The process was patented (in 1722) by Henry Clay, of Birmingham, who used it to make mostly small objects such as tea caddies, trays and jewelry boxes. It was not until the early 19th century that the firm of Jennens and Bettridge began fully to exploit the extraordinary lightness and flexibility of the material, producing papier mache canterburys, chairs, tables and even bed ends.

A circular vitrine in mahogany with ormolu mounts, 24in. diam. (Brogden & Co.) $639

American Colonial inlaid mahogany tea cart with glass top and tray, 30in. high. (Coles, Knapp & Kennedy) $341

A 19th century French table de ecrire of shield-shape in kingwood with terrazzo top. (P. Wilson & Co.) $732

A mid-Georgian mahogany and rosewood crossbanded architect's table, 37in. wide. (Christie's) $3,790

A 17th century oak chair table, the whole raised on turned legs with sleigh feet. (Butler & Hatch Waterman) $2,175

A 20th century oval marble top table, America, 31in. wide. (Robt. W. Skinner Inc.) $550

A French Empire walnut
pier table, circa 1810, 3ft.
wide, top Italian.
$8,046

A George II mahogany
architect's table with adjustable hinged top, 2ft.8in.
wide, circa 1760.
$9,116

A Louis XVI-style mahogany
and ormolu mounted table
en chiffoniere, circa 1900,
2ft.6in. wide.
$877

A Louis XVI-style mahogany
and ormolu mounted table
ambulante, stamped 'P. Sor-
mant, Paris', circa 1900, 1ft.
9in. wide.     $1,433

Mid 19th century circular
Huali table with panelled
top, 1ft.6½in. diam.
$776

A maple and pine hutch
table, New England, circa
1780, 48in. diam. (Robt.
W. Skinner Inc.)
$850

A 19th century Chinese
carved padoukwood and
Cantonese porcelain moun-
ted table, 57cm. diam.
(H. Spencer & Sons)
$1,463

A small Regency brass-inlaid
rosewood kidney-shaped
table with galleried top,
circa 1810, 2ft.11in. wide.
$8,250

A late George III small satinwood tripod table, 1ft.9½in.
wide open, circa 1810.
$1,009

A Charles II style oak chair-table with a hinged seat enclosing two secret compartments, 3ft.5in. wide.
$2,767

Pine and maple tip table, possibly New York, circa 1800, 21½in. wide. (Robt. W. Skinner Inc.)
$1,250

A Regency rosewood library table on brass-capped splayed legs, 3ft.3in. wide, circa 1815.
$3,418

A George II mahogany tripod table with a baluster gallery, 2ft.1in. wide, circa 1755.    $3,300

A George II mahogany tripod table with rectangular needlework top, 2ft.8½in. wide, circa 1750.
$7,590

A George IV rosewood and marble-topped occasional table, 1ft.8¼in. diam., circa 1830.    $2,116

Mid 18th century George II mahogany tripod table, 2ft.2½in. diam.
$19,800

A late George II mahogany architect's table with fitted interior and a candlestand, 3ft. wide, circa 1750.
$2,604

A George IV circular mahogany table on three large paw feet, 28¾in. diam. (Lawrence Fine Art)
$861

# FURNITURE

A Regency circular tip-up top tripod table on a vase-shaped pedestal, 31in. diam. (Lawrence Fine Art)$1,257

A Chippendale cherry tea table, New England, circa 1780, 36in. wide. (Robt. W. Skinner Inc.)$550

A George III mahogany tripod table on a baluster stem and tripod base, 26 x 22in. (Lawrence Fine Art) $509

A Central Asian octagonal table, the sides with shaped arches, the whole inlaid with mother-of-pearl. (P. Wilson & Co.)          $137

A George III kidney shape occasional table in king-wood and rosewood, 37½in. wide. (Lawrence Fine Art) $7,128

Queen Anne tiger maple and maple tea table, New England, circa 1760, 31½ x 21½in. (Robt. W. Skinner Inc.) $3,100

A Louis XIV-style harewood and tulipwood table ambulante, inlaid with gilt metal mounts, circa 1880, 59cm. wide.          $926

Early 18th century architect's walnut veneered table, with hinged adjustable top, 31in. wide. (Anderson & Garland) $7,980

A 19th century Empire-style ormolu mounted mahogany circular specimen table, circa 1880, 21in. diam. (Neales)          $1,160

A George II red walnut occasional table supported on four cabriole legs, 47 x 21in. (Locke & England) $5,200

A Country Federal painted tip table, the top with black and red painted chequerboard, top 19¼ x 19in. (Robt. W. Skinner Inc.) $1,400

A painted dough table with drop leaves and breadboard ends, probably Mass., circa 1800, 36in. long. (Robt. W. Skinner Inc.) $3,000

Chippendale mahogany birdcage tea table with tilting circular top, Rhode Island, circa 1760, 35in. diam. (Robt. W. Skinner Inc.) $3,000

A small hardwood octagonal table with plain top, inlaid with ivory and mother-of-pearl and carved with Kufic designs. (P. Wilson & Co.) $110

Late 19th/early 20th century mahogany tray-top silver table with claw and ball feet, 33 x 19in. (P. Wilson & Co.) $462

A Louis XV-style kingwood and floral marquetry two-tier etagere, 2ft.7½in. wide, circa 1900. $760

An early George III mahogany tripod table with single-piece circular tip-up top, 31in. diam. (Lawrence Fine Art) $509

William and Mary pine and maple tavern table, New England, circa 1730, top 21 x 29½in. (Robt. W. Skinner Inc.) $1,000

A 19th century Chinese hardwood altar table with rectangular top, 69in. long. (Lawrence Fine Art) $726

An early Victorian rosewood breakfast table with rectangular top, 54 x 36in. (Lawrence Fine Art) $726

A cherry hutch table, Cherry Valley, N.Y., circa 1750, 45in. diam. (Robt. W. Skinner Inc.) $500

Queen Anne maple tea table with inscription on underside 'W D 1794', New England, 39½in. long. (Robt. W. Skinner Inc.) $7,500

A Victorian burr walnut teapoy with rising lid, 48cm. diam. (Osmond Tricks) $655

An Edwardian mahogany and satinwood crossbanded two-tier tray-top tea table, 35in. wide. (Anderson & Garland) $694

Victorian mahogany ornate occasional table, 1890. (British Antique Exporters) $210

A tavern table with drawer, oak rectangular overhanging top, 31in. wide. (Robt. W. Skinner Inc.) $375

A Victorian circular games table in walnut, the top with marquetry inlay and chequer board. (Butler & Hatch Waterman) $775

# PEMBROKE TABLES

**T**ABLES of one kind or another have been around almost as long as man himself. Originally little more than a plank on legs, the table gradually developed in shape and style to accommodate all tastes and permit a number of uses. Many, designed or found suitable for a particular purpose at a particular time, outlive the fashion which established their style, but most lend themselves quite happily to an alternative use to that for which they were originally intended. One of the more universal uses to which tables are put is that of providing a platform from which meals may be eaten and enjoyed. It is only common sense, therefore, to select for this purpose a table whose design and manufacture are of a standard that will enhance, rather than detract from, the fullest possible appreciation of a well cooked meal.

This useful table, introduced during the 1760s, was, according to Sheraton, named after the Countess of Pembroke, who was the first to place an order for one.

Essentially, the Pembroke table has a rectangular top with a drawer and small flaps that are either squared or oval in shape. Beyond this, there are any number of different bases ranging from elegant center columns with tripod splay feet to bulbous, turned pine legs as on the late Victorian examples.

Owing to wide variations in style and quality, price too, Pembroke tables may be used anywhere from salon to toolshed.

The better examples make excellent dining tables for two, or four at a pinch.

A George III mahogany Pembroke table, the oval top with narrow kingwood crossbanding, 36½in. long extended. (Lawrence Fine Art)   $5,702

Georgian mahogany Pembroke table, 1820. (British Antique Exporters)   $218

A Regency rosewood and brass inlaid occasional table of serpentine outline, 26¾ x 37½in. extended. (Lawrence Fine Art)   $9,394

An Edwardian breakfast trolley with single drawer and simulated drawer with metal latticework grille to base, 19 x 29in. (Butler & Hatch Waterman)   $3,354

A late Georgian mahogany Pembroke table with two-flap top, 27 x 36½in. extended. (Lawrence Fine Art)   $2,147

A small Regency mahogany Pembroke table, 2ft. wide, circa 1810.   $875

# FURNITURE

## PEMBROKE TABLES

A late 18th century George III satinwood Pembroke table on square tapering legs. $1,900

A late 18th century Sheraton mahogany oval Pembroke table, 31in. wide. (Banks & Silvers) $1,015

A mid 18th century Cuban mahogany Pembroke table on turned tapering supports, 30in. wide. (D. M. Nesbit & Co.) $381

A George III mahogany and rosewood crossbanded Pembroke table, 2ft.8½in. wide, circa 1810. $1,389

A Federal mahogany inlaid Pembroke table, circa 1790, 34in. wide. (Robt. W. Skinner Inc.) $650

A Federal mahogany inlaid Pembroke table, possibly Duncan Phyfe, N.Y. City, circa 1795, top 21 x 36in. (Robt. W. Skinner Inc.) $1,600

A George III mahogany and rosewood crossbanded rectangular Pembroke table, circa 1790, 2ft.6in. wide. $800

A George III mahogany crossbanded rectangular Pembroke table, 2ft.4in. wide, circa 1790. $2,187

A late George III mahogany Pembroke table, the flap top with fluted edge, 35¾ x 39in. extended. (Lawrence Fine Art) $792

384

A George III mahogany Pembroke table with two rectangular drop leaves and two drawers, circa 1800, 2ft.3in. wide.  $828

A George III rosewood and mahogany Pembroke reading table, 108cm. wide. (H. Spencer & Sons) $1,860

Federal cherry inlaid Pembroke table, New England, circa 1790, 36in. long. (Robt. W. Skinner Inc.) $2,200

A George III mahogany Pembroke table with two-flap top, 30¼ x 41in. (Lawrence Fine Art) $4,435

A George III satinwood Pembroke table, the oval top crossbanded in rosewood, circa 1785, 2ft.4in. wide. $2,722

Late 19th century mahogany Pembroke table with single beaded drawer and blind drawer. (P. Wilson & Co.) $352

An early 19th century rosewood games table, the top with two drop flaps, 107cm. long. (H. Spencer & Sons) $4,216

A George III mahogany Pembroke table with oval two-flap top, 33 x 41½in. extended. (Lawrence Fine Art)    $3,492

Federal mahogany Pembroke table, New England, circa 1800, 20in. wide. (Robt. W. Skinner Inc.) $950

# SIDE TABLES

SIDE tables are the root from which occasional tables grew, dating from the 15th century and resembling in their earliest form, a kind of chest of drawers under a table top. They were used in large households only, for storage of cutlery, linen and condiments in the dining room and, true to the fashion of the time, were made of oak. Few of these have survived and as such command exceptionally high prices.

There are quite a few to be found, however, dating from the William and Mary period, which although expensive, are a good investment.

Slightly better side tables from this period have shaped stretchers with S scroll legs ending in volutes.

From about 1850 fine tapering legs gave way to massive turned ones with heavy brass cup castors and the whole look of side tables became bulbous and rather ugly.

An early Georgian mahogany side table having one drawer with brass ring handles, 33½in. long. (Outhwaite & Litherland)$1,625

A William and Mary oak side table with a drawer and shaped apron, circa 1700, 84cm. wide.                                    $489

A leather top library table with three drawers, by Gustav Stickley, 66½in. wide. (Robt. W. Skinner Inc.)                 $1,250

A mahogany side table fitted with decorative brass drop handles and escutcheons, 30in. wide. (Butler & Hatch Waterman)$248

A 19th century rectangular mahogany side table with three drawers, 9ft.6½in. wide. (Anderson & Garland)     $3,192

A Louis XV provincial oak table with removable rectangular top, 45½ x 32in. (Lawrence Fine Art)                $1,327

# FURNITURE

A George II mahogany serving table with satinwood crossbanded serpentine top, 60in. wide. (Dacre, Son & Hartley) $2,356

A George III mahogany rectangular side table with fluted apron, 58in. wide. (Dreweatt Watson & Barton) $3,275

Late 18th century French oak table rustique with petrin, 65½in. long. (Lawrence Fine Art) $805

Victorian mahogany three-tier dinner wagon, 1870. (British Antique Exporters) $383

A 19th century mahogany inlaid two-drawer side table with brass ball feet, 28¼in. high. (Robt. W. Skinner Inc.) $850

A Jacobean-style oak serving table, by Maples & Co., 7ft. wide. (Capes, Dunn & Co.) $387

A Victorian rosewood stretcher table on quadruple splayed legs, 4ft. wide. (Vidler & Co.) $572

An early 19th century Swiss walnut and pine table, the top with trellis inlay, 62 x 22¼in. (Dreweatt Watson & Barton) $1,179

# FURNITURE

SIDE TABLES

A 19th century carved Oriental hardwood side table with cross stretcher. (Worsfolds) $340

One of a pair of oak neo-Greek pier tables on boldly scrolled cabriole legs, 5ft. 2½in. wide, 1840's. $4,125

George II mahogany pier table with later marble top, 45½in. wide. (Reeds Rains) $3,059

A William and Mary oak side table with molded rectangular hinged top, 31in. wide. (Christie's) $1,287

A George III mahogany side table in the Chippendale style, 39in. wide. (Lawrence Fine Art) $1,078

A 19th century Dutch marquetry side table of shaped outline, 32in. wide. (Lawrence Fine Art) $1,257

A 19th century carved pine side or serving table, made by I. B. Webber, Taunton, 69in. wide. (Lawrence Fine Art) $1,078

A Spanish walnut serving table, circa 1680, 5ft.6½in. long. $1,287

One of a pair of George III-design carved pine pier tables, circa 1900, 3ft.9in. wide. $1,215

An Italian painted pier table with parcel gilt ribbon and leaf decoration, 4ft.9in. wide.          $2,475

A late 17th century oak rectangular table with shaped apron, 33½ x 21in. (Dreweatt Watson & Barton)          $503

Federal mahogany inlaid banquet table, New England, circa 1800, 45½in. wide. (Robt. W. Skinner Inc.)          $1,000

A George III mahogany rectangular table fitted with a drawer at each end,  33 x 19½in. (Dreweatt Watson & Barton)          $799

Federal mahogany serving table, America, circa 1800, 20 x 29in. (Robt. W. Skinner Inc.)          $750

A George I walnut side table, with three drawers, 2ft.6in. wide, circa 1725.          $5,940

A late 17th century walnut rectangular table on bobbin turned legs and stretchers, 32½in. wide. (Dreweatt Watson & Barton)          $1,087

Late 19th century rococo Revival walnut pier table with serpentine-shaped marble top, 82in. wide. (Robt. W. Skinner Inc.)          $3,300

A spindle-sided table with lower shelf, by Gustav Stickley, circa 1905, 36in. wide. (Robt. W. Skinner Inc.)          $3,400

## SOFA TABLES

THE sofa table, was originally introduced to the world by Sheraton towards the end of the 18th century. He suggested that the length should be five feet six inches, (with flaps raised) the width two feet and the height 28 inches.

Basically, of course, this is simply the Pembroke table stretched a bit into more elegant proportions and it is interesting to consider how, given the fundamental idea of a table with drawers and flaps, three such successful designs as the Pembroke, sofa and Regency supper tables can be produced.

Earlier sofa tables were made of mahogany or, occasionally, satinwood but later, in the early 19th century a variety of woods was used including rosewood, amboyna and zebra wood. These are good tables in every sense of the word and, as such, command high prices. Although the 19th century examples are the more flamboyant with their use of exotic woods, inlaid brass and lyre end supports, it is the more austerely elegant late 18th century variety which are the most sought after and, therefore, the most expensive.

The Regency supper table is basically a sofa table with the flaps being hinged from the long sides instead of the short, and having one long drawer in the apron with a dummy front at the opposite end.

Usually made of mahogany or rosewood, the Regency supper table was popular from the beginning of the Regency period through to the start of the Victorian and, although there was little variation in the style of the tops, bases varied considerably in pursuit of changing fashions.

**A Regency mahogany sofa table with lion paw castors, 5ft.10in. wide, circa 1810. $16,016**

**A light mahogany sofa table with reeded legs, 1830, 114cm. wide extended. (Chelsea Auction Galleries) $738**

**A Regency brass inlaid roswood veneered sofa table, 4ft.9in. open, circa 1820. $8,624**

A George III mahogany
sofa table crossbanded in
satinwood, 5ft. wide, circa
1790.     $12,375

A late Regency mahogany
sofa table, the top with
twin flaps, 56in. wide,
open. (Christie's)
$561

A Regency rosewood sofa
table in the manner of
Gillow of Lancaster, 4ft.
11in. wide, circa 1815.
$9,075

A Regency rosewood sofa
table with two-flap top
with a satinwood band,
58¼in. extended. (Lawrence
Fine Art)   $3,643

A Regency rosewood sofa
table with D-end leaves and
beaded edging, 57 x 28in.
overall.  (Morphets)
$1,660

A William IV sofa table veneered in faded figured rosewood with satinwood band-
ing, 3ft. closed. (Woolley &
Wallis)        $885

A Regency rosewood and
satinwood inlaid sofa table
with two drawers, turned
knobs and with brass
castors, 60in. wide overall.
(Dacre, Son & Hartley)
$5,332

A late Regency rosewood
sofa table, the two-flap top
with wide calamanderwood
crossbanding, 59in. extended.
(Lawrence Fine Art)
$1,331

A Regency mahogany, rose-
wood crossbanded and box-
wood and ebony lined sofa
table, 52in. wide, open.
(Christie's) $3,931

**SOFA TABLES**

A Regency rosewood pedestal sofa table, the top with rounded corners, 4ft.11in. wide open, circa 1815. $1,872

A Regency mahogany sofa table with brass paw feet and castor terminals. (Outhwaite & Litherland) $2,194

A George IV mahogany sofa table with two rounded flaps, 36 x 62½in. (Lawrence Fine Art) $603

A Regency rosewood sofa table crossbanded in satinwood and with box and ebony outlining, 153cm. wide, extended. (Osmond Tricks) $9,072

A George III mahogany sofa table, 150cm. wide extended. (H. Spencer & Sons) $980

A late Regency rosewood sofa table with two-flap top, 41½ x 27in. and 66in. extended. (Lawrence Fine Art) $2,818

A Regency satinwood sofa table with rosewood crossbanding to the two-flap top, 37 x 26¼in. deep and 57½in. extended. (Lawrence Fine Art) $2,235

A small Regency rosewood sofa table, the crossbanded top with D-shaped leaves, circa 1810, 35½in. wide. (Neales) $409

A George III rosewood and crossbanded sofa table, inlaid with satinwood stringing, 2ft.11in. wide, circa 1800. $2,633

## WORKBOXES & GAMES TABLES

WELL before the introduction of playing cards, in the 15th century, proficiency at chess, backgammon and dice was considered to be an essential part of the education of anyone intending to take his place in society. Indeed, all forms of gaming were so popular that *The Complete Gamester* was felt to be almost compulsory reading and, in the edition of 1674, we find the declaration ". . . he who in company should appear ignorant of the game in vogue would be reckoned low bred and hardly fit for conversation." Since there were, at that time, dozens of games widely played, including glecko, primero, ombre, picquet, basset, quadrille, commerce and loo, to name but a few, there must have been a considerable number of people wandering about with inferiority complexes.

And another thing, people in society rarely messed about with gambling for loose change; in many of the higher gaming establishments, the dice were rarely thrown for less than £100 a throw and, in a letter to an acquaintance, the Countess of Sutherland complained mildly of her husband's habit of gambling £5,000 a night on basset.

Early games were played on marked boards (as chess and draughts) which were placed either on the floor or on a table. Towards the end of the 17th century, however, the business of losing a fortune was civilized somewhat by the introduction of beautifully made gaming tables specifically designed for players of particular games.

Although a few earlier pieces do exist, it was during the 18th and 19th centuries that gaming tables really came into their own, often being combined with a workbox.

A Sheraton-style inlaid mahogany sewing box on stand with two carrying handles, 20th century. (P. Wilson & Co.) $385

Fine Regency work table, 1820. (British Antique Exporters) $527

A Victorian rosewood two-tier sewing table, 41cm. diam. (Osmond Tricks) $302

A Regency mahogany work table on four short sabre legs with brass castors, the whole inlaid with ebony stringing, 22in. wide. (Lawrence Fine Art) $1,815

A Victorian burr walnut work table, 22in. wide. (Russell Baldwin & Bright) $475

Victorian rosewood workbox on scroll feet, 1840. (British Antique Exporters) $368

A Federal curly and bird's-eye maple and mahogany work table, 1795, top 20½ x 17in. (Robt. W. Skinner Inc.)          $475

A Chinese carved hardwood games table, circa 1870, 3ft. 3in. wide.          $1,072

A George III mahogany work table, circa 1790, 1ft.8in. wide, formerly with a sewing bag.          $1,188

A French kingwood parquetry and ormolu mounted table a ouvrage, 2ft.1in. wide, circa 1880.          $1,275

A George III satinwood work table with two-flap top, 2ft. 7in. wide, circa 1795.          $944

A Biedermeier games and work table, the top with a sliding reversible panel inlaid as a chessboard, 24½in. wide. (Lawrence Fine Art)          $1,078

A papier mache worktable, stamped 'Jennens and Bettridge', Birmingham, circa 1850, 29¼in. wide. (Robt. W. Skinner Inc.)          $500

An Edwardian rosewood work and games table, 76cm. wide. (H. Spencer & Sons)          $467

A Victorian papier mache work table with gilt borders, circa 1850, 1ft.7in. wide.          $614

An early 19th century rosewood work/games table with a hinged top, 54cm. wide. (H. Spencer & Sons) $457

A 19th century Dutch mahogany and marquetry games table with two flaps, 43 x 56½in. (Lawrence Fine Art) $1,900

A 19th century French kingwood and marquetry table en chiffonier in the Transitional style, 50cm. wide. (H. Spencer & Sons) $635

A George III rosewood-veneered work table with canted corners, circa 1780, 1ft.6in. wide. $1,267

A Victorian mahogany workbox on platform base. (Taylors) $169

A George III mahogany and rosewood banded and boxwood line inlaid work table, 20in. wide. (Dreweatt Watson & Barton) $769

An inlaid walnut games and work table of bow-ended form, 2ft.4in. wide, circa 1860. $1,790

A 19th century French kingwood games table on gilt metal mounted, fluted, ebonized supports, 24½in. wide. (Reeds Rains) $691

A classical Revival mahogany and mahogany venee work table, probably New York, circa 1815, 22½in. wide. (Robt. W. Skinner Inc.) $3,300

A Regency rosewood and boxwood lined games and reading table, 30in. wide. (Christie's) $4,212

A Federal tiger maple work table with four cock-beaded drawers, circa 1815, 16¼in. wide.(Robt. W. Skinner Inc.) $4,700

A Regency rosewood writing and games table, 29in. wide. (Christie's) $1,053

A Regency rosewood work table decorated with inlaid scrolling brass bands and stringing, 19in. wide. (Anderson & Garland) $2,660

A Victorian inlaid walnut sewing table with rising lid. (Butler & Hatch Waterman) $248

Mid 19th century Victorian mahogany work table, the top inlaid with chequer board in coromandel and sycamore, 20in. wide. (P. Wilson & Co.) $242

Victorian rosewood center column games table on platform base, 1840. (British Antique Exporters) $937

An early 19th century Chinese Export black and gold lacquer sewing table, 27in. wide. (Christie's) $561

A Victorian burr-walnut sewing table with floral inlay, 2ft. wide. (Russell Baldwin & Bright) $799

# WRITING TABLES & DESKS

BETWEEN 1775 and 1825 there were a number of beautifully made desks designed in a delicately feminine manner yet strongly built so that many have survived in good condition to the present day.

There is a fascination in any piece of furniture which has an action like that which is incorporated in this desk, for, when the drawer is opened, the tambour automatically rolls back into the frame to reveal a fitted compartment which may be used for storing paper and envelopes. The drawer also acts as a support for the flap, which can now be lifted from the centre of the desk and folded forward to provide an ample, leather covered writing surface.

Tambours were widely used during this period, both vertically and horizontally, to cover everything from desk tops to night commodes.

Made of thin strips of wood glued on to a linen or canvas backing, they run in grooves on the frame and follow any path the cabinet maker wishes them to take.

Another elegant and highly desirable writing table which was made from the end of the 18th century until about 1825 and then again during the Edwardian period when the styles of this era were revived, is described by Sheraton in his Drawing Book as "a Lady's Drawing and Writing Table". It adopted the name Carlton House table from the residence of the Prince of Wales for whom the design was originally prepared.

Basically a D-shaped table on fine square tapering legs terminating in brass cup castors, this particular writing table has a bank of drawers and compartments ranged round the sides and curved back and is usually made of mahogany or satinwood.

A sponge painted pine lift-top desk, Vermont, circa 1800, 24¾in. wide. (Robt. W. Skinner Inc.) $1,200

A Regency period rosewood veneered gilt and brass inlaid bonheur du jour in the manner of John McLean, 26½in. wide. (Woolley & Wallis) $5,244

A marble top library table, America, circa 1865, 36in. wide. (Robt. W. Skinner Inc.) $850

An Edwardian lady's mahogany cylinder bureau with revolving top, 76cm. wide. (H. Spencer & Sons) $585

A figured walnut mid Victorian bonheur du jour with arabesque inlay and gilt metal mounts, 35in. wide. (Woolley & Wallis) $1,265

An Edwardian Carlton House-design mahogany desk, 41¾in. wide. (Woolley & Wallis) $1,625

A late George III mahogany center or library table, circa 1810, 4ft.1in. long. $7,590

A mahogany Carlton House writing table in late George III-style decorated with ebony stringing, 56in. wide. (Dreweatt Watson & Barton) $3,480

A George III library table inlaid with ebonized stringing, 4ft. wide, circa 1800. $17,556

A George III tulipwood-veneered bonheur du jour, on square tapering legs, circa 1790, 2ft.6in. wide. $7,590

A Louis Phillipe writing table in kingwood with inset tooled leather top, circa 1840, 2ft.2in. wide. $3,466

A Sheraton period rosewood and inlaid combined work and writing table, 14.3/8in. x 18,1/8in. (Geering & Colyer) $2,340

A 19th century French ebonized and boulle bonheur du jour with pull-out writing slide, 30in. wide. (Morphets) $1,562

One of a pair of George III serpentine tables in the manner of John Cobb, 2ft. 6in. wide, circa 1770. $31,350

Schoolmaster's painted desk, America, circa 1800, with slanted writing surface, 30½in. wide. (Robt. W. Skinner Inc.) $2,500

A late George III library drum table, 4ft.4in. diam., circa 1805. $8,910

A 19th century amboyna table in French style by W. Williamson & Sons, 31in. wide. (Dreweatt Watson & Barton) $2,812

A late Regency Irish mahogany writing table with ropetwist and brass beaded borders, 54 x 27in. (Dreweatt Watson & Barton) $2,960

A Regency escritoire in rosewood with leather inset top, on a plain stand, 66cm. wide. (Osmond Tricks) $2,030

Louis XVI kingwood and parquetry bureau de dame, demi-lune shaped with pierced brass gallery, 3ft.2in. wide. (Capes, Dunn & Co.) $649

A mahogany bonheur du jour surmounted by pierced brass gallery, circa 1780, 3ft.5in. wide. $979

A French rosewood and ormolu mounted bonheur du jour, circa 1890, 3ft. 3in. wide. $994

A Victorian serpentine fronted walnut and kingwood crossbanded bonheur du jour in the French style, circa 1860, 4ft.5in. wide. $2,121

A George III mahogany and sabicu lady's writing cabinet, 1ft.3in. wide, circa 1800. $907

## WRITING TABLES & DESKS

A George III mahogany and crossbanded tambour-top kneehole writing desk, 3ft.9in. wide, circa 1800.
$13,305

A George IV brass-inlaid rosewood-veneered library table, circa 1820, 3ft.10in. wide.       $3,801

A serpentine-fronted writing table by Edwards & Roberts. (Taylors)     $1,300

A Victorian walnut bureau de dame with gilt metal mounts, circa 1870, 2ft.8in. wide.       $1,316

Late Victorian inlaid rosewood lady's writing desk. (Barber's Fine Art)
$520

A Gillow & Co. small mahogany writing desk with a semi-cylindrical raised back portion, 29in. wide. (Lawrence Fine Art)
$1,694

A mahogany slope-top clerk's desk, by Gillows of Lancaster, circa 1835, 37in. wide. (Neales) $1,812

A Victorian burr-walnut small writing table on swept cabriole legs, 29in. wide. (Woolley & Wallis)
$1,298

A 19th century French bonheur du jour, the ebonized ground decorated with panels of foliate scrolls, 38in. wide. (Lawrence Fine Art)
$2,217

Mid Victorian lady's mahogany writing desk on French cabriole supports, 47½in. wide. (Reeds Rains) $1,048

A George IV rosewood library table, circa 1830, 5ft.2½in. wide. $1,552

A Chinese carved hardwood writing table with dragon motifs, circa 1900, 2ft.11½in. wide. $929

A George III satinwood reading and writing tripod table, the top crossbanded with rosewood, 21in. wide. (Lawrence Fine Art) $4,276

A late 19th century mahogany French bureau plat, with inset tooled leather top, 65 x 35½in. (Banks & Silvers) $3,045

A Louis XVI small kingwood desk or jewel cabinet banded in purple heart, 15 x 39in. high. (Dreweatt Watson & Barton) $39,150

A late 19th century satinwood tambour fronted writing desk with gilt brass gallery, 76cm. wide. (H. Spencer & Sons) $1,906

A Louis XVI-style bonheur du jour, veneered in exotic woods, 31in. long. (Outhwaite & Litherland) $2,244

Federal mahogany inlaid desk with fold-out writing surface, New England, circa 1810, 40½in. wide. (Robt. W. Skinner Inc.) $2,500

# WRITING TABLES & DESKS FURNITURE

Victorian mahogany banker's desk, 1860. (British Antique Exporters) $1,936

A 19th century escritoire in the Louis XVI manner, the whole with boulle inlay. (W. H. Lane & Son) $1,040

A Louis XVI-style plum-mottled mahogany and brass mounted bureau a cylindre, circa 1880, 4ft. 3in. wide. $1,807

Georgian pine clerk's desk, 1800. (British Antique Exporters) $343

Victorian oak twin pedestal, bevelled panelled roll-top desk, 1880. (British Antique Exporters) $1,278

A yewwood writing and shelf unit with open shelves above two glazed doors, 28in. wide. (Lawrence Fine Art) $1,210

A Federal pine grain painted schoolmaster's secretary, New Hampshire, circa 1800, 37in. wide. (Robt. W. Skinner Inc.) $1,200

Early 20th century Chippendale design twin pedestal mahogany finish desk, 37 x 62in. (P. Wilson & Co.) $2,074

Victorian mahogany cylinder desk, 1860. (British Antique Exporters) $1,670

# TRUNKS & COFFERS

THE coffer, or chest, is one of the earliest forms of furniture.

It was used as a convenient, safe receptacle for clothes and valuables, doubling as a seat and even, in the case of the larger ones, as a bed.

It was Henry II, in 1166, who really started the boom in coffers when he decreed that one should be placed in every church to raise money for the crusades. Despite the holy cause, all those coffers were fitted with three locks whose keys were held separately by the parish priest and two trustworthy parishioners, just in case any insular minded local felt that he could put the money to better use.

On most early coffers, the stiles form the legs but others were made without such refinements, being made to be fastened down to the floor. There were still other designs, which were entirely of plank construction, the front and back being lapped over the sides and fastened with dowels or hand wrought nails. The side planks extend down below the bottom of the coffer to raise it off the damp, straw covered floor.

The 16th century saw a notable advance in the method of construction of coffers A number of wide upright stiles were joined with mortise and tenon joints to top and bottom rails, muntins (vertical framing pieces) being added to make the panelled framework.

Decoration on these coffers was usually confined to the panels and took the form, particularly in the early models, of a linenfold design.

A carved oak joined chest with rectangular hinged lid, possibly 17th century, England, 63½in. wide. (Robt. W. Skinner Inc.) $600

A Charles I oak chest with four-panel rectangular top, circa 1640, 4ft.4in. wide. $2,035

A pine painted blanket chest, Page County, Virginia, 1822, with lift-top, 45in. wide. (Robt. W. Skinner Inc.) $1,500

An oak and elmwood chest with simple panelled top and sides, 4ft.1in. wide, circa 1620. $1,139

# FURNITURE

A 17th century oak coffer, the two panel hinged lid having fluted stiles, 3ft. 3½in. wide. (Capes, Dunn & Co.) $365

A 17th century Adige cypress wood chest with rectangular hinged cover, 72in. wide. (Lawrence Fine Art) $1,771

A 19th century Italian gilt cassone in Renaissance style, with hinged cover, 68in. wide. (Lawrence Fine Art) $670

William and Mary blanket chest with lift-top, possibly Rhode Island, circa 1740, 37½in. wide. (Robt. W. Skinner Inc.) $1,300

A painted pine blanket chest, New England, circa 1820, 40in. wide. (Robt. W. Skinner Inc.) $1,300

A 17th century oak mule chest with three 'cushion' front panels and drawers with brass knob handles, 3ft.9in. wide. (Edgar Horn) $545

An early 18th century yewwood mule chest, with rising top, 4ft. wide. (Geering & Colyer) $1,950

An early 17th century iron Armada chest with two side handles, the hinged lid with complicated lock, 82cm. wide. (Osmond Tricks) $1,575

A blanket box decorated in polychrome green, black and red floral designs, New England, circa 1820, 34in. wide. (Robt. W. Skinner Inc.) $1,900

An early 18th century
brass studded leather covered, dome-top marriage
chest, 3ft.10in. wide.
(Woolley & Wallis)
$1,232

An early 18th century oak
love chest, two panel front
and dummy drawer, 25in.
wide. (Coles, Knapp &
Kennedy)     $256

An 18th century French brass
bound kingwood coffret forte,
veneered in radiating designs
with gilt metal clasps, 21 x
14 x 12in. (Lawrence Fine
Art)        $2,217

Mid 17th century oak
chest with one long drawer,
on plank feet, 51½in. wide.
(Christie's)     $965

A late 17th century oak mule
chest with scroll carved frieze,
on later stand, 51in. wide.
(Dacre, Son & Hartley)
$413

A Federal grain-painted blanket chest, original red-umber
and dark brown graining,
New England, circa 1820,
41½in. wide. (Robt. W. Skinner Inc.)        $600

An early 16th century oak
standing chest with planked
hinged top, probably French,
56 x 23 x 42in. (W. H. Lane
& Son)      $2,337

A miniature walnut blanket
box on ogee bracket base,
circa 1790, 9½in. high.
(Robt. W. Skinner Inc.)
$2,300

An oak and mahogany mule
chest with hinged top and
block panelled front, 4ft.
6in. wide. (Vidler & Co.)
$442

A 16th century heavy oak planked coffer, the corners with shaped iron bracket mounts, 56 x 28 x 23in. (W. H. Lane & Son) $861

Early 19th century Scandinavian floral painted pine dower chest, 18¼in. deep. (Robt. W. Skinner Inc.) $200

A 17th century oak coffer with triple panel top, 52in. long. (Lawrence Fine Art) $483

A 19th century polychrome painted trunk, the exterior with painted scenes of Mexican life, 32¾in. wide. (Robt. W. Skinner Inc.) $500

A 17th century Spanish leather and brass decorated coffer, 47in. wide. (Robt. W. Skinner Inc.) $500

Victorian pine trunk with brass carrying handles, 1850. (British Antique Exporters) $131

A 17th century inlaid walnut cassone, Italy, on hairy paw feet, 50¼in. wide. (Robt. W. Skinner Inc.) $400

A George II rosewood and maple blanket chest on molded square legs, 49in. wide. (Christie's) $2,061

WARDROBES are, surprisingly, quite close relations to corner cupboards, for both were born in recesses in walls. Wardrobes were late developers, however, failing to break free from their enclosing walls until the second half of the eighteenth century.

Presses with shelves and drawers were in fairly widespread use by the end of the seventeenth century, before which clothes had been stored in trunks and chests. It had sufficed, for a very long time, to store clothes by packing them flat in horizontal containers but, with the advent of a more sophisticated and clothes-conscious society in which both sexes tended to have increased numbers of garments, it became common sense to hang them vertically, both for general convenience and to save creasing and crushing.

Although the vogue for wardrobes of different kinds seems to have dissipated as abruptly as it arose, a few nice examples have remained with us.

All the fashionable decorative quirks found in other pieces of furniture appear on wardrobes, including dentil cornices, applied moldings and canted front edges. Chippendale favoured serpentine fronts, often with bombe fronted drawers below, while Sheraton and Hepplewhite both featured bow-fronted designs. Adam's hallmark on the other hand, was a frieze decorated with low relief carving depicting classical motifs, or panels inlaid with designs of contrasting woods.

Various styles of feet abound, including bracket, ogee and, the superbly sweeping French-style foot with a shaped apron.

A gentleman's rosewood, kingwood, parquetry inlaid and ormolu mounted wardrobe, 8ft. wide. (Vidler & Co.)
$4,440

Victorian walnut triple armoire, 1880. (British Antique Exporters)
$250

An Aesthetic movement ash combination wardrobe and a similar dressing table, 43in. wide.(Reeds Rains)
$432

Victorian oak armoire in Art Nouveau style, 1900. (British Antique Exporters)
$206

Fine Victorian mahogany and walnut armoire with two keys, 1865. (British Antique Exporters)
$648

A 20th century mahogany hanging wardrobe with single shelf, 48in. wide. (P. Wilson & Co.)
$605

# WARDROBES & ARMOIRES

An early 19th century Dutch press with brass ring handles and lock plates, 6ft.1in. x 9ft. 8in. high. (Anderson & Garland)    $4,921

An 18th century Chippendale poplar kas, Hudson Valley, New York, 56in. wide. (Robt. W. Skinner Inc.)    $1,700

An 18th century Dutch figured walnut wardrobe, 6ft.3in. wide. (Geering & Colyer)    $3,537

A Victorian walnut wardrobe with single large mirror panel door, 39in. wide. (Butler & Hatch Waterman) $186

A Scandinavian painted kas, dated 1818, 67in. long. (Robt. W. Skinner Inc.)    $2,000

A Louis XV provincial oak armoire with brass barrel hinges and escutcheon plates, 60in. wide. (Lawrence Fine Art)    $1,073

A Louis XV oak armoire, 4ft. 1in. wide, circa 1760.    $1,455

A Georgian mahogany sectional fitted wardrobe with four pairs of double doors, 80in. wide. (Dee & Atkinson)    $787

A mid 18th century Breton walnut armoire with a drawer in the base, 4ft.10in. wide.    $2,604

A late 18th century mahogany clothes press, the drawers with original oval brass plates, 4ft. wide. (Woolley & Wallis)   $2,080

A George III mahogany breakfront clothes press, 6ft.6in. wide, circa 1770, later pediments.
$2,926

A Georgian mahogany linen press fitted with brass ring handles, 93in. high. (Anderson & Garland)   $2,128

A George III mahogany and satinwood crossbanded gentleman's wardrobe, 4ft. wide, circa 1780.
$1,433

An early George III breakfront gentleman's wardrobe, 5ft.11in. wide, circa 1770.   $4,125

A Louis XV carved oak armoire with foliate vase and scroll motifs, 5ft.6in. wide, circa 1770.
$1,960

A Georgian mahogany gent's wardrobe, the interior fitted with brass hanging rail, 51in. wide. (Butler & Hatch Waterman)
$527

An 18th century French provincial oak armoire fitted with two panelled doors, 52in. wide. (Banks & Silvers)   $978

A French provincial oak armoire. (Russell Baldwin & Bright) $2,375

# WASHSTANDS

WASH basins and ewers were introduced as early as the 16th century when Sir John Harrington deemed it essential to "wash all the instruments of the senses with cold water".

Soap balls had been manufactured since the 14th century; toothbrushes had had to wait until the end of the 17th, but it was not until midway through the 18th century that furniture designers thought to design an article specifically for the housing and use of these essential aids to personal hygiene.

Many of the late 19th century washstands were made to house a multitude of drawers, cupboards and mirrors which give them a bulky appearance and allow little in the way of improvement.

They usually have marble tops, nearly always white, although sometimes variegated.

A mahogany toilet pedestal with enclosed locker top and brass side carrying handles, 1ft.5in. wide. (Warner Sheppard & Wade) $226

A Federal mahogany washstand, circa 1795, 39in. high, 23in. wide. (Robt. W. Skinner Inc.) $550

A Dutch marquetry and mahogany washstand with rouge royale marble inset top, 2ft.9in. wide, circa 1840. $1,250

Victorian mahogany marble top washstand, 1860. (British Antique Exporters) $231

A late 18th century mahogany corner washstand with splay feet. (Elliott & Green) $189

Victorian mahogany and maple, tiled back, marble top washstand, 1865. (British Antique Exporters) $366

# WHATNOTS

FORMERLY of French design, the whatnot made its English debut in about 1790 and was enthusiastically received as the ideal display piece for books and bric a brac.

The earlier examples are generally of rather simple designs and usually of rosewood or mahogany. Subsequent styles, late Regency and Victorian, are often found to be quite elaborate with shaped shelves and fretwork galleries, while some of the Victorian whatnots were made to fit into a corner or enlarged up to four feet in length and designed to be placed against a wall.

The whatnot is one of those pieces which could have been called anything at all. The original French name was etagere, but this apparently taxed the memory or linguistic talents of our ancestors to the extent that they fell back on just the kind of name we would be likely to use today; thingamebob, oojah or whatsit.

A Victorian four-tier walnut whatnot with serpentine fronted display shelves, 3ft. 9in. high. (Edgar Horn)   $286

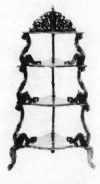

A mid Victorian mahogany four-tier serpentine fronted corner whatnot. (P. Wilson & Co.)   $628

A Victorian mahogany four-tier whatnot with tray top, 16½ x 10½ x 35in. high. (Butler & Hatch Waterman)   $260

Late 18th century mahogany four-tier square top whatnot. (Elliott & Green)   $702

A Victorian ebonized and amboyna etagere, circa 1860, 2ft.4in. wide.   $643

A 19th century lacquer nest of corner tables of triangular form with slightly bowed fronts.   $1,099

A Victorian mahogany corner whatnot with four graduated bow-front tiers, 80cm. wide. (H. Spencer & Sons)   $621

A Regency mahogany four-tier whatnot, circa 1810, 1ft.5in. wide. $1,078

## WINE COOLERS

RECORDS indicate that there were wine coolers in use as early as the 15th century, and examples from the following two centuries are to be seen in many a contemporary tapestry or painting.

They were made for cooling the wine in ice or cold water, and were usually of oval or bowl shape, supported on legs and made in a variety of materials including bronze, copper, silver or even marble and other stones. Some of the silver pieces in particular were very extravagant affairs, and one, in the inventory of the possessions of the Duke of Chandos, is recorded as weighing over two thousand ounces.

Wine coolers made of wood with lead liners were first introduced in about 1730, and these were often supported on cabriole legs with finely carved paw feet.

Some have a nice little brass tap on the side for ease of emptying. Others have brass carrying handles so they could be lifted out of the way with minimal risk of slopping the contents over the guest of honour.

Cellarettes were introduced in about 1750 and, at first, were usually of octagonal shape, the earliest often having short feet decorated with carved foliage

Most are made of mahogany with brass bandings, are lined with lead and partitioned to take nine bottles. At first they were of quite large proportions to take the wide green bottles used at the time but, as these slimmed, cellarettes followed suit.

Later in the 18th century, cellarettes tended towards an oval shape, delicately inlaid with urns and shells and supported on slightly splayed, square tapering legs.

A George III mahogany and brass banded wine cooler on stand with hinged octagonal top, 27in. wide. (Christie's)          $1,614

A George III mahogany and brass bound oval wine cooler with lead liner, 24in. wide. (Dreweatt Watson & Barton) $2,292

A late Georgian small mahogany wine cellarette with brass ring handles at the sides, 20 x 19in. (Lawrence Fine Art)          $726

A George III mahogany wine cooler with three plain brass bands and carrying handles, 22in. (Lawrence Fine Art) $2,654

A Victorian mahogany sarcophagus-shaped wine cooler, minus lining, in the Chippendale-style, circa 1850, 29in. long. (P. Wilson & Co.) $605

Late 18th century mahogany octagonal wine cooler on stand. (Elliott & Green) $4,840

A George III mahogany and brass bound wine cooler with hinged octagonal top, 22in. wide. (Christie's) $5,047

A George III mahogany oval wine cooler with line inlay, 24in. (Woolley & Wallis) $2,398

A Regency small mahogany wine cooler with brass ring handles and paw feet, 16½in. high. (Lawrence Fine Art) $2,514

A George III mahogany octagonal wine cooler with lead-lined interior, circa 1785, 1ft.11in. high. $2,464

A Regency period mahogany sarcophagus-shaped cellaret with original inset brass roller casters, 26in. high. (Woolley & Wallis) $812

George III mahogany cellarette with brass bindings, 18in. diam. (Stalker & Boos) $800

413

A large Sunderland rummer
with bucket bowl, circa
1800, 21cm. high.
(Christie's) $1,085

A pink stained spa beaker
of barrel shape, circa 1840,
12cm. high.      $230

A Sunderland rummer with
bucket bowl, on a spreading
stem and square lemon-
squeezer base, circa 1800,
14cm. high. (Christie's)
$317

A Bohemian ruby glass
beaker, the bowl cut with
panels, circa 1850, 11.5cm.
high.           $300

A Sunderland rummer on a
spreading stem and square
lemon-squeezer base, circa
1800, 17.5cm. high.
(Christie's) $795

A Silesian engraved beaker,
circa 1740-50, 10cm. high.
$475

A Vienna beaker of waisted
form, painted by Anton
Kothgasser, 11cm. high.
(Lawrence Fine Art)
$2,402

A Bohemian Zwischengold
beaker, the flared body with
faceted sides, circa 1730,
9cm. high.
$1,086

A 19th century Bohemian
bulbous base glass beaker
with hand-painted panel.
(Woolley & Wallis)
$352

# GLASS

A Venini glass bottle and stopper, swollen cylindrical, tall neck and spherical stopper, 1950's, 33.5cm. high. $312

A wine bottle of dark brown glass, of depressed spherical form with kick-in base, circa 1710, 14cm. high. (Lawrence Fine Art) $201

An early 18th century clear glass serving bottle and stopper, 11in. high. $512

An early 18th century green glass sealed wine bottle, 20cm. high.  $218

A serving bottle with lightly molded panelled cylindrical body, early 18th century, 20.5cm. high. (Christie's) $217

A Galle enamelled glass bottle with silver stopper, circa 1900, 17.5cm. high. $1,844

A Stourbridge bottle-shape vase with wide trumpet mouth, of opaque white glass, 35.5cm. high. (Lawrence Fine Art)$144

A rare mid 17th century green glass sealed wine bottle, 19.5cm. high.  $3,750

One of a pair of Bohemian ruby and white overlay glass bottles, 10¾in. high. (Christie's)  $238

# BOWLS

An iridescent Loetz glass
bowl of broad shallow form
with inverted rim on three
white glass feet, 27.5cm.
diam.        $250

An iridescent glass bowl of
squat bulbous form and
overall pale gold lustre, by
Loetz, circa 1900, 12cm.
high.        $250

Francois Decorchemont bowl
with serpent handles, circa
1925, 13.5cm. diam.
        $9,072

An Argy Rousseau pate de
cristal ashtray in the form
of a flower calyx, 1920's,
9.25cm. wide. $440

A superb Man in the Moon bowl
by Emile Galle, circa 1890,
11cm. diam.  $11,740

An unusual Galle enamelled
glass bowl of milky gray
ground, circa 1900, 10cm.
high.        $1,250

Galle carved cameo glass bowl
overlaid with white and deep
rose pink, 6.75cm. high.
        $3,750

An American cut glass fruit
bowl, circa 1900, 10½in.
diam.        $350

A small bowl of circular section by Francois Decorchemont, circa 1929, 10.5cm.
diam.        $3,201

A Majorelle wrought iron mounted Daum glass bowl in amber glass with dark mottling at the rim, 1920's, 26.5cm. diam. $562

A large leaf-shaped bowl by Venini, circa 1950, 'Made in Italy', 33.5cm. wide. $320

A Decorchemont pate de cristal bowl, circa 1935, engraved number 'C 399', 13.5cm. diam. $1,206

A Venini handkerchief bowl, the gray/green glass internally decorated with variegated white latticinio design, circa 1955, 22.5cm. high. (Christie's) $1,215

A Lalique opalescent glass powder bowl and cover, 1920's, 13.5cm. diam. $375

An Argy Rousseau pate de cristal bowl, 1920's, globular body in gray glass mottled in ochre, 6.7cm. $522

A Galle cameo glass bowl in pink/gray glass overlaid with purple and gray/green, circa 1900, 28cm. wide. $531

A Flygors glass bowl, heart-shaped, in clear glass with opaque black inner layer, 1950's, 21.5cm. max. width. $218

A Tiffany iridescent glass centerpiece with a design of lily pads, circa 1917, 25cm. diam. $750

# BOXES

## GLASS

A Lalique circular box and cover of flattened form, 25.5cm. (Lawrence Fine Art) $518

A Galle cameo glass box and cover, gray glass overlaid in orange and red-brown, circa 1900, 15.5cm. wide. $1,403

A Galle cameo glass box and cover of lozenge shape, circa 1900, 22cm. $893

A Charder cameo glass box. with knopped cover, 1920's, 12.5cm. diam. $156

A Bohemian overlay and enamelled casket, the body in opaque-white overlaid on clear glass, circa 1840, 10.5 x 13cm. $501

An Argy Rousseau pate de cristal box and cover, 1920's, 14cm. high. $3,689

A Lalique opalescent glass box, the circular cover molded with six chubby birds in flight, circa 1930, 17.25cm. diam.$281

Glass powder box by R. Lalique, decorated with dancers in Greek costume, 7cm. diam., circa 1920. $277

A Lalique glass box, the cover molded with raised blisters and thorny strands, 7.75cm., 1930's. $250

A pair of Georgian cut glass and brass candlesticks each on four ball feet, 11¼in. high. (Christie's) $935

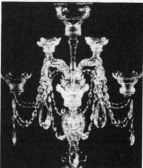

A Georgian cut glass eight-light centerpiece candelabrum, on a baluster-shaped support with a faceted domed base on a square foot, 21in. high. (Christie's) $1,980

Pair of Georgian cut glass and ormolu candlesticks, each with a scalloped urn-shaped candle-cup over a scalloped dish hung with prisms, 9.5/8in. high. (Christie's)    $700

A Lalique glass flower-form candleholder, circa 1930, 23cm. high. $357

A pair of Georgian cut glass double-light candelabra, each with a circular finial over a scalloped cup hung with prisms, 21in. high.(Christie's) $1,320

A taperstick, the plain nozzle set on a balustroid stem, 5¼in. high, circa 1750. $814

Two of a set of four Georgian cut glass candelabra, each with a pear-shaped finial above a scalloped circular dish, 18¼in. high. (Christie's) $1,540

One of a pair of Regency cut crystal and ormolu table candelabra, 16½in. high. (Banks & Silvers) $4,495

A pair of Georgian cut glass candlesticks, each with a scalloped urn-shaped candle-cup hung with prisms, 11¼in. high. (Christie's)    $825

# DECANTERS

An 18th century English green glass tapered decanter with lozenge stopper. (Woolley & Wallis) $396

An engraved silver-plated tantalus on ball feet containing three square cut-glass decanters. (Cooper Hirst)     $500

A French 'boulle-de-savon' opaline oviform decanter and stopper, 26.5cm. high, together with a goblet, circa 1835. (Christie's) $578

A Liberty Tudric pewter and Powell green glass decanter, circa 1900, 30cm. high. (Christie's) $272

A dated enamelled carafe, the opaque white panel inscribed Thos. Worrall 1757, 22cm. high. (Christie's) $8,393

Late 19th century silver mounted cut glass decanter, with domed lid, Germany, 12in. high. (Robt. W. Skinner Inc.) $325

A fine green Bristol glass decanter inscribed 'Shrub'. (Martel Maides & Le Pelley) $216

Early 19th century set of three English green glass ships decanters with triple ring necks and mushroom stoppers. (Woolley & Wallis) $946

An engraved decanter of mallet form, the body inscribed Calcavella, circa 1770, 24cm. high.     $869

A Documentary Waterford flask of elliptical form with short cylindrical neck, circa 1783-1799, 20.5cm. long. $735

'Susanna och gubbarna', an Orrefors clear glass decanter and stopper designed by Edward Hald, circa 1935, 23.5cm. high. (Christie's) $462

A Bohemian enamelled 'Milchglas' decanter and stopper, circa 1770, 29.5cm. high. $351

A WMF silver plated pewter mounted green glass decanter, circa 1900, 38.5cm. high. (Christie's) $476

An oak tantalus containing three square cut-glass decanters with prismatic stoppers. (Cooper Hirst) $256

An overlay carved decanter and stopper, probably Webb, circa 1880, 32cm. high. $451

A 'Lynn' decanter of mallet shape, the body lightly molded with horizontal ribs, circa 1775, 23cm. high. (Christie's) $723

A Galle enamelled glass bottle of flattened flask shape with stopper, 30.25cm. high. $425

An enamelled Bohemian decanter, the shoulder faceted body painted in tones of puce and white, circa 1860, 30cm. high. $484

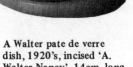

An Iittala glass leaf-form dish, designed by Tapio Wirkkala, circa 1955, 25cm. wide.
$516

A Walter pate de verre dish, 1920's, incised 'A. Walter Nancy', 14cm. long.
$2,412

A Barbini clear glass dish, the relief figure of a swimming woman in opaque purple glass decorated in gold, 39.5cm. wide.
$510

Early 20th century cut glass compote with flaring bowl, America, 10½in. diam. (Robt. W. Skinner Inc.)     $300

A cut glass charger with scalloped rim, America, circa 1880, 12in. diam. (Robt. W. Skinner Inc.)
$200

Early 20th century cut glass compote on round foot with starburst bottom, America, 7in. diam. (Robt. W. Skinner Inc.)
$175

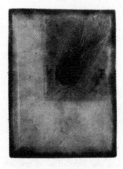

A circular dish, the base molded radials impressed Cork Glass Co., circa 1800, 18cm.          $585

A sweetmeat glass supported on a scallop-edged foot, 6¼in. high, circa 1770.
$88

A small rectangular Walter pate de verre dish, 1920's, 11.5cm. wide. $851

# GLASS

## DRINKING SETS

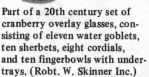

Part of a 20th century set of cranberry overlay glasses, consisting of eleven water goblets, ten sherbets, eight cordials, and ten fingerbowls with undertrays. (Robt. W. Skinner Inc.) $500

A Lalique glass drinking set, the decanter 26.5cm. high, 1930's.            $520

Part of a thirty-nine piece Schott & Gen. Jenaer Glas heat-resistant teaset, designed by W. Wagenfeld, teapot 14cm. high. (Christie's) $1,012

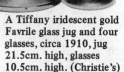

An Art Deco decanter and set of six matching tots in smoked and frosted glass. (Capes, Dunn & Co.) $117

A Tiffany iridescent gold Favrile glass jug and four glasses, circa 1910, jug 21.5cm. high, glasses 10.5cm. high. (Christie's) $652

A 19th century engraved wine ewer of ovoid pedestal form and a pair of goblets. (H. Spencer & Sons) $290

A Lalique glass liqueur set, 1930's, decanter 20cm. high.            $737

'Bahia', a Lalique drinking set comprising a jug and six tumblers in clear and satin-finished amber glass, circa 1930, jug 23cm. high, glasses 13cm. high. (Christie's) $516

Part of an Orrefors engraved glass drinking set, designed by Vicke Lindstrand, 1940's, the decanter 29.5cm. high. $650

423

An engraved goblet set on a facet-cut stem with conical foot, circa 1780, 18cm. high. $234

An engraved color-twist goblet with large ogee bowl, possibly Jacobite, circa 1770, 18cm. high. $2,340

A Dutch-engraved wine goblet, the bowl supported on a fine Newcastle-type light baluster stem, circa 1750, 21cm. high. $2,006

A Dutch engraved goblet, with a folded conical foot, circa 1750, 24cm. high. $802

An Austrian/Bohemian enamelled glass goblet, 1840's, 13cm. high. $515

Mid 19th century Bohemian ruby stained bell-shaped glass goblet and cover. (Reeds Rains) $3,348

An engraved goblet with large ogee bowl, the stem enclosing an opaque-white gauze corkscrew, circa 1760, 19.2cm. high. $250

A Jacobite goblet, the bucket bowl engraved with rose, half-opened and closed buds, moth on reverse, circa 1750, 17.5cm. high. $401

Early 17th century Venetian goblet in slightly grayish metal, 19.5cm. high. $2,006

A 17th century Façon de
Venise serpent-stem goblet,
23.2cm. high.
$2,675

A Richardson vitrified goblet with baluster stem,
enamel painted in shades
of gray with water carriers,
17cm. high. (Christie's)
$162

A Dutch stiple-engraved
Friendship goblet, the bowl
supported on a facet-cut
stem, circa 1770, 21.7cm.
high.        $5,517

A Dutch-engraved goblet
with pointed funnel bowl,
circa 1750, 18cm. high.
$769

A 16th century Venetian
goblet of grayish metal
with bell-shaped bowl,
15cm. high.
$3,511

A Bohemian Zwischengold
goblet, circa 1730, 16.5cm.
high.        $1,170

A Jacobite portrait goblet,
the bowl engraved with a
half-length portrait of
Prince Charles Edward,
circa 1750, 19.5cm. high.
$5,684

An amber-flashed Williamite
goblet, probably Bohemian,
circa 1840, 14.4cm. high.
$267

An engraved composite-
stem goblet, the bowl supported on a blade knop
over inverted baluster stem,
circa 1765, 19cm. high.
$752

A small Daum rectangular section cameo glass jug, circa 1900, 11cm. long. (Christie's)  $380

A claret jug, the bottle shape glass body with star-cut base and with a vine branch handle, 27cm. high. (Lawrence Fine Art) $461

An engraved claret jug of neo-classical form, possibly Stourbridge for Phillips & Pierce, circa 1880, 32cm. high.               $224

Mid 19th century Clichy filigree jug with applied loop handle, 35.6cm. high.              $484

A Victorian silver-mounted glass double-necked claret jug, by Heath & Middleton, London, 1895, 12.1/8in. high.              $1,252

A Venini glass jug, cylindrical, shaped spout, green glass banded in milky blue, 1950's, 24.5cm. high.   $204

A Victorian claret jug, the cylindrical glass body with swelling base, by Charles Edwards, 1878, 25.7cm. high. (Lawrence Fine Art) $864

A large Schneider mottled glass pitcher, in red glass streaked with yellow, 1920's. $322

A Webb silver mounted cameo glass claret jug, 1881, 25cm. high.              $568

A Wm. Hutton & Son silver and green glass cruet jug, London hallmarks for 1903, 18cm. high, 8oz.14dwt. (Christie's)  $190

A green glass Art Nouveau wine jug of slender trumpet form with pewter mounts and handles, 11in. high. (Capes, Dunn & Co.)  $83

A late Victorian claret jug, with pink glass body and with domed cover and harp handle, by E. S. Jones, Birmingham 1897, 29.8cm. high. (Lawrence Fine Art)  $605

A Bohemian white and clear overlay glass jug, decorated with stylized morning glory and arrowhead foliage, 13in. high. (Christie's)  $238

A French 'turquoise' opaline tapering oviform jug with scroll handle, circa 1835, 16cm. high. (Christie's)  $491

A Venini glass jug in clear glass striped with green, purple and blue, 29.5cm. high, 1950's.  $195

A Galle enamelled glass jug, the ovoid body with faceted neck and angled handle, 1890's, 21cm. high.  $387

Mid 16th century Venetian filigree ewer, the whole in 'vetro a reticello' 37.6cm. high.  $6,353

A Richardson vitrified ewer, enamel painted in shades of gray with water-carriers by a fountain, registration lozenge for 1843, 24.5cm. high. (Christie's)  $434

# MISCELLANEOUS

# GLASS

Late 19th century wheel etched and enamelled humidor, Russia, 8¼in. high. (Robt. W.Skinner Inc.)          $140

A 19th century lithophane of William Penn's Treaty with the Indians, 6½ x 8¼in. (Robt. W. Skinner Inc.)          $240

'Orange-Julep' syrup dispenser, circa 1920, 14¼in. high. (Robt. W. Skinner Inc.)          $500

A Lalique glass figure of a naked woman with a wreath of flowers falling to her feet, circa 1935, 21cm. high.          $385

A stained glass panel with scene of mediaeval punishment, 18¾ x 15in. (Capes Dunn & Co.)          $2,337

A sea-blue frosted and bubbled glass figure of Pierrot, by Walter Nancy, France. 9½in. high. (Chelsea Auction Galleries)          $1,430

A Kosta etched cameo glass plate of frosted gray glass overlaid with amber and dark brown, 1950's, 34.75cm. diam. $150

One of a pair of Bohemian gilt and overlay lustres, circa 1860, 29.5cm. high.          $802

An Irish wine glass rinser, circa 1790, 9.8cm. high.          $752

Lalique frosted glass mascot, 'Crouching Mermaid', 4in. high. (Dacre, Son & Hartley)    $299

A St. Louis macedoine wafer stand with ogee bowl, the base filled with parts of colored canes and ribbons, 3½in. high. (Christie's)    $495

A jelly glass, the conical bowl engraved with a stag's head and peacock, 3½in. high, circa 1760.    $227

'Cherry Chic' syrup dispenser, manufactured by J. Hungerford Smith, New York, circa 1925, 11½in. high. (Robt. W. Skinner Inc.)    $1,450

'Victoire', a Lalique car mascot in molded pale amethyst clear and satin finished glass, France, circa 1930, 24.7cm. wide. (Christie's)    $7,484

'Hires' syrup dispenser, Phila., patented 1920, 14¼in. high. (Robt. W. Skinner Inc.)    $340

A Facon de Venise bucket with loop handle, probably early 17th century, 14.3cm. diam.    $2,675

A 19th century lithophane of Ruth with Sheaf of Wheat, 7.7/8 x 6.1/8in. (Robt. W. Skinner Inc.)    $95

Late 19th century Webb ivory cameo rose jar of squat spherical form, 5¾in. high. (Robt. W. Skinner Inc.)    $1,150

# GLASS

A Baccarat fruit weight, the clear glass set with a leafy spray bearing two pendant ripe pears, 8cm. diam. $1,170

A Baccarat flat-bouquet weight with star-cut base, 9cm. diam. $5,852

A Clichy swirl weight with central green-and-white rose, 5.8cm. diam. $1,086

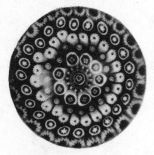

A miniature St. Louis concentric-millefiori weight, 5.2cm. diam. $384

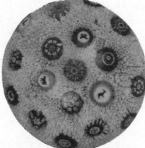

A Baccarat carpet-ground weight, the ground of white corrugated canes with pink centers, 8cm. diam. $4,180

A Baccarat thousand-petal rose weight, 7.9cm. diam. $5,684

A Clichy flat-bouquet weight, the clear glass set with three sprays bound with a ribbon, 8.5cm. diam. $15,884

A St. Louis concentric-millefiori weight, the central cane surrounded by seven rows of canes in pastel shades, 8cm. diam. $1,170

A Clichy convolvulus weight, the clear glass enclosing a white flower with mauve edge, 7.6cm. diam. $6,520

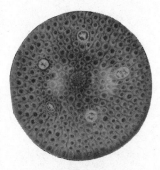

A St. Louis carpet-ground weight, the ground of closely-packed pink crimped canes, 7.5cm. diam. $3,009

A Baccarat 'tulip-bud' weight with star-cut base, 8.1cm. diam. $1,254

A St. Louis four-color crown weight, 5.7cm. diam. $916

A Baccarat sulphide color-ground weight, 8.5cm. diam. $785

A St. Louis pom-pom weight, the translucent cranberry-red ground set with swirling white threads, 7cm. diam. $1,421

A Baccarat carpet-ground weight, dated B1848, 7.3cm. diam. $3,845

A Clichy swirl weight with central deep pink-and-white cane, 7.9cm. diam. $1,421

A St. Louis mushroom weight with star-cut base, 7.3cm. diam. $1,755

A Clichy moss-ground pat-terned-millefiori weight, 6.8cm. diam. $7,356

A Lalique glass perfume bottle, circular with spherical stopper, 1930's, 22cm. high.          $258

A Lalique glass perfume bottle with conical stopper molded with flowering brambles.          $193

A Lalique glass perfume bottle, 'Coeur Joie' for Nina Ricci, of pierced heart-shape molded with flowers, 1920's.          $161

A Galle cameo glass perfume atomiser of flattened bulbous shape, circa 1900, 22.3cm. high.  $829

A Lalique glass perfume bottle, flattened, square body with central oval depression, 1930's, 12.75cm. high.          $387

Lalique perfume bottle decorated with stylized flowers, 11.75cm. high, circa 1925. $345

A Lalique glass perfume bottle for Worth, 'Dans la Nuit', 1930's, 26cm. high.          $368

Daum Nancy perfume bottle, straight diamond shaped bottle, circa 1900, 4½in. high. (Robt. W. Skinner Inc.) $300

A French 'Gorge De Pigeon' opaline flared cylindrical scent bottle and stopper, circa 1835, 11.5cm. high. (Christie's) $404

# GLASS

## SCENT BOTTLES

A Victorian cut glass heart-shaped double scent bottle, by S. Mordan & Co.,bearing the registered design mark for 1869, 3.1/8in. high. (Anderson & Garland) $714

One of a pair of Lalique glass perfume bottles, molded as sea urchins, 9.5cm. high, 1930's. $195

A Daum cameo glass perfume bottle and stopper of ovoid shape with cone-shaped stopper, circa 1900, 14.5cm. high. (Christie's) $544

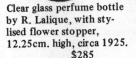

Clear glass perfume bottle by R. Lalique, with stylised flower stopper, 12.25cm. high, circa 1925. $285

A set of three Lalique glass perfume bottles in leather carrying case, 1920's, 8.75cm. high. $1,021

A Lalique glass perfume bottle of rectangular shape with stepped recessed panels, 18.5cm. high. $258

A ruby-ground cameo scent bottle with silver mount, Thos. Webb & Sons, circa 1885, the silver London, 1886-87, 11cm. high. (Christie's) $506

A Lalique perfume bottle decorated with female figures in Greek costume, 15.5cm. high, circa 1925. $400

A Lalique glass perfume bottle for Molinard, with spherical stopper, 1930's. $387

433

# SHADES

A Tiffany Studios leaded glass shade, inset with a floral design in deep blue and mauve glass, circa 1900, 46cm. diam. $3,750

A Galle cameo glass lamp shade on Austrian earthenware base, circa 1900, 50cm. high. $1,925

A cameo glass hanging shade, attributed to Loetz, the mottled pink/white body overlaid in deep red, circa 1900/10, 40cm. max. width. $357

A Galle cameo glass flower form shade, the white body overlaid in deep pink/red/brown, circa 1900, 21.5cm. max. width. $1,237

An Art Deco wrought iron hanging light, attributed to Edgar Brandt, circa 1925, 37cm. high. $500

One of a pair of Daum glass and metal wall lights, fitted for electricity, circa 1925, 60cm. wide. (Christie's) $2,585

A pendant lamp shade of shallow bowl shape, signed 'Maxonade Paris', 1ft.6in. diam. (Capes, Dunn & Co.) $231

A Marvin cold-painted metal lamp with Muller Freres cameo glass shade, circa 1905. $1,000

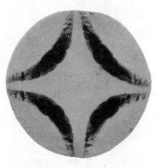

A Lalique opalescent glass hanging shade molded with swags of fruit, circa 1930, 31cm. diam. $343

# GLASS

## TANKARDS

A Bohemian enamelled and gilt tankard and cover in opaque-pink glass with applied scroll handle, 20cm. high, circa 1840-60.
$1,003

A bell-shaped mug with gadrooned lower part and everted folded rim, mid 18th century, 11cm. high. (Christie's) $259

One of a pair of Liberty Tudric mugs designed by A. Knox with original green glass liners by J. Powell & Son, circa 1900, 13cm. high. (Christie's)
$162

## TUMBLERS

A Bohemian pale green flared octagonal tumbler on spreading foot, mid 19th century, 12cm. high. (Christie's)
$491

A Baccarat enamelled cut glass tumbler, the plaque decorated in colored enamels on gilt foil, 8.5cm. high. (Christie's)
$723

A Bohemian octagonal flared tumbler with waisted foot, circa 1845, 13cm. high. (Christie's)
$462

A Bohemian cobalt blue octagonal tumbler with waved foot, circa 1845, 13cm. high. (Christie's)
$462

One of a pair of cut glass tumblers with sterling silver mountings, Russia, circa 1900, 4in. high. (Robt. W. Skinner Inc.)
$300

A Bohemian pale blue hexagonal waisted tumbler decorated in silver, circa 1835, 12cm. high. (Christie's) $607

Early 20th century Tiffany Art glass vase, New York, 4¼in. high. (Robt. W. Skinner Inc.)    $700

Libbey cut glass flower center with sawtoothed rim, Ohio, circa 1910, 9½in. diam. (Robt. W. Skinner Inc.)$700

An aurene vase by Steuben Glass Works, New York, circa 1920, 8in. high. (Robt. W. Skinner Inc.)    $1,700

An opalescent and floral engraved and blue stained 'Reflets' vase, by R. Lalique, France, circa 1928, 5in. high. (Woolley & Wallis)    $246

A pair of Bohemian ruby glass vases of slender ovoid pedestal form, 45.5cm. high. (H. Spencer & Sons)    $1,225

A Bacchantes Lalique opalescent glass vase, circa 1930, 25cm. high.    $3,668

Late 19th century Galle cameo glass vase, signed, France, 8¼in. high. (Robt. W. Skinner Inc.)    $350

Early 20th century red Tiffany glass vase with pulled blue iridescent design, 3¼in. high. (Robt. W. Skinner Inc.)    $2,100

A large cut glass vase with tulip-shaped body, America, circa 1890, 18in. high. (Robt. W. Skinner Inc.)    $850

436

Late 19th century Galle multi-color cameo glass vase, signed, 7in. high. (Robt. W. Skinner Inc.) $375

Late 19th century Webb Burmese glass vase, England, 2½in. high. (Robt. W. Skinner Inc.) $250

A Muller Fres. Art Glass vase of baluster form in pink flashed with silver, signed. (Osmond Tricks) $170

A Lalique satin and clear vase, thistle-shaped, 4½in. high. (Capes, Dunn & Co.) $48

Late 19th century Galle cameo vase in shades of green on shades of peach to tan ground, signed, 17¼in. high. (Robt. W. Skinner Inc.) $700

Tiffany blue iridescent Art glass vase, New York, circa 1900, 3¾in. high. (Robt. W. Skinner Inc.) $1,250

An Italian 17th century ormolu mounted amethyst-tinted vase, 34.5cm. high. $1,504

Blue aurene vase by Steuben Glass Works, N.Y., circa 1910, signed, 10½in. high. (Robt. W. Skinner Inc.) $700

Early 20th century Quezal Art Glass vase, New York, signed, 8¼in. high. (Robt. W. Skinner Inc.)$575

Late 19th century two-color cameo glass vase with white foliage decoration on cranberry ground, 12in. high. (Robt. W. Skinner Inc.) $1,700

A Galle double overlay cameo glass vase with bulbous base, circa 1910, 15cm. high. (Christie's) $544

An Orrefors gray tinted bottle-shaped vase with curly handles, designed by Simon Gate, circa 1930, 23.5cm. high. (Christie's) $952

A large Daum vase of stretched pear-shape, circa 1920, 44cm. high. (Christie's) $476

An opalescent blue stained glass vase by Lalique entitled Salmonides. (Phillips) $2,400

Victorian brown cameo over opal vase, by George Woodall, circa 1895, 8in. high. (Giles Haywood) $2,562

'Bacchantes', a Lalique molded glass vase, France, circa 1930, 25cm. high. (Christie's) $2,993

A Daum cameo glass tall slender baluster vase with waisted base, circa 1900, 52cm. high. (Christie's) $1,769

A Verlys molded glass vase, France, circa 1930, 28.5cm. high. (Christie's) $258

A Galle cameo glass and fire-polished shaped cylindrical vase, circa 1900, 19.9cm. high. (Christie's) $706

An Orrefors clear glass vase of tall tapering shape, circa 1940, 28cm. high. (Christie's) $298

Late 19th century Galle cameo glass vase with cylindrical neck on bulbous base, France, 4in. high. (Robt. W. Skinner Inc.) $250

A Galle cameo glass vase of tapering cylindrical shape with flared neck, circa 1900, 20.5cm. high. (Christie's) $1,224

A Verlys pale amber-colored molded glass vase with everted rim, France, circa 1930, 22.5cm. high. (Christie's) $128

A large Fulvio Bianconi vase of flattened flaring cylindrical shape, 1957, 39cm. high. (Christie's) $2,041

A vase in clear and frosted glass of ovoid shape, signed Muller Luneville, France, circa 1930, 20cm. high. (Christie's) $230

Quezal floriform vase with ruffled rim and gold interior, New York, circa 1910, 5.3/8in. high. (Robt. W. Skinner Inc.) $600

A Fratelli Toso two-handled 'murrina' vase in cobalt blue, white and green, circa 1910, 32.5cm. high. (Christie's) $952

# VASES
# GLASS

Late 19th century Daum
Nancy acid finished bud
vase, France, 4½in. high.
(Robt. W. Skinner Inc.)
$225

A Galle molded blown and
cameo glass vase of tapering
baluster form on circular
foot, circa 1900, 29.2cm.
high. (Christie's)
$7,484

A 19th century French
green glass vase, the tulip-
shaped bowl with crenellated
rim, 36cm. high. (Lawrence
Fine Art)        $102

Late 19th century Galle
cameo glass vase, signed,
France, 6in. high. (Robt.
W. Skinner Inc.)
$200

A Lalique opalescent glass
vase with molded nodule
decoration, 7in. high. (P.
Wilson & Co.) $220

A Webb cameo vase of deep
funnel form, on everted
conical foot, circa 1910,
25cm. high.        $317

A Daum vase with barrel-
shaped body with four lug
handles, circa 1930, 26.5cm.
high. (Christie's)
$1,115

A Galle cameo glass soli-
fleur vase with shaped
conical base, circa 1900,
30.8cm. high. (Christie's)
$1,020

A Lalique opalescent glass
globular vase with molded
leaf decoration, 7in. high.
(P. Wilson & Co.)
$187

Mid 19th century French opaque-opaline glass baluster vase handpainted in colored enamels, 17½in., with companion vase, now as a lamp. (Edgar Horn) $372

A Kosta cameo glass vase designed by Gunnar Wenneberg, circa 1900, 17cm. high. (Christie's) $408

A large Loetz vase with twisted body and quatrefoil neck, circa 1900, 43.6cm. high. (Christie's) $1,088

Late 19th century Galle cameo glass vase, flared rim on teardrop shape, signed, 8in. high. (Robt. W. Skinner Inc.) $325

A Lalique vase in clear and satin-finished glass, engraved France, circa 1930, 24cm. high. (Christie's) $298

A Webb faceted vase with embossed Art Nouveau floral design and signature, 9in. high. (Capes, Dunn & Co.) $62

A Steuben green jade vase, Corning, New York, circa 1920, 10½in. high. (Robt. W. Skinner Inc.) $400

A Delatte enamelled glass vase, slender ovoid with flared rim and pad foot, 1920's, 21.25cm. high. $170

A 20th century opaline 'Danaides' vase, signed R. Lalique, France, 7.1/8in. high. (Robt. W. Skinner Inc.) $600

A small wine glass supported
on a plain stem, 5¾in. high,
circa 1770.          $121

A mixed-twist wine glass
with conical foot, circa
1760, 15.5cm. high.
$535

A wine glass with large ogee
bowl, 6¼in. high, circa 1760.
$97

A Jacobite wine glass, the
flared bucket bowl decorated with multi-petal rose and
bud, circa 1750, 16.5cm.
high.          $919

A Jacobite firing glass, the
small ogee bowl engraved
with crowned thistle, on
thick circular foot, circa
1760, 9cm. high.
$1,504

A Dutch light baluster
wine glass, the ogee bowl
engraved with a man-o'-war,
7in. high, circa 1750.
$488

A cordial glass with ogee
bowl on multi-spiral air-
twist stem, circa 1760,
16cm. high. $434

A green-tinted wine glass
with ovoid bowl set on a
hollow stem, 1750-70,
15.6cm. high. $367

A wine glass with slender
bell bowl, 6½in. high, circa
1750.          $137

# GLASS

## WINE GLASSES

A deceptive wine glass, the thickened ogee bowl set on a double-series opaque-twist stem, circa 1760, 14cm. high.          $802

A Williamite glass, the ovoid bowl decorated with an equestrian portrait of William III, circa 1800, 15cm. high.          $1,003

A 'Lynn' wine glass with rounded funnel bowl, circa 1760, 14cm. high.          $300

A mixed-twist wine glass, the bowl with rounded base and everted rim, circa 1760, 16cm. high.          $217

A Jacobite firing glass or syllabub glass set on a hollow knop and everted foot, circa 1750, 10cm. high. $752

A Jacobite wine glass with mercury-twist stem and conical foot, circa 1750, 16cm. high.          $351

A mixed-twist wine glass with bell bowl, on conical foot, circa 1760, 17.5cm. high.          $250

The 'Beves' 'Amen' glass engraved with the Jacobite version of God Save the King, circa 1750, 18cm. high.          $20,900

A disguised Jacobite glass, inscribed 'The Immortal Memory', circa 1750, 16cm. high.          $2,340

# WINE GLASSES

An early cordial glass, the waisted bowl with solid base, circa 1720, 16cm. high.          $484

An opaque twist Jacobite wine glass, the bell bowl engraved with a rose, circa 1770, 17.5cm. high. (Christie's)     $317

A baluster wine or cordial glass with waisted bowl, circa 1710, 16.3cm. high.          $535

A color-twist wine glass the bell bowl set on a double-series opaque-twist stem, circa 1770, 17cm. high.          $869

An 18th century serpent-stemmed glass, the funnel bowl supported on a merese, 18cm. high. (Christie's)          $259

A Wiener Werkstatte glass, designed by Otto Prutscher, circa 1910, 21cm. high.          $1,560

An 18th century commemorative wine glass with ogee bowl, 5in. high. (Woolley & Wallis)     $362

An unrecorded signed Royal armorial goblet by Wm. Beilby, circa 1762, 25cm. high. (Christie's)          $75,254

An 18th century engraved wine glass on facet cut stem with central knop. (Woolley & Wallis)          $286

# GLASS

## WINE GLASSES

A small wine glass, the ogee bowl engraved with a wild flower and bird, 5½in. high, circa 1770.        $121

An 18th century cordial glass with funnel bowl on double air-twist stem to conical foot. (Woolley & Wallis)        $65

A gilt wine glass, the facet-cut stem with central swelling, circa 1770, 16cm. high.        $317

A Jacobite cordial glass with drawn-trumpet bowl and multi-spiral air-twist stem, circa 1745, 16cm. high.        $769

A firing glass of possible Jacobite significance, circa 1760, 11.5cm. high.        $250

A light baluster wine glass engraved by Jacob Sang, Amsterdam, 1757, 19.2cm. high. (Christie's)        $8,683

A composite-stemmed wine glass consisting of drawn-trumpet bowl with multi-spiral air-twist shank, circa 1750, 18cm. high.        $317

A firing glass with drawn-trumpet bowl inscribed 'The Friendly Hunt', circa 1750, 9cm. high.        $250

A Jacobite portrait glass, the funnel bowl engraved with a portrait of Prince Charles Edward, circa 1750, 15.5cm. high.        $1,839

# GOLD

Early 19th century Swiss three-color gold box with diamond-set thumbpiece, 8cm., unmarked.
$1,392

Early 19th century Swiss gold and enamel box set with rose diamonds. (Phillips)$4,080

A George III 18kt. gold snuff box, by Alexander J. Strachan, 1806, the cover 1807, 7.5cm. (Lawrence Fine Art)
$1,441

A 20th century Cartier gold cigarette box, Paris, 263gr. (Robt. W. Skinner Inc.)
$2,300

Mid/late 19th century Austro-Hungarian jewelled gold and enamel 'Historismus' model of the rollicking cook, 8cm. high.
$957

A jewelled two-color gold cigarette case, the reeded body set with diamonds, St. Petersburg, 1908-17, 9.8cm.    $3,395

A circular French two-color gold and lacquer powder box, circa 1780, 3¼in. diam.
$439

A gold presentation kovsh of bowl form, by J. C. Klinkosch, Vienna, circa 1880, 12.5cm.
$3,700

A Swedish two-color gold portrait snuff box by F. Fyrwald, maker's mark, Stockholm, 1794, 6.1cm
$10,013

# GOLD

An early 19th century Russian three-color gold bangle, hallmarked St. Petersburg 1825. (Woolley & Wallis) $3,045

Early 18th century gold mounted carved ivory snuff box. (Phillips)$1,500

A gold snuff box, maker's mark Am, Vienna, 1840, 2½in. wide. $502

Steuben gold aurene thorn vase, three graduated cylinders with applied nodes, circa 1920, 6.1/8in. high. (Robt. W. Skinner Inc.) $450

A French gold portrait snuff box, by Pierre-Andre Montauban, Paris control marks for 1809-1819, 7.3cm. $7,402

A Horta gold double locket set with a sapphire and fourteen small diamonds, circa 1900, 3.5cm. diam. (Christie's)$1,632

Early 18th century gold mounted shell snuff box. (Phillips) $2,160

A Kerr 14kt. gold travel timepiece, Newark, N.J., 1917, 120gr. (Robt. W. Skinner Inc.) $700

A 19th century gold framed malachite snuff box. (Phillips) $4,320

One of a pair of heavily carved malachite groups of predatory birds, late Qing Dynasty, 20.5cm. high. (Christie's) $1,140

An 18th/19th century lapis lazuli mountain of slender slightly concave cross-section, 26cm. wide. (Christie's) $3,706

A large malachite vase formed as an irregular upright tree trunk issuing from rockwork, late Qing Dynasty, 26cm. high. (Christie's) $683

A malachite flattened baluster vase and cover, late Qing Dynasty, 12cm. high. (Christie's) $285

A Chinese 20th century carved agate Foo dog in tones of smoky brown, gray and white, 5.3/8in. high. (Robt. W. Skinner Inc.) $650

A chalcedony agate group carved as a lady standing holding a scroll, another beside her, late Qing Dynasty, 23cm. high. (Christie's) $498

A green hardstone stele carved with Guanyin astride a caparisonned lion, late Qing Dynasty, 62cm. high. (Christie's) $1,853

A carnelian agate group of two lady Immortals, late Qing Dynasty, 16.5cm. high. (Christie's) $455

A rock crystal vase and cover, the high domed cover with a plain globe finial, late Qing Dynasty, 23.5cm. high. (Christie's) $855

# HORN

Rhinoceros horn cup, Chinese, possibly 18th century, the handle composed of a group of intertwined dragons, 4¾in. high. (Robt. W. Skinner Inc.) $1,300

A 17th century pressed-horn plaque with the Raising of Lazarus, 6 x 5cm.. $506

A 19th century rhinoceros horn cup, China, 5½in. high. (Robt. W. Skinner Inc.) $1,300

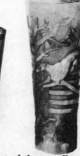

An 18th century horn figure of Kuan Yin, stained an amber color, 5½in. high. (Lawrence Fine Art) $273

A set of three well-carved horn beakers with silver mounts by W. Thornhill & Co., hallmarked London 1882, 10in. and 6in. (Woolley & Wallis) $892

Late 16th century English shoe horn cut from an ox horn, 9¾in. long. $2,711

A red stained horn figure of Kuan Yin, seated on the back of a kylin, 5¾in. high. (Lawrence Fine Art) $259

An 18th century rhinoceros horn libation cup finely carved with many travellers walking, on horseback and in boats, 17cm. high, with fitted box. (Christie's) $5,132

A horn carving of Shou Lao, on a wood stand, 18.5cm. high. $288

# ICONS

An icon painted in two registers with the Mother of God and the Beheading of John the Baptist, circa 1700, 31.8 x 27cm. $1,108

The Hodigitria Mother of God, inscribed 'through the hand of Nicholas Lamboudi of Sparta', 15th century, 67 x 47.5cm. $28,512

The Kazan Mother of God encased in a silver gilt oklad, maker's mark P.T., Moscow, 1899-1908, 31.2 x 26.8cm. $1,188

An icon of Christ Pantocrator, maker's mark E.U., Moscow, 1899-1908, 22.5 x 17.8cm. $712

An icon of Christ Pantocrator, maker's mark of F.V., Moscow 1830, 32 x 27cm. $1,980

Saint Sergei of Radonejh, maker's mark S.G., Moscow 1908-26, 31 x 27cm. $1,029

The Mother of God of the Burning Bush, bearing fake assay marks for Moscow, 1908-1917, 71 x 57cm. $5,702

The Virgin Hodigitria, Cretan, 1480-1520, 40.5 x 32.5cm. $7,268

Christ Pantocrator, encased in a silver gilt oklad, Moscow 1880, 32 x 27.5cm. $950

A 19th century icon, in the style of the early 17th century, of The Solovki Deisis, 31 x 26.2cm.
$1,821

The Resurrection of Christ From The Tomb, maker's mark P.A., Moscow, 1832, 31 x 26.5cm. $1,267

The Mother of God of Life-Giving Source, probably Constantinople, dated 1778, 52.8 x 39.3cm.
$1,663

A 19th century icon of The Kazan Mother of God, 31 x 26.4cm.      $760

Early 17th century icon of St. Onouphrios The Great, signed by E. Lambardos, 55.5 x 36.5cm.
$60,192

The Iverskaya Mother of God, maker's mark A.E., Moscow 1908-17, 31 x 26.5cm.      $950

The Kazan Mother of God, maker's mark of I. A. Alexceev, Moscow, 1908-17, 27.3 x 22.7cm.
$1,267

A 19th century icon of The Mother of God 'Helper of Those Who Are Lost', 53.5 x 45cm. $1,267

The Sainted Hierarchs of Rostov, James and Dimitre, late 18th century, 34.5 x 27.5cm.      $601

Saint Nicholas, probably Byzantine, early 15th century, shown bust length, 36.5 x 27.5cm.
$4,118

A four-part icon with the Kazan Mother of God, within a repousse and silver oklad, maker's mark I.A., Orel, 1865, 22 x 18.5cm.
$712

The Tikhvin Mother of God painted on a gold ground, maker's mark A.V., Moscow, 1790, 30.2 x 26cm.
$1,584

A 19th century Russian icon of St. Nicholas the Miracle Worker, maker's mark for N. Dubrovin over 1830, 12½ x 10¾in. (Robt. W. Skinner Inc.)
$300

The Anastasis painted in miniature on a gold ground, 19th century, 22.4 x 17.8cm.
$1,346

Christ Pantocrator, encased in a repousse and chased silver oklad, Moscow 1899-1908, maker's mark S.G., 31.5 x 27.2cm.  $918

The Mother of God of Life-Giving Source painted on gold ground, 1870, 36.2 x 30.4cm.  $1,821

An ivory plaque carved in low relief with twelve Festivals, early 16th century, 6.1 x 5.7cm.
$1,663

Saints Zosima and Savatii, the oklad with a silvered metal revetment, 18th century, 32 x 26.7cm.
$1,742

The Saviour depicted in an Italianate manner encased in a repousse and silver gilt oklad, maker's mark T.G., St. Petersburg, 1850, 31.5 x 26cm.     $823

An 18th century Greek triptych, gold ground, 12.5 x 15cm.     $1,029

Christ Pantocrator painted on a sand colored ground, the icon encased in a parcel gilt oklad, 31.5 x 27cm., Moscow 1880.  $712

Late 17th century icon of St. Nicholas, 31.2 x 26.6cm.     $792

Christ Pantocrator painted on a light-brown ground, maker's mark S.G., Moscow 1899-1908, 32 x 27.2cm.     $760

An icon of the 'Six Days' (Shestodnev), 19th century, 53 x 44cm.  $1,663

An icon painted in two registers, contained within a repousse and silver gilt oklad, late 18th century, 48.5 x 39.5cm.     $3,326

A 19th century brass bound triptych, the central panel with the Deisis, the side leaves with the Holy Trinity, 8.8 x 23.5cm.  $792

Christ enthroned upon an elaborate baroque throne, encased in a gilt metal oklad, 18th century, 21 x 15.5cm.     $792

An 18th century four-case roironuri inro, with a metal ojime and a tubular netsuke, 19th century. (Christie's) $447

A four-case inro decorated in gold and silver hiramakie, unsigned, with a brown agate ojime and large amber netsuke. (Christie's) $1,177

A 19th century three-case roironuri inro, signed Jokasai, with glass ojime and guri hako netsuke. (Christie's) $657

A three-case roironuri inro, signed Jokasai, with glass ojime and guri hako netsuke, 19th century. (Christie's) $657

Late 18th/early 19th century three-case gold fundame inro, with attached ivory bead ojime. (Christie's) $843

A 19th century five-case inro decorated with a jardiniere containing miniature trees. $343

A four-case kinji inro with pink glass melon-shaped ojime and shinchu kagami-buta netsuke. (Christie's) $2,743

A 19th century ivory three-case lacquered inro decorated in red and gold takamakie flakes. $687

A 19th century four-case inro with attached wood ojime and wood octagonal netsuke. (Christie's) $1,433

A 19th century four-case inro, probably Kajikawa School, with attached metal ojime. (Christie's) $1,413

Early 19th century four-case roironuri inro, Somada School. (Christie's) $478

A 19th century seven-case kuronuri inro with an attached ribbed glass bead ojime, signed Minkoku. (Christie's) $589

Late 19th century three-case inro, signed Koma Yasutada saku, with an attached agate ojime and a netsuke, 19th century. $1,530

Early 19th century three-case kuroronuri inro decorated in gold and silver hiramakie, takamakie and ivory, unsigned, with small coral bead ojime.(Christie's) $258

A 19th century four-case kinji inro, signed Shokasai. (Christie's) $530

A 19th century four-case inro, signed Eisai Nariaki Shotatsu, with an attached glass bead ojime.(Christie's) $647

Early 19th century four-case kinji inro, signed Shokosai. (Christie's) $776

A four-case kinji inro with attached gold fundame bead ojime and ivory netsuke. (Christie's) $717

# INSTRUMENTS

A walnut cased combined timepiece, barograph, aneroid barometer and thermometer, signed Chadburn & Son, 26¾ x 14in. (Lawrence Fine Art) $559

A marine chronometer in a brass mounted rosewood case, the lid with a separate glass panel, inscribed D. McGregor & Co. (Woolley & Wallis)   $843

A marine chronometer by J. R. Arnold No. 578, diam. of bezel 105mm. $3,828

An eight-day marine chronometer by Hatton & Harris No. 570, diam. of bezel 133mm.   $7,975

A 19th century terrestrial globe inscribed Phillips 30 inch Reference Globe. (Boardman) $1,337

A 3½in. brass refracting telescope on stand, length of tube 47in., signed Ross London.   $934

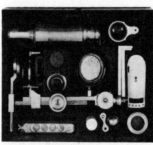

A Dollond ebony octant with ivory scale 0°–105°, English, circa 1840, 9½in. radius.   $510

A brass monocular microscope, the tube of the 'Jones Most Improved' type, circa 1800, size of case 21 x 17cm. (Lawrence Fine Art)   $958

A two-day marine chronometer by Morris Tobias No. 794, diam. of bezel 115mm. $1,914

A two-day marine chronometer by John Bruce No. 786, diam. of bezel 125mm. $2,552

A Victorian marine bronze sextant with an ebony grip brass sight with two optics. (Woolley & Wallis) $524

A 36-hour marine chronometer by Leroy No. 821, diam. of bezel 82mm. $925

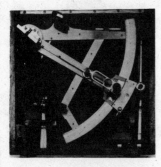

A Cary brass sextant with gold scale, numbered 3856, 11¾ x 11¼in. (Lawrence Fine Art) $1,929

Late Victorian brass transit theodolite by Troughton & Simms, London. (Reeds Rains) $496

A Henry Crouch brass binocular microscope, circa 1890, 1ft.4in. high, together with two eyepieces. $560

A small terrestrial globe by Nathaniel Hill. (Bearnes) $936

Late 18th century brass sextant, signed H. Ould, Dartmouth, 11½in. radius. $1,754

A two-day marine chronometer by James Poole No. 5818, diam. of bezel 125mm. $1,674

Pocket terrestrial globe, globe rotates freely in a hinged fish skin case, London, 1817, 3in. deep. (Robt. W. Skinner Inc.) $850

A Simpson part amputation set, in a fitted mahogany case. $835

A locomotive timepiece with 4in. diam. dial, English, circa 1925, 15in. high. $285

A mahogany Hadley's quadrant, English, circa 1750, 18in. radius. $2,073

Late 18th century sand clock, the two sand glasses mounted in a brass frame, 5½in. high. $638

A brass Culpeper-type monocular microscope on three scrolled legs, 10¼in. high, contained in its mahogany case. $642

Mid 19th century English ship's wheel with ten turned mahogany spokes, 68cm. diam. $1,116

Early 20th century Kelvin & White Ltd. ship's binnacle, 53in. high, together with a Brown Brother's ship's wheel, circa 1920. $1,515

Early 20th century brass sextant by H. G. Blair & Co., 6½in. radius, with two telescopes. $350

A Crichton oxidized brass 'Y'-type theodolite, 10in. high, in a mahogany case, with a tripod. $803

A 5½in. Cary star globe contained in mahogany case, English, circa 1870. 9in. wide.                    $638

An 18th century signed brass and wrought-iron wall spitjack, England, 11in. high. (Robt. W. Skinner Inc.)$800

Mid 19th century, English, Cary brass pillar sextant, No. 2544, 18½in. high. $2,552

Surveyor's cased brass compass, New York, circa 1840, 15in. long. (Robt. W. Skinner Inc.)        $325

An ebony octant by S. A. Cail, English, circa 1800-20, 9¾in. radius. $606

Mid 19th century English ebony octant by H. Hughes, 9½in. radius, in shaped mahogany case. $574

Early 20th century White Thompson & Co. ship's binnacle compass, 54in. high.        $797

Surveyor's brass transit with wooden case, silvered dial marked 'Blunt & Co., N.Y.', circa 1845, 12in. high. (Robt. W. Skinner Inc.) $450

A Hurlimann, Ponthus & Therrode brass aeronautical fleurais-type sextant, French, circa 1915, 6in. radius.    $1,196

A Spencer & Co. ebony sextant, English, circa 1800, 14in. radius. $1,754

A japanned and brass microscope with coarse and fine focusing, by W. Watson & Son Ltd., London. (Reeds Rains)    $193

A ship's sextant, complete with all fitments and in mahogany case, by George Lee & Son. (Butler & Hatch Waterman)    $483

A 2in. brass refracting telescope, the 27½in. brass tube with rack and pinion focusing, in its wooden case.    $433

An English 20th century, 7in., G. Phillip & Son star globe in mahogany case.    $574

A William IV terrestrial globe by C. Smith & Son, 172 Strand, 2ft.11½in. high.    $2,534

Early 19th century mahogany cased quadrant, ebony with inset ivory scale, London, 13½in. long. (Robt. W. Skinner Inc.)    $450

A James Ayscough mahogany Hadley's quadrant, English, circa 1760, 17½in. radius.    $3,190

Brass reflecting telescope, marked Fran. Watkins, Charing Cross, London, circa 1780, 28in. long. (Robt. W. Skinner Inc.) $1,300

A brass spectroscope with two prisms, telescope and collimeter, signed John Browning, London, 12½in. (Lawrence Fine Art) $223

A C. Gould improved pocket compound microscope, made by W. Cary, in its fitted mahogany case. $465

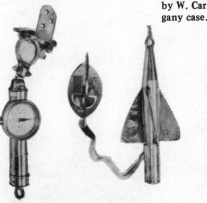

A half-hour sandglass, the two glass bulbs joined by wax and silk thread binding, English, circa 1800, 7¼in. high. $829

Early 20th century Thos. Walker 'Harpoon' depth finder, English, 6½in. long. $239

An 18in. Malby's celestial globe on stand, 45in. high. $1,477

A. T. Cooke & Sons brass transit theodolite, 15½in. high. $468

Late 19th century coromandel and brass inlaid marine chronometer. (Reeds Rains) $1,100

Continental mid 19th century ebony octant, No. 2003, inscribed C. Johansson, 10in. radius. $717

# INSTRUMENTS

Victorian treadle sewing machine with cast iron stand, 1880. (British Antique Exporters) $61

Early 18th century boxwood nocturnal, the shaped and pierced handle stamped 'Both Bears', 8½in. long. $1,771

A Watson & Sons high power binocular microscope numbered 79995. (Lawrence Fine Art) $226

Rosewood stereo viewer, table top, manufactured by Alex. Becker, N.Y., circa 1859. (Robt. W. Skinner Inc.) $400

A 1lb brass and bell metal beam scale, maker De Grave Short & Co. Ltd., in a 15in. case/stand. (Anderson & Garland) $130

Mid 19th century S. Maw, Son & Thompson enema or stomach pump apparatus, English, 12½ x 7½in. $202

Portable combination graphoscope, 5½ x 9in. base, for viewing stereo cards and cabinet cards, circa 1890. (Robt. W. Skinner Inc.) $80

Penny operated British Fillalita fuel dispenser in the form of a 1930's Shell petrol pump, 20in. high. (Reeds Rains) $174

A mutoscope in cast iron octagonal shaped case, electrically lit, 22in. high. $822

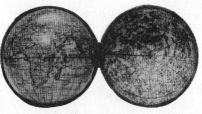

A London Stereoscopic Co. 'Jewel' kaleidoscope, English, circa 1860, tube 12in. long.        $569

A 2¾in. pocket terrestrial globe, English, circa 1770, 3¼in. diam.    $822

A Dollond brass telescope solar eyepiece, English, circa 1860, Dawes patent, 8in. long.        $379

A cased set of Jacobus Listingh coin weights, Dutch, dated 1659, 3½ x 6¼in., in leather slip case.
$3,542

Late 19th century English Oertling brass precision balance, 23in. wide.
$480

A Kelvin & Hughes Ltd. ship's binnacle compass, English, circa 1940, 53in. high.        $860

A Hammond No. 1 typewriter, American, with piano type ebony keys, circa 1884.
$695

A mahogany zograscope, English, circa 1800, 25in. high.        $354

Rowsell's parlor graphoscope, folding table model, base 23 x 12in., circa 1875. (Robt. W. Skinner Inc.)
$200

One of a matching set of six Regency campana-shaped cast-iron garden urns, 16in. diam. (Boardman) $1,605

A pair of 17th century iron rushlight holders. (Cooper Hirst) $273

A Victorian cast-iron umbrella and stick stand in the form of the young Hercules. (P. Wilson & Co.) $390

A James I iron fireback. (Russell Baldwin & Bright) $500

One of a pair of cast-iron andirons with tapering fluted capitals, 1576, 24in. high. $263

Late 19th century cast-iron architectural panel, the cast mask of 'King Neptune', 23 x 23in. (Robt. W. Skinner Inc.) $300

An 18th century wrought-iron door knocker, 10½in. high. $558

A National currant cleaner by Parnall, Bristol. (Coles, Knapp & Kennedy) $36

A 19th century Indo-Persian leather covered shield dahl, 18¼in. diam. (Geering & Colyer) $27

A cast-iron group of a boar being attacked by dogs, base signed P. J. Mene and dated 1846, 10¼in. high. $343

Late 18th century wrought iron broiler, probably Pennsylvania, 20in. long. (Robt. W. Skinner Inc.) $360

Two late 18th century cast iron cooking pots, one 6½in. diam., the other 11in. diam. (Robt. W. Skinner Inc.) $250

One of a pair of Japanese iron cylindrical vases, signed Saikyo Inoue zo, 6½in. high. (Christie's) $1,235

Cast-iron fireback with cherubs and fruit. (Barber's Fine Art) $248

One of a pair of cast metal campana-shaped garden urns on fluted circular pedestal bases, 24¼in. high. (Neales) $455

One of a pair of steel andirons in the form of standing foxes. (Anderson & Garland) $984

Pair of cast-iron firedog female figure heads, inscribed 1625, together with basket. (Barber's Fine Art) $248

A cast-iron garden ornament of Cupid on a circular base, 39in. high. (Lawrence Fine Art) $708

Late 17th/18th century South German steel lock and key, 6½ x 3.5/8in. $2,128

Late 19th century cast iron fountain, stamped 'Robert Wood & Co. Makers Phila.', 40in. high. (Robt. W. Skinner Inc.) $2,300

An early coffee grinder by Parnall. (Coles, Knapp & Kennedy) $63

One of a pair of Victorian cast iron campana-shaped garden urns. (Strides) $900

A Victorian cast iron spiral staircase, by Hayward Bros., London, circa 1880, 141in. high, 25in. radius. (Neales) $507

Victorian cast iron fire surround in Art Nouveau style, circa 1885. (British Antique Exporters) $227

An 18th/19th century shield, circular with domed center, 20½in. diam. $534

One of a pair of cast iron garden urns of campana form, circa 1830, 2ft. high. $2,710

Late 18th century cast iron bake kettle, original fitted cover with deep flange, 13¼in. deep. (Robt. W. Skinner Inc.) $325

# IVORY

An ivory carving of an old man raking up leaves, signed Mitsuka, late Meiji period, 22cm. high. (Christie's) $740

A Preiss carved ivory nude figure, 1930's, 21cm. high. $1,560

An ivory tusk vase and flat cover with seated elephant finial, signed Onizawa, Meiji period, 69.4cm. high overall. (Christie's) $1,261

A stained ivory carving of a Sumo wrestler, signed Ryusui, Meiji/Teisho period, 22cm. high. (Christie's) $717

A carved ivory okimono of a farmer leaning on a bamboo pole, signed Ittei, Meiji period, 16cm. high. (Christie's) $1,672

An ivory figure of a noble fisherman 5¼in. high. (Lawrence Fine Art) $302

An ivory okimono of a monkey with a toad and its young on his back, 2¼in. high. (Lawrence Fine Art) $331

An okimono of a monkey and toad, 2¾in. wide. (Lawrence Fine Art) $171

Late 19th century ivory carving of a Chinese scholar, 18.4cm. high. (Christie's) $315

# IVORY

An ivory okimono of
Hotei, signed Munetak,
Meiji period, 14.7cm. wide.
(Christie's) $709

A sectional wood and ivory
carving of a ferryboat of
travellers, Meiji period,
46.5cm. long. (Christie's)
$1,340

Late 19th century ivory
carving of a scholar, signed
Toyokazu, 17.6cm. wide.
(Christie's) $1,024

Late 19th century carved
ivory and wood okimono
of an old man, signed
Hoshin, 12.2cm. high.
(Christie's) $595

Late 19th century carved
ivory okimono of a kneeling
hunter aiming a matchlock
rifle, 10.6cm. high. (Christie's)     $630

Late 19th century ivory
carving of a Rakan holding
a ju-i sceptre, signed Mitsu-
hide. (Christie's) $394

A carved ivory okimono of
a kneeling hunter, signed
Yoshimitsu, Tokyo School,
late Meiji period, 17.4cm.
high. (Christie's)
$1,497

Late 19th century ivory
carving of a fisherman,
signature tablet missing,
33cm. high. (Christie's)
$1,734

Late 19th century ivory
carving of a standing caparisonned elephant, 23.2cm.
high. (Christie's)
$1,892

# IVORY

Late 19th century carved sectional ivory okimono of of two farmers, signed Ippitsusai, 13.7cm. wide. (Christie's) $867

Late 19th century sectional ivory carving of two fishermen in a boat, 23.3cm. long. (Christie's) $709

An ivory okimono of a group of players, all wearing floral engraved robes, 1¾in. wide. (Lawrence Fine Art) $201

Late 19th century ivory okimono of a seated man reeling back as a serpent emerges from a basket, signed Shoraku, 12.8cm. high. (Christie's) $709

Late 19th/early 20th century ivory Samurai, Japan, 5¼in. high. (Robt. W. Skinner Inc.) $125

An ivory okimono of the Seven Gods of Good Fortune in a boat, 2½in. wide. (Lawrence Fine Art) $360

A Japanese ivory model of a boat with an exotic bird's head figurehead, 17in. wide. (Christie's) $1,250

An ivory carving of a fisherman holding a boy in his left arm, another boy standing at his side, signed Kozan to, Meiji period, 35.2cm. high. (Christie's) $2,049

A 19th century Japanese ivory okimono of frogs, toads and turtles under attack from a snake, 3in. (Woolley & Wallis) $100

# IVORY

A carved ivory tray of finger citron form with shallow rounded sides, 8in. long, Qianlong.          $743

An ivory panel, 14½in. long, Guangxu, wood stand.          $711

An ivory filigree casket of shaped rectangular form, 10¼in., Guangxu.          $1,164

A 19th century ivory figure of a maiden standing holding a sceptre with a bat terminal, 11.7/8in. high.          $1,164

Pair of ivory figures on shaped wood and ivory bases, circa 1800, 9¼in. high, Dieppe.          $3,190

An ivory figure of a maiden, 10in. high, mark of Qianlong, Guangxu, wood stand.          $840

A 17th century ivory figure of the infant Buddha, 5¼in. high.     $905

A 18th century inlaid ivory brushpot, 5in. high.          $905

A 17th century carved ivory figure of Buddha, seated cross-legged, on wood stand, 4¾in. high.          $970

An ivory brushpot of shaped oval section, the exterior carved in high relief, 6.7/8in. high, with fixed wood stand. $743

A 16th century English knife with ivory handle and single edged blade, 6.5/8in. long. $287

Carved ivory okimono of a laughing Chinese boy, Japan, circa 1900, 6in. high. (Robt. W. Skinner Inc.) $275

An 18th century Dieppe ivory figure of Perseus, 6¾in. high. $1,276

A 19th century ivory table screen, 10¾ x 9¾in. $711

A well carved ivory figure of a Dignitary, 9in. high, Ming Dynasty, wood stand. $905

Early 18th century oval ivory portrait medallion, by Jean Mancel, 3.7/8in. $893

An 18th century ivory brushpot of irregular section, 6in. high, with wood stand. $3,072

Late 17th/early 18th century ivory portrait roundel, attributed to Jean Cavalier, 3¼in. diam. $797

An ivory carving of a girl holding a sickle and carrying a basket of flowers, signed Mitsutoshi, Meiji period, 19.4cm. high. (Christie's) $473

An 18th/19th century ivory cane handle, 3.5/8in. $207

A 19th century French carved ivory figure of a girl, 39cm. high. (H. Spencer & Sons) $734

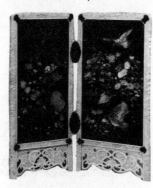

A Japanese one-piece carved ivory figure of a man, 23cm. high. (H. Spencer & Sons) $170

Late 19th century ivory mounted two-leaf table screen, 22.8 x 12.5cm. (Christie's) $1,901

One of a pair of late 19th century ivory tusk vases inlaid in Shibayama style, signed Masahisa and Masayoshi, 29.2cm. high. (Christie's) $1,433

An ivory figure of Venus signed Richard Garbe 1955, 46cm. high. (Christie's) $2,041

A Japanese carved ivory figure group, signed on inset red lacquer panel, 19.5cm. high. (H. Spencer & Sons) $361

A large ivory carving of a fisherman, signed Shuzan, Meiji period, 32.3cm. high. (Christie's) $1,497

# IVORY

Late 19th century ivory tusk vase and flat cover, inlaid in Shibayama style, signed Masayasu, 31cm. high.(Christie's) $1,553

An ivory carving of an elephant, a large lotus flower on its back, inlaid in Shibayama style, signed Kansai Kazuyuki, Meiji period, 14.8cm. long. (Christie's) $1,433

A Japanese one-piece carved ivory figure of a standing man with his arm raised to support a cockerel, 32cm. high. (H. Spencer & Sons) $519

A Japanese one-piece carved ivory figure of a fisherman wearing breeches, a short kimono and grass apron, 28.5cm. high. (H. Spencer & Sons) $1,356

A Dieppe carved bone wall mirror, 84cm. high. (H. Spencer & Sons) $496

An ivory figure of a woman wearing traditional costume, signed, 8in. high. (Lawrence Fine Art) $216

A Chinese ivory tusk vase intricately carved with many figures, buildings and trees, 18.5cm. high, with hardwood stand. (H. Spencer & Sons) $683

An ivory bas relief attributed to Richard Garbe, of a cupid bending a vine for a goose, circa 1930, 19.5cm. high. (Christie's) $706

A Richard Garbe carved ivory relief of a young woman on a wooden base, inscribed 1946, 28cm. high. (Christie's) $3,538

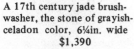

A 17th century jade brush-washer, the stone of grayish-celadon color, 6¼in. wide
$1,390

A mottled grayish jade square seal carved in the archaic taste, probably Qing Dynasty, 9.5cm. square.
(Christie's)     $926

A white jade figure of a pony, details of mane and hair incised, 4½in. long.
$646

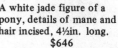

A Qianlong jade vase of pale celadon color, signed with six-character mark, 6¾in. high. (Robt. W. Skin-ner Inc.)     $600

A flecked spinach green jade rectangular box and cover with dragon head loose ring handles, Qing Dynasty, 23cm. wide, with wood stand.
(Christie's)
$2,566

A 19th century small spin-ach jade vase of shouldered form, 3¾in. high, seal mark of Qianlong.     $711

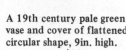

A 19th century pale green vase and cover of flattened circular shape, 9in. high.
$808

Late 18th century celadon jade group formed as a hollowed section of bam-boo beside a gu-shaped quatrefoil vase, 16cm. high, with wood stand.
(Christie's)  $855

Dark green spinach jade covered urn of bronze form, on giltwood base.
(Stalker & Boos)
$1,200

# JADE

A small celadon jade teapot, China, possibly 18th century, 4in. high. (Robt. W. Skinner Inc.) $400

An 18th century spinach green two-handled bowl, 26cm. wide, with fitted box. (Christie's) $5,987

A gray and green jade carving of a striding dragon, Six Dynasties or later, 11cm. long. (Christie's) $2,280

Chinese green celadon bowl, possibly Yuan, 12.5/16in. diam. (Robt. W. Skinner Inc.) $1,100

One of a pair of jadeite carvings, each of two crested water-birds, 4½in. high. $840

A 17th century jade flask carved in the form of a hollowed gourd, 5.1/8in. high. $1,099

A 19th century green jade carving of a finger-citron, 6.7/8in. high. $840

A brown and pale celadon jade leys jar, zhadou, Ming Dynasty, 13.1cm. diam. (Christie's) $3,421

An 18th century pale celadon jade rectangular table screen carved with the eight Daoist Immortals, 29 x 19cm., with wood stand. (Christie's) $6,130

A diamond and aquamarine brooch, by J. E. Caldwell & Co., circa 1915. (Robt. W. Skinner Inc.) $2,100

A Victorian gold and turquoise bracelet in the form of a strap, in original case from J. Mayer, Lord St., London, with letter of presentation dated 1858. (Lawrence Fine Art) $1,512

An opal and diamond pin set in platinum and gold. (Robt. W. Skinner Inc.) $400

Garnet necklace and brooch, the brooch in the form of two feathers. (Robt. W. Skinner Inc.) $350

A cameo pendant and pair of earrings en suite, in original fitted case from Hall & Co., Manchester. (Lawrence Fine Art) $2,062

A diamond bow brooch with large center diamond with six radiating baguettes, 2½in. wide. (Capes, Dunn & Co.) $4,567

An 18kt. yellow gold bracelet, composed of large oval links, 71.5gr., French hallmarks. (Robt. W. Skinner Inc.) $1,350

An amethyst, diamond and seed pearl brooch. (Robt. W. Skinner Inc.) $525

An 18kt. yellow gold necklace, by Manfredi, Italy, clasp set with 3 sapphires, an emerald and 2 rubies, 67.2gr., 17in. long. (Robt. W. Skinner Inc.) $1,750

Large shell cameo brooch, depicting an Egyptian court scene in a 14kt. yellow gold frame. (Robt. W. Skinner Inc.) $425

A gold, enamel and diamond bracelet, circa 1855. (Robt. W. Skinner Inc.) $1,600

An Art Deco sapphire, diamond and garnet ring in a platinum mount. (Robt. W. Skinner Inc.) $1,000

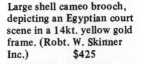

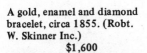

An 18kt. gold and steel necklace, "Bonds" interlocking oval links of gold and steel, 15½in. long. (Robt. W. Skinner Inc.) $575

A Victorian suite of pearl, diamond and enamel jewellery, in original fitted leather case. (Robt. W. Skinner Inc.) $2,000

Diamond horseshoe brooch, set with 25 diamonds weighing a total of approx. 1.7kt. (Robt. W. Skinner Inc.) $850

A portrait brooch, miniature portrait of a woman within a gold, pearl and enamel frame. (Robt. W. Skinner Inc.) $100

An Art Nouveau sterling silver and plique-a-jour brooch/pendant, French hallmark. (Robt. W. Skinner Inc.) $475

A hardstone cameo and pearl pin/pendant. (Robt. W. Skinner Inc.) $300

# JEWELRY

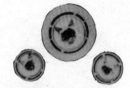

A pair of rubillite and diamond earclips, by Bulgari, Italy, cabochon stones weighing approx. 5.50kt., pave-set with 24 diamonds. (Robt. W. Skinner Inc.) $1,500

A silver and gold portrait ring, two ivory miniatures of gentlemen in a flipover mount encircled by rose-cut diamonds. (Robt. W. Skinner Inc.)$1,600

A 14kt. gold and crystal pin and earrings, each centered by a yellow cat. (Robt. W. Skinner Inc.) $225

Gold, emerald and pearl bracelet, India, hinged, 44gr. (Robt. W. Skinner Inc.) $275

Diamond solitaire, center old mine diamond weighing approx. 1.85kt. in a yellow gold mount. (Robt. W. Skinner Inc.) $850

A Victorian gold bracelet, flexible gold band completed by a buckle clasp and tassel, 24gr. (Robt. W. Skinner Inc.) $500

Etruscan Revival antique gold and coral necklace and pendant. (Robt. W. Skinner Inc.) $1,000

Group of Victorian jewellery consisting of onyx hoops, onyx button screwback earrings and a black enamel brooch with matching earrings. (Robt. W. Skinner Inc.) $375

An 18kt. gold brooch, as a cat with ruby eyes, a diamond collar and a pearl resting at its feet, 17.8gr. (Robt. W. Skinner Inc.)$250

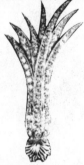

A diamond brooch in the form of a leek, naturalistically formed. (Lawrence Fine Art) $590

Pair of gold, diamond and enamel rings, as lions heads. (Robt. W. Skinner Inc.) $700

An Art Deco diamond and pearl tassel complete with a platinum chain. (Robt. W. Skinner Inc.)$2,600

478

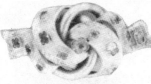

Gold earrings, circa 1870, Etruscan Revival mounts supporting a 19mm. gold pendant ball. (Robt. W. Skinner Inc.)$475

An antique gold and emerald pin, stylized knot surmounted by thirteen emeralds. (Robt. W. Skinner Inc.)       $250

A pair of large gold hoop earrings with wire twist decoration, circa 1870. (Robt. W. Skinner Inc.)
$225

Gold, emerald, ruby and pearl bracelet, Indian, 48gr. (Robt. W. Skinner Inc.)
$425

An openwork gold hinged bangle with eleven graduated diamonds. (Reeds Rains)       $1,391

Gold coin bracelet, consisting of six Indianhead five dollar gold coins in gold bezels. (Robt. W. Skinner Inc.)       $1,200

An antique diamond bow brooch, set with approx. 113 diamonds, weight approx. 3kt. (Robt. W. Skinner Inc.) $1,350

An 18kt. gold, enamel and diamond ring and earclips, total weight approx. 2.85kt. (Robt. W. Skinner Inc.) $1,700

A shell pattern agate pendant the gold ribbon pattern mount set with 17 diamonds. (Reeds Rains) $1,065

An Art Deco silver and enamel pendant, Germany. (Robt. W. Skinner Inc.) $275

Pair of gold coin earrings, five dollar U.S. gold coins, one dated 1898, the other 1900, in gold bezels. (Robt. W. Skinner Inc.)$400

An 18kt. gold and diamond pin, as a cat with black enamel jacket, 20gr. (Robt. W. Skinner Inc.) $375

Yellow sapphire and diamond ring, the sapphire approx. 14.82kt., the two diamonds .35kt. (Robt. W. Skinner Inc.) $850

An opal butterfly with wings and tail highlighted by diamonds, in a yellow and white gold mounting. (Robt. W. Skinner Inc.) $325

A black opal and diamond ring, in a platinum mount. (Robt. W. Skinner Inc.) $500

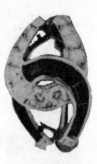

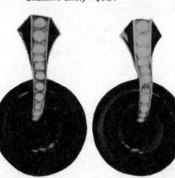

A platinum, diamond and ruby ring, interlocking horseshoe. (Robt. W. Skinner Inc.) $1,000

Victorian onyx and pearl earrings highlighted by black enamel. (Robt. W. Skinner Inc.) $525

An antique gold and seed pearl locket, circa 1860, by Carlo Guilliano. (Robt. W. Skinner Inc.)$1,700

A 14kt. gold and crystal pin, gold horseshoe centering a reverse crystal of a horse. (Robt. W. Skinner Inc.) $150

A hardstone stone cameo with green background, the frame highlighted by black onyx bands. (Robt. W. Skinner Inc.) $525

Shell cameo pendant, profile of an angel in a 14kt. yellow gold frame. (Robt. W. Skinner Inc.) $200

An antique ring set with emeralds and rose-cut diamonds in the form of a clover. (Robt. W. Skinner Inc.) $300

Gold and diamond clip and bracelet, by Cartier, approx. total weight 1.70kt. (Robt. W. Skinner Inc.)$700

Sapphire and diamond ring, the cushion-cut sapphire 9kt., encircled by 14 round diamonds. (Robt. W. Skinner Inc.) $9,000

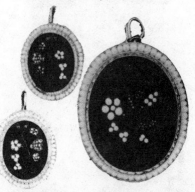

An oval locket of granulation and wire twist decoration centering a reverse crystal depicting a cat. (Robt. W. Skinner Inc.) $950

A suite of enamel and pearl jewelry, circa 1870, consisting of a brooch and earrings. (Robt. W. Skinner Inc.) $900

An 18kt. gold, ruby, emerald and diamond ring, by D. Webb, diamonds weighing approx. .40kt. (Robt. W. Skinner Ine.) $1,400

A diamond flower spray brooch . (Lawrence Fine Art) $806

A 14kt. gold and crystal pin/pendant, reverse painted crystal of two cats in a gold frame. (Robt. W. Skinner Inc.) $250

Diamond bow brooch, silver top gold pin set with diamonds, weight approx. 7kt. (Robt. W. Skinner Inc.) $2,800

# JEWELRY

A Victorian bracelet, mesh strap with foxtail link slide and tassel highlighted in pearls and black enamel. (Robt. W. Skinner Inc.) $550

A diamond and quartz bar brooch, by Tiffany & Co., diamonds weighing approx. 1.50kt. (Robt. W. Skinner Inc.)     $1,700

A ring, the centre diamond weighing approx. .85kt., flanked by sapphire and ruby, each weighing approx. .50kt. (Robt. W. Skinner Inc.)     $400

A natural pearl necklace, by Tiffany & Co., consisting of 80 pearls with a diamond clasp, .50kt., length 20in. (Robt. W. Skinner Inc.) $1,500

An emerald clover brooch, Tiffany & Co., set with twenty-five square-cut emeralds, weight approx. 8.50 karats. (Robt. W. Skinner Inc.)     $5,900

Sapphire and diamond bracelet, 18kt. yellow gold mount set with 35 oval sapphires weighing approx. 7kt., the pairs of diamonds weighing approx. .35kt. (Robt. W. Skinner Inc.)$1,050

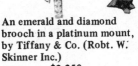

An emerald and diamond brooch in a platinum mount, by Tiffany & Co. (Robt. W. Skinner Inc.) $2,250

Nine 14kt. gold charms, as an orchestra of cats, 122.3gr. (Robt. W. Skinner Inc.)     $900

A Victorian gold locket, shaped cartouche centering an oval disc highlighted by pearls. (Robt. W. Skinner Inc.)     $475

A Victorian bar pin, the gold bar decorated with Etruscan beadwork. (Robt. W. Skinner Inc.) $275

A Lalique gold, diamond, opal and enamel choker buckle, circa 1900, 7.5cm. wide. $22,704

A jade and diamond pin, the oval jade plaque in a platinum and enamel frame highlighted by tiny diamonds. (Robt. W. Skinner Inc.)     $1,000

Victorian gold bar pin, decorated with gold filigree and bead decoration, highlighted by a center diamond and seed pearls. (Robt. W. Skinner Inc.)    $225

A Victorian gold mesh bracelet, as a buckle with pearl highlights and fringe. (Robt. W. Skinner Inc.) $275

Victorian gold pin, rectangular bar with applied bicolor gold bird. (Robt. W. Skinner Inc.)    $200

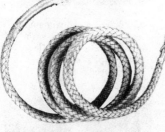

A gentleman's 14kt. gold and jade ring, the gold mount of Greek key design. (Robt. W. Skinner Inc.) $375

An antique gold snake bracelet, a woven mesh band terminating in a coiled tail. (Robt. W. Skinner Inc.) $650

An antique gold pin, a swallow with pave pearl body and jewelled eye. (Robt. W. Skinner Inc.)    $175

A Danish Art Nouveau hammered silver brooch set with lapis lazuli, Continental silver marks, circa 1910, 12cm. long. (Christie's) $190

18kt. gold suite of tiger claw jewellery, circa 1875, claws set in filigree mounts with center tiger as a pin. (Robt. W. Skinner Inc.) $475

An antique gold and amethyst pendant, the center stone set into an Etruscan-style frame. (Robt. W. Skinner Inc.) $475

An amethyst and diamond bangle on an heavy gold triple band. (Lawrence Fine Art)  $1,100

A Guild of Handicrafts Ltd. silver enamel and amethyst buckle/cloak clasp, designed by C. R. Ashbee, circa 1902, 13.75cm. wide.     $9,223

An Art Deco diamond, onyx and chrysophase pin. (Robt. W. Skinner Inc.) $290

A Japanese black and gilt tea dust lacquer box, cover and liner of lobed oval form, 10.3cm. wide. (H. Spencer & Sons) $881

A shibayama and cinnabar lacquer table cabinet with brass trefoil loop handle to the top, 27cm. wide. (H. Spencer & Sons) $271

An 18th/early 19th century red lacquer square box and cover with canted corners, 32cm. square. (Christie's) $855

Early 19th century nashiji tebako decorated in gold hiramakie with kiri mon, 14.3x 12cm. (Christie's) $1,010

Late 19th century pair of large gold lacquer cylindrical vases, 36.5cm. high. (Christie's) $8,316

Japanese lacquer writing box of square form with all over gilt decoration, 9in. square. (Stalker & Boos)$475

A 19th century kinji kodansu with hinged outer door, 11.7 x 10.4 x 8.8cm. (Christie's) $2,020

Japanese lacquer on tortoiseshell plate of circular petal form, 11in. diam. (Stalker & Boos) $325

Late 19th century two-tiered jubako decorated in gold, silver and brown hiramakie and okibirame, 14 x 13 x 11.8cm. (Christie's) $1,307

An 18th century red, yellow and green lacquer circular box and domed cover, 29cm. diam. (Christie's) $1,568

A 19th century Japanese red lacquer and shibayama jardiniere and stand, 22.5cm. high. (H. Spencer & Sons)     $316

A 19th century mokkogata kobako, 9cm. wide. (Christie's)   $1,544

A 19th century four-tiered red lacquer jubako of gourd shape, 34.6cm. high. (Christie's)     $416

Late 19th century gold and silver lacquer shaped rectangular two-leaf table screen, each leaf 49 x 24.3cm. (Christie's) $8,910

A 19th century roironuri circular hokai box and cover, 56cm. high. (Christie's)$4,990

Early 19th century suzuri-bako with canted corners, 24.5 x 15.2cm. (Christie's) $2,138

One of a pair of Chinese cinnabar lacquer vases of baluster form, 23.5cm. high. (H. Spencer & Sons) $129

A 19th century roironuri tebako, signed Setsuyu, 22.5 x 21cm. (Christie's) $1,782

Late 19th century rose mother-of-pearl satin glass fairy lamp, with Clarke's glass candle cup, 5in. high. (Robt. W. Skinner Inc.) $150

Late 19th century jewelled cast brass fairy lamp with clear glass 'wee-fairy' candle cup, 4in. high. (Robt. W. Skinner Inc.) $100

Late 19th century Webb decorated Burmese lamp with ruffled base, England, liner signed S. Clarke's Fairy, 5½in. high. (Robt. W. Skinner Inc.) $400

A slag glass and gilt metal table lamp, America, circa 1910, 23½in. high, shade 17¾in. diam. (Robt. W. Skinner Inc.) $175

Late 19th century peach-blow fairy lamp on three-legged brass stand, possibly Mt. Washington, 8½in. high. (Robt. W. Skinner Inc.) $350

Slag glass and patinated metal table lamp, stamped Sale M Bros., 16½in. high. (Robt. W. Skinner Inc.) $175

Late 19th century blue swirled, ruffled satin glass lamp with matching base, 7½in. high. (Robt. W. Skinner Inc.) $110

Late 19th century cranberry blown-molded two-faced owl pyramid, 4¼in. high. (Robt. W. Skinner Inc.) $60

Late 19th century pink enamelled satin glass lamp with matching base, 7½in. high. (Robt. W. Skinner Inc.) $160

# LAMPS

Late 19th century swirled pink and white satin glass lamp, England, 5½in. high. (Robt. W. Skinner Inc.) $275

Late 19th century KPM painted bisque three-faced nursery lamp, Germany, 4in. high. (Robt. W. Skinner Inc.) $100

Late 19th century pale pink Parian rose light with clear pressed glass cup, 3¾in. high. (Robt. W. Skinner Inc.) $160

Lead Favrile glass and bronze table lamp, by Tiffany Studios, circa 1910, 25¼in. high. (Robt. W. Skinner Inc.)$5,300

One of a pair of late 19th century mirrored red velvet wall sconces with clear diamond point lights, 16in. high. (Robt. W. Skinner Inc.) $225

Reverse painted and gilt metal table lamp, by Bradley & Hubbard, circa 1910, 23¼in. high. (Robt. W. Skinner Inc.) $300

One of a pair of late 19th century pint blown molded satin glass lamps, France, 8¾in. high. (Robt. W. Skinner Inc.) $90

Late 19th century baccarat pressed glass amberina fairy lamp, France, with cut-out air vents, 4½in. high. (Robt. W. Skinner Inc.) $130

Iorio dogwood paperweight lamp on opalescent ground, 1981, 5in. high. (Robt. W. Skinner Inc.) $50

Late 19th century pink milk glass lighthouse, France, 7in. high. (Robt. W. Skinner Inc.) $100

Late 19th century decorated Burmese centerpiece with four nosegay vases, England, 4½in. high. (Robt. W. Skinner Inc.)$700

Late 19th century lemon yellow camphor striped satin glass fairy lamp on metal stand, 11.1/8in. high. (Robt. W. Skinner Inc.) $150

Early 20th century pairpoint puffy boudoir lamp, Mass., 8in. high. (Robt. W. Skinner Inc.) $700

Late 19th century Burmese glass epergne on mirrored plateau, 16in. high. (Robt. W. Skinner Inc.) $800

Late 19th century blue and white camphor splashed lamp with matching base, glass liner signed Clarke, 7in. high. (Robt. W. Skinner Inc.) $90

Late 19th century Webb Burmese lamp with velvet mirrored stand, 7.3/8in. high. (Robt. W. Skinner Inc.) $200

Late 19th century Meissen lithophane and porcelain fairy lamp, Germany, 6in. high. (Robt. W. Skinner Inc.) $500

Late 19th century pink and white end-of-the-day lamp with matching pedestal base, 10.3/8in. high. (Robt. W. Skinner Inc.) $150

A 20th century Austrian bronze figural electric lamp, in the form of a pavilion, 10in. high. (Robt. W. Skinner Inc.)     $650

Late 19th century four light rose verre moire (Nailsea) epergne with mirrored plateau, 10in. high. (Robt. W. Skinner Inc.) $325

Late 19th century Webb & Sons Fairy lamp, the plain shade and clear liner fitting into a decorated ruffle, 10in. high. (Robt. W. Skinner Inc.)     $600

Late 19th century Steven & Williams cased satin glass fairy lamp with matching base, England, 6in. high. (Robt. W. Skinner Inc.) $340

One of a pair of late 19th century Cricklite brass and glass table lamps, 16in. high. (Robt. W. Skinner Inc.) $350

A painted Parian castle of round turreted form, with Clarke's porcelain candle plate, 5¾in. high, Germany. (Robt. W. Skinner Inc.) $300

Late 19th century formal diningroom Cricklite centerpiece, England, 29¾in. high. (Robt. W. Skinner Inc.) $600

Late 19th century Burmese shade on Doulton Burslem base, base signed S. Clarke's Fairy patent trademark, 5¼in. high. (Robt. W. Skinner Inc.) $250

An Art Deco figure table lamp in green patinated metal, signed Limousin, 16½in. high. (Capes, Dunn & Co.)$207

Late 19th century yellow mother-of-pearl satin glass lamp with bulbous base, 8in. high. (Robt. W. Skinner Inc.) $225

Late 19th century Webb peachblow fairy lamp in matching base, England, the base having a ruffled and fluted rim, 5½in. high. (Robt. W. Skinner Inc.) $550

Late 19th century Pairpoint reverse painted table lamp, Mass., base and shade signed, 21in. high. (Robt. W. Skinner Inc.) $300

One of a pair of mid 19th century gilt metal mounted French porcelain lamp columns, 57cm. high. $1,080

A pair of 19th century French porcelain and gilt metal decorative oil lamps, 30in. high, overall. (Geering & Colyer) $992

A 19th century papier-mache figure of St. Nicholas, with functioning lantern, 27in. high. (Theriault's) $1,050

A Grueby pottery lamp with Bigelow & Kennard leaded shade, circa 1905, 17¾in. diam. (Robt. W. Skinner Inc.) $2,500

A Victorian brass oil standard lamp converted to electricity. (Morphets) $237

A Tiffany apple blossom table lamp with pierced base. (Wm. Doyle Galleries Inc.) $22,000

One of a pair of gilt-metal hall lanterns of square shape, 1ft.11½in. high, circa 1880. $781

A Mary Gregory stoneware oil lamp. (R. K. Lucas & Son)     $145

Late 19th century pink mother-of-pearl satin glass lamp with matching base and clear glass candle cups, 6in. high. (Robt. W. Skinner Inc.)     $80

A Loetz glass and gilt metal table lamp. (Christie's) $5,040

Late 19th century formal diningroom Cricklite centerpiece, England, 21in. diam. (Robt. W. Skinner Inc.) $425

Late 19th century Clarke's pyramid nursery lamp/food warmer, England, 10½in. high. (Robt. W. Skinner Inc.) $180

Late 19th century bisque-fired Christmas tree fairy lamp and clear Cricklite base, Austria and England, 5.1/8in. high. (Robt. W. Skinner Inc.) $150

One of a pair of gilt metal electric table lamps. (Fox & Sons)     $396

A Roycroft copper lamp with Steuben gold iridescent glass shade, circa 1910, 16in. high. (Robt. W. Skinner Inc.) $1,400

# LEAD

Late 17th century oval lead
jardiniere decorated with
typical strapwork and dated
'1689', 2ft.high. (Crowther,
Syon Lodge Ltd.)
$5,250

A 19th century American
lead George Washington figure, 58in. high. (Robt. W.
Skinner Inc.)
$1,500

A pair of lead jardinieres on
lion paw feet, decorated with
figures representing 'The
Four Seasons', dated 1769,
1ft.7in. high. (Crowther,
Syon Lodge Ltd.)
$2,250

Pair of late 19th century
cold-painted lead figures of
Beefeaters, signed Limousin,
12½in. high. (Edgar Horn)
$159

A George I lead cistern
dated 1725, 3ft.5in.
(Woolley & Wallis)
$1,824

An early 19th century lead
sculpture in the form of a
seated cherub, 42cm. high.
(Osmond Tricks) $529

Britain's 1950's lead French
Foreign Legion and the
Arabs. (Hobbs & Chambers)
$238

A 19th century lead figure
of a young boy playing the
pipes, 31in. high.
$516

A Mignot lead figure of Napoleon,
with various other portrait figures,
and other 1st Empire figures of
various regiments. (Christie's)
$696

# MARBLE

Pair of 19th century carved Carrara marble sphinxes, 2ft.5in. high. (Crowther, Syon Lodge Ltd.) $8,750

A white marble bust of a young woman by W. J. McLean, 1ft.2½in. high. (Capes, Dunn & Co.) $188

A beige marble table, the end sections carved with floral and scrollwork, 44 x 21½ x 31in. high. (Stalker & Boos) $1,100

A lifesize marble statue, 'Innocence Avoiding The Serpent', by Angelo Bienaime, 4ft.3in. high. (Crowther, Syon Lodge Ltd.) $11,875

Late 17th century pink marble relief of Venus Marina, 9.1/8in. high. $1,674

Marble bust of Apollo, head turned down gazing to the right, 18¾in. high. (Robt. W. Skinner Inc.)$3,100

One of a pair of gilt metal mounted Breche Violette marble vases with fruiting finials, 19in. high. (Christie's) $2,295

A late George III white and sienna marble mantelpiece, the frieze with a central floral inlaid tablet in the manner of Bosi, 68in. wide. (Christie's) $3,912

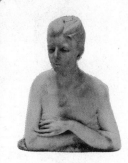

White marble portrait bust of a woman, 21in. high. (Robt. W. Skinner Inc.) $700

A late 19th century Italian white marble bust on pedestal, signed Lombardi, Roma 1878, 5ft.9in. overall. (Edgar Horn) $2,091

A late George III white and sienna marble mantelpiece with breakfront stepped top, 62in. high. (Christie's) $3,477

Marble copy of head of Apollo Belvedere, 19in. high, on fitted stand. (Robt. W. Skinner Inc.) $1,700

Head and torso of marble Bacchus, probably 1st or 2nd century B.C., 8in. high. (Robt. W. Skinner Inc.) $1,500

One of a pair of 19th century French white marble and ormolu urns, 10½in. high. $907

A Venetian white marble wellhead, the Lion of St. Mark sculptured in relief, dated 1394. (Crowther, Syon Lodge Ltd.) $10,000

Late 14th century white marble head, possibly of Frederick II, 17¾in. high. (Robt. W. Skinner Inc.) $1,300

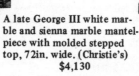

A late George III white marble and sienna marble mantelpiece with molded stepped top, 72in. wide. (Christie's) $4,130

A 15th century Italian carved marble head of a king, mounted on a wooden base, 14½in. high. (Robt. W. Skinner Inc.)$1,000

A gentleman in uniform, signed Tassie F, black velvet ground and turned ivory frame. (Christie's) $1,139

William Pitt, by Tassie probably after Flaxman, on blue ground. (Christie's) $1,708

James Tassie, signed W. Tassie F, inscribed and dated 1799, a portrait commemorating his death in his 64th year. (Christie's) $797

Hugh, 1st Duke of Northumberland, K.G., signed with a 'T', inscribed and dated 1780, on black ground. (Christie's) $740

A gentleman in profile, signed T F, the portrait molded onto gray glass ground. (Christie's) $546

Major M. Macalister of the Glengarry Fencibles, signed Tassie F, inscribed and dated 1796, on blue ground. (Christie's) $911

William, 1st Earl of Mansfield, signed Tassie F, dated 1779, on blue ground. (Christie's) $1,025

Philip Dormer Stanhope, 4th Earl of Chesterfield, by Tassie after Gosset, integral white paste ground. (Christie's) $660

Admiral Lord Duncan, signed Tassie F, inscribed and dated 1797, on green ground. (Christie's) $854

Late 18th century Anglo-Indian ivory-veneered toilet mirror, 3ft.1½in. high by 1ft.10in. wide.
$3,300

A gilt framed mirror, comprising center section surrounded by five smaller sections, 53in. high. (Outhwaite & Litherland)
$3,780

An electrotype dressing glass, the shaped rectangular frame decorated with a mandoline, goblet, bow and quiver, 50.5cm. (Lawrence Fine Art)
$489

A George II walnut and parcel-gilt looking glass with rectangular bevelled plate, 4ft.1in. high, circa 1740.
$3,135

A William and Mary oyster walnut cushion-framed wall mirror, 1ft.6in. high, circa 1700.
$731

One of a pair of George II giltwood mirrors, 4ft.9½in. high, 2ft.5½in. wide, circa 1740.
$18,975

A George III carved and gilt framed girandole, circa 1770, 2ft. wide.
$1,243

A Victorian dressing glass with rectangular bevelled glass plate, by Rosenthal & Jacobs, 1887, 61.3cm. wide. (Lawrence Fine Art)
$806

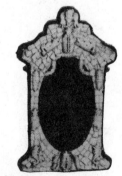

A Dieppe ivory and bone mirror with feathers, serpents and a crest, 32in. high. (Dreweatt Watson & Barton)
$348

# MIRRORS

Chippendale walnut and parcel gilt looking glass, circa 1780, 53½in. high. (Stalker & Boos) $2,250

An Oriental lacquer dressing mirror, China, circa 1800, with shield-shaped glass, 30¾in. high. (Robt. W. Skinner Inc.) $500

A late George II giltwood chinoiserie mirror with tall pagoda cresting, 6ft.7in. high, circa 1755. $14,025

A George II giltwood wall mirror, 35.5 x 19.25in. (Woolley & Wallis) $1,652

Late 18th century Chinese mirror painting of a lady seated under a tree, 14.5 x 11.7in. (Woolley & Wallis) $3,289

A George I carved giltwood and gesso looking-glass, 3ft. 10in. high, circa 1725. $3,418

One of a pair of 19th century gilt frame oval wall mirrors, the sides each with a three-arm candlebranch, 43 x 60in. high. (Lawrence Fine Art) $3,326

An Italian carved giltwood and gesso decorated rococo frame triptych dressing table mirror, 3ft.5½in. high. (Woolley & Wallis) $504

WMF silvered metal dressing mirror, 14in. high. (Reeds Rains) $458

A George III carved giltwood wall mirror, 2ft. wide, circa 1760.          $2,356

An Edwardian Sheraton-style satinwood dressing table mirror, the box base fitted with three drawers, 21in. wide. (P. Wilson & Co.)          $99

Mid 19th century carved giltwood mirror of early Georgian design, 60in. high. (P. Wilson & Co.) $1,159

An Edward VII photograph frame in the Art Nouveau style, Birmingham 1902, 21cm. high. (H. Spencer & Sons)          $297

William IV mahogany cheval robing mirror with pillar supports, 2ft.10½in. wide. (Capes Dunn & Co.)          $713

An early 19th century carved giltwood and gesso girandole in neo-classical Regency style, 2ft.10in. x 2ft.2in. (Edgar Horn)          $297

Early 19th century walnut and walnut veneer cheval mirror, 55½in. wide.(Robt. W. Skinner Inc.)          $850

A 19th century Dutch mantel mirror in a walnut marquetry frame, 42in. wide. (P. Wilson & Co.)          $327

An early George III giltwood wall mirror with 'C' scroll pediments, 38 x 23½in. overall. (Woolley & Wallis)          $3,055

A 19th century French rococo-style gilt carved wall mirror, 51½in. high. (Robt. W. Skinner Inc.) $1,100

Mid 19th century oval gilt wall mirror carved in the Chippendale style, 28in. high. (P. Wilson & Co.) $286

One of a pair of early George III carved giltwood pier-glasses, 6ft. high, 2ft.5in. wide, circa 1770. $26,400

One of a pair of late 18th century Flemish cushion-shaped pier mirrors with pierced and embossed ormolu mounts, 7ft.6in. high. (J. R. Bridgford & Sons) $5,980

A Victorian over mantel mirror having arched ebonized frame, 76 x 50in. (P. Wilson & Co.) $280

A Queen Anne giltwood small wall mirror, 3ft.5in. high, circa 1705. $1,188

A George III walnut and parcel gilt wall glass, 26 x 49in. (Christie's) $1,123

Late 19th century Venetian-style mirror, Italy, 51in. high. (Robt. W. Skinner Inc.) $700

A 19th century Italian ebonized walnut pier mirror. (Reeds Rains) $687

A 19th century mahogany oval swing framed mirror, 11½ x 8½in. (Butler & Hatch Waterman) $75

An early George III Carton-Pierre mirror, circa 1760, 3ft.7in. high. $3,520

A George III carved giltwood looking glass, 52in. high. (Dreweatt Watson & Barton) $1,090

An 18th century Queen Anne wall mirror, walnut veneer on pine, 17¼in. high. (Robt. W. Skinner Inc.) $700

A Victorian mahogany cheval robing mirror. (Hobbs & Chambers) $239

A giltwood toilet mirror of George II-style with arched bevelled plate, 32½in. high.(Christie's) $5,356

Victorian mahogany toilet mirror, 1860. (British Antique Exporters)$61

Victorian mahogany oval toilet mirror, 1860. (British Antique Exporters) $333

A Queen Anne green japanned toilet mirror, the lower part of bureau form, circa 1710, 1ft.6½in. wide. $3,203

A George I giltwood mirror, circa 1720, 4ft.3in. high. $4,681

A Victorian oak cheval mirror with arcaded apron and stepped shaped trestle ends, 35in. wide. (Christie's) $687

An early George I giltwood looking glass, circa 1720, 4ft.10in. high. $5,051

A George II giltwood wall mirror, the later bevelled plate within a sanded border, circa 1730, 5ft.3in. high. $4,928

A Federal mahogany mirror clock, by Asa Munger, Auburn, New York, circa 1830, 39in. high. (Robt. W. Skinner Inc.) $1,500

Victorian mahogany barley-twist support cheval mirror, 1860. (British Antique Exporters) $601

An 18th century Queen Anne decorated mirror, possibly America, 27½in. high. (Robt. W. Skinner Inc.) $425

Victorian mahogany toilet mirror, 1860. (British Antique Exporters) $243

Late 18th century decorated Chippendale mirror, possibly America, 41½in. high. (Robt. W. Skinner Inc.) $3,000

Early 20th century shipbuilder's model of the turret deck steamer 'Duffryn Manor', English, 44in. long, in glazed mahogany case.                    $3,190

Early 20th century shipbuilder's model of the cargo vessel 'Nailsea Manor' built by Bartram & Sons Ltd. of Sunderland, 54in. long.                    $2,871

A shipbuilder's model of the schooner yacht 'America', American, circa 1850, 28in. long.                    $4,785

Late 19th century shipbuilder's half-block model of a steam yacht, English, 53in. long.                    $1,435

Early 19th century prisoner-of-war boxwood model of the 48-gun Ship-of-the-Line 'Glory', 20 x 28in.
                    $19,140

Early 19th century prisoner-of-war bone model of an 84-gun Second Rate Ship-of-the-Line, 19½ x 24in.    $13,557

Mid 19th century shipping diorama, depicting the three-masted clipper 'Solway', together with a fishing smack, English, 39in. wide.                    $797

A boxwood, lime and walnut model of 'H.M.S. Endeavour', made by Brian Hinchcliffe, English, modern, 30in. long.
                    $7,975

Late 19th century shipbuilder's half-block model of a Barquentine 'Sound of Jura', English, 67in. long.     $1,754

Mid 19th century English contemporary model of a sailing ship hull, 9in. long.     $271

Early 20th century model of the Clyde steamer 'Duchess of Fife', made by N. S. Forbes, 54in. long.   $4,147

An early 20th century American steamship model, diorama scene in mahogany case, 48in. wide. (Robt. W. Skinner Inc.)     $600

A Bing battleship 'H.M.S. Powerful', German, circa 1912, 29in. long.     $1,346

Early 19th century prisoner-of-war bone model of a frigate, 7in. long, under glass dome.     $1,435

Mid 19th century English sailor-made half-block model of a clipper, 34in. wide.     $446

Mid 19th century English sailor-made half-block ship model of a paddle steamer, 30in. wide.     $669

A painted tinplate model of an early 4-funnel torpedo boat, by Bing, circa 1912, 16in. long. (Christie's) $348

Late 19th century English shipbuilder's half-block model of a yacht, 24in. long. $510

Mid 19th century English model of the brig 'Vanda', probably sailor-made, 15in. long. $1,116

A bone prisoner-of-war model of a 90-gun ship-of-the-line, 8¾in. long overall, standing on a straw-work plinth. (Lawrence Fine Art) $3,891

Early 19th century prisoner-of-war bone model of an 80-gun Ship-of-the-Line, 18 x 24in. $15,152

Model of H.M.S. Prince, 1670, 27in. long. (Barber's) $840

A half-block model of the Coaster 'S.S. Ardnagrena', Scottish, built by G. Brown & Co., Greenock, 1908, 42in. wide. $1,075

A shipbuilder's model of Lord Ashburton's steam yacht 'Venetia', Scottish, 1893, 67½in. long. $10,367

A late 19th/early 20th century ships model of a harbour dredger, 78in. long. (Boardman) $963

A tinplate model of a three-funnel ocean liner, with clockwork mechanism operating two propellers, by Bing, circa 1920, 15½in. long. (Christie's) $928

A prisoner-of-war bone ship model with turned brass guns, in a glazed mahogany case, 18in. long overall. (Lawrence Fine Art) $3,630

Mid 19th century sailor-made model of a whaling ship, probably English, 21in. long. $542

A contemporary model of a Bristol slaver, English, circa 1810, 45in. long. $2,233

Mid 19th century contemporary model of the schooner 'Shar', English, 51in. long. $531

A wooden framed working model of a single screwing boat 'The Swift', circa 1904, Greenock, 32½in. long. (Christie's) $293

A model of a paddle steamer 'Caledonian', English, circa 1900, 56in. long. $797

A gauge 1 painted brass clockwork model of the Great Central Railway 4-4-0 locomotive and tender, circa 1910. (Christie's) $812

A gauge O clockwork model of an American styled 0-4-0 locomotive and tender No. 3501, by J. Distler, Germany. (Christie's) $440

Hornby gauge O clockwork 4-4-2 tank locomotive, No. 6954, finished in L.M.S. maroon and black lined in gold. $102

Hornby gauge O clockwork 4-4-2 tank locomotive, No. 2221, finished in G.W.R. green and black lined gold. $102

A Marklin gauge 1 tinplate bogie kaiserwagen, German, circa 1901, 11in. long. $871

A rake of four gauge 1 Great Northern Railway teak passenger carriages, all by Marklin, circa 1925. (Christie's) $344

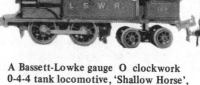

A Bassett-Lowke gauge O clockwork 0-4-4 tank locomotive, 'Shallow Horse', No. 109. $665

A fine scale Bassett-Lowke gauge O clockwork 4-2-2 locomotive 'Princess of Wales', No. 2601. $429

Hornby gauge O clockwork 4-4-0 locomotive 'Bramham Moor', No. 20, with six-wheeled tender. $285

A Stevens & Brown painted tin train, 'Thunderer' black and red engine, green tender and two yellow passenger cars, America, 1870's, engine 7in. long. (Robt. W. Skinner Inc.) $3,000

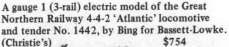

A Bassett-Lowke gauge O clockwork 4-6-2 locomotive 'Flying Scotsman', No. 4472.                          $506

A gauge 1 (3-rail) electric model of the Great Northern Railway 4-4-2 'Atlantic' locomotive and tender No. 1442, by Bing for Bassett-Lowke. (Christie's)                          $754

Marx wind-up 'Bunny Express' train, circa 1920. (Robt. W. Skinner Inc.)  $600

An early H. J. Wood live steam 4in. gauge 2-2-2 brass locomotive, 'Fire King', English, dating from circa 1860.                          $871

A Marklin tinplate 'Rocket' gauge 1 train set, German, circa 1909. $40,392

A 3½in. gauge copper and brass spirit fired 2-4-0 locomotive, No. 715, English, circa 1880's, 17¼in. long. $1,584

A Marklin gauge 1 clockwork 0-4-0 locomotive with matching four-wheeled tender, German, circa 1898, 11in. long.                          $950

A Hornby 'O' gauge 4-4-0 electric 'Eton' locomotive and tender, circa 1930, finished in Southern green livery and transfer printed in gold to the tender. $451

A Bassett-Lowke gauge 'O' electric 'Flying Scotsman', English, circa 1935, finished in British Railways Caledonian blue and black lined cream. $645

A Hornby 'O' gauge 4-4-2 electric locomotive 'Lord Nelson', finished in Southern region, together with an SR tender, circa 1900. $290

A Hornby 'O' gauge 'Bramham Moor' 4-4-0 clockwork locomotive and tender, finished in LNER apple green, with brass nameplate to each side, circa 1925. $451

One of two Marklin gauge '1' tinplate passenger coaches, hand-painted, German, circa 1902. $1,742

A 2½in. gauge live-steam coal-fired engineered model of a 2-6-2 Pannier Tank locomotive, 24in. long, modern. $1,935

A hand-built 'O' gauge locomotive, No. 1038, the 4-4-0 electric locomotive finished in LMS maroon and black lined yellow, with matching six-wheeled tender. $387

A 3½in. gauge live-steam 2-4-0 locomotive, 27½in. long, circa 1880's. $1,548

Late 19th century cast iron 'Speaking Dog' mechanical bank, by J. & E. Stevens Co., 7¾in. long. (Robt. W. Skinner Inc.) $1,000

Late 19th century cast iron clown mechanical bank, 9½in. high. (Robt. W. Skinner Inc.) $500

A cast iron 'Eagle and Eaglets' mechanical bank, by J. & E. Stevens, patented 1883, 6¾in. long. (Robt. W. Skinner Inc.) $350

Late 19th century cast iron owl money bank. $156

A cast iron novelty bank, by J. & E. Stevens Co., the building with front door opening to reveal a cashier, American, late 19th century. $322

A tinplate monkey mechanical bank, German, circa 1930, 6½in. high. $387

A cast iron two frogs mechanical bank, American, late 19th century, 8½in. long. $580

A 20th century Kenton cast iron flatiron building bank, America, 8¼in. high. (Robt. W. Skinner Inc.) $200

A cast iron 'Always Did 'Spise a Mule' money bank, American, circa 1897, by J. Stevens & Co., 10in. long. $903

A Celstina paper roll 'orguinette', No. 8425 with twenty reeds, together with eighteen paper rolls, American, circa 1890.          $823

Late 19th century elaborately carved cylinder musical box case, German.
$396

Late 19th century Nicole Freres interchangeable cylinder forte-piano musical box on stand, Swiss.
$2,851

A 19.5/8in. polyphon disc musical box, 36in. high, German, circa 1900.
$1,900

A Swiss organ Celeste cylinder musical box, the 49cm. cylinder playing twelve airs, circa 1880.   $1,742

A 9½in. Symphonion disc musical box, 11in. wide, together with one metal disc, German, circa 1900.
$380

An 11in. polyphon disc musical box number 165096, the table model with duplex combs with periphery drive. (Lawrence Fine Art)
$598

A bells-in-sight cylinder musical box, the 5.7/8in. cylinder playing ten airs. (Lawrence Fine Art)      $546

An automatic barrel piano, the 48-note coin operated movement playing from a 33in. pinned wooden cylinder, 49½in. (Lawrence Fine Art)   $1,264

A J. Navarro horn gramophone with 10in. turntable, Continental, circa 1905. $792

A mid 19th century Nicole Freres key-wound musical box, the 47cm. cylinder musical box playing twelve airs, Swiss. $1,188

A 14¾in. Symphonion disc musical box with center drive motor, together with thirteen discs, German, circa 1900. $1,552

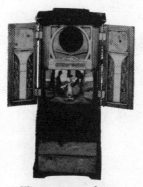

A Klingsor gramophone complete with 10in. turntable, Swiss, circa 1925. $792

A Schmidt & Co. 'Ariosa' organette, for use with annular discs, with eighteen reeds, German, circa 1904. $475

An 11in. polyphon disc musical box, contained in rosewood veneered case, 16in. wide, with twelve discs, German, circa 1900. $570

A Continental horn gramophone with 12in. turntable, the trumpet horn with brass rim, circa 1910. $506

A 19th century Swiss musical box by J. Heller, playing twelve airs. (Locke & England) $3,472

A Continental horn gramophone with 10¾in. turntable and Imperator soundbox, circa 1910. $633

A Continental horn gramo-
phone with 11½in. turn-
table and Hispano Suiza
soundbox, 1905.
$950

A singing bird box, the silver plated case with lid
opening to small singing
bird, 3¾in. wide.
$950

An Edison concert phono-
graph with Bettini spider
diaphragm, American, circa
1902.    $2,059

An 11in. Sirdar polyphon
disc amusement machine,
35½in. wide, German,
circa 1900.
$2,692

A Gramophone Co. horn
gramophone with 8in.
diam. turntable, English,
circa 1900.    $380

A late 19th century German
19.5/8in. polyphon disc
musical box on stand, together with eleven metal discs.
$2,059

A Euphonika 'Herophon'
organette with twenty-four
reeds, German, circa 1905.
$554

A Swiss mid 19th century
key-wound mandoline
cylinder musical box, No.
2451, the 33cm. cylinder
playing four operatic tunes.
$1,346

A Mandoline sublime
harmony cylinder musical
box the 33cm. cylinder
playing six airs, Swiss,
circa 1880.    $1,188

A large horn gramophone with 10in. diam. turntable and Maestrophone soundbox, Continental, circa 1910. $982

A Charles Ullmann 'Bells, Drums and Castanets In Sight' cylinder musical box, circa 1880. $3,009

A horn gramophone with 12in. turntable and Exhibition soundbox, probably French, 1905. $792

A Clementi chamber barrel organ, the 17-key movement with 46cm. pinned wooden barrel, English, circa 1810.$2,692

An Edison spring motor phonograph with Bettini Type D reproducer, American, circa 1903. $1,552

A 17¼in. Stella disc musical box on stand with periphery driven movement, together with thirty-four metal discs, Swiss, circa 1900.     $3,168

A Columbia type A gramophone No. S7138, American, circa 1900.$411

A Czechoslovakian late 19th century 12-key serinette with 18cm. pinned wooden barrel playing six tunes on wooden pipes. $554

A late 19th century J. M. Draper 'English' cardboard strip organette with fourteen reeds,     $475

A Polyphon disc musical box, 15½in.                    $1,156

A jewelled 3¾in. rectangular gilt brass singing bird box, with key and case. (Anderson & Garland) $870

An 11¾in. Symphonium disc musical box, German, early 20th century, 18in. wide, with eighteen metal discs. $645

Fine Victorian walnut polyphon and clock, with handle, 1870. (British Antique Exporters)          $1,720

A Symphonion Eroica triple disc coin-operated musical box. (Christie's) $6,000

A coin operated walnut veneered upright polyphon disc musical box playing 19¾in. discs. (Lawrence Fine Art) $2,795

A 10½in. Symphonion table top disc musical box. (Reeds Rains)          $1,054   £850

A rosewood cased standing cylinder music box, by B. A. Bremond, Switzerland, 41½in. wide. (Robt. W. Skinner Inc.) $3,250

A 15½in. polyphon disc musical box, number 84941, together with eight discs, 21½in. wide. (Lawrence Fine Art)   $1,464

A painted brass side-drum of The 16th/5th Queen's Royal Lancers, by Premier, dated 1941, battle honors to Cambrai, 1917. (Wallis & Wallis)     $179

A bird's eye maple and gilt gesso harp, by Erard Co., Paris, circa 1850, 69½in. high. (Robt. W. Skinner Inc.)     $1,400

Early 19th century four or six-keyed ebony flute by Cusson, Valenciennes, in mahogany case.     $814

A cased pair of five-keyed cocuswood flutes by Monzani & Co., London, circa 1815, in mahogany case. $1,709

Victorian walnut organ, 1880. (British Antique Exporters)     $111

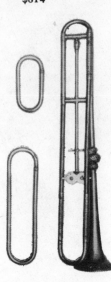

A brass slide trumpet by J. A. Kohler, London, circa 1850, in case. $1,221

A brass side drum well painted with ERII Arms and the badge and battle honors of The 1st Bn. Grenadier Guards. (Wallis & Wallis)     $386

A presentation set of Union pipes by Robt. Reid, North Shields, 1830.     $5,860

An English violon-
cello by T. Dodd,
London, unlabelled,
circa 1800, length
of back 75.4cm.,
in travelling case.
$211,640

A French violin
by Emile Blondelet,
Paris, 1923, length
of back 35.8cm.,
and a bow, in case.
$1,465

A French violin by
Francois Louis
Pique, Paris, 1810,
length of back
36.4cm.
$8,465

An English violon-
cello ascribed to J.
Morrison, length
of back 29in., circa
1900, in travelling
case. $1,465

A treble viola con-
verted from a Par-
dessus De Viole,
length of body,
34.3cm., in case.
$1,139

A French pedal harp
by Holtzmann, Paris,
5ft.4in. high, circa
1780.  $1,302

An eight-keyed box-
wood clarinet by G.
Wood, London,
length 23in., circa
1830.    $244

A Gothic double-
action pedal harp
by S. & P. Erard,
London, 5ft.9¾in.
high, circa 1829.
$2,442

# MUSICAL INSTRUMENTS

A Scottish viola by
James W. Briggs,
Glasgow, 1927,
length of back
16½in.
$2,604

An Italian violin by
Enrico Clodoveo
Melegari, Turin,
1884, length of
back 35.4cm.
$8,495

An English violin
by Geo. Craske,
Stockport, 1845,
length of back
36cm., and a bow.
$1,790

A German violon-
cello by J. C.
Hammig, 1797,
length of back
73.4cm., and a bow,
in canvas cover.
$2,930

An Irish harp by
John Egan, Dublin,
34¾in. high, circa
1825, in case.
$1,628

A six-keyed box-
wood clarinet by
Wood & Ivy, Lon-
don, length 65.6cm.,
circa 1840.
$179

A double-action
pedal harp by F.
Dizi, London, 5ft.
6¼in. high, circa
1820. $748

Mid 17th century
Venetian guitar,
School of Sellas,
length of back
46.6cm., in case.
$8,140

An English violin
by Richard Duke,
London, unlabel-
led, length of back
14in., and two
bows. $1,628

An English viola
by Thos. Simpson,
and A. Richardson,
1935, length of
back 43.3cm., and
a bow, in case.
$1,139

An Italian violin
length of back
35.3cm., in case.
$10,093

An English violin
by G. Craske, Stock-
port, length of back
35.2cm., in case.
$3,256

A violoncello by
Antonio Stradivari
Co., circa 1690,
length of back
30in., in case.
$407,000

A Scottish violin,
by Thos. Hardie,
Edin., 1852, length
of back 14.1/8in.
$1,953

A violin labelled
Pietro Mazzetti Stru-
mentajo di S.A.R.
fecit Ann. 1798,
length of back 14in.
$1,953

A French violin by
Chas. Jean Baptiste
Collin-Mezin, Paris,
1895, length of
back 35.8cm.
$1,628

A violoncello converted in England, circa 1800, from a viola da Gamba, circa 1700, length of back 74.5cm., in case.
$8,465

An English violin by a member of the Panormo family, length of back 35.3cm., and a bow, in case.
$5,372

A Cremonese violin by N. Amati, circa 1630, length of back 35.3cm., in case.
$27,676

A French violin, workshop of J. Hel, length of back 36cm., and a bow, in case.
$1,546

A double bass, unlabelled, length of back 45¼in., in canvas cover.
$1,790

A violin by Joseph filius Andrea Guarneri, Cremona, 1714, length of back 35.3cm., in case.
$130,240

An English violin by Wm. Robinson, London, 1929, length of back 14in., in case.
$1,221

A Flemish violin, labelled Antonius & Hieronymus Fr. Amati, circa 1720, length of back 14¾in.
$1,953

  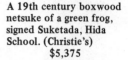

A 19th century boxwood netsuke of a monkey seated on the back of a recumbent puppy, signed Josui. (Christie's) $494

A 19th century boxwood netsuke of a mermaid and octopus, signed Shoko, Hida School. (Christie's) $2,150

A 19th century boxwood netsuke of a green frog, signed Suketada, Hida School. (Christie's) $5,375

Late 19th century wood netsuke of a wasp inside a rotten pear, signed with a kao. (Christie's) $4,181

A 19th century hako netsuke, in gold and black lacquer, signed Koman, together with another. (Christie's) $530

A carved wood and ivory netsuke of a courtier throwing beans at an oni, signed Kokoku, Tokyo School. (Christie's) $2,269

A 19th century circular ivory netsuke, signed Meikosai, 6.6cm. diam. (Christie's) $214

Late 19th/early 20th century boxwood netsuke of six apes surrounding a chestnut, a seventh seated inside the nut, signed Masateru. (Christie's) $2,031

A wood and ivory netsuke of Hotei, signed Meikei, Tokyo School, circa 1900. (Christie's) $3,583

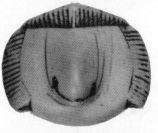

A 19th century ivory netsuke of a cat pursuing a mouse in a paper lantern, Japan. (Robt. W. Skinner Inc.)      $325

An 18th century ivory netsuke of a fledgling sparrow, unsigned. (Christie's)      $597

A boxwood netsuke study of an Oshidori, by the Kyoto School artist Masanao.      $52,800

Early 18th century ivory netsuke of a grazing horse with inlaid eye pupils. (Christie's)  $1,075

A 19th century ivory okimono-style netsuke of two Sumo wrestlers, signed Shomin. (Christie's)      $299

An ivory netsuke of a wiry old hound sitting and scratching its ear, 1½in. long. (P. Wilson & Co.)      $58

Late 18th/early 19th century well-carved cypresswood netsuke of a Chinese sennin playing kemari, unsigned. (Christie's)      $329

A well-carved boxwood netsuke of a rat and her young, signed Ikko, 19th century. (Christie's)    $776

A 19th century black lacquered netsuke in the form of a cannon, unsigned, together with another. (Christie's)      $106

Early 19th century boxwood netsuke of a recumbent wild boar, signed Mitsumasa, and kao, Nagoya School. (Christie's) $4,539

An 18th century wood netsuke of a karashishi holding a ball between its paws, signed Tametake. (Christie's) $1,530

Mid 19th century ivory netsuke modelled as a group of seven rats, signed Tomonobu, Edo School. (Christie's) $836

An 18th century ivory netsuke of Zensai (or Otsugo), unsigned. (Christie's) $955

An ivory netsuke of an open peony flower, the stalk forming the cord attachment, unsigned, circa 1800. (Christie's) $286

Late 18th century ivory netsuke of a grazing horse, unsigned. (Christie's) $896

Mid 19th century marine ivory okimono-style netsuke of a skeleton kneeling behind a large skull, signed Tomonobu, Edo School. (Christie's) $537

Late 19th/early 20th century netsuke in unstained boxwood formed as a rush basket, Chokusai. (Christie's) $1,177

Late 19th century boxwood netsuke of a seated courtier, signed Ikkosai (Toun) to, Tokyo School. (Christie's) $1,015

# NETSUKE

A 20th century pale fruit-wood netsuke formed as a stylized bronze frog of the Han dynasty. (Christie's) $353

Late 18th century carved wood netsuke of a seated karashishi, signed Tame-taka, Nagoya School. (Christie's)$4,539

A 19th century stained box-wood netsuke of the Demon of the Rashomon.(Christie's) $305

A 19th century boxwood netsuke of a human skull, signed Shuzan. (Christie's) $883

A 19th century lightly stained ivory manju netsuke carved and pierced in Ryusa style, unsigned.(Christie's) $453

An ivory netsuke modelled as an old woman and a basket, signed. (Lawrence Fine Art)     $251

A boxwood netsuke of two monkeys, by the Tamba School artist Toyomasa. $36,000

Mid 19th century ivory okimono-style netsuke of three musicians surrounding a seated Shishimai dancer, signed Ono Ryo-min, and kao, Edo School. (Christie's)     $740

A wood netsuke of two frogs wrestling on a lotus leaf, signed Sosai, late Meiji period. (Christie's) $211

An early 17th century small saucer or spice plate with plain rim, 4in. diam. $988

Pair of Kayserzinn pewter candlesticks on three feet, circa 1900, 30.5cm. high. (Christie's) $476

Early 19th century pewter porringer, Conn., Jacob's mark no. 107 for Saml. Danforth, 3½in. diam. (Robt. W. Skinner Inc.) $425

Late 17th century ball-knopped candlestick, with maker's mark CB on the foot rim, 22cm. high. $567

A Flemish broad-rimmed dish (Kardinaalschotel), probably by Cornelis Peeters I, circa 1700, 12¾in. diam. $993

Mid 18th century Swiss prismenkanne, by J. Weber of Zurich, 15¾in. high. $638

Late 16th/early 17th century French pewter pichet, 5½in. high. $574

Early 17th century pewter 'Jan Steen' jug with domed cover, Holland. (Christie's) $6,612

A pewter pump lamp with two wick whale oil burner, maker's mark on base 'I. Neal's patent, May 4th, 1842', 8in. high. (Robt. W. Skinner Inc.) $350

A Glasgow pear-shaped pewter pint measure, circa 1826, 6½in. high. $127

Early 19th century pewter pint mug, maker's mark T.D. & S.B., America, 4½in. high. (Robt. W. Skinner Inc.) $650

A Scottish pear-shaped pewter quart measure, circa 1826, 8¼in. high. $430

One of a pair of pewter five-branch candelabra, probably Dutch, circa 1900, 45.5cm. high. (Christie's) $476

Late 17th century small Stuart plate or saucer, with cast roped border, 12.5cm. diam. $1,986

One of a pair of early 18th century Continental pricket candleholders, unmarked, 31in. high. $681

A Scottish crested pewter tappit hen, circa 1800, 11¾in. high. $733

A late 14th/early 15th century hansekanne with squat baluster body on flared foot, 8½in. overall. $5,742

A pewter beaker engraved in 'wriggled-work', circa 1700, 6.5/8in. high. $478

An early 18th century North German pewter deep bowl, with scrolled caryatid handles, 9¼in. across handles. $606

A 16th century pair of pewter pricket candlesticks, probably German, 17½in. high. $2,153

A Liberty Tudric two-handled rose bowl on raised circular foot, 24cm. diam. (Christie's) $340

A Dutch 'wriggled-work' pewter beaker by the Master IZ of Amsterdam, circa 1700, 6.7/8in. high. $606

A Liberty Tudric pewter and Clutha glass bowl on stand designed by Archibald Knox, circa 1900, 17cm. high. (Christie's) $434

A 'Victoria' radio loud-speaker with cast white metal figure of a female piper, circa 1925, 21in. high. $475

Late 17th century Stuart octagonal based candlestick, 18.2cm. high. $6,527

Set of three 19th century Scottish pewter baluster shaped measures, pint, half-pint and gill. (Dreweatt Watson & Barton) $261

Late 18th century Swiss stegkanne, by Johann H. Petersohn of Bern, 32cm. high. $1,064

Early 19th century pewter
gimbal lamp, America,
6in. high. (Robt. W. Skinner Inc.)    $350

A large Charles II charger,
probably by Wm. Wette,
circa 1670, 23in. diam.
$1,419

A Regency oval tureen and
cover, on four claw-and-
ball feet, circa 1820, 16½in.
long overall.    $737

A German Tailor's Guild pewter cup and cover, circa 1697,
24¾in. high.    $1,595

Pair of Chinese pewter
altar candlesticks, now
mounted as lamps, 34in.
high. (Stalker & Boos)
$500

A William and Mary 'wriggled-
work' portrait beaker, made
by J. Kenton of London,
circa 1689-94, 13cm. high.
$3,831

An 18th century Swiss
bauchkanne, by Pier
Antoin Simaval, 13in.
high.        $567

A 'wriggled-work' plate,
made by John Duncombe,
circa 1720, 22.7cm. diam.
$652

An early 18th century Swiss
pewter stitze of tapering
form with moulded girdle,
11¼in. high.  $717

'Westfalischer Bauer', gelatin silver print, 8 x 6¼in., by Albert Renger-Patzsch, late 1940's or early 50's. (Christie's)    $471

'Baby Blossom', by Julia M. Cameron, albumen print, 13½ x 11in., 1860's. (Christie's) $1,488

'Our Marquis', portrait of Lionel Tennyson, by Julia M. Cameron, albumen print, 10 x 7in., 1860's. (Christie's) $124

'Twisted Tree, Lobos State Park, California 1950', 10 x 8in., by Minor White. (Christie's)    $520

'Parlormaid and under parlormaid ready to serve dinner', gelatin silver print, image size 13½ x 11½in., by Bill Brandt, 1930's. (Christie's) $930

H.R.H. Queen Elizabeth, The Queen Mother, four gelatin silver prints, two 10 x 8in., and two 10 x 7in., by Cecil Beaton, 1940's. (Christie's) $173

Untitled, portrait of Harriette, albumen print, 11 x 9in., by Robert T. Crawshay, 1860's. (Christie's) $520

Portrait of a young girl, Eaton Place, London, by Bill Brandt, 9 x 7½in. (Christie's)    $744

Roger Fenton in a borrowed kepi, photogalvanograph, 8 x 6in., by Hugh Welch Diamond, printed credit 'London. Published May 1857.' (Christie's) $496

# PHOTOGRAPHS

'Finlay of Colonsay, Deerstalker', calotype, 9 x 6½in., by David O. Hill and Robert Adamson, circa 1846. (Christie's) $372

'Twinka', gelatin silver print, 14 x 11in., by Judy Dater, 1970. (Christie's) $272

'Paul Getty, the richest man in the world', 9½ x 7¾in., by Bill Brandt. (Christie's) $806

'Preambule', gelatin silver print mounted on tissue, 14¾ x 11in., by Herbert Lambert, signed and dated 1924. (Christie's) $235

Female Nude, 9½ x 7¼in., by Bill Brandt. (Christie's) $744

'The Conversation Piece', by Oscar Gustave Rejlander, albumen print, unmounted, 8¼ x 6½in., 1860's or 70's. (Christie's) $210

'Tabacco', gelatin silver print, 14 x 10¼in., by Mario Giacomelli, 1950's. (Christie's) $173

Last photograph of Lincoln, 1865, copy enlargement 8 x 10in. (Robt. W. Skinner Inc.) $45

'Ballnight', (Charity Ball — New York City), 11¾ x 8½in., by Robert Frank. (Christie's) $396

# PHOTOGRAPHS

'On A Riverboat', (Yom Kippur — East River, New York City), 9 x 13½in., by Robert Frank. (Christie's)          $1,178

'Mother and Child', 9 x 13½in., by Robert Frank. (Christie's)          $744

'The Terra Nova in the McMurdo Sound', toned gelatin silver print, 23½ x 29¾in., by Herbert Ponting, 1910-12. (Christie's)          $396

'The Bull Ring, Mexico City', gelatin silver print, 8¾ x 10½in., by Rune Hassner, circa 1950. (Christie's)          $49

'High School, Edinburgh', calotype, 5¾ x 7¾in., by David O. Hill and Robert Adamson, Edinburgh 1844. (Christie's)          $3,224

Untitled, two veiled girls, photogravure, image size 6 x 8in., by Charles Puyo, dated 1896. (Christie's)          $496

The Beatles, gelatin silver print, 12 x 16in.,
by Norman Parkinson, circa 1963. (Christie's)
$173

'Muscle Beach, Venice, California', framed
gelatin silver print, 11 x 19in., by Max Yavno,
circa 1940. (Christie's) $620

Farmyard Scene, salt print, 7 x 8¾in., signed
and dated in the negative 'G. Shepherd Nov.
10, 1853'. (Christie's) $396

'The Welsh Fish Girls', albumen print, 11 x
13in., signed in ink Robert Crawshay Photo,
1860's. (Christie's) $1,054

Untitled, lady at her toilette, albumen print,
7½ x 9¾in., by Charles Puyo, late 19th or
early 20th century. (Christie's) $620

'Mrs Cameron & Julie. Little H. Hse. 1858',
photographer unknown, salt print, 4¼ x 5¾in.
(Christie's) $248

A Norwegian family group, half-plate daguerreotype portrait, maker's label P. A. Eyde, Bergen, dated 1858. (Christie's)    $235

'The Dream', by Julia Margaret Cameron, albumen print, 12 x 9½in., 1869. (Christie's) $1,612

Autographed portrait of Andy Warhol and friends, gelatin silver print, 9½ x 9in., signed Cecil Beaton and Andy Warhol, 1964. (Christie's) $297

'Lamp Standard and Ventilating Shaft, erected over the Subway, Southwark Street, London', albumen print, 12 x 7½in., photographer unknown. (Christie's)    $310

An albumen Civil War print, 3¼ x 4¼in., showing four soldiers and chaplain, all wearing Masonic aprons. (Robt. W. Skinner Inc.) $55

'Welsh Miner', 9½ x 6½in., by Robert Frank. (Christie's)    $471

'King Arthur', by Julia M. Cameron, albumen print, 14 x 11in., 1874. (Christie's) $1,364

Quarter plate tintype, Union private full length pose, musket with bayonet at side, in wood frame with gold mat. (Robt. W. Skinner Inc.)    $70

Portrait of Marlene Dietrich, gelatin silver print from a 1930's negative, 8 x 6in., signed Cecil Beaton. (Christie's)    $173

# PHOTOGRAPHS

Henry Herschel Hay Cameron, by Julia Margaret Cameron, albumen print, 14½ x 10¾in. circa 1870's. (Christie's) $372

'Joachim', albumen print, 12¾ x 10¼in., by Julia M. Cameron, 1868. (Christie's) $4,960

'Pakistani Girl, Karachi Market', gelatin silver print, 12½ x 10¼in., dated 1958, by Dorothea Lange. (Christie's) $272

Isabel Somers-Cocks, by O. G. Rejlander or Lewis Carroll, albumen print, 7¼ x 5¾in., early 1860's. (Christie's) $434

'Maidens in Waiting', image size 13½ x 10in., 1951, by Bert Hardy. (Christie's) $198

Julia Jackson, albumen print, 9½ x 7¾in., by Julia M. Cameron, 1860's. (Christie's) $161

H.R.H. Duchess of Kent, gelatin silver print, 10 x 8in., by Cecil Beaton, 1940's. (Christie's) $93

Nude framed gelatin silver print, image size 13½ x 11¼in., by Bill Brandt, July 1956. (Christie's) $744

Alfred Tennyson, autographed portrait, albumen print, 11½ x 9¼in., by Julia M. Cameron, 1867. (Christie's) $1,488

# PIANOS

A square piano by Patrick
Butler, Dublin, 1798, 5ft.
2½in. long. $2,442

A William IV rosewood case
table piano, maker's label
Thos. Butcher, London, 5ft.
10in. long. (Woolley &
Wallis)          $506

Mid 18th century compos-
ite English spinet, 6ft.0½in.
long.          $1,790

A single manual harpsichord
by Delf, 4½ octave keyboard,
in mahogany case, 6ft.2in.
long. (P. Wilson & Co.)
          $1,834

An upright piano by
Bechstein. (Worsfolds)
          $968

A grand piano by Bechstein,
Berlin, probably about 1880,
in black ebonized case, 6ft.
9in. long. (P. Wilson & Co.)
          $589

A 19th century French
grand piano in inlaid
mahogany case, by Bois-
selot et Fils of Marseilles.
(Butler & Hatch Water-
man)          $1,354

An American organ by the
Estey Organ Co. of Battle-
borough, in mahogany case.
(Worsfolds)          $264

An English two-manual
harpsichord by J. & A.
Kirckman, London 1722,
7ft.11in. long.
          $24,420

A young lady by Michaelo Albanesi, signed and dated 1840, rectangular 3in. $391

An officer of The 1st Foot Guards, called Captain Wm. Paxton-Jervis by George Engleheart, circa 1812, rectangular 3¼in. $2,310

A young girl by William Bone after Romney, signed and dated 1832, enamel, rectangular 2.7/8in. $858

A miniature portrait of a gentleman by Andrew Plimer, 6.8cm. (Lawrence Fine Art) $1,237

An artist by Jacques Le Brun, signed and dated 1787, seated on a crimson chair, 3in. diam. $1,305

An early 19th century miniature portrait of General Eyre, 7.2cm., English. (Lawrence Fine Art) $429

Duc D'Aumale by Edward de Moira, signed and dated 1864, rectangular 5¼in. $652

Madame Perregaux attributed to Mademoiselle G. Capet, after Vigee-Lebrun, rectangular 3¾in. $435

A young lady by Thomas Hargreaves, circa 1800, with tightly curled auburn hair, oval 3¼in. $429

A young lady by Joseph Philippe Oorloft, signed and dated 1831, oval 2¼in. $783

A gentleman by Rosalba Carriera, circa 1710, 3¼in. $4,135

A young lady, School Guerin, circa 1810, oval 9.8cm. $304

Lady Russell by John Barry, circa 1805, wearing a white dress, oval 8.3cm. $957

A young lady by Ignazio Pio Vittoriano Campana, circa 1785, 2½in. diam. $1,044

Frances Parker, by Thos. Richmond, circa 1800, with long brown hair, oval 2½in. $462

A nobleman by Francisek Smiadecki, circa 1650, oil on copper, oval 2in. $1,287

A gentleman, by the artist signing V., circa 1785, 2½in. oval. $462

A gentleman, perhaps by John Hazlitt, circa 1790, wearing a black jacket, oval 7.6cm. $495

A young girl holding a rabbit, German School, circa 1815, oval 2.7/8in. $792

James, Duke of York, by Henry P. Bone, after Van Dyck, signed and dated 1845, enamel, oval 2¼in. $2,145

An officer, attributed to Jean Louis Voille, circa 1775, oval 2.1/8in. $478

An officer, English School, circa 1800, three-quarters dexter, oval 3in. $412

Etienne Francois, Marquis D'Aligre by Augustus Dubourg, after Van Loo, signed and dated 1789, 2¾in. diam. $1,741

A gentleman by Andrew Plimer, circa 1805, wearing a double-breasted jacket, oval 7.7cm. $1,122

A lady, French School, circa 1710, her hair upswept, oval 1¾in. $195

King Edward VII, as Prince of Wales, by Wm. C. Bell, after Winterhalter, circa 1850, oval 2in. $561

King George III by Samuel Collins, circa 1780, with hair en queue, oval 2.3/8in. $1,188

A young officer of The 18th (Royal Irish) Regt. of Foot, in the manner of Peter Paillou, circa 1800, oval 2½in. $429

A lady by Charles Pierre Cior, signed circa 1800, 2¼in. diam. $435

Charlotte Anne Freill, by John Smart, signed with initials and dated 1788, oval 2¾in. $10,230

Colonel Robert Frith, by Robert Bowyer, after John Smart, circa 1800, oval 2½in. $1,452

A lady by Jean Baptiste Isabey, signed circa 1795, 2.7/8in. diam. $4,135

Louis XVII, as Dauphin, by Francois Dumont, circa 1790, wearing a blue jacket with scarlet collar, oval 1¾in. $2,089

A young lady possibly by Jean Louis Voille, signed, circa 1790, oval 7cm. $696

General Jean Andoche Junot, Duc d'Abrantes by Sophie Lienard, signed circa 1840, on porcelain, oval 5.1/8in. $2,176

A gentleman called Prince De Metter by Ferdinand Georg Waldmuller, circa 1830, oval 6in. $870

Ferdinand Philip Louis
Charles Henry, Duke D'
Orleans by Madame de
Mirbel, oval 4.1/8in.
$2,611

An elderly lady by Walter
Stephen Lethbridge, circa
1800, signed in full on the
verso, oval 3½in.
$1,155

Colonel Paty by Charles
Claude Noisot, signed
and dated 1824, oval 3in.
$696

A double sided miniature
of Lord Hervey by John
Smart, signed and dated
178(?), oval 1½in.
$4,950

An officer by Giuseppe
Rota, signed and dated
1810, 2.3/8in. diam., the
reverse glazed to show a
lock of hair. $391

A Young Clansman, English
School, circa 1790, 2¼in.
oval.        $3,300

A gentleman by Joseph
Franz Goez, signed and
dated 1798, with powdered
hair en queue, oval 2½in.
$609

A young nobleman ascribed
to Benjamin Arlaud, circa
1700, oval 2¼in. $435

A lady by Jeremiah Meyer,
circa 1775, with high piled
hair adorned with pearls,
oval 2in.     $1,023

A gentleman by Louis Lie Perin-Salbreux, signed circa 1790, 2.1/8in. diam.
$1,523

A lady by Charles Robertson, circa 1780, wearing a low-cut pink dress, oval 1.5/8in.     $495

A lady, French School, circa 1790, her hair adorned with a ribbon, 2½in. diam.
$1,305

Lady Mary Villiers by Henry P. Bone, after Hanneman, signed and dated on the verso 1844, oval 4.1/8in.
$2,062

Emperor Franz I by Johann Christian Fiedler, circa 1730, wearing a powdered wig, oval 2in.     $957

A General by Louis Marie Sicardi, signed and dated (18)10, octagonal 2¾in.
$20,900

A lady playing a hurdy-gurdy by Pierre Pasquier, signed circa 1780, 2¾in. diam.     $609

Princess Louisa of Stolberg-Gedern, set within the lid of a circular gold mounted ivory box, 2¼in. diam.
$1,654

A gentleman by Sampson Towgood Roch(e), signed and dated 1805, oval 2¾in.
$627

A lady by Andrew Plimer, circa 1790, wearing a low-cut white dress, oval 5.3cm.    $693

A young lady by Madame J. Doucet de Suriny, circa 1795, 2¾in. diam.    $565

Queen Alexandra attributed to Charles J. Turrell, circa 1910, head and shoulders to dexter, oval 5cm.    $1,815

Henry, Prince of Wales, by Henry P. Bone, after Robert Peake, the Elder, signed and dated 1845, oval 4in.    $1,732

The Bath of Venus by Jacques Charlier, rectangular 2¾in.    $1,392

A young boy in the manner of Joseph Saunders, circa 1780, oval 1.5/8in.    $363

Mid 17th century miniature on ivory, said to be Nell Gwynn, 1.7/8in. high. (Robt. W. Skinner Inc.)    $250

A young lady by Ofnet, signed, wearing a white dress, 4in. diam. $652

An 18th century miniature on ivory of a young lady, 1½in. high. (Robt. W. Skinner Inc.)    $500

Eugene Grasset, 'Jean D'Arc, Sarah Bernhardt', circa 1900, lithographic poster, 116 x 71cm. $218

Absinthe Robette by Privat Livemont, lithograph printed in colors, 1896, 104 x 75.2cm. (Christie's) $468

A lithographic poster, Gaby Montbreuse, by Anton Girbal, 1924, 159 x 116cm. $325

Purgatif Geraudel, by Jules Cheret, lithograph printed in colors, 1891, 243.5 x 85cm. (Christie's) $437

'Suzy Deguez Dans Ses Danses D'Art', by Eugene Grasset, 197 x 77.5cm., circa 1900. $587

YOU CAN BE SURE OF SHELL
A poster 'The Quay, Apple-dore', by Brynhild Parker, no. 341, together with nos. 464 by R. Miller and 468 by G. Chapman. $794

Early 20th century American motor-car illustration by Clarence P. Helck, 19¾in. wide. (Robt. W. Skinner Inc.) $2,000

YOU CAN BE SURE OF SHELL
A poster 'Brimham Rock, Yorkshire', by Graham Sutherland, no. 507. $454

'Monaco Monte Carlo', by Alphonse Mucha, 1897, 110 x 76cm. $1,067

A motorcycle racing poster by Gamy, France, 1913, 7.5/8 x 35¼in. (Robt. W. Skinner Inc.) $170

An automobile racing poster, France, circa 1906, entitled 'Circuit des Ardennes, Belges 1906-Duray, 6 Gagnant', by E. Montaut, 35¼in. wide. (Robt. W. Skinner Inc.) $230

Lithographic poster, 'Internationale Kunst Ausstellung', by Frans Stuck, 84 x 36cm., circa 1905. $242

'Chocolat Ideal', by Alphonse Mucha, circa 1900, 85 x 58cm. $533

Edouard Bernerd, 'Arlette Montal', 1920's, lithographic poster, 128 x 85cm. $150

A lithographic poster, Maria del Villar, by Lion Astric, 1920's, 104 x 79cm. $156

'Bar', by E. Dantan, circa 1925. $800

A theatrical poster, chromolithographed on paper by 'The Donaldson Litho. Co. Newport, Ky.', entitled 'Hunting Escaped Slaves'. (Robt. W. Skinner Inc.) $75

'Exposition Internationale Anvers 1930', by Marfurt, lithographic poster, 104 x 74cm. $312

543

A poster 'Kimmeridge Folly, Dorset', by Paul Nash, no. 505.          $567

A U.S. Army Recruiting poster, American Lithograph Co. N.Y. 1909, image 35½ x 24¾in. (Robt. W. Skinner Inc.)          $80

A lithographic poster, 'Lorenzaccio', 1899, 37 x 104cm. $459

A lithographed print, 'Rose', signed in the block 'Mucha', 1897, 107.5 x 46cm.
          $1,658

Poster advertising the Grand Prix at the Nurburgring, 1947. (Onslows)          $960

A poster 'Newlands Corner', by John Armstrong, no. 340.
          $567

'8 Bells' comedy poster, by Strobridge Lithograph Co., Ohio, circa 1910, 40 x 30in. (Robt. W. Skinner Inc.)
          $110

A lithographed print, 'Carnation', signed in the block 'Mucha', 105 x 44cm., 1897.
          $701

Late 19th century applique quilt made up of green and red cotton prints on natural white ground fabric, 8ft.6in. x 6ft.9in. (Robt. W. Skinner Inc.) $2,200

An applique quilt composed of red and green calico patches on a white cotton field, America, circa 1845, 80 x 92in. (Robt. W. Skinner Inc.) $1,000

Mid 19th century patchwork and applique quilt, New England, 6ft.8in. x 6ft.5in. (Robt. W. Skinner Inc.) $1,600

A 19th century patchwork cotton quilt, with unusual tulip border motifs, America, 92 x 92in. (Robt. W. Skinner Inc.) $1,300

A 19th century cotton piecework quilt, American, with a centre star motif, 90 x 91in. (Christie's) $1,000

An applique album quilt, New Jersey and Pennsylvania, 1853, 7ft.9in. x 8ft.7in. (Robt. W. Skinner Inc.) $3,000

A Serab runner with camel colored field, 3ft.8in. x 7ft.6in. (Robt. W. Skinner Inc.) $900

Eastern Caucasian/Shirvan prayer rug, dated, with ivory field, 3ft.11in. x 4ft. 10in. (Robt. W. Skinner Inc.) $1,900

Early 20th century Afshar rug, the soft gold field with all over floral trellis design, 4ft.1in. x 6ft.1in. (Robt. W. Skinner Inc.) $1,200

Early 20th century Afshar rug, the midnight blue field with vivid red stepped medallions, 4ft. x 5ft.6in. (Robt. W. Skinner Inc.) $800

Late 19th century Turkoman/Yomud asmalyk, 4ft. 4in. x 2ft.6in. (Robt. W. Skinner Inc.) $4,000

Early 20th century Persian Maslaghan rug with open red field, 6ft.3in. x 3ft.1in. (Robt. W. Skinner Inc.) $1,600

Late 19th/early 20th century Caucasian/Kuba rug, the blue field with pink, yellow and red roses, 3ft.10in. x 6ft.5in. (Robt. W. Skinner Inc.) $1,600

Mid 19th century Turkoman/Tekke Main carpet, 6ft.8in. x 8ft.3in. (Robt. W. Skinner Inc.) $4,750

Late 19th century Caucasian rug with yellow field, 4ft.3in. x 7ft. (Robt. W. Skinner Inc.) $750

Early 20th century Ersari Ensi rug, on a rust colored field, (Robt. W. Skinner Inc.)  $375

Late 19th century hooked rug, New England, 4ft.10in. x 2ft.7in. (Robt. W. Skinner Inc.)  $2,200

Late 19th century Trans-caucasian Village rug with soft red field, 6ft.8in. x 4ft.9in. (Robt. W. Skinner Inc.)  $2,300

Early 20th century Baluch rug/Turbat-I-Haidari, 3ft.2in. x 6ft. 2in. (Robt. W. Skinner Inc.)  $550

Mid 19th century Soumak bag face, 1ft.7in. x 1ft. 4in. (Robt. W. Skinner Inc.)  $1,850

Mid 20th century Heriz-Area carpet with rust red field, 9ft.9in. x 6ft. 4in. (Robt. W. Skinner Inc.)  $1,200

Late 19th/early 20th century Anatolian Manastir prayer rug, 5ft. x 3ft.5in. (Robt. W. Skinner Inc.)  $650

Eastern Caucasian/Kuba rug, dated H1322, the dark blue field with ivory, blue green and red Leshgi stars, 4ft.3in. x 5ft.4in. (Robt. W. Skinner Inc.)  $1,800

Late 19th/early 20th century Malayer rug with open cream colored field, 7ft. 1in. x 4ft.1in. (Robt. W. Skinner Inc.)  $1,500

Late 19th century Qas Qai rug with midnight blue field with red diamond medallion, 2ft.3in. x 1ft. 9in. (Robt. W. Skinner Inc.) $750

A Kuba rug with red field woven with rows of stylized flowerheads, 5ft.5in. x 2ft.9in. (Lawrence Fine Art)    $733

Early 20th century Soumak rug, rust-orange field with light and dark blue and black medallions, 3 x 5ft. (Robt. W. Skinner Inc.) $850

Serapi carpet, madder rust field with all over floral design, 9ft.3in. x 11ft.7in. (Robt. W. Skinner Inc.) $7,250

Late 19th century Shirvan Kelim, 4ft.9in. x 10ft.6in. (Robt. W. Skinner Inc.) $800

Early 20th century Feraghan/Sarouk rug, with open ivory field, 3ft.7in. x 5ft. (Robt. W. Skinner Inc.) $425

A 20th century East Caucasian/Shirvan rug with a dark blue field, 4ft.9in. x 6ft.9in. (Robt. W. Skinner Inc.)    $4,200

A Shiraz Kelim woven with four broad bands, 9ft.8in. x 5ft.4in. (Lawrence Fine Art) $861

An East Caucasian/Daghestan prayer rug, dated 1301=1883, 3ft.7in. x 5ft. (Robt. W. Skinner Inc.) $850

# RUGS

Mid 20th century Hamadan area rug with dark blue field, 4ft. x 2ft.5in. (Robt. W. Skinner Inc.) $170

Early 20th century Yomud Chuval, red, ivory and blue chuval guls on a rust brown field, 2ft.6in x 3ft.6in. (Robt. W. Skinner Inc.) $275

Early to mid 19th century Yomud Main carpet with chestnut brown field, 5ft. 2in. x 9ft.9in. (Robt. W. Skinner Inc.) $11,000

Late 19th century Anatolian Village rug, peach field with turquoise, cochineal, gold and ivory medallions, 6ft. 6in. x 7ft.6in. (Robt. W. Skinner Inc.) $1,400

Early 20th century Serab corridor carpet with camel field, 9ft.2in. x 4ft.4in. (Robt. W. Skinner Inc.) $3,400

Late 19th/early 20th century Kashan/Mohtashem mat with dark blue floral medallion, 2ft.2in. x 2ft. 6in. (Robt. W. Skinner Inc.) $650

Mid 20th century Bidjar rug with brick red field filled with herati motifs, 3ft.7in. x 5ft.4in. (Robt. W. Skinner Inc.) $1,000

Early 20th century Kerman pictorial saddle cover, 3ft. x 3ft.8in. (Robt. W. Skinner Inc.) $550

An Oriental silk rug with coral field, 5ft.6in. x 3ft. 11in. (Woolley & Wallis) $873

549

A Qum rug, the field divided into squares woven with flowering plants, sprays and boteh, 6ft.7in. x 4ft.8in. (Lawrence Fine Art) $1,276

Late 19th/early 20th century Turkoman/Yomud asmalyk, woven in the usual trellis of ashik motifs, 3ft.11in. x 2ft.6in. (Robt. W. Skinner Inc.) $1,500

Tabriz-style Persian rug with multi-colored floral and medallion design on mainly red ground, 90 x 53in. (Reeds Rains) $756

Early 20th century Armenian Kazak rug with a rusty red field, 4ft.10in. x 7ft.10in. (Robt. W. Skinner Inc.) $1,500

An Isfahan pictorial rug with beige and floral meander border with dark blue guard stripes, 3ft. x 2ft.6in. (Capes, Dunn & Co.) $725

Early 20th century Karagashli rug, red sawtoothed and blue stepped medallions on dark blue field, 3ft.7in. x 5ft.11in. (Robt. W. Skinner Inc.) $2,300

Mid 19th century Central Anatolian Yatak, 5ft.4in. x 6ft.8in. (Robt. W. Skinner Inc.) $6,200

Tabriz-style Persian rug, 83 x 52in. (Reeds Rains) $675

Mid 19th century Central Anatolian Village rug, 3ft. 10in. x 4ft.11in. (Robt. W. Skinner Inc.) $3,000

An Eastern Caucasian/Shirvan prayer rug, 3ft.7in. x 5ft. 3in. (Robt. W. Skinner Inc.) $6,100

Late 19th century Kuba rug, trees, boteh and chickens on an ivory field, 3ft.1in. x 4ft.5in. (Robt. W. Skinner Inc.) $4,000

A Kuba rug with blue field, 6ft.10in. x 3ft.8in. (Lawrence Fine Art) $1,355

Late 19th/early 20th century Southwest Persian bag face, possibly Bahktiari, 1ft.11in. x 2ft.3in. (Robt. W. Skinner Inc.) $425

Late 19th/early 20th century double Soumak bags, 11 x 22½in. (Robt. W. Skinner Inc.) $1,100

Late 19th century Turkoman/Ersari Main carpet, the rust and red field with Mina Khana all over design, 9ft. x 10ft. (Robt. W. Skinner Inc.) $31,000

Early 20th century Turkish rug, 3ft.4in. x 4ft.9in. (Robt. W. Skinner Inc.) $150

Early 20th century Kazak/Gendje rug, field of diagonal stripes filled with S-hooks, 3ft.11in. x 5ft.9in. (Robt. W. Skinner Inc.) $2,400

Late 19th/early 20th century Caucasian/Daghestan rug with a yellow field, 3ft.5in. x 4ft.11in. (Robt. W. Skinner Inc.) $650

Late 19th century East Anatolian/Village rug, the field woven in two large square panels, 4ft. x 6ft. 8in. (Robt. W. Skinner Inc.) $1,200

Early 20th century Bahktiari rug , woven in a grid of squares, 4ft. x 6ft. 1in. (Robt. W. Skinner Inc.) $275

Mid 20th century Kerman rug, the ivory field with magenta medallion, 4ft. 3in. x 7ft. 1in. (Robt. W. Skinner Inc.) $1,000

Mid 20th century Bahktiari carpet with blue field, 5ft. x 7ft.7in. (Robt. W. Skinner Inc.) $1,050

Late 19th century Caucasian/Kuba Kelim bag, 2ft. 1in. x 2ft. (Robt. W. Skinner Inc.) $250

Late 19th century Eagle Kazak, double 'Eagle' medallions, within a wide ivory 'crab' border, 4ft.8in. x 7ft. (Robt. W. Skinner Inc.) $3,100

Pair of late 19th/early 20th century Kurdish saddle bags, each panel approx. 1ft.9in. x 1ft. 8in. (Robt. W. Skinner Inc.) $300

Pictorial Shirvan, dated 1311, (1894 A.D.), with inscription, 5ft.3in. x 6ft. 2in. (Robt. W. Skinner Inc.) $3,500

Mid 20th century Bidjar rug with red field, 2ft. 7in. x 4ft.4in. (Robt. W. Skinner Inc.) $575

Mid 18th century Boston School, Adam & Eve sampler, 6¾ x 11½in. (Robt. W. Skinner Inc.) $7,000

Sampler by Ann Foss of Houghton, Le Spring, 1813, 12½ x 17in. (Christie's) $504

A Charles II Border Band sampler, circa 1660, 13 x 6¼in.        $739

Early 19th century Adam and Eve sampler by Eliz. Tredick, New Hampshire or Southern Maine, 11 x 16in. (Robt. W. Skinner Inc.) $1,600

A needlework sampler by Susanna H. White, Marblehead, dated 1806, 14½ x 19in. (Robt. W. Skinner Inc.) $14,000

A needlework sampler made by Sarah Johnson, Newport, Rhode Island, 1769, 9 x 16in. (Robt. W. Skinner Inc.) $21,000

A Georgian needlework sampler by Maria Coster, in the tenth year of her age, 1819, 1ft.5in. x 1ft.1in. $904

Sampler by Janet Anderson, depicting Inverary Castle, 1823, 18 x 19in. (Christie's)$960

A Boston School needlework sampler, made by Sarah Henderson in 1765, aged 12, 21 x 18½in. (Robt. W. Skinner Inc.)   $20,000

Mid 18th century English gold fob seal, with pierced scroll handle, 2.7cm.
$261

An English gold fob seal, 3.2cm., circa 1830.
$174

An English gold double-sided swivel fob seal with ribbon-bound reeded pendant, 4.6cm., circa 1790.
$413

Early 19th century English gold fob seal of large size, oval with reeded and fluted mount, 5cm.    $696

Mid 18th century English gold fob seal with smoky-quartz matrix, 3.2cm.
$478

An English gold fob seal of oblong form, with plain foiled citrine matrix, 4cm., circa 1835.    $369

Early 19th century English gold fob seal with plain oblong bloodstone matrix, 3.8cm.    $478

A gold double-sided swivel fob seal with scrolled wire-work mount in the form of two serpents, 5cm., circa 1810.    $1,654

An English gold fob seal with armorial-engraved oblong citrine matrix, 4.1cm., circa 1835.
$435

Late 18th century English gold double-sided swivel fob seal of oval form, 5.3cm.     $652

An English gold fob seal with pendant ring and the chalcedony matrix engraved with armorials, 3.2cm., circa 1835.     $217

An early 19th century two-colored gold fob seal, matrix detached. 2.9cm.     $239

Early 19th century Swiss gold musical fob seal with central winder, 4.2cm. high. $870

A two-color gold and hard-stone articulated triple desk seal by Faberge, St. Petersburg, 1908-17, 9.1cm. $5,224

Early 19th century Swiss gold and enamel musical fob seal, 4.2cm. $1,174

An early 19th century English three-color gold fob seal, 5.3cm.     $652

An English gold fob seal, the oblong carnelian matrix engraved with armorials, 3.6cm., circa 1835. $239

An English gold fob seal, the oval chalcedony matrix engraved with initials MK, 2.7cm., circa 1785.     $261

Shibayama decorated ivory elephant from the Meiji period, 11in. high. $3,120

Late 19th century aikuchi tanto, the kinji koshirae and hilt decorated in a Shibayama style, 38cm. long. (Christie's) $5,108

A Shibayama vase and cover of lozenge section, 4in. high, circa 1900. $1,548

One of a pair of Japanese enamelled silver Shibayama vases each inset with ivory panels and with dragon handles, 12¼in. high, circa 1900. (Anderson & Garland) $2,464

A Japanese Shibayama two-leaf table screen, the panels inset with mother-of-pearl and soapstone, 9¼in. high x 10¼in. wide. (Christie's) $2,282

Late 19th century large ivory vase, each side with a shaped panel inlaid in Shibayama style, 33cm. high. (Christie's) $3,208

Late 19th century silver filigree mounted gold lacquer fan, 39.5cm. high. (Christie's) $2,020

A Shibayama miniature cabinet, the sides decorated in silver and gold lacquer, 5¼in. high, circa 1900. $1,548

A 19th century Japanese Shibayama tusk vase with flat ivory cover, 67.5cm. high overall. (H. Spencer & Sons) $734

# SILHOUETTES

A colored profile of Lieut. Robert Conry by Charles or John Buncombe, circa 1810, oval 3¼in.  $527

A full-length profile of Wm. Pitt, by Wm. Wellings, signed and dated 1781, rectangular 10½in. $3,010

An Etruscan profile of Captain W. Sotheby, by Jacob Spornberg, signed and dated Bath 1793, oval 3½in. $3,260

A colored profile of an officer of the Life Guards called Nunn Davie, by C. Buncombe, circa 1795, oval 4¾in.  $1,028

An Etruscan profile of a lady of the Anstey Family by Jacob Spornberg, signed and dated Bath 1793, oval 8.6cm. $3,511

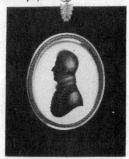

A bronzed profile of an officer of the Light Dragoons called George Baker by John Field, circa 1810, oval 3in. $727

A full-length profile of William, 1st Marquess of Lansdowne by Wm. Hamlet the elder, inscribed and dated 1785 on the reverse, 8¾in. rectangular. $1,129

A full-length profile of John, Earl of St. Vincent, by Wm. Wellings, signed and dated 1783, oval 11¼in.  $3,260

A full-length profile of a young lady of the Gosset Family, circa 1780, rectangular 11½in. $2,445

557

A gentleman by George Bruce, circa 1796, in profile to sinister, oval 5in. $376

A verre eglomise profile of a young girl, Continental School, circa 1780, 5cm. diam. $577

William, 17th Earl of Erroll, by John Miers, circa 1807, oval 9.8cm. $602

Lieut. A. Robotiier by Mrs. Isabella Beetham, circa 1785, 8.6cm. oval. $477

A young lady by Thos. Wheeler, in profile to sinister, painted on plaster, circa 1790, oval 9.5cm. $251

A lady by J. Thomason, circa 1795, in profile to sinister, painted on plaster, oval 8.6cm. $401

A gentleman by Mrs. Isabella Beetham, circa 1785, 3½in. oval. $376

A young lady by John Miers, painted on ivory, signed circa 1805, 4cm. oval. $251

A lady by Mrs. M. Lane Kelfe, signed and dated Bath 1784 on the verso, oval 9cm. $351

# SILHOUETTES

A gentleman by J. Thomason, inscribed 1797 on the reverse, oval 12.7cm., with verre eglomise border.     $376

A bronzed profile of a lady by John Field, signed Miers and Field, circa 1810, 5.7cm. oval.  $1,129

Mrs. McDowell Grunt, by John Miers, circa 1785, oval 8.6cm. $1,028

A lady, in profile to dexter, painted on plaster, circa 1795, oval 4in. $251

A gentleman by John Thomason, circa 1790, 1½in. diam. $201

A lady by John Miers, circa 1790, in profile to dexter, oval 9cm.     $477

A young lady by J. Thomason, in profile to dexter, painted on plaster, circa 1790, oval 8.5cm.     $376

Miss Mary Ann Lovell as a child, by W. Phelps, 1786, painted on plaster, oval 8.5cm.     $1,066

An officer by A. Charles, signed and inscribed on the verso, circa 1790, oval 10cm.  $853

# BASKETS

A 19th century oval bread basket, worked to simulate a cane basket, 1875, 13¾in. wide, 23½oz. (Capes, Dunn & Co.)            $1,820

A Dutch neo-classic design cast silver-colored metal basket of navette shape, 15.5in. wide, circa 1880, 30oz. (Neales) $669

A Russian oval dessert basket, 38cm. wide overall, maker's mark G.F.B,B., St. Petersburg, 1805, 1200gr. $6,950

A George II shaped oval cake basket, by Philips Garden, 1753, 14¼in. long, 58oz. (Christie's) $3,742

A Victorian hallmarked silver basket with scroll base and feet, London 1886, 19oz. (Locke & England)     $450

An oval Adam basket by Wm. Plummer, London, 1783, 14½in. (Wooley & Wallis) $2,321

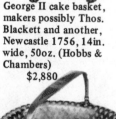

George II cake basket, makers possibly Thos. Blackett and another, Newcastle 1756, 14in. wide, 50oz. (Hobbs & Chambers)     $2,880

A chased and pierced silver basket by Thomas Parr, 1743. (Bonham's)    $5,040

A George V fruit basket of shaped circular form with swing handle, Sheffield, 1934, 25cm. diam., 806gr. (H. Spencer & Sons)     $159

A George II large oval cake basket, by David Willaume II, 1730, 15¼in., 86oz. (Christie's)     $19,278

A George III oval cake basket by John Emes, 14in. long, 27oz. (Russell Baldwin & Bright)     $906

A parcel gilt and enamel bread basket of circular form with rope-twist handles, Moscow, 1884, 38cm.     $4,354

An oval dessert basket by Charles Stuart Harris, London 1903, 30cm., 30oz. (Lawrence Fine Art) $1,237

Victorian openwork cake basket with cast swing handle, by Henry Wilkinson, London 1860. (Reeds Rains) $314

A parcel gilt trompe-l'oeil bread basket on scrolled feet, maker's mark P.L., Moscow, 1883, 37cm. $2,828

An early George III shaped oval cake basket by E. Romer, 1769, 37.3cm., 41oz. (Lawrence Fine Art) $1,512

A George IV silver gilt oval cake basket in George III-style, by P. Rundell, London, 1822, 13¾in. wide, 39oz.10dwt. $10,621

An early George III shaped oval cake basket, by Wm. Plummer, 1765, 37.5cm., 47oz. (Lawrence Fine Art) $2,449

A George III shaped oval cake basket, by John Romer, 1765, 13in. long, 34oz. (Christie's) $1,822

Late 19th century sterling silver sugar basket, by S. Kirk & Son Co., Maryland, 7in. high. (Robt. W. Skinner Inc.) $325

A George II Irish cake basket, by John Gumley, Dublin, circa 1740, 35.2cm., 39oz. (Lawrence Fine Art) $1,925

A Victorian cake basket, by John Figg, London, 1840, 12in. diam., 44oz. (Dreweatt Watson & Barton) $1,090

A George III boat-shaped cake basket on spreading foot, by Paul Storr, 1801, 14.7/8in. long, 30oz. (Christie's) $3,417

A George III shaped oval cake basket with pierced swing handle rising from shells, 1763, 37cm., 35.5oz. (Lawrence Fine Art) $835

A Catherine II covered beaker with 19th century inscription to the rim. (Woolley & Wallis) $330

A silver gilt and niello beaker of cylindrical form, maker's mark J.N. in script, Moscow, 1838, 7.7cm. $478

A trumpet-shape parcel gilt beaker by P. Semyonov, maker's mark, Moscow, circa 1775, 18cm. $1,261

A North German trumpet-shaped beaker, 22.1cm. high, unmarked, circa 1660, 590gr. $2,505

One of six Victorian goblets, engraved with crest and initials, 1883, maker's mark overstruck with that of Frazer & Haws, 6½in. high, 109oz. (Christie's) $4,276

A tapering cylindrical beaker by Antoni Magnus, Deventer, ?1664, 18.4cm. high, 362gr. $50,090

A silver gilt and niello beaker of campana form, maker's mark A.K., Moscow, 1835, 7.4cm. $652

A German tapering cylindrical beaker, by Philipp Jacob Drentwett III, Augsburg, circa 1690, 5½in. high, 10oz. 12dwt. (Christie's) $1,253

A German parcel gilt beaker, by Christoph Muller, Breslau, circa 1710, 5oz.5dwt., 5in. high. $2,695

A William IV beaker, by
Joseph and John Angell,
London, 1836, 5oz.2dwt.
$446

One of a pair of cylindrical
beakers with an applied
molded strap handle, Bos-
ton, 1790-1810, 3.1/8in.
high, overall, 8oz.
(Christie's)   $550

A Dutch parcel gilt beaker,
13cm. high, probably for
Hindrik Muntinck, Gronin-
gen, apparently 1655, 225gr.
$2,392

A William III silver gilt beaker, circa 1700, 8cm. high.
(Lawrence Fine Art)
$792

One of a pair of French
beakers, by Joseph Moillet,
Paris, 1725, 6oz.1dwt.,
2¼in. high.  $1,636

A parcel gilt campaign
beaker, 3¼in. high, 3oz.
10dwt. (Christie's)
$1,000

An 18th century trumpet-
shaped North European
beaker, 5¾in. high. (Geering & Colyer) $285

One of a pair of George III
silver gilt beakers, by Wm.
Holmes, London, 1801,
3½in. high, 11oz.11dwt.
$1,012

A parcel gilt beaker of tapering cylindrical form, by F.
Petrov, maker's mark, Moscow, 1759-74, 17.5cm.
$1,392

A shaped circular bowl with two S-scroll twisted wire handles, by B. Schaats, N.Y., circa 1690-1700, 5.3/8in. diam., 6oz. (Christie's)
$35,200

An inlaid silver Indian-style bowl, by Tiffany & Co., for the Columbian Exposition, circa 1893, 6¼in. high, 56oz. 10dwt. (Christie's)
$63,800

A Dutch octagonal brandy bowl, probably by J. H. Raapsvelt, Leeuwarden, circa 1680, 8oz.10dwt., 8¼in. wide overall.
$4,235

A silver bowl with Thos. Farrer mark, hallmarked London 1731, 9½in. diam. (Robt. W. Skinner Inc.)
$1,050

Mid 19th century silver mounted coconut bowl, probably America, 6¾in. diam. (Robt. W. Skinner Inc.) $125

A silver two-handled punch bowl, London 1905, 10½in. diam. (Edgar Horn)
$518

A parcel gilt circular bowl, by Anton Gunter Dieckmann, initialled and dated 1732, 15.4cm. diam.
$2,588

A child's Victorian christening bowl and matching spoon by John Russell, Glasgow 1888, in fitted case. (Reeds Rains)
$148

A large two-handled bowl, by James Ramsay, London, 1934, 14in. diam., 166oz.14dwt.
$2,593

A William IV Scottish punch bowl, by J. McKay, Edinburgh 1831, 27cm., 34oz. (Lawrence Fine Art) $1,375

A copper and silver applied bowl, by Gorham Manuf. Co., Providence, 1883, 3¼in. high. (Christie's) $605

A 19th century French sugar bowl, stand and cover, post 1838 .950 standard mark, 18cm. across stand, 21oz. (Lawrence Fine Art) $357

A footed bowl, by Whiting Manuf. Co., circa 1875-85, 5in. high, gross weight 22oz. (Christie's) $2,640

A Scandinavian circular two-handled bowl and cover, 14.8cm. high, maker's mark C.M., circa 1760, 560gr. $3,757

A large punch bowl, by Walker & Hall, Chester 1906, 21.7cm. high, 69oz. (Lawrence Fine Art) $1,650

A Faberge sugar bowl, set with two 18th century Russian coins, St. Petersburg marks, circa 1890-95, 3in. diam. (Geering & Colyer) $2,480

A Maltese sugar bowl and cover, probably by Mario Schembri, circa 1775, in Italian style, 10oz.16dwt., 6in. high. $1,444

A silver gilt two-handled bowl by Jakob Kessbayr, 17cm. wide, Augsburg, circa 1625, 280gr. $6,262

A silver gilt box with three rounded corners, the lid inset with an enamel plaque signed W. Sawers 1922, 2oz. 17dwt., 9cm. long.(Christie's) $230

An Austrian hammered silver and silver gilt box with carved ivory finial, Austrian silver marks for 1925, 12oz. 10dwt., 8.2cm. high. (Christie's) $680

An octagonal covered sugar box, by Thos. Dankenmair, 13.5cm. wide, Augsburg, 1716, 148gr. $2,088

A shaped circular toilet box by Francois Thomas Germain, 9cm. diam., Paris, 1750, 275gr. $9,600

A hammered silver and silver gilt cheroot case and vesta combined, unmarked, possibly American, circa 1890, 4oz., 9.4cm. long.(Christie's) $476

Late 17th century Estonian parcel gilt toilet box, by F. Lemke, Reval, 4oz.6dwt., 3½in. diam. $1,251

An Italian sugar box and cover, Turin, circa 1790, 8oz.14dwt. $3,850

A silver gilt double lid toilet box, probably German, circa 1750, unmarked, 3in. wide. $1,540

A silver and ivory trinket box of ovoid form with ball feet, Birmingham 1923. (Locke & England) $728

A French pepperbox, by Simon-Thadee Puchberger, Aix, 1769, 3¼in. wide, 150gr.     $1,117

A Guild of Handicrafts hammered silver box and cover, London hallmarks for 1907, 2oz., 7.25cm. long. (Christie's)     $312

A small Liberty & Co. silver and enamel pill box, Birmingham, 6.75cm. diam., 1914.     $156

An Italian sugar box and cover, maker's mark G.T., Venice or Padua, circa 1780, 4in. wide, 130gr.     $1,925

A Liberty & Co. silver box and cover, the tapering swollen cylindrical body and domed cover set with small turquoise stones, together with two silver match box covers.     $368

An early George II circular box by Charles Kandler, London, 1727, 5in. diam., 15oz.18dwt. $5,313

A Charles II toilet box, maker's mark only IL a flower below, London, circa 1680, 4¼in. wide.     $1,518

A plain silver tobacco box of cushion outline, with maker's mark for Robert McGregor, circa 1830. (Christie's)  $260

A William and Mary plain circular box and cover, by Elizabeth Haslewood, Norwich, 1691, 2½in. diam., 1oz.9dwt. (Christie's)     $1,474

# CANDELABRA

One of a pair of three-light candelabra, by Thomas Bradbury & Sons, London, 1898/1902, 18¼in. high, 132oz.16dwt.
$1,548

One of a pair of candelabra, in Louis XVI style, by Odiot, 55.8cm. high, circa 1870, 11450gr.    $7,095

A 20th century silver plated on copper two-branch candelabrum.    $75

One of a pair of late Georgian cut glass table candelabra, each with a square base, 25in. high. (Lawrence Fine Art)
$1,821

Mid 19th century pair of French silver gilt five-light candelabra each on shaped circular base and baluster stem, maker's mark H.S., 21½in. high, 279oz. (Christie's)    $6,237

One of a pair of WMF electroplated candlesticks, each cast as a young woman supporting a flower sprouting to form the four candleholders, 48cm. high, circa 1900.
$2,838

One of a pair of George III table candlesticks, by John Green & Co., Sheffield, 1802, 52cm. overall. (Lawrence Fine Art)
$1,375

Pair of 19th century Regency-style silver candelabra, labelled Peruzzi, Florence, 16½in. high. (Robt. W. Skinner Inc.)
$700

One of a pair of Morton's patent Sheffield plated three-light candelabra, 35cm. extending to 49cm. (Lawrence Fine Art) $547

One of a pair of Victorian four-light candelabra, maker J.A. JS., London 1833, 22½in. high, 136oz. (Anderson & Garland)        $2,080

One of a pair of Georg Jensen Danish silver candelabra, 9in. high, 76 troy oz. (Stalker & Boos)        $4,000

A Victorian six-light candelabrum centerpiece on shaped triangular base and three shell feet, by Benjamin Smith III, 1845, 34¼in. high, 320oz. (Christie's)        $7,371

A Victorian four-light candelabrum, by John Mortimer and John S. Hunt, 1839, 26½in. high, 174oz. (Christie's) $3,402

One of a pair of sterling silver five candle candelabra, Adams style, 16½in. high, 75 troy oz. (Stalker & Boos)        $1,900

One of a pair of William IV Sheffield plate candelabra, by J. Dixon & Sons, 21¼in. high. (Woolley & Wallis)        $619

One of a pair of late 19th century silver candelabra, St. Petersburg, 20.5cm.        $1,654

Pair of George III candelabra, by W. Tucker & Co., Sheffield, 1809, 23in. high. (Dreweatt Watson & Barton)        $4,033

One of a pair of Victorian candelabra, each four lights, by Wm. Moulson for Lambert & Rawlings, London, 1851, 25¾in. high, 9110gr.        $14,839

# CANDLESTICKS                    SILVER

One of four George III silver gilt candlesticks with detachable nozzles, by John Parsons & Co., Sheffield, 1785, 11½in. high. (Christie's) $8,553

One of a pair of William III candlesticks, maker's mark IL, a coronet above and pellet below, circa 1695, 7in. high, 30oz. (Christie's) $4,783

One of a pair of Edwardian candlesticks with trumpet-shaped foot, by Gilbert Marks, 1902, 13in. high, 41oz. (Christie's) $4,847

One of a pair of George III desk candlesticks, probably by Wm. Abdy, London, 1770, 6¾in. high. $1,084

Pair of George II silver table candlesticks with cherub columns, by Simon Jouet, London, 1747, 9¾in. high, 42oz. (Hobbs & Chambers) $2,394

One of four Georgian table candlesticks, one by Wm. Cafe, 1759, the others by R. Sharp, 1789, all London, 81oz.11dwt. $4,785

One of a pair of early Victorian silver candlesticks, by Henry Wilkinson & Co., Sheffield 1840, 10.1/8in. high. (Geering & Colyer) $582

One of a pair of French table candlesticks, 20.4cm. high, maker's mark P.H., Lille, 1757, 800gr. $4,174

One of two Sicilian table candlesticks, almost matching, makers' marks G. and A.M., Palermo, 1786 and circa 1790, 23oz., 7¾in. high. $1,925

One of a pair of late Victorian table candlesticks by Hawksworth Eyre Ltd., Sheffield 1896, 30.3cm. high. (Lawrence Fine Art)
$632

One of a pair of Queen Anne candlesticks, by John Bache, London, 1705, 7in. high. (Woolley & Wallis)
$2,499

One of four George II table candlesticks, by Wm. Gould, London 1743/4, 7½in. high.
$6,600

One of a pair of silver Edwardian neo-classical-style table candlesticks, London 1906, 9¼in. high. (Capes, Dunn & Co.)
$442

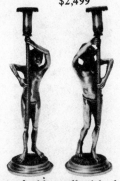

Pair of table candlesticks, by J. M. Wendt, the stems in the form of a male and female aboriginal, Adelaide, circa 1875, 20.5cm. high, 1330gr.
$12,375

One of a pair of mid 18th century German candlesticks, maker's mark that of the Muller family, 7.3/8in. high, 15oz.3dwt. (Christie's)
$3,991

One of a pair of Spanish table candlesticks, Antonio Ruiz, Cordoba, circa 1780, 29oz.3dwt., 9¾in. high.
$3,080

One of a pair of dressing table candlesticks by F. W. Sponholtz, 12cm. high, Danzig, circa 1775, 310gr.
$2,296

One of a set of four George II Sheffield plate circular candlesticks, 11in. high. (Woolley & Wallis)
$533

# CARD CASES (Various Materials)     SILVER

A mother-of-pearl card case in the form of a purse. (Lawrence Fine Art) $47

An early Victorian shaped rectangular silver card case by Nathaniel Mills, Birmingham 1846, 10.2cm. (Lawrence Fine Art) $343

A tortoiseshell card case, inlaid in tinted mother-of-pearl with long-tailed birds among flower branches. (Lawrence Fine Art) $68

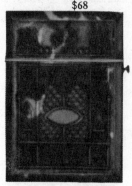

A mother-of-pearl card case, engraved with scrolling foliage and set on each side with tortoiseshell panels. (Lawrence Fine Art) $82

A Chinese ivory card case, deeply carved with numerous figures and buildings in landscapes. (Lawrence Fine Art) $88

A pressed tortoiseshell card case, molded on either side with a Gothic facade. (Lawrence Fine Art) $68

A Chinese ivory card case, carved in shaped panels with figures and buildings in garden and river scenes. (Lawrence Fine Art) $61

A Victorian shaped rectangular silver card case, by R. Thornton, Birmingham 1873, 9.8cm. (Lawrence Fine Art) $61

An Indian card case inlaid with mosaic panels and borders of tinted ivory and metal. (Lawrence Fine Art) $14

A mother-of-pearl card case, the center panel carved with a bird on a flower branch. (Lawrence Fine Art) $47

A Victorian shaped rectangular silver card case, by R. Thornton, Birmingham 1866, 11cm. (Lawrence Fine Art) $68

A card case, inlaid with a diamond pattern of tortoise-shell and engraved mother-of-pearl. (Lawrence Fine Art) $32

A papier mache card case, inlaid with mother-of-pearl and gilt with a Chinese river scene. (Lawrence Fine Art) $13

A tortoiseshell card case, inlaid in engraved mother-of-pearl . (Lawrence Fine Art) $82

A mother-of-pearl card case, the center panel carved with a bird perched in a flowering branch. (Lawrence Fine Art) $13

A mother-of-pearl card case, the center panel carved with four long-tailed birds. (Lawrence Fine Art)$61

A Victorian shaped rectangular silver card case, by Edward Smith, Birmingham 1852, 10.1cm. (Lawrence Fine Art) $330

A pale tortoiseshell card case, inlaid with flowers in mother-of-pearl and metal. (Lawrence Fine Art) $41

# CARD CASES (Various Materials)   SILVER

An ivory card case, engraved with a crest, a motto and a monogram. (Lawrence Fine Art)   \$13

An early Victorian calling card case by Nathaniel Mills, Birmingham 1850, 60gr. (H. Spencer & Sons) \$299

A Japanese ivory card case, lacquered in black and gold with birds, tree-stumps and rocks. (Lawrence Fine Art) \$55

A tortoiseshell card case, inlaid in silver pique with formal scrolling flower branches. (Lawrence Fine Art)   \$47

A Japanese ivory and Shibayama card case, inlaid in tinted mother-of-pearl and hardstones. (Lawrence Fine Art)   \$110

A tortoiseshell card case, inlaid with borders of flowers in engraved mother-of-pearl. (Lawrence Fine Art) \$47

A mother-of-pearl card case, inlaid in a trellis pattern with an engraved bird and flowers, with paua shells. (Lawrence Fine Art) \$32

An early Victorian silver calling card case by N. Mills, Birmingham 1843, 72gr. (H. Spencer & Sons) \$247

A mother-of-pearl card case inlaid with diamond panels, the borders with alternate panels of triangular paua shell and mother-of-pearl. (Lawrence Fine Art) \$14

574

One of a pair of George III plain bulbous-shaped casters, Newcastle, circa 1760, maker probably John Kirkup, 11oz. (Christie's)     $391

One of a pair of George I casters, probably Jacob or Samuel Margas of London, circa 1720, 18oz.2dwt., 6in. high.     $1,676

One of a pair of baluster casters, by Reynier De Haan, maker's mark, The Hague, 1781, 24.2cm. high, 888gr.     $4,174

A George I caster, marked Glover Johnson, London, 1718, 7in. high, 6oz.10dwt.     $2,733

An Elkington silver sugar caster, maker's marks and Birmingham hallmarks for 1938, 5oz.2dwt., 8.5cm. high. (Christie's)     $298

A Victorian sugar caster, London, 1895, 8in. high, 8oz. (Hobbs & Chambers)     $185

William and Mary silver muffineer, London, 1691-2, maker's mark CA, 7in. high, 9 troy oz. (Robt. W. Skinner Inc.)     $475

A George III caster in the form of a turret, by Solomon Hougham, Solomon Royes and John East Dix, 1817, 11.3cm. high. (Lawrence Fine Art)     $2,500

One of a pair of George III silver shakers, London, 1796-7, 7in. high, 7 troy oz. (Robt. W. Skinner Inc.)     $325

# CENTERPIECES

A William IV centerpiece by Joseph and John Angel, London 1837, 21in. high, 71oz. (Woolley & Wallis) $889

A George V table centerpiece with a central trumpet vase, maker's mark WH & Co. Ltd., London 1910, approx. 3657 gr., 40.5cm. high. (H. Spencer & Sons) $1,790

An electroplate centerpiece and mirror plateau, circa 1870, 49cm. high. $838

A large Continental shaped oval centerpiece embossed and chased overall in rococo style, 12¼in. high, import marks for 1906, 149oz. (Neales) $7,102

A copper applied centerpiece bowl, by Whiting Manuf. Co., New Jersey, circa 1882, 9in. diam. (Christie's) $1,980

A WMF electroplated metal centerpiece of boat form, circa 1900, 46cm. wide. $523

A table centerpiece in the form of a fruiting vine branch supporting a bowl, 27in. high. (Anderson & Garland) $442

A Victorian oval table centerpiece on four foliage and paw feet, by Stephen Smith, 1872, 19in. long, 135oz.(Christie's) $4,922

An early Victorian table centerpiece by E. & J. Barnard, London 1852, 2485 gr., 46cm. high. (H. Spencer & Sons) $2,044

One of a pair of Queen Anne chamber candlesticks, by C. McKenzie, Edinburgh, 1706, 3.5/8in. sq., 13oz.3dwt.
$4,686

One of a pair of early 18th century chamber candlesticks, possibly Jersey, circa 1715, 4¼in. diam., 12oz. 9dwt.      $9,684

One of a set of four George III circular chamber candlesticks, by Wm. Sharp, London, 1817, 5½in., one nozzle 1799, 38oz.17dwt.
$3,592

One of a pair of Victorian chamber candlesticks, by Walker Knowles & Co., Sheffield, 1849, 19oz. 15dwt., 6in. diam.
$2,025

One of a pair of George III round chamber candlesticks, by John Crouch I and Thos. Hannam, London 1793, 18oz. (Dreweatt Watson & Barton)
$850

A George III circular chamber candlestick, maker John Mewburn, London 1817, 12oz. (Woolley & Wallis)      $725

One of a pair of George III chamber candlesticks, by Smith, Tate, Nicholson and Hoult, Sheffield, 1818, 5¾in. diam., 23oz.2dwt.
$1,392

One of a pair of Sheffield plate chamber candlesticks, circa 1810, 6½in. wide.
$468

One of a pair of early Victorian chamber candlesticks, by S. Walker & Co., Sheffield, 1838, 6in. diam., 21oz. 16dwt.      $1,202

# CHOCOLATE POTS

Late 19th century copper
and silver chocolate pot,
9¼in. high. (Robt. W.
Skinner Inc.)
$2,800

A Queen Anne chocolate pot
of tapered cylindrical form,
Dublin, 1706, 10¾in. high,
1025gr.        $4,373

A German baluster choco-
late pot, by Jakob Wilhelm
Kolb, Augsburg, 1767-69,
18oz.10dwt. all in, 10¼in.
high.        $3,850

A Queen Anne large plain
tapering cylindrical chocolate pot, by John Jackson
I, 1705, 11in. high, gross
33oz. (Christie's)
$6,237

Late 18th century French
silver chocolate pot, 8in.
high, 23 troy oz. including
wooden handle.
$2,000

Silver chocolate pot,
maker's mark for Wm.
Fawdery, London, circa
1710, approx. 12 troy oz.
(Robt. W. Skinner Inc.)
$350

# CIGARETTE BOXES

Liberty & Co. silvered metal
and enamel cigarette box,
circa 1905, 22.5cm. wide.
$150

A Ramsden & Carr silver
cigarette box and cover,
London, 1903, 19cm. wide.
$937

A cigarette box, maker's mark
HIT, Russian, circa 1890,
21oz.8dwt. all in, 6.5/8in.
wide.        $451

An enamelled silver cigarette
case, probably German, circa
1910, thumbpiece missing,
3½in. high.        $502

A silver Imperial presentation
cigarette case by Faberge,
Moscow, 1908-17, 9.8cm.
high.        $1,348

An enamelled cigarette case,
German, circa 1905, 9cm.
high.        $401

A 1930's cigarette case, silver
and two-color gold colored
metal, with stripes of black
lacquer, 11.75cm. wide.
$451

An Omar Ramsden silver
cigarette case, with gilt
interior, 1923, 9.5cm.
$170

A silver cigarette case with
sapphire-set thumbpiece by
Faberge, Moscow, 1908-17,
11cm.
$1,305

A silver and enamel cigarette case by I. Khlebnikov,
Moscow, circa 1880, 9.5cm.
$1,000

An enamelled cigarette case,
probably German, circa 1910,
oblong, painted in pastel
shades, 3½in. high.
$1,191

An Art Deco sterling silver
cigarette case with black and
silver ground in a crackle pattern with red enamel zigeraut
decoration on one side. (Robt.
W. Skinner Inc.)   $200

# CLARET JUGS

## SILVER

A Victorian claret jug, by James Le Bass, Dublin, 1840, fully marked, 30cm. high, 38oz.4dwt.
$1,328

A Victorian Irish claret jug, maker J. S. (Russell Baldwin & Bright)   $1,150

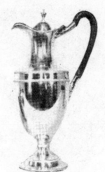

A George III solid silver claret jug, by Hester Bateman, London, 1784, 12½in. high, approx. 20 troy oz. (Stalker & Boos)
$2,000

A Hukin & Heath electroplated claret jug, designed by Christopher Dresser, 22cm. high, 1880's.
$260

A William IV claret jug, by E., E., J. & W. Barnard, London, 1836, 30oz.10dwt., 12¼in. high.   $1,435

A Victorian silver mounted claret jug, by Chas. Reily & George Storer, London, 1850, 11in. high.$975

A Victorian claret jug, maker's mark WWW, 1866, 14in. high, 37oz.14dwt. all in.
$1,161

A Victorian silver mounted claret jug. (Russell Baldwin & Bright)   $925

A Victorian glass claret jug with silver top and leaf matt and strapwork handle, maker W. E., London, 1873, 12in. high. (Woolley & Wallis)
$1,548

One of a pair of George III
silver coasters decorated
with embossed vines, 1816.
(Hobbs & Chambers)
$1,105

One of a pair of William IV
shaped circular wine coaster,
by Thomas Blagden & Co.,
Sheffield, 1830, 18.5cm.
diam. (Lawrence Fine Art)
$1,437

One of a pair of George III
coasters, by Wm. Plummer,
London, 1779, 4¾in.
(Dreweatt Watson & Barton)
$1,090

One of a pair of Omar Ramsden silver wine coasters,
London, 1934, 14cm. diam.
$4,540

One of a pair of George III
wine coasters, makers
John and Thos. Settle,
Sheffield 1816, 7in. diam.
(Hobbs & Chambers)
$1,088

One of a pair of early Victorian
decanter stands, by C., C.T. and
G. Fox, London, 1839/41.
(Woolley & Wallis)
$1,612

Pair of George IV wine
coasters by Benjamin Smith,
London 1823, 5⅜in. diam.
$4,092

One of a pair of George IV
brass bound mahogany wine
coasters, 12½in. high.
(Christie's)    $2,829

Two of a set of four George III
circular wine coasters, by R.
Emes and E. Barnard, 1809
and 1810, 15.6cm. diam. (Lawrence Fine Art)$2,437

One of a set of four early
Victorian shaped circular
wine coasters, by Hyman
Wilkinson & Co., Sheffield
1842, 14cm. diam.
(Christie's)  $1,474

One of a pair of George III
plain coasters, by Robert
and Samuel Hennell, 1803,
5¼in. (Christie's)
$1,853

One of a pair of George III
circular coasters, by Jabez
and Thos. Daniel, London,
1773. (Woolley & Wallis)
$1,369

# COFFEE POTS

A George II baluster coffee pot, by Fuller White, London, 1756, 9¾in. high, 25oz. 4dwt. all in. $3,110

A sterling silver repousse coffee pot, New York, circa 1850, 11½in. high, 35½ troy oz. (Robt. W. Skinner Inc.) $500

A George III silver pear-shaped coffee pot, possibly by Wm. Cox, London 1775, 11.3/8in. high, 28oz.10dwt. gross. (Geering & Colyer) $595

A George II silver coffee pot of plain form, by J. Payne, London 1754, 22oz. (Locke & England) $2,480

A George II coffee pot of tapering cylindrical form, by Edward Feline, 1732, 6.75in. high, 14oz. gross. (Neales) $1,091

A George II baluster coffee pot, by Thos. Whipham, London, 1755, 23oz.18dwt. $1,768

A George I coffee pot of tapering cylindrical form, by P.I., 1717, 7½in. high, 18oz. 10dwt. (Neales) $1,740

A Chinese coffee pot, the scroll handle, finial and spout in the form of bamboo, 22.5cm., 26oz. (Lawrence Fine Art) $576

A George I tapered cylindrical coffee pot by Philip Elliot, Exeter, 1726, 9¼in. high, 21oz.9dwt. all in. $4,061

582

A silver gilt coffee pot by
J. C. Krause, 24.1cm. high,
Konigsberg, 1757, 645gr.
(all in). $3,757

An early Victorian coffee pot,
by Charles Reily & George
Storer, 1841, 30.7cm. overall
height. (Lawrence Fine Art)
$893

A vase-shaped coffee jug
and stand, by Paul Storr,
London, 1814, 28.3cm.
high, 1830gr.
$5,844

An Italian coffee pot with
carved wood handle, 31.3cm.
high, Genoa, 1768, 1110gr.
$7,931

A silver gilt coffee pot by M.
Ovchinnikov, in Empire
style, maker's mark, Mos-
cow, 1896, 22cm. high.
$3,917

A George III plain baluster
coffee pot, by J. Kentember,
1773, 11¼in. high, 25oz.
19dwt. gross. (Neales)
$1,340

A George I tapered cylindrical coffee pot, marked John
Wisdome, London, 1719,
9½in. high, 23oz.15dwt. all
in. $4,061

A George II Irish coffee pot,
by Thomas Walker, Dublin
1736, 9in. high, 27oz. all
in. (Woolley & Wallis)
$2,540

A baluster coffee pot, by
Franz T. Baltzer, 20cm.
high, Munster, circa 1785,
320gr. (all in). $2,092

## COFFEE POTS

A German coffee pot, by Gustav Friedrich Gerich, Augsburg, 1805, 22oz. all in, 10½in. high.
$1,309

A William IV melon panelled baluster coffee pot by E., E. J. & W. Barnard, London 1834, 29oz. (Woolley & Wallis)     $870

A George I plain tapering cylindrical coffee pot, by Thos. Mason, 1725, 9¾in. high, gross 27oz. (Christie's) $4,762

A George II coffee pot by Thomas Whipham, London, 1745, 9½in. high. (Woolley & Wallis)
$1,607

George II silver coffee pot, by Edward Vincent, London, 1738, 8in. high, 19oz. (Hobbs & Chambers)
$1,827

A Queen Anne plain tapering cylindrical coffee pot, by Isaac Dighton, 1705, 9in. high, gross 23oz. (Christie's)$6,804

A George II coffee pot, by Wm. Williams I, London, 1743, 24oz.14dwt., 9½in. high.        $1,187

A North Italian coffee pot, maker's mark A.T., circa 1770, 31oz.2dwt. all in, 11½in. high.
$4,428

A George III baluster coffee pot, by Walter Brind, 1773, 10½in. high, 22oz. gross. (Neales)    $1,522

584

A Queen Anne plain tapering cylindrical coffee pot, by Joseph Ward, 1703, 9in. high, gross 18oz.10dwt. (Christie's) $6,577

A Maltese coffee pot, apparently Francesco Arnaud, circa 1780, 30oz.15dwt., 11in. high. $4,620

A George III coffee pot, by Hester Bateman, London, 1775, 12¼in. high, 27oz. 4dwt. all in. $2,087

A George III coffee pot in the neo-classical style, London 1792, 34cm. high, 790 gr. (H. Spencer & Sons) $880

A Belgian coffee jug, maker's mark MH conjoined below a crown, Mons, circa 1730, 9oz.15dwt., 6in. high. $6,160

A George III coffee pot, London, 1781, 24½oz. (John D. Fleming & Co.) $1,196

A George III coffee pot, by John Kentember, London, 1770, 26oz.7dwt., 10¾in. high. $1,816

A George II coffee pot, by Ayme Videau, London, 1738, 6¾in. high, 12oz.16dwt. all in. $949

A George I tapering cylindrical coffee pot on molded rim foot, by John East, London 1722, 23.2cm. high, 24oz. (Christie's) $3,931

# CREAM JUGS

A 19th century Dutch cow creamer, Import marks for 1892, 17.5cm., 7.8oz. (Lawrence Fine Art) $522

A William IV silver cream jug on four feet, London, 1835, maker's mark R.P.G. B., 5oz.10dwt. (Geering & Colyer) $119

A George III cream jug formed as a cow, by John Schupper, 1764, 4oz.6dwt. (Christie's) $4,989

A George II cream jug, by Chas. Woodward, London, 1748, 4oz.16dwt., 4¼in. high. $586

An early Victorian melon-shaped silver cream jug, 6oz. $206

A George III cream jug, London, 1795, 5½in. high, 3oz. (Hobbs & Chambers) $179

Late 19th century Dutch silver cream jug, 3½oz. $100

Late Victorian silver cream jug by Smith, Sissons & Co., 1897. $156

A Belgian cream pot with scroll handle, maker's mark T.B. crowned, Namur, circa 1750, 12.3cm. high, 155gr. $1,669

A two bottle cruet frame, by Adam Jansens, maker's mark, Maastricht, 1784-86, 27.1cm. wide, 680gr. excluding cut glass bottles and stoppers.          $6,956

George IV seven-bottle silver cruet stand on paw feet, 1824.   $562

An oval two-bottle cruet with two cut glass spirit bottles with silver stoppers, Dutch, 18th century. (Christie's)     $760

An oval two-bottle cruet with two silver mounted spirit bottles of a later date, London, 1775. (Christie's) $651

A Victorian basket design egg cruet, by Robert Hennell III, London, 1856, 9½in. long, 28oz. (Woolley & Wallis)          $619

An Italian two-bottle cruet frame, by Gaspare Ravizza, Turin, circa 1755, 11oz. excluding two blue glass liners, 8in. high.
                  $2,214

George III four-bottle silver cruet, by R. & S. Hennell, with blue glass bottles, 9½in. high, 1809.          $687

A George III cruet stand, by Hester Bateman, 1783, the bottle mounts Birmingham, 1871 by Henry Matthews, 21.5cm. high. (Lawrence Fine Art)          $187

A George II Warwick cruet, by Milne & Campbell, Glasgow, circa 1750, 9¼in. high, 49oz.13dwt. $3,275

A silver caudle cup, London, 1683, 8½oz. (Wm. Doyle Galleries) $1,200

A Guild of Handicrafts hammered silver plated cup and cover set with garnets designed by C. R. Ashbee, circa 1896, 29cm. high. (Christie's) $2,177

Silver caudle cup by Henry Greene, London 1720-21, 7oz. (Wm. Doyle Galleries) $650

A Wakeley & Wheeler silver cup and cover designed by R. Y. Gleadowe, Birmingham silver marks for 1938, 30oz.10dwt., 37cm. high. (Christie's) $10,206

A James Powell & Son silver and green glass two-handled cup, London hallmarks for 1909, 19oz.12dwt., 22.8cm. high. (Christie's) $748

A Charles I silver gilt recusant chalice, the bulbous knop applied with four angels' heads. (Woolley & Wallis) $744

A George III cup and cover by Robert Sharp, London 1800, 15in. high, 71oz. (Woolley & Wallis) $1,860

A Continental silver gilt nautilus cup, 17in. high. (Woolley & Wallis) $1,364

A Regency period silver gilt campana-shape cup and cover by Paul Storr, London 1818, 15in. high, 108oz. (Woolley & Wallis) $4,318

One of a pair of George III
cups and covers, by Smith
& Sharp, London, 1773,
9¼in. high, 32oz.15dwt.
$3,124

A George III parcel gilt
fox's mask stirrup cup,
by Thomas Pitts, 1771,
5½in. long, 5oz. (Christie's)
$3,189

A George III silver mounted
ostrich egg cup, 26cm. high.
(Lawrence Fine Art)
$412

A silver gilt standing cup
by A. Kessbair I, 22.6cm.
high, Augsburg, circa 1680,
290gr.       $1,670

Tiffany sterling silver loving
cup, New York, 1891, 9in.
high, 13 troy oz. (Robt. W.
Skinner Inc.) $500

A parcel gilt standing cup
by Marx Merzenbach, 14cm.
high, Augsburg, circa 1670,
75gr.       $5,009

A George III maritime vase-
shaped presentation cup
and cover, by Robert Sal-
mon, London, 1793, 14in.
high, 43 troy oz. (Reeds
Rains)     $3,550

A German parcel gilt standing cup, 20cm. high, probably by Gerhardt Sanders ,
Wesel, 1692-93, 348gr.
$1,980

A George III silver gilt cup
and cover by John Houle,
London 1812, 38cm. high,
101oz. (Lawrence Fine Art)
$2,475

One of a pair of George III
entree dishes and covers,
by Richard Cooke, London,
1807, 11in. diam., 134oz.
$5,310

An early George I straw-
berry dish, Britannia Standard 1717, 22.5cm., 17.5oz.
(Lawrence Fine Art)
$1,375

Mid 19th century Kirk
repousse sterling covered
vegetable dish of oval form,
Maryland, approx. 100 troy
oz. (Robt. W. Skinner Inc.)
$2,100

A George II dish, possibly
John Carnaby, Newcastle,
circa 1735, 7oz.17dwt.,
6¼in.       $977

A silver gilt and plique a
jour enamel kovsh of wide
boat form with flattened
trefoil-shaped handle, Moscow, circa 1880, 14.7cm.
long.       $1,654

Late 16th/early 17th cen-
tury Hungarian parcel gilt
circular dish, unmarked,
24.2cm. diam., 415gr.
$4,950

A Baptismal two-handled
basin by J. A. Lamoureux,
56cm. wide overall, Riga,
circa 1730, 2080gr.
$3,339

A George III neo-classical
sauce dish and cover, by J.
Wakelin and W. Taylor,
London 1785, 8.5in. high.
(Woolley & Wallis)
$1,302

One of a pair of oblong
entree dishes and covers, by
Paul Storr, London 1812,
31cm. wide, 3750gr.
$6,680

One of a pair of William IV entree dishes and covers, by Paul Storr, London, 1836, 10¾in. diam., 113oz.7dwt. $4,147

One of a pair of early 19th century rectangular entree dishes on stands, 15in. across handles. (Woolley & Wallis) $666

A William IV entree dish and cover by Paul Storr, London 1835, complete with a Sheffield plate warmer and liner, 60oz. (Morphets) $4,420

A George III silver gilt fluted circular dish of shallow form, by E. C. Farrell, London, 1818, 10in. diam., 17oz.3dwt. $4,373

One of a pair of late Regency Sheffield plate oval meat dishes and matching covers, 16in. (Woolley & Wallis) $533

A William IV entree dish by Paul Storr, on four foliate scroll feet, London, 1833, 34oz. (Morphets) $780

One of a set of four Sheffield plated entree dishes , covers and detachable handles by M. Boulton, 25.3cm. (Lawrence Fine Art) $446

A lapis lazuli dish with silver couple on round cornered rectangular stone, 4¼in. long. (Robt. W. Skinner Inc.)$275

A shaped oval dish by H. Swierink, Amsterdam, 1766, 52cm. wide, 1580gr. $3,547

A George II oval shaving ewer by John Delmester, London, 1759, 8¼in. high, 19oz.11dwt. all in. $2,655

A Portuguese ewer, circa 1580, 18oz.2dwt., 9in. high. $6,160

One of a pair of late 18th century Portuguese ewers, maker's mark G.I.P., 58oz. 14dwt., 10¼in. high. $10,010

A helmet-shaped ewer in the style of the early 18th century, maker's mark T.C., 21.5cm. high, 22oz. (Lawrence Fine Art) $1,732

Pair of large vase-shaped ewers, by Messrs. Carrington, 1905 and 1906, height without plinth 17½in., 231oz. (Christie's) $11,340

A Victorian ewer by Henry Heyde, London, 1859, 14in. high, 27oz.6dwt. all in. $1,435

A Victorian 'Cellini' pattern ewer, Charles Boyton, London, 1884, 11½in. high, 32oz.3dwt. $1,139

A helmet-shaped ewer by Johann Breckerfelt, 21.9cm. high, maker's mark, Wesel, 1723-24, 620gr. $4,620

A pyriform ewer with a flaring fluted neck, by Conrad Bard & Son, Phila., 1850-59, 29oz.10dwt. (Christie's) $880

A Norwegian parcel gilt spoon, by Jost Alberszenn, (Bergen), circa 1620, with leaf-engraved and later crested bowl, maker's mark only. $963

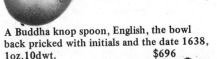

A Buddha knop spoon, English, the bowl back pricked with initials and the date 1638, 1oz.10dwt. $696

A Dutch fish server, by Jan Diederik Pont, Amsterdam, 1757, 8oz.13dwt., 15in. long. $3,080

A serving fork and spoon, by Gorham Manuf. Co., circa 1870, 11in. long, 6oz.10dwt. (Christie's) $385

A Georgian Irish silver punch ladle. (Russell Baldwin & Bright) $550

A 127-piece canteen of Dubarry pattern cutlery, Sheffield, 1930, in original oak case with two fitted drawers, 168oz. (Worsfolds) $3,840

Pair of George III stork cast ribbon pullers with gilt beak, maker possibly E. Holmes, London 1801. (Woolley & Wallis) $246

A William IV fiddle, thread and shell table service, by Samuel Hayne and Dudley Cater, 1836, 248oz. (Christie's) $11,389

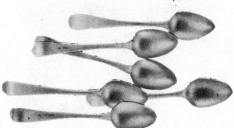

A set of six teaspoons, maker's mark of Joseph Lownes, Phila., circa 1785-1815, each with a pointed oval bowl, 6.1/8in. long, 3oz. (Christie's) $495

Mid 17th century Hungarian silver gilt spoon, probably Pozsony. $660

An early George II Hanoverian rat-tail pattern basting spoon, maker John Gibbons or Goram, London, 1730, 5.5oz. (Woolley & Wallis)     $464

An early 19th century fiddle pattern basting spoon by Robert Keay, Perth, 4oz. (Woolley & Wallis)           $166

Mid 17th century German parcel gilt spoon with fig-shaped bowl, possibly by F. W. Kiel.           $1,237

An Old English pattern basting spoon, maker Alexander Thompson, circa 1775, 6.5oz. (Woolley & Wallis)       $522

A silver gilt spoon by Michael Hafner, maker's mark, Augsburg, circa 1695.           $825

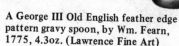

A George III Old English feather edge pattern gravy spoon, by Wm. Fearn, 1775, 4.3oz. (Lawrence Fine Art)       $288

A 17th century trefid spoon, the stem of circular form, flattened and tapering to the terminal, 17cm. long. (H. Spencer & Sons)       $541

A Norwegian spoon, the bowl engraved with a spray within strapwork, circa 1612.           $577

A 57-piece service of fiddle, thread and shell pattern cutlery for twelve place settings, maker's mark CWF, 1933, 136oz. (Lawrence Fine Art)       $1,873

A 19th century service of fiddle, thread and shell pattern cutlery for twelve place settings, by several silver makers, 142oz. (Lawrence Fine Art)       $429

# SILVER

## FLATWARE

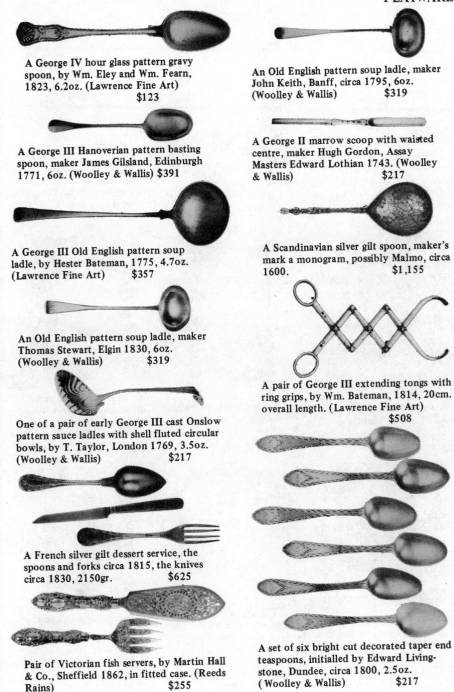

A George IV hour glass pattern gravy spoon, by Wm. Eley and Wm. Fearn, 1823, 6.2oz. (Lawrence Fine Art) $123

A George III Hanoverian pattern basting spoon, maker James Gilsland, Edinburgh 1771, 6oz. (Woolley & Wallis) $391

A George III Old English pattern soup ladle, by Hester Bateman, 1775, 4.7oz. (Lawrence Fine Art) $357

An Old English pattern soup ladle, maker Thomas Stewart, Elgin 1830, 6oz. (Woolley & Wallis) $319

One of a pair of early George III cast Onslow pattern sauce ladles with shell fluted circular bowls, by T. Taylor, London 1769, 3.5oz. (Woolley & Wallis) $217

A French silver gilt dessert service, the spoons and forks circa 1815, the knives circa 1830, 2150gr. $625

Pair of Victorian fish servers, by Martin Hall & Co., Sheffield 1862, in fitted case. (Reeds Rains) $255

An Old English pattern soup ladle, maker John Keith, Banff, circa 1795, 6oz. (Woolley & Wallis) $319

A George II marrow scoop with waisted centre, maker Hugh Gordon, Assay Masters Edward Lothian 1743. (Woolley & Wallis) $217

A Scandinavian silver gilt spoon, maker's mark a monogram, possibly Malmo, circa 1600. $1,155

A pair of George III extending tongs with ring grips, by Wm. Bateman, 1814, 20cm. overall length. (Lawrence Fine Art) $508

A set of six bright cut decorated taper end teaspoons, initialled by Edward Livingstone, Dundee, circa 1800, 2.5oz. (Woolley & Wallis) $217

# FRAMES

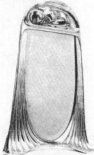

An Austrian electroplated mirror, cast with crouched nude figure above, 51.75cm. high, circa 1900. $851

A white metal and colored enamel dressing mirror in the Art Nouveau style, attributed to the March Bros., 50cm. high. (Lawrence Fine Art)        $256

An Edwardian silver framed standing table mirror, Birmingham, 1904, 16in. high. (P. Wilson & Co.)        $264

Late 19th century shaped silver photograph frame, 24.2cm. high. (Christie's)        $772

A WMF electroplated frame, border cast with young woman gazing at her reflection, circa 1900, 37cm.        $663

A cartouche-shaped easel dressing table mirror frame, makers T. May & Co., Birmingham, 1904, 17½ x 18in. overall. (Woolley & Wallis)        $1,161

Late 19th century Howard & Co. rococo-style sterling silver dressing mirror, New York, 33in. high. (Robt. W. Skinner Inc.)        $7,500

A Charles II toilet mirror, the border and cresting chased with chinoiserie figures, by Anthony Nelme, 1684, 23in. high. (Christie's)        $20,370

One of a pair of silver coloured metal frames, each swivel mounted in angled open supports, 31cm. high, 1930's.        $260

One of a pair of George III goblets, by R. Sharp, London, 1794, 6¼in. high, 17oz.17dwt.
$1,518

One of three Desny electro-plated goblets, conical bowl and small conical foot connected by angled flange, 1920's, 12cm. high.          $737

One of a rare set of five goblets, by J. Lownes, Phila., circa 1790-1820, 5½in. high, 38oz. (Christie's)
$9,900

A 17th century Portuguese chalice, unmarked, 20oz. 8dwt., 9¾in. high.
$1,444

One of a pair of presentation Art Nouveau goblets, by Omar Ramsden and Alwyn Carr, London 1913, 5in. high. (Woolley & Wallis)     $1,041

A small parcel gilt chalice, by G. Tcherch, circa 1850, 10.2cm.          $478

A 17th century Flemish silver mounted glass goblet, unmarked, the bowl probably Liege, 8¼in. high. (Christie's)  $680

One of a set of six Victorian goblets, by J. Dixon & Sons, two uninscribed, Sheffield 1862/66 and four inscribed and dated 1868, 46oz., 6½in. high. (Woolley & Wallis)
$2,142

A presentation goblet, American, possibly Savannah, circa 1857, 7½in. high, 9oz.10dwt. (Christie's)  $1,320

An ornate early Victorian silver inkstand with two silver mounted glass inkwells. $468

A 19th century hallmarked Danish silver inkstand, Copenhagen, 16 troy oz. (Robt. W. Skinner Inc.)      $310

A Victorian two-bottle inkstand, by Henry Holland, London, 1877, 35oz., 11in. wide. $1,031

A Victorian inkstand, by E. Barnard & Sons, London, 1895, 14in. wide, 1772gr. $1,625

A Victorian inkstand, by Walker & Hall, Sheffield, 1898, 10½in. wide, 20oz. $437

George IV silver inkstand on bun feet, 5oz., dated 1822.      $531

A Victorian inkstand, London, 1880, maker's mark WBJ, 34cm. long, 1642gr. (H. Spencer & Sons)      $458

A Victorian inkstand, by C. Reily and G. Storer, London, 1843, 12½in. wide, 32oz. 6dwt. excluding inkwell. $2,087

A large electroplate two-bottle inkstand, by Edward Barnard & Sons of London, 1840-46, 12¾in. long.          $910

A Spanish inkstand, by Blas Antonio Santa Cruz, Cordoba, 1771, 58oz.6dwt., 12in. wide.          $3,658

Late Victorian, cyclist's novelty inkwell, Birmingham, 1896, 5¼in. wide. (Capes, Dunn & Co.)          $494

A silver gilt, presentation, rectangular inkstand, by C. T. & G. Fox, London, 1857, 11½in. long. (Woolley & Wallis)          $4,998

A late George III rectangular inkstand with two silver mounted ink bottles flanking the central wafer box, by T. & J. Settle, Sheffield, 1819, 30cm. long. (Lawrence Fine Art)          $2,500

A silver mounted emu egg inkwell, by J. M. Wendt, maker's mark, Adelaide, circa 1870, 21cm. high.          $5,426

A George III silver gilt rectangular inkstand on four lion's paw feet, by Digby Scott and Benjamin Smith, 1804, 11¼in. long, 65oz. (Christie's)          $18,144

Sheffield plated inkstand fitted with two ink pots and pen tray, 16in. long. (Stalker & Boos)          $650

# JUGS

# SILVER

A George III vase-shaped hot water jug, maker's mark RG, possibly Richard Gardner, 1787, 12¾in. high, 25oz. gross. (Christie's) $1,594

A William and Mary small jug with bulbous body, by Thos. Havers, Norwich, 1689, 2in. high, 1oz.5dwt. (Christie's) $1,134

A Spanish jug, by Antonio Fernandez Clemente, Salamanca, 1759, 23oz. 6dwt., 9½in. high. $3,273

Tiffany sterling silver water pitcher of circular bulbous form, circa 1880, 8¾in. high, approx. 30 troy oz. (Stalker & Boos) $900

A George III neo-classical vase-shaped hot water jug by Thos. Wallis I, London 1775, 12in. high, 26oz. (Woolley & Wallis) $1,091

Silver milk pitcher, maker's mark Hayden & Gregg, 1846-52, 6 5/8in. high, approx. 14 troy oz. (Robt. W. Skinner Inc.) $650

A sterling silver repousse water pitcher, marked S. Kirk & Son, Baltimore, 1846-61, 11.1/8in. high, 32 troy oz. (Robt. W. Skinner Inc.) $750

A frosted silver kvass jug with reeded neck and scroll handle, Moscow, 1888, 10cm. high. $261

George II silver covered baluster jug by Pent Symonds, Exeter, 1739, 9½in. high, 27oz. (Hobbs & Chambers) $4,410

# SILVER

A goldwashed silver and coral rattle whistle, hallmarked Birmingham, 1862, 6in. long. (Robt. W. Skinner Inc.) $290

A Victorian trophy, by E. Barnard & Sons, London, 1894, 88oz.10dwt. excluding the ebonized wood plinth, 18in. wide. $4,191

A Rein & Son 'London Dome' silver plated hearing trumpet, English, circa 1865, 6¾in. long. $430

A recipe cocktail shaker, the outer sleeve of which revolves to reveal the correct ingredients. (Phillips) $108

Art Deco gold and silver compact with French-cut sapphire and gold mounts, housing a lighter and a lipstick. (Robt. W. Skinner Inc.) $300

A plated cocktail shaker in the form of a dumbbell. (Phillips) $168

A Sheffield plate 'Skep' honey pot, unmarked, circa 1800, 5in. high. $628

Late 19th century American ebony walking cane, with silver handle, 35½in. long overall. (Reeds Rains) $165

A George III kitchen nutmeg grater with reeded handle, by Phipps & Robinson, London 1786, 11cm. long. (Christie's) $477

# SILVER

A George III oval Argyle, marked Aldridge & Green, London, 1781, 4¼in. high, 12oz.9dwt. all in.
$2,312

A George III presentation trowel with faceted stained ivory handle, 38cm. long, Dublin 1789.
$2,499

A snuffer's tray and a pair of snuffers, by G. Cardon, the tray 22cm. wide, Dunkerque, circa 1745, 403gr.
$2,505

A George III hanging nutmeg grater, by John Reily, London, 1817, 4in. high.
$638

One of a pair of silver gilt Argyles in George III-style, marked J. B. Carrington, London, 1902, 6in. high, 49oz.6dwt. $4,061

A silver gilt and horn linctus dropper, hallmarked London 1884.
$960

A Michelsen silver cocktail shaker designed by Kay Fischer, Danish silver marks, circa 1935, 18oz.5dwt., 24.5cm. high. (Christie's)
$706

Pair of silver and glass spirit bottles, the trompe-l'oeil basketwork covers tied with a silver rope, St. Petersburg, 1880, 29cm. $2,960

A French table bell, 10.2cm. high, maker's mark J.D., Paris, 1761, 138gr.
$5,009

A late Victorian chamber pot, with a scroll handle. (Woolley & Wallis) $619

A George I lemon strainer, London, 1722, 6½in. wide over handles, 1oz.13dwt. $669

A table bell in the form of a tortoise, maker's mark JB, London, 1897, 6¼in. long. $701

A silver-plate figure of an elephant, the howdah in the form of a gu-shaped vase, 10in. high. $291

A set of twelve George III buttons, possibly by John Orme, London, circa 1780, 1oz.19dwt. $3,280

A glass and silver trompe-l'oeil spirit bottle, with rope-bound wicker holder, St. Petersburg, 1884, 23cm. high. $2,176

A table bell by Godert Van Ysseldijk, 14.5cm. high, maker's mark, The Hague, 1767, 306gr. $742

Late 19th century silver koro with pierced shaped handles, the cover signed Shiono, 9.4cm. high. (Christie's) $946

An electroplated epergne and mirror plateau, 24½in. high, circa 1850. $1,276

# SILVER

A William and Mary mug of tapered cylindrical form, maker's mark IC over a star, London, 1691, 4½in. high, 419gr.          $2,967

A christening mug by Pierre Maingy, Guernsey, circa 1763, 2½in. high, 2oz.19dwt.          $622

A Victorian christening mug, by Stephen Smith, 1872, 9.6cm. high.          $125

A George III Irish Provincial mug, by Carden Terry, Cork, circa 1780, 13oz.3dwt., 4¾in. high.          $949

Victorian silver gilt christening mug of faceted baluster form, Sheffield, 1859, 7oz. 4dwt., 4½in. high.          $437

Silver christening mug of inverted bell shape with scroll handle and cast foot, London 1869, 2½oz. (P. Wilson & Co.) $115

A Queen Anne mug, Britannia Standard 1706 by M. E. Lofthouse, 12.4cm. high, 13.2oz. (Lawrence Fine Art)          $467

An early 18th century silver cann, probably Boston, possibly by Samuel Edwards, 4in. high, 6 troy oz. (Robt. W. Skinner Inc.)          $900

A 19th century silver mug with loop handle simulating bamboo, 4½in. high.          $737

One of a pair of James II baluster mugs, by G. Garthorne, London, 1688, 4in. high, 19oz.2dwt.
$3,436

A Channel Islands christening mug with circular body, circa 1690-1730, 6.3cm. high. (Lawrence Fine Art)
$742

One of a pair of William and Mary baluster mugs, probably by J. Chadwick, London, 1691, 3¼in. high, 7oz.11dwt.
$3,592

A George III silver baluster shaped mug, maker's mark B.C., 4.7/8in. high, London 1776, 6oz.18dwt. (Geering & Colyer)    $419

A 19th century South American mug, stamped Leiba, 12oz.2dwt., 4¼in. high.         $578

Mid 18th century footed silver cann, maker's mark on base 'I. Edwards', 5¼in. high, 10 troy oz. (Robt. W. Skinner Inc.)
$1,400

One of a pair of canns of pyriform with 'S' scroll handles, by Samuel Edwards, Boston, 1730-62, 5½in. high, 22oz. (Christie's)
$3,300

A Victorian engine-turned christening mug with leaf capped reverse scroll handle, by Rawlings & Sumner, London, 1850, 8oz. (Christie's)    $156

A George I mug, by Wm. Darker, London, 1726, 10oz.10dwt., 5in. high.
$768

A George III oval mustard
pot, by Hester Bateman,
London, 1787, 3in. high.
$258

A George III oval mustard
pot, by Joseph Scammel,
London, 1793, 5½in. high.
$193

George III silver mustard
pot of plain cylindrical
form with scroll handle,
3½oz.      $106

A George III shaped oblong
mustard pot, by Edward
Capper, London, 1797, 3¾in.
high.      $258

A French silver gilt double
compartment salt cellar
and a mustard pot, maker's
mark apparently F.A.T.,
Paris, circa 1860, 4in. high,
1289gr.     $3,658

A Victorian mustard pot
formed as Mr Punch,
maker JBH, London 1878,
10cm. high, 6.5oz.
(Christie's)   $785

A drum mustard pot, mar-
ked Edward Aldridge,
London, 1764, 3oz.16dwt.
$343

George III silver mustard
pot with scroll handle,
4oz., 1801.    $218

A Victorian octagonal
mustard pot, by Robert
Garrard, 1851, 18oz.8dwt.
$387

20th century sterling silver nef, probably Germany, 17½in. long, 34 troy oz. (Robt. W. Skinner Inc.) $1,100

Late 19th century Dutch or German nef, modelled as a galleon with putti and dolphin chased hull, 23½in. high, 114oz.16dwt. of silver-colored metal. $3,225

A large silver nef made by Neresheimer & Co. of Hanau, with import marks for Berthold Muller. $3,840

## PORRINGERS

A silver Guild of Handicrafts single-handled porringer, London hallmarks for 1900, 3oz.12dwt., 19cm. wide. (Christie's) $788

A Gorham sterling silver porringer of circular form with two side mounted 'C' scroll handles, 4½in. diam., 7 troy oz. (Stalker & Boos) $200

A Kirk sterling silver porringer with reticulated handle, 4¼in. diam., 8 troy oz. (Stalker & Boos) $350

A James II two-handled porringer, maker's mark PR in monogram, 1685, 3.1/8in. high, 6oz.10dwt.(Christie's) $1,708

Late 18th century Boston-style silver porringer, 5in. diam., 8 troy oz. (Robt. W. Skinner Inc.) $400

A James II small two-handled porringer with half fluted body, London, 1685, 3½oz. (Christie's) $542

One of a pair of William and Mary trencher salt cellars, London, 1690, diam. 7cm., with a pair of 18th century spoons, 7oz.     $908

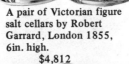

One of a pair of salts of fluted shell-shape, by Whiting Manuf. Co., circa 1865, 4in. long. (Christie's)     $286

One of a pair of Queen Anne trencher salt cellars, by Wm. Pearson, London, 1710, 2½in. wide, together with a pair of salt spoons, 4oz.14dwt.     $872

One of four George II circular salt cellars, by Paul de Lamerie, two 1730, two 1731, Britannia Standard, 27oz. (Christie's) $8,505

A pair of Victorian figure salt cellars by Robert Garrard, London 1855, 6in. high. $4,812

A German silver gilt salt, maker's mark F. above a wheel (Rosenberg no. 498), Augsburg, 1600-10, 3oz., 2¼in. high. $1,117

A silver shell-shaped salt on domed foot, maker's mark J.D. (Latin), 1857, 7cm.     $652

Five Victorian salt cellars with matching spoons, London 1869, 6½oz., in case. (Capes, Dunn & Co.) $208

A C. R. Ashbee hammered silver salt, set with amber London hallmarks for 1900, 1oz.12dwt., 5cm. high. (Christie's)     $380

One of a set of four early George II compressed circular salt cellars by Edward Wood, London 1735/36, 16oz. (Woolley & Wallis) $393

A silver gilt boat-shaped salt, maker's mark C.B., St. Petersburg, circa 1810, 9cm. $391

One of a set of six George II salt cellars, by Paul Crespin, London, 1734, 3.5/8in. diam., 60oz.     $8,437

One of a pair of George II oval-shaped sauceboats, by Wm. Skeen, London, 1755, 16oz. 4dwt., 6¾in. high. $738

One of a pair of George IV oval sauceboats, by Edward Farrell, London, 1829, 8¾in. high, 29oz.10dwt. $2,233

One of a pair of George III Irish oval sauceboats, by Matthew West, Dublin, 1775, 23oz.17dwt., 8¾in. long. $1,816

One of a pair of late Victorian cast rococo sauceboats, by Charles Stuart Harris, London 1897, 21oz. (Woolley & Wallis) $667

One of a pair of George III oval sauceboats, by Wm. Skeen, London, 1767, 6¾in. high, 16oz.15dwt. $1,563

One of a pair of George III oval ogee sauceboats, possibly by W. Vincent, 1771, 8¼in. long, 27oz. (Neales) $1,125

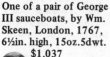

One of a pair of George III sauceboats, by Wm. Skeen, London, 1767, 6½in. high, 15oz.5dwt. $1,037

One of a pair of George II sauceboats in the rococo style, London 1759, 19cm. high, 37.6oz. (Lawrence Fine Art) $2,310

An oval sauceboat chased with foliage, unmarked, circa 1740, 7in., 15oz.11dwt. $4,842

An oval sauceboat with scroll handle, unmarked, circa 1750, 12cm., 5oz.5dwt. $1,093

One of a pair of oval sauceboats by J. A. G. L'Herminotte, Maastricht, 1768-70, 16.5cm., 745gr. $5,009

One of a pair of Regency-style scallop shell bowl sauceboats, makers Carrington & Co., London 1907. (Woolley & Wallis) $762

A George III oval silver snuff box, by Joseph Angell, London, 1817, 4¼in. wide. (Christie's)   $1,125

A French gold snuff box of rectangular pocket-fitting form, circa 1830, 8.3cm. wide.    $1,567

A French cartouche-shaped snuff box, 7.9cm. wide, Paris, 1738.   $1,253

A George IV Scottish gilt lined oblong snuff box, the hinged cover with a plaque of Pegasus, maker's or retailer's mark Home, Edinburgh, 1824, 3¼in. long. (Christie's)    $997

A 19th century Swiss gilt metal singing bird box, 10.5cm. wide. (H. Spencer & Sons)    $936

A George III snuff box in the form of a purse, maker's mark RB incuse, 1814, 6.3cm. (Lawrence Fine Art)    $288

A silver gilt cartouche-shaped snuff box, probably German, circa 1760.    $625

A George III oblong silver gilt snuff box, marked Linnit & Atkinson, London, 1812, 3in. wide.    $1,483

A large German hardstone snuff box of cartouche form, after the manner of the designs of M. Engelbrecht of Augsburg, circa 1740-50, 12cm. wide.   $2,524

A Scottish hand decorated sycamore snuff box, by Paterson of Mauchline, circa 1845, 3½in. wide.    $476

An English oval pressed horn snuff box, by John Obrisset, 1712, the lid decorated with the arms of Sir Francis Drake, oval 4in.    $326

An early Victorian oblong snuff box, engine turned, by Rawlings & Sumner, London, 1837, 8.6cm. wide.    $1,171

An English gilt metal and agate snuff box of cartouche form, Birmingham, mid 18th century, 2¾in. wide.
$201

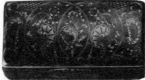

A silver and niello snuff box of rectangular form, maker's mark N.M., Moscow, mid 19th century, 9.2cm. wide.
$435

A gilt metal and mother-of-pearl snuff box, probably German, 2¾in. wide, circa 1740.
$476

A silver gilt and niello snuff box, maker's mark O.B., Moscow, 1834, 6.6cm. wide.
$522

A ram's horn snuff mull with plain silver rim and stand-off butterfly hinge, unmarked. (Christie's)
$65

An ivory snuff box, probably German, circa 1730, 3,1/8in. wide.
$376

An oval parcel gilt and niello snuff box, maker's mark D. L., Moscow, 1836, 7.1cm. wide.
$1,741

A French silver gilt snuff box, probably by E. Septier de la Selliere, Paris, 1752, 3¼in. wide.
$2,695

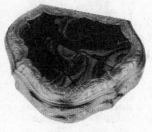

An English gilt metal and hardstone snuff box, Birmingham, circa 1750, 2½in. wide.
$201

An English gilt metal and aventurine snuff box, probably Birmingham, mid 18th century, 2½in. wide.
$226

An English gilt metal and agate snuff box, Birmingham, circa 1750, 2¼in. diam.
$125

A tortoiseshell pique snuff box, probably English, circa 1730, 3 1/8in. wide.
$451

# TANKARDS

George III lidded tankard with later repousse 'C' scroll, London, 1763, 29.2oz. gross. (Dee & Atkinson)   $496

A George III tapering cylindrical tankard, by J. W. Storey and W. Elliot, 1813, 7¾in. high, 57oz. (Christie's) $4,082

A Bayreuth black glazed brown stoneware cylindrical tankard with hinged silver gilt cover and ball thumbpiece, circa 1720, 23.5cm. high. (Christie's) $1,769

A late Victorian baluster tankard with molded girdle, by J. Round, Sheffield 1900, 21.5cm. high, 25oz. (Lawrence Fine Art)   $742

A parcel gilt tankard by N. Schlaugitz, Danzig, circa 1685, 16.4cm. high, 655gr. $2,713

A George III tankard, maker's mark of C. Hougham overstriking another, 1789, 18.5cm. high, 23oz. (Lawrence Fine Art) $893

A silver handled tankard, maker I.L., Newcastle, 1757, 10 troy oz., 4¾in. high. (Giles Haywood) $237

An Omar Ramsden hammered silver tankard, London hallmarks for 1914, 16oz., 12.5cm. high. (Christie's) $842

A George II baluster quart tankard by Fuller White, London 1754, 25.5oz. (Woolley & Wallis) $1,397

A German parcel gilt tankard, possibly by Marx Schaller II, Augsburg, circa 1655, 14.3cm. high, 440gr. $3,340

A silver gilt tankard by H. C. Lau(e)r, 15cm. high, Nuremberg, circa 1610, 290gr. $3,547

A James II·lidded cylindrical quart tankard, by Dorothy Grant, London, 1688, 6in. high, 19.75oz. (Woolley & Wallis) $2,975

A George III baluster tankard, possibly by Wm. Chatterton, London, 1775, 8½in. high, 33oz.6dwt. $2,733

A Queen Anne double quart lidded tankard, by John Downes, London 1708, 8in. high, 32oz. (Woolley & Wallis) $1,295

A George III bulbous-shaped lidded tankard by P., A. and W. Bateman, London, 1800, 8½in. high, 25oz.3dwt. (Banks & Silvers) $906

A George III tapered cylindrical tankard, maker's mark WG London 1779, 22oz. 14dwt., 7½in. high. $1,252

A Liberty & Co. 'Cymric' silver tankard designed by Archibald Knox, 1901, 19.25cm. high. $5,104

A George III baluster tankard with reeded spreading foot, by T. Powell, London, 1775, 8¾in. high, 31oz.6dwt.$1,834

A Victorian parcel gilt tea caddy by Joseph Angell, London, 1860, 7¾in. high, with a caddy spoon by G. Unite, Birmingham, 33oz. 9dwt. $3,280

Late 19th century Faberge silver tea caddy in the form of a large tea packet, Moscow, 13cm. wide. $11,320

One of a set of three George III tea caddies by D. Smith and R. Sharp, London, 1763, 5½in. high, 27oz. 2dwt., with a fitted shagreen case. $2,214

A Victorian tea caddy, repousse with mythological figures, London, 1875, 3½in. high, 5oz. (Hobbs & Chambers) $236

A late Victorian tea caddy in the Art Nouveau style, Chester 1900, 213gr. (H. Spencer & Sons) $209

A George III tea caddy, by Robt. Hennell I, London, 1788, of shaped oval form, 10oz.18dwt., 5¾in. high. $1,327

A George III tea caddy, by Peter and Wm. Bateman, London, 1814, 3¾in. high, 5oz.11dwt. $911

A George III square tea caddy, by Aaron Lestourgeon, 1772, 14oz.5dwt. (Christie's) $2,164

A George III oval tea caddy, by C. Aldridge & H. Green, London, 1778, 5in. high, 15oz.4dwt $2,186

A conical shaped tea kettle, by Mappin & Webb, possibly designed by C. Dresser, complete with stand and spirit burner. (Reeds Rains) $64

A Portuguese tea kettle, apparently Lisbon, circa 1750, and an English stand, Lewis Herne & Francis Butty, London, 1760, 99oz. 10dwt., 17in. high. $2,695

A late Victorian tea kettle, burner and stand, the oval stand on four 'S' scrolling supports, Sheffield 1899, maker's mark H.S., 1068 gr. total gross. (H. Spencer & Sons) $327

A George II inverted pear-shaped tea kettle, stand and lamp, by Wm. Cripps, 1744, gross 84oz. (Christie's) $2,041

Late 19th century sterling silver hot water kettle on stand, by Dominick & Haff, New York, 11½in. high. (Robt. W. Skinner Inc.) $800

A George V oval spirit kettle on stand. (Russell Baldwin & Bright) $425

An early Victorian circular panelled kettle on stand by J. & G. Angell, London, 1841, 86oz. (Woolley & Wallis) $1,736

A tea kettle and stand by The Goldsmiths & Silversmiths Co. Ltd., 1930, 31cm. high, 66oz. all in. (Lawrence Fine Art) $951

A Victorian tea kettle on stand, by Martin, Hall & Co., 1879, 30.5cm. high, 44oz. (Lawrence Fine Art) $1,325

# TEAPOTS

# TEAPOTS

A George IV teapot by R. Emes and E. Barnard, 1827, 26.5cm., 21oz. (Lawrence Fine Art)  $495

A George III teapot, by Cornelius Bland, London, 1789, 13oz.6dwt., 6in. high.  $977

A George II compressed circular teapot, by A. Videau, London, 1747, 4¾in. high, 26oz.9dwt. all in.  $2,811

A silver teapot by Paul Storr, 1832, 14oz.  $3,360

George III plain octagonal teapot on stand, by Henry Nutting, London, 1797, 23.3oz. gross. (Barber's Fine Art) $744

A George II inverted pear-shaped teapot, by George Methuen, London, 1750, 6in. high, 18oz.16dwt. all in.  $1,562

An early George III inverted pear-shape teapot by Robert Gordon, Edinburgh 1760, 20oz. all in. (Woolley & Wallis)  $992

George II silver teapot of pear form with turned finial on squat domed cover, London 1740-1, 5,7/8in. high. (Robt. W. Skinner Inc.)  $425

A George III oval serpentine panelled teapot on a matching oval stand, by M. Plummer, London 1795, teapot 18oz. all in. (Woolley & Wallis)  $1,165

An early Indian Colonial oval teapot, by John Hunt, circa 1800, 26.5oz. all in. (Woolley & Wallis)  $1,102

A William IV compressed circular panelled teapot by Chas. Fox, London, 1834, 25oz. all in. (Woolley & Wallis)  $406

A George IV teapot, the compressed spherical body on a molded foot rim, by James C. Edington, 1829, 26.5cm. 22oz. all in. (Lawrence Fine Art)  $518

A Charles Boyton hammered silver teapot, London hallmarks for 1933, 21oz. 19dwt., 12.5cm. high. (Christie's) $680

Part of a late 19th century Chinese three-piece teaset, by Woshing, Shanghai, 41oz. 6dwt. all in, the teapot 5¼in. high.          $1,155

A George III teapot of rounded cushioned rectangular form, London 1816, 625gr. (H. Spencer & Sons)          $202

A Chinese Export teapot in the English taste, Shanghai, circa 1790, 32cm. across, 26oz. all in. (Lawrence Fine Art)          $4,034

A fine quality George III silver teapot, 31oz. (Cooper Hirst) $473

A George IV rectangular ogee boat-shaped teapot by Joseph Angell, London, 1822. (Woolley & Wallis) $369

A George III cylindrical teapot with crested flush-hinged cover, by Charles Wright, 1772, 4.75in. high, 13oz. gross. (Neales) $570

An early Victorian teapot by Joseph II and Albert Savory, London 1846, 20.5cm. high, 25oz. (Lawrence Fine Art)$495

A pear-shaped teapot by J. C. Girschner, 12cm. high, Augsburg, 1763-65, 300gr. (all in). $3,130

A George III compressed circular teapot, by Wm. Burwash and R. Sibley, London 1805, 22oz. all in. (Woolley & Wallis) $508

A George III teapot on stand by Robert and David Hennell 1797, 28cm. across teapot, 17.7oz. all in. (Lawrence Fine Art)          $550

A George IV Irish teapot and cover of baluster form, by J. Keating and J. Fry, Dublin 1821, 1155gr. (H. Spencer & Sons)          $528

617

# SILVER

A composite silver gilt four-piece tea service , together with two dessert spoons, two dessert forks, two dessert knives and a pair of sugar tongs, 1820/22, all London, 55oz.4dwt. $3,045

A five-piece tea and coffee service on tray, by Ellis & Co. Ltd., Birmingham 1936 and 1937, coffee pot 24.5cm. high, 152oz. all in. (Lawrence Fine Art) $2,882

A silver gilt five-piece tea service, the teapot and hot water jug with ebonized scroll handles, by Messrs. Dobson, 1897, 1904, 1905 and 1907, hot water jug 18cm. high, 42oz. (Lawrence Fine Art) $1,100

A George IV three-piece tea service of panelled squat globular form, by
Charles Fox, London 1825, 1458 gr. (H. Spencer & Sons)    $861

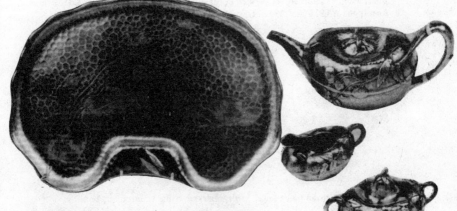

A hammer-textured silver-colored four-piece tea service by
Tiffany & Co., tray 15in. wide, circa 1890, 70oz. gross.
(Neales)                                    $3,484

A late Victorian five-piece tea and coffee service, including a tea kettle
on stand, by Charles Boyton, 1898, kettle 31.5cm. high, 102oz.
(Lawrence Fine Art)                              $1,801

A silver-gilt tea and coffee service in Slavonic taste, by Elkington & Co.,
Birmingham 1910 and 1913, tray 18¼in. wide, 87oz. gross. (Neales)
$1,340

A George IV three-piece teaset, fully marked William Bateman, London,
1828, 43oz.4dwt. (all in).                    $1,092

An Elizabeth II four-piece tea and coffee service in the late Georgian
style, of girdled circular pedestal form, Sheffield 1968, 2907gr., together
with a two-handled tea tray, Sheffield 1912, 2925gr., 58cm. long.
(H. Spencer & Sons)                    $1,845

A five-piece tea and coffee service, the plain baluster bodies each on a
spreading foot rim, by Mappin & Webb, 1919, coffee jug 20.5cm. high,
68oz. (Lawrence Fine Art)                    $1,210

A Chinese four-piece tea and coffee service on tray, maker's mark of
Bisansha, tray 52.5cm. across, 135oz. (Lawrence Fine Art)
$3,026

A Victorian four-piece ovoid tea and coffee set, maker's mark of Frederick
Elkington struck over that of E. Barnard & Sons, London, 1874, 95oz.
12dwt. all in.                              $2,967

An oval George III boat-shape six division toast rack, by John Emes, London, 1805, 7.5oz. (Woolley & Wallis) $212

Edwardian plated toast rack on bun feet.
$22

A Victorian electroplated toast rack designed by C. Dresser, by Hukin & Heath, 1881, 12.5cm. high. (Lawrence Fine Art) $165

Late 19th century silver plated on brass toast rack with pierced base. $25

A George III lyre-shaped toast rack with scroll ends and ring handle, maker Nathaniel Smith & Co., Sheffield, 1798, 5oz. (Woolley & Wallis) $328

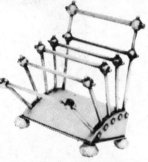

A Victorian electroplated letter rack in the style of Christopher Dresser, by Hukin & Heath, 12.9cm. high. (Lawrence Fine Art) $156

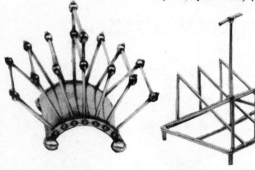

A Hukin & Heath electroplated toast/letter rack, designed by Christopher Dresser, 12.25cm. high, circa 1882. $227

A James Dixon & Son electroplated toast rack designed by C. Dresser, 1880's, 13.5cm.
$3,831

A Hukin & Heath electroplated toast/letter rack designed by Christopher Dresser, 12.5cm. high, 1880's.
$214

An early 19th century
Sheffield plate oval tea tray
with baized wood base,
23in. (Woolley & Wallis)
$571

William IV snuffer's tray,
Sheffield, 1830, 10in. wide.
(Hobbs & Chambers)
$217

A Queen Anne circular tazza
with stem foot, by Thos.
Parr, London, 1705, 10in.
(Woolley & Wallis)
$1,190

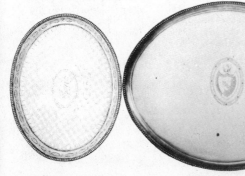

A George III oval teapot stand
by Hester Bateman, on four
ball and claw supports, London 1786, 16.9cm. (Lawrence
Fine Art)          $430

A George III oval salver with
four beaded shaped feet and
rim, by John Hutson, 1789,
17½in., 55oz. (Christie's)
$2,708

A Queen Anne plain circular footed waiter, probably
London, 1706, 24.5cm.
diam., 16oz. (Christie's)
$842

A Victorian shaped circular
salver on four pierced scroll
feet, by John S. Hunt, 1857,
23½in. diam., 140oz.
(Christie's)      $2,847

A William IV shaped circular salver on three foliate
feet, by J. Mackay, Edinburgh, 1833, 37cm. diam.,
40oz. (Christie's)$644

A George IV shaped circular salver on four scroll
bracket feet, by Robert
Garrard, 1823, 17¾in. diam.,
97oz. (Christie's)
$3,402

A late Victorian silver salver with gadrooned border, 18¼in. diam., London 1897, maker's mark J.F.C., approx. 90oz. 4dwt. (Geering & Colyer) $949

A George III salver with raised shaped shell pattern border, makers Thos. Hanman, London 1763, 12in. diam. 29oz. (Dee & Atkinson) $922

A William IV silver-gilt shaped circular salver, by Paul Storr, London 1836, 10in. diam., 24oz.11dwt. $2,392

A George IV shaped oblong two-handled tea tray, by Wm. Bateman I, London 1826, 68.5cm. across handles, 137oz. (Lawrence Fine Art) $4,620

A George III oval salver on four volute supports, by Thos. Jones, Dublin 1786. 13¾in. wide, 27oz.16dwt. $1,745

An oblong two-handled tea tray with plain centre, by Ellis & Co. Ltd., Birmingham 1940, 63cm. across handles, 106oz. (Lawrence Fine Art) $1,237

An early George III salver by Robert Rew, London 1760, 13in. diam., 35oz. (Woolley & Wallis) $1,276

A George III silver plate, makers Fras. Butty and N. Dumee, London 1769. (Dee & Atkinson) $369

One of two George II salvers in sizes, 38cm. and 24cm. diam., by George Wickes, London 1746, 74oz.1dwt. $4,529

An early George III shaped circular salver, by R. Rew or Rugg, London 1762, 10¼in. diam., 20oz.17dwt. $638

A George II salver by Ebenezer Coker, 1755, 10in. diam., 18oz. (Neales) $696

A hallmarked English silver salver, London 1767, 13½in. diam., approx. 37 troy oz. (Robt. W. Skinner Inc.) $800

A Sheffield plated rectangular tea tray with two scroll leaf and shell handles, 73.5cm. across handles. (Lawrence Fine Art) $691

An early Victorian rectangular electroplated tea tray with two ornate cast handles, 26in. overall. (Woolley & Wallis) $124

A two-handled tea tray by Mappin & Webb, Sheffield 1935, 67.2cm. across handles, 114oz. (Lawrence Fine Art) $1,152

An Adam circular salver, the center engraved with the coat-of-arms of the Purchas Family, maker probably Wm. Chawner, London 1778, 15in. diam., 51oz. (Woolley & Wallis) $1,885

A Regency rectangular salver by Rebecca Emes & Edward Barnard, London 1817, 12in., 32oz. (Woolley & Wallis) $1,102

A George II shaped circular salver on three stepped hoof supports, by C. Woodward, 1745, 19.5cm. diam., 10.6oz. (Lawrence Fine Art) $522

A German silver gilt circular ecuelle, cover and stand, 19.7cm. diam., Augsburg, 1745-47, 530gr.
$6,679

A George III soup tureen and cover, by Edward Fennell, London, 1789, 51oz.8dwt., overall width 16in.      $2,794

One of a pair of electroplated sauce tureens, by Henry Wilkinson & Co., 21.5cm. across handles. (Lawrence Fine Art)
$331

One of a pair of George III boat-shaped sauce tureens and covers, by Peter, Ann & William Bateman, London, 1802, 9½in. wide over handles, 36oz.4dwt.
$4,373

A Regency pierced Sheffield plate rectangular soup tureen, the part fluted lid with reeded leaf tie ring handle, 11.5in. (Woolley & Wallis)
$812

One of a pair of George III sauce tureens and covers, by Robt. Sharp, London, 1802, 54oz.13dwt., 9¾in. wide.      $2,724

A George III two-handled oval soup tureen and cover, by Wm. Fountain, 1806, with liner by R. Garrard, 1862, 11¼in. long, 138oz. (Christie's) $5,443

George III boat-shaped silver soup tureen, Edinburgh, 1802.
$4,080

A Georg Jensen silver two-handled tureen and cover, Danish silver marks, circa 1930, 62oz., 25cm. high. (Christie's) $4,354

An 18th century Queen Anne, silver plated tea urn, probably England, 13in. high. (Robt. W. Skinner Inc.)        $350

An early George III tea urn, by Thos. Whipham and C. Wright, London, 1763, 21¼in. high, 97oz.14dwt. all in.        $3,036

Sheffield silver plated hot water urn with Federal-style high domed cover, England, circa 1810, 18. 7/8in. high. (Robt. W. Skinner Inc.) $325

A George III two-handled plain circular tea urn, by George Eadon & Co., Sheffield, 1802, 19¾in. high, gross 142oz. (Christie's)
        $2,494

A George III oval tea urn on stand, by John Emes, London, 1805, 9in. across, 97oz. all in. (Woolley & Wallis) $1,612

A Victorian silver samovar, London, 1884, 40oz. (John D. Fleming & Co.)
        $1,196

A George III tea urn, the vase-shaped body with spool-shaped cover and pedestal foot, maker's mark W. M., Edinburgh, 1804, 15in. high, 48oz.14dwt.        $1,310

A German two-handled samovar and lamp, by Johann G. Kohlheim, Berlin, 1804-15, 20¾in. high, 154oz. gross excluding wooden base. (Christie's) $2,619

A George III two-handled vase-shaped tea urn, by D. Smith and R. Sharp, 1785, 21¼in. high, 111oz., in a fitted wood case.(Christie's)
        $3,189

One of a pair of George III neo-classical sugar vases by John Carter, London 1774, 6.5in. high, 16.5oz. (Woolley & Wallis)    $917

A George III neo-classical set of a pair of tea vases and a matching sugar vase by D. Smith and R. Sharp, London 1770, 42.5oz. (Woolley & Wallis)

$1,798

Late 19th century silver vase with melon-shaped body, signed on the base Masayoshi, 25.8cm. high. (Christie's)

$1,010

A late 19th century silver baluster vase with tall tapering hexagonal trumpet neck, signed Sadayoshi koku, 35cm. high. (Christie's)

$1,010

A Victorian replica of the Warwick vase and plinth, the vase with maker's mark of J. S. Hunt, 1865, the plinth with maker's mark of Hunt & Roskell, 1866, London, 8079gr.   $10,934

An electroplated vase, circa 1900, probably WMF, on an open four-legged base, 38.25cm.

$397

An Alwyn Carr silver two-handled vase, cylindrical, raised on circular foot, 1920, 16.25cm. high.

$516

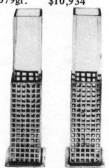

A pair of Argentor silvered metal vases, after a design by Josef Hoffman, circa 1920, 17cm. high.

$391

A large silver globular vase with trumpet-shaped neck, signed Takasaki Koichi koreo seizo and dated Meiji 33 (1900), 63cm. high, 210oz. (Christie's)   $3,564

A silver gilt rectangular vinaigrette, by William Boot, circa 1820, 4cm. wide. (Christie's) $325

An early Victorian silver gilt rectangular vinaigrette, by Nathaniel Mills, Birmingham 1837, 4.1cm. (Lawrence Fine Art) $389

An oblong silver castletop vinaigrette chased with a view of Windsor Castle, by Nathaniel Mills, Birmingham, 1837. (Christie's)$597

An early Victorian rectangular viniagrette, by Francis Clarke, Birmingham 1843, 4.3cm. (Lawrence Fine Art) $179

A scallop-shaped vinaigrette, the grill engraved with a basket of flowers, by Matthew Linwood, 1806, 3cm. wide. (Christie's) $227

A large oblong silver gilt vinaigrette, by Samuel Pemberton, Birmingham, 1814. (Christie's) $455

A 19th century Continental vinaigrette, the top inset with a fossilized quartz stone, 2.5/8in. overall. (Banks & Silvers) $1,957

A silver gilt shell vinaigrette, the body formed from a small cowrie, circa 1800. (Christie's) $570

A Scottish silver mounted mottled jasper vinaigrette with chased foliage rims, circa 1820, unmarked. (Christie's) $427

An oblong silver castletop vinaigrette chased with a view of Newstead Abbey, by Nathaniel Mills, Birmingham, 1838. (Christie's) $597

An oblong silver gilt vinaigrette, by Joseph Taylor, Birmingham, 1813. (Christie's) $312

A 19th century Chinese oblong silver gilt vinaigrette with chased body, unmarked. (Christie's) $455

# VINAIGRETTES

An oblong silver gilt castle-top vinaigrette chased with a view of Westminster Abbey, by Taylor & Perry, Birmingham, 1839. (Christie's) $712

An oblong silver castletop vinaigrette chased with a view of Abbotsford House, by N. Mills, Birmingham, 1837. (Christie's) $541

A Victorian rectangular vinaigrette, the cover chased with a view of York Minster, by Joseph Willmore, 1842, 4cm. wide. (Christie's) $422

Victorian shaped rectangular vinaigrette, by Yapp & Woodward, 1848, 3.5cm. wide. (Christie's) $195

A silver gilt vinaigrette of scallop shape, by Matthew Linwood, Birmingham, 1802. (Christie's) $398

Silver gilt cushion-shaped vinaigrette, by John Shaw, circa 1810, 3.2cm. wide. (Christie's) $195

An oblong silver gilt vinaigrette with pierced foliage panel on the cover, by J. Bettridge, Birmingham, 1827. (Christie's) $213

An unusual, silver gilt vinaigrette chased as a crown, by Joseph Willmore, Birmingham, 1820, with suspension ring. (Christie's) $1,069

A George III vinaigrette in the form of a purse, by John Shaw, Birmingham 1819, 2.8cm. (Lawrence Fine Art)

A large oblong silver castle-top chased with St. Paul's Cathedral on matted ground, by N. Mills, Birmingham, 1842, 4.8cm. long. (Christie's) $1,025

A George IV silver gilt rectangular vinaigrette, with maker's marks of T. & S. Pemberton, Birmingham, 1821, 3.4cm. (Lawrence Fine Art) $100

An oblong silver castletop vinaigrette chased with a view of Kenilworth Castle, by Nathaniel Mills, Birmingham, 1839. (Christie's) $455

# SILVER

One of a pair of Elkington plate wine coolers, 1840, 30cm. tall. (Chelsea Auction Galleries) $649

One of a pair of Paul Storr silver wine coolers. (Christie's) $50,000

One of a pair of 19th century Sheffield plate wine coolers. (Capes, Dunn & Co.) $516

An Austrian wine cooler, maker's mark G.H., Vienna, 1795, 120oz. excluding plated liner, 12½in. high. $5,198

One of a pair of wine coolers with reeded side handles with grape bunch body mounts, circa 1815, 8¾in. high. $1,032

One of a pair of George III campana vase-shaped wine coolers, by Philip Rundell, 1819, 11¼in. high, 186oz. (Christie's) $12,474

One of a pair of Victorian wine coolers, by Elkington, Mason & Co., 29cm. high. (Lawrence Fine Art) $1,025

A Sheffield plate vase-shaped wine cooler chased with fruiting vines, lacking liner. (Christie's) $227

One of a pair of Sheffield plate two-handled campana-shaped wine coolers, by T. & J. Creswick & Co., circa 1820, 26.5cm. high. (Christie's) $1,677

A six-color glass overlay snuff bottle with 'snowflake' ground, 1820-80.
$5,108

A silver Mongolian snuff bottle, the neck inset with coral and turquoise beads and silver beading, stopper attached by a chain.
$567

A glass overlay snuff bottle, the bubble-suffused ground decorated in green with fruiting pods and gourds, 1800-50.
$156

A white jade snuff bottle with stopper, 18th century.
$,7236

A gold snuff bottle of flattened pear shape, weight of bottle 120gm. $993

An Imperial style ivory snuff bottle, four character Qianlong mark on the base, with matching stopper.
$8,514

A lapis lazuli snuff bottle of flattened rectangular form, in rich blue stone, 1800-50.
$993

An agate snuff bottle of flattened rounded form with indented base, 1800-50.
$737

An 18th century carved Peking glass snuff bottle of transparent ruby-red metal well carved in high relief.      $624

A turquoise matrix snuff bottle, the pale greenish stone suffused with a metallic black matrix, 1820-80.
$1,489

A Suzhou agate snuff bottle, the mushroom-colored stone with dark inclusions.
$1,560

A small chalcedony snuff bottle of flattened baluster form, the stopper with a third white bird perched on top.
$652

A celadon jade double gourd snuff bottle, 2½in. high. (Lawrence Fine Art)
$172

A glass inside-painted snuff bottle, by Shi Chuan, signed, well painted with a Manchu warrior.
$425

An 18th century glass overlay snuff bottle with clear bubble-suffused ground.
$2,696

A blue beryl snuff bottle of flattened rectangular form, the stone of pale blue tone suffused with rivering, 1800-80.
$993

An agate snuff bottle, the stone of richly colored caramel and white suffused in 'thumbprint' bands, 1780-1850.   $1,702

A rare tourmaline snuff bottle, the stone of rich deep bottle-green color, incised mark of Daoguang on the base, 1820-80.
$2,838

A pale amber soapstone model of a seated monkey warrior, 27.2cm. high, with carved stand. (Christie's) $498

A 19th century small blue-john vase on cylindrical socle, 5in. high. (Christie's) $1,020

A 17th century alabaster group of Bacchus and Ceres, South Italian, 17¾in. high. $993

A sandstone head of a youth, mounted on wooden base, 12¾in. high. (Robt. W. Skinner Inc.) $800

A portion of carved stone frieze, on wooden stand, 11in. long. (Robt. W. Skinner Inc.) $225

A sandstone head of youth, possibly from Petra, on a gray marble pedestal, 13.3/8in. high. (Robt. W. Skinner Inc.) $400

A carved alabaster figure of Venus arising from the sea, signed Richard Garbe A.R.A. 1933, 64.5cm. high. (Christie's) $1,769

A 17th/18th century soap-stone figure of a Lohan, 2½in. high. $646

Cast stone group of the Virgin and Child, circle of Hans Von Judenburg, circa 1410, 27½in. high. $55,352

A 17th century alabaster bust of Aristotle, on black marble base, 11½in. high. $585

A brass sundial, mounted on a stone pillar, raised on a stepped base, 42in. high. (Banks & Silvers) $522

A terracotta group of Venus and Cupid, signed L. Tinant, 14in. high. (Lawrence Fine Art) $322

Ceramic Roman funerary head, light tan clay with traces of light brown finish, on wooden base, height of head 6in. (Robt. W. Skinner Inc.)$275

A large carved stone 19th century wall fountain, the bowl in the shape of a carved scallop shell, 5ft.1in. high. (Crowther, Syon Lodge Ltd.) $1,500

An Etruscan terracotta head of woman, on wooden base, 14¼in. high. (Robt. W. Skinner Inc.) $550

A soapstone figure of a Lohan, Jiaquing, the head with features picked out in black and red, 13cm. high. $903

A plaster portrait bust of The Hon. Mrs Maryanna Marten by Augustus John, 24in. high. (Woolley & Wallis) $1,353

An early 18th century Dutch stone group representing some marshal allegory, 4ft. 4in. high. (Crowther, Syon Lodge Ltd.) $5,625

A pair of 18th century woven tapestry panels of pastoral scenes in muted colors of blue crimson, green and brown, each 31 x 22in. (Dreweatt Watson & Barton) $702

Mid 19th century English woolwork picture, 15 x 21in.          $1,355

A framed needlework family record clock, wrought by 'Mary B. Clark 1832', 17 x 16½in. (Robt. W. Skinner Inc.)$475

A mid 18th century George II stumpwork coat of arms worked with the Royal Arms and motto in faded colors on a red silk damask ground, 4ft. wide.
$1,155

Mid 18th century Boston School needlework picture of a shepherdess and piper in a landscape, 19 x 14in. (Robt. W. Skinner Inc.)
$63,000

A late 17th century Eastern quilted cream damask coverlet with tufted border, 60 x 38in., and matching pillow cover, possibly Indian or Chinese in origin. (Dreweatt Watson & Barton)          $2,600

One of a pair of mid 19th century English wool-work pictures, portraying HMS Duncan and HMS Cambrian, 10½ x 14½in. $877

Mid 17th century Charles I stumpwork picture, 11¾ x 17½in. $3,203

A Charles I silk embroidered picture of the Sacrifice of Isaac, circa 1640, 9½ x 11¾in. $1,170

A feather cushion covered in purple and gold brocade woven with a displayed eagle, 15¼in. square. (Christie's) $856

Mid 19th century English sailor-work wool picture, stitched in eight colors, 20½ x 22in. $765

Mid 18th century Boston needlework picture, wool and silk yarns worked in all over cross stitches, 16 x 21in. (Robt. W. Skinner Inc.) $19,000

One of a set of three wool and silk Templeton's curtains, designed by Bruce Talbert, circa 1880, together with two pelmets. $3,121

A Leek Embroidery Society panel, 1880's, 63.5 x 71.5cm. $127

One of two pairs of Morris & Co. printed cotton curtains, designed by Wm. Morris, 'Corncockle' design, 1880's, 216 x 139cm.   $340

One of a pair of Morris & Co. wool curtains and matching pelmet, designed by Wm. Morris, 1880's, 'Bird' pattern, 250 x 240cm.
$3,547

A Morris & Co. panel, embroidered in pastel silks, 1880's, 54.5 x 55.5cm.  $193

A Morris & Co. panel, embroidered in blue, green and brown silks, 1880's, 129.5 x 52cm. $269

Early 20th century polychrome embroidered tablecloth with needlework border, 7 x 7ft. (Robt. W. Skinner Inc.) $150

Mid 18th century crewel embroidered pocketbook, America, 7 x 11in. (Robt. W. Skinner Inc.) $1,300

A 'Turkeywork' picture, circa 1850, 21 x 19½in. $326

Late 19th century painted tin clockwork bowing man, 7½in. high. (Robt. W. Skinner Inc.)    $150

A custom crafted Colonial-style doll's house, circa 1980, with ten rooms of furniture, rugs, textiles and accessories, 28in. high, 53¾in. long. (Robt. W. Skinner Inc.)    $1,500

Gunthermann wind-up painted tin merry-go-round, Germany, 1920's and 1930's, 10in. high, 10.3/8in. diam. (Robt. W. Skinner Inc.)    $1,300

Late 19th century Connecticut clockwork dancing black couple, 10½in. high. (Robt. W. Skinner Inc.)    $2,200

A carved and painted rocking horse with horsehair mane and tail, glass eyes and leather bridle and saddle, America, circa 1880, 72in. long. (Robt. W. Skinner Inc.)    $1,800

Mid 20th century life-size young donkey, probably Steiff, 39in. high, 39in. long. (Robt. W. Skinner Inc.)    $150

A painted toy of a skater, with clockwork mechanism, by A. F. Martin, French, circa 1890, 8½in. high. (Christie's)    $812

A Britains set No. 434, R.A.F. Monoplane, with two pilots and four R.A.F. personnel, in original box. (Christie's)  $1,392

An F. Martin 'Le Gai Violiniste', in original clothes, French, circa 1910, 7¾in. high.    $348

A J.E.P. tinplate P.2 Alfa Romeo
racing car, French, circa 1930,
20½in. long.          $411

A Meccano non-constructional car,
finished in red and blue, circa 1935,
8¾in. long.          $760

Group of various paperdolls, including Miss Ida Rehan, 14in. high, by
Raphael Tuck & Sons, 1894. (Theriault's)          $475

Early 20th century goatskin goat
pulltoy, baa's when head is pressed
down, Germany, 16½in. high.
(Robt. W. Skinner Inc.)$700

Late 19th century cast iron baby chick
pulltoy, patented 1881, 5in. high.
(Robt. W. Skinner Inc.)  $900

A Bing tinplate De Dion vehicle, the
clockwork mechanism driving the rear
axle, 6in. long, German, circa 1910.
          $792

A Carette lithographed limousine,
complete with driver, German, circa
1910, 8½in. long.   $2,059

A Bub tinplate and clockwork road-
ster, with tinplate driver, 36cm.
long overall.          $1,786

Turner steel four door sedan, circa 1924,
26½in. long. (Robt. W. Skinner Inc.)
          $900

Britains King's Troop Royal Horse Artillery No. 39, with gun-limber,
six-horse team with postillions and five-man galloping escort. $221

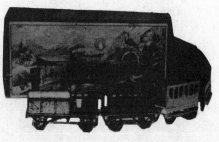

A large Steiff rocking elephant,
45in. long, German, circa 1925.
          $633

An M. J. tinplate pull-along train,
French, circa 1905, 11in. wide.
          $348

A Bing lithographed open tourer, the
clockwork mechanism driving the
rear axle, 12½in. long, German, circa
1930.          $316

Lehmann tinplate postal delivery van,
No. 786, German, circa 1927, 7¼in.
long.          $871

A tinplate Lineol ambulance, No. WH 2517, German, circa 1938, 12in. long.          $570

American six-piece carved wooden polar bear with socket head, by Schoenhut of Philadelphia. (Theriault's)          $200

Late 19th century boy and hoop painted tin toy, possibly by Stevens & Brown, America, 7½in. high. (Robt. W. Skinner Inc.)          $2,700

A mechanical walking crocodile, possibly by Decamps, 34in. long, French, circa 1915.  $792

Dent cast iron three horse hook and ladder, early 1900's, 29in. long. (Robt. W. Skinner Inc.)$400

A tinplate 'Rudy' walking ostrich, the underside marked 'Nifty', 8½in. high, German, circa 1925.          $190

A Gunthermann tinplate four-seat open tourer and passengers, German, circa 1910, 7½in. long. $3,484

Late 19th/early 20th century painted walking gait wooden horse toy, America, mounted on an iron frame, 28in. long. (Robt. W. Skinner Inc.)          $600

Six-piece carved wooden leopard, by Schoenhut of Philadelphia, 7in. (Theriault's)    $175

A Lehmann 'Halloh' gyroscopic motor cycle, No. 683, clockwork, German, circa 1920, 8½in. long.    $1,267

American toy of a young boy, 4in. tall, on 'wheeled' skis, standing on a wooden and cardboard ski slope, by Schoenhut of Phila., 27in. overall. (Theriault's)    $200

An English 20th century wood rocking horse, 41½in.    $348

Late 19th century painted tin horse drawn coach, overall length 29in. (Robt. W. Skinner Inc.)    $2,200

Goodwin clockwork doll and carriage, doll with papier mache head, 11in. high, 9½in. long, 1868. (Robt. W. Skinner Inc.)    $900

A Gunthermann tinplate vis-a-vis motor car, German, circa 1900, 11in. long.    $2,534

A Lehmann Ikarus tinplate aeroplane, No. 653, German, 10½in. long.    $1,425

Marx wind-up 'Buck Rogers' space ship, New York, 1927, 12in. long. (Robt. W. Skinner Inc.) $430

A tinplate mechanical lobster, German, circa 1910, 8½in. wide. $506

A Lehmann tinplate 'Berolina' convertible motor car, No. 686, German, circa 1915, 6¾in. long. $950

A Lehmann tinplate 'Oh My', No. 690, the articulated figure holding the clockwork mechanism, circa 1920, 10½in. high. $300

Japanese porcelain child's teaset, each piece illustrates a scene from Little Orphan Annie, circa 1920. (Theriault's) $450

A roly-poly Santa, Germany, probably early 20th century, 10in. high. (Robt. W. Skinner Inc.) $150

Early 20th century clock-work musical trained golden mohair bear, Germany, 7¼in. high. (Robt. W. Skinner Inc.) $150

American carved wooden five-piece goose, with two-part articulated head and throat, by Schoenhut of Philadelphia. (Theriault's) $225

Late 19th century Martin clockwork drunkard, 8in. high. (Robt. W. Skinner Inc.) $100

# TOYS

An early French mechanical tricyclist, circa 1890, 8¼in. long. $1,108

Late 19th century German clockwork diorama, 13½in. wide. (Robt. W. Skinner Inc.)     $700

Late 19th century painted 'Dandy Dan' riding horse toy, America, 3ft.9in. long. (Robt. W. Skinner Inc.)     $525

A tinplate Toonerville Trolley. (Phillips) $492

An F. Martin tinplate pianist, the clockwork mechanism moving the arms and torso of the pianist, French, circa 1910, 6in. high.     $554

Late 19th century yellow Victorian doll's house and furniture, 26¾in. wide. (Robt. W. Skinner Inc.)     $300

A painted metal model lighthouse with winding staircase on exterior, electrified, 40in. high. (Robt. W. Skinner Inc.)$200

Victorian wooden doll's house, cottage style, with working door with brass knob at front, circa 1890. (Theriault's) $1,450

Lithographed tin balloon man, triple animation, Germany, 1930, 6.5/8in. high. (Robt. W. Skinner Inc.)     $425

645

Britain's set of South African Mounted
Infantry in its original box. (Phillips)
$780

A Bing tinplate and clockwork limousine,
9¾in. long, circa 1910. $2,337

Part of a set of Britain's 21st Lancers, Royal Scots
Greys (2nd Dragoons), and The 9th Queen's Royal
Lancers, No. 24. $133

Britain's Army Building No. 1739, circa
1940, a model of gunners' quarters.
(Phillips) $1,200

Eight British Boer War soldiers wearing
tropical helmets, in their original box.
(Wallis & Wallis) $85

An Edwardian painted wooden model of a
Noah's Ark, containing approx. 120 pain-
ted carved wooden animals, 56cm. long.
(H. Spencer & Sons) $885

A Marx Buck Rogers spaceship, Pat. 1927,
lithographed tin, 12in. long. (Robt. W.
Skinner Inc.) $175

Post war tinplate pedal car 'Austin Devon'
with battery operated headlamps, 60in.
long. (Reeds Rains) $241

# TOYS

Early 20th century Bing lithographed tin garage, Germany, with key-wind open car and closed sedan type car, 5½in. and 6½in. (Robt. W. Skinner Inc.)    $325

Cast iron model of a Leyland Lion single decker bus. (Phillips)    $900

A painted tin wind-up tanker, by J. Fleischmann, Germany, 1950's, 19in. long. (Robt. W. Skinner Inc.)    $200

A Marx Charlie McCarthy & Mortimer Snerd auto, 1939, lithographed tin, 16in. long. (Robt. W. Skinner Inc.)    $500

Twelve German made solid pewter model Boer soldiers, 45mm. high, circa 1900, in their original red box. (Wallis & Wallis)    $92

A Carette tinplate and clockwork limousine, circa 1910.    $1,716

A Britain's boxed set of a Royal Horse Artillery gun team. (Phillips)    $7,440

A child's painted wooden rocking horse, probably Mass., with leather upholstered seat, 31in. high. (Robt. W. Skinner Inc.)    $1,000

A horse-drawn governess cart by Purvis, with varnished top, double seat and original hair stuffed buttoned loose cushions. (Anderson & Garland) $558

A horse-drawn Irish jaunting cart by Hughes, Galway, four-seater, with iron double step to front and rear step. (Anderson & Garland) $505

Nickel plated steel high wheel bicycle, the 'Expert Columbia' model, by The Pope Manufacturing Co., wheel diam. 52in. (Robt. W. Skinner Inc.) $1,800

A four-wheeled dog cart, to suit donkey or pony, either single or a pair up to 12 hand 2. (Andrew Grant) $1,096

An open-lot horse-drawn gipsy caravan on four wheels, interior comprising double bunk bed, drawers and cupboards, canvas top with interior lining. (Anderson & Garland) $997

A 19th century C-spring brougham, the interior in buttoned American cloth with braided pockets and window blinds, maker W. & F. Thorn of London. (Osmond Tricks) $4,788

Open lot gypsy caravan by O. Cave & Son, Dewsbury. (Reeds Rains) $2,240

An Edwardian ice cream cart in good condition. (Bearnes) $744

A Royal Mail pennyfarthing bicycle painted in black with red coachline, with original leather seat. (Anderson & Garland) $1,662

A wicker and bentwood baby carriage, labelled Whitney, raised on wooden wheels, America, circa 1895, 55in. long. (Robt. W. Skinner Inc.) $300

Late Victorian Romany or Showman's travelling wagon, by Thos. Tong, Lancashire, circa 1899-1900, 158in. long by 78in. wide. (Reeds Rains) $3,668

A 19th century britschka in the original yellow livery of Lord Hylton of Ammerdown, nr. Bath, with original buttoned cushions, maker G. & T. Fuller. (Osmond Tricks) $15,960

A Rolls Royce 20-25 post vintage thorough-
bred 25.3 H.P. four-seater tourer motor car,
the body by Hooper, with a current M.O.T.
Certificate. (Anderson & Garland)
$20,615

1948 Rolls Royce Silver Wraith, chassis
no. WYA-55, with electric window behind driver. (Robt. W. Skinner Inc.)
$13,000

A Clement model ACR rear entrance four
seat Tonneau, four cylinder engine, overhead
inlet valve, 14 hp., wooden wheels with 810 x
90 pneumatic tyres. (Christie's)
$29,900

1914 B.S.A. solo motorcycle, single cylinder
engine, 557cc., three speed transmission,
belt drive. (Christie's)          $3,120

1933 Austin 7 black/maroon saloon, reg. no.
KX 9941, clock mileage 27,832, current
MOT, 7.8 h.p., petrol driven. (Giles
Haywood)                    $2,343

1920 Lafayette touring car, aluminium V-8,
burgundy with black fenders, one of five
made, completely restored and running.
(Robt. W. Skinner Inc.) $16,500

1932 Riley Gamecock Special Series Sports
... four cylinder engine, monobloc,
... d, 1087cc., chassis no.
... ual transmission. (Christie's)
$7,150

An ABC Skootamota, Model No. 1B, built
and registered between 1919 and 1922.
(Osmond Tricks)              $943

1933 Rolls Royce Henley convertible, coachwork by 'Brewster', Model No. 270 AJS, engine no. Y95F. (Robt. W. Skinner Inc.) $150,000

1951 Sunbeam S8 crank-driven motorbike, 500cc., reg. no. PHA 363, clock and true mileage 12,195. (Giles Haywood) $843

1929 Austin Seven 'Top Hat' two-door saloon, four cylinder engine, side valve, 750cc., manual gearbox, chassis no. 96614. (Christie's) $2,600

1929 Amilcar CGSs Competition two seater, four cylinder engine, 1074cc., chassis no. 20158. (Christie's) $5,850

Bentley S2 Continental two-door carriage by H. J. Mulliner, chassis no. BC86BY. (Andrew Grant) $21,285

1921 B.S.A. 986cc. solo motorcycle, frame no. 1296, engine no. 1268, twin cylinder. (Christie's) $1,430

1923 Ariel 498cc. solo motorcycle, single cylinder engine, three-speed transmission, frame no. 9905, engine no. S12358. (Christie's) $780

1929 Sunbeam 16 hp. four door saloon, chassis no. 5291K, six cylinder engine, overhead valve, 2040cc. (Christie's) $6,500

1952 Armstrong Siddeley Hurricane three position drophead Coupe, six cylinder engine, overhead valve, 2.3 litre, chassis no. 1812323. (Christie's)                    $5,200

1928 Rolls Royce Phantom 1 boat tailed four seat tourer, replica coachwork by Bampton, chassis no. 25CL, six cylinder engine, overhead valve, 7668cc. (Christie's)                    $24,700

1931 Morris Cowley three-quarter sliding-head coupe with dickey, four cylinder engine, side valve, 1550cc., 11.9 hp. (Christie's)                    $3,640

1965 Daimler Majestic Major saloon, eight cylinder enginer, vee, 4561cc., Borg-Warner automatic transmission, chassis no. 147670. (Christie's)                    $2,080

1934 Rover 10 hp., Sports saloon, four cylinder engine, overhead valve, 1389cc., manual gearbox, semi- elliptic suspension, chassis no. 402102. (Christie's)                    $2,860

A Benz Kontra, 2.7 litre engine, horizontally opposed twin cylinder, 9.3 hp., circa 1898/9. (Christie's)                    $6,500

1959 Rover 80 four door saloon, four cylin-  ngine, overhead valve, 2286cc., chassis  ~61, disc front brakes, drums at  )                    $4,420

1930 Austin 7 Ulster-type Sports two seater, four cylinder engine, side valve, 747cc., manual gearbox, chass no. 105354.(Christie's)                    $3,380

1935 Bentley 3½ litre two door fixed head foursome Coupe, six cylinder engine, overhead valve, twin carburettor, 3669cc., chassis no. B84D9. (Christie's) $15,600

1934 Rolls Royce 20/25 Sports saloon, coachwork by Freestone & Webb, six cylinder, overhead valve, 3700cc., chassis no. GWE 25. (Christie's) $14,300

1954 M.G. TF Sports two seater, four cylinder engine, 1250cc., overhead valve, manual gearbox, chassis no. 80616/2295. (Christie's) $8,710

1967 OSI 20 MTS 2 + 2 Coupe, coachwork by Bertone, six cylinder engine, vee, overhead valve, 1998cc., chassis no. EX 54CD01507. (Christie's) $4,170

1952 Bristol 401 Sports saloon, six cylinder engine, overhead valve, 1971cc., manual gearbox, chassis no. 401/1214. (Christie's) $5,460

1953 Morris Minor Series MM, four cylinder, engine, side valve, 918cc., chassis no. FBE11/178224. (Christie's) $910

1930 Chevrolet Universal sedan, six cylinder engine, 3200cc., overhead valve, chassis no. 12AD75107. (Christie's) $2,860

1947 Lagonda 2.6 litre Sports saloon, six cylinder engine, double overhead camshaft, 2580cc., chassis no. 2. (Christie's) $1,950

A papier-mache tray of rounded rectangular form, gilt painted with flowering plants on a black ground, 30in. wide., circa 1840 $645

A Regency mahogany two-handled rectangular wine tray, on melon feet, 13½ x 9¾in. (Geering & Colyer) $910

A 19th century Japanese black and gold lacquer tray, 23.5in. wide. (Woolley & Wallis) $1,935

'Coca Cola' advertising tip tray, round, America, circa 1905. (Robt. W. Skinner Inc.) $200

A set of five late 18th century pink-ground counter trays, width 13cm. and 9cm. $566

'Clysmic' advertising tip tray, oval, copy reads 'Clysmic, King of Table Waters' (Robt. W. Skinner Inc.) $50

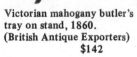

18th century metal tray decorated with a bird, urn and floral displays. $340

Victorian mahogany butler's tray on stand, 1860. (British Antique Exporters) $142

Papier mache tray by Jennens & Bettridge of London, 2ft. 1½in. wide, circa 1850. $800

Late 19th century full bodied bull molded weathervane, America. (Robt. W. Skinner Inc.) $900

A copper gilded eagle figure weathervane, America, circa 1880, 33in. high. (Robt. W. Skinner Inc.) $2,250

Late 19th century American full bodied prancing horse weathervane in solid cast zinc, 33in. long (Robt. W. Skinner Inc.) $4,000

Late 19th century American copper cod fish weathervane, 32in. long. (Robt. W. Skinner Inc.) $3,700

Late 19th century running horse weathervane, America, 66in. high. (Robt. W. Skinner Inc.) $1,400

Mid 19th century copper Gabriel weathervane, America, 41¾in. long. (Robt. W. Skinner Inc.) $1,200

Late 19th century full bodied running copper horse weathervane with directionals, America, horse 32in. long. (Robt. W. Skinner Inc.) $1,700

Molded full bodied rooster weathervane, Cushing Factory, Mass., circa 1883, original gold leaf, red painted comb and wattles. (Robt. W. Skinner Inc.) $2,100

Late 19th century American copper pig weathervane, 33in. long. (Robt. W. Skinner Inc.) $4,750

A Maori wood handclub, 15¼in. long. $5,808

A pair of 17th century Spanish carved wood gilt and polychrome statuettes of a Royal Couple, 10¼in. high. (Lawrence Fine Art) $530

A 19th century English carved oak ship's figurehead, carved in the form of a lion's head, 109cm. high. $829

One of a pair of carved and pierced sandalwood picture frames with Japanese folded silk and paper pictures, 19½ x 14in. (Edgar Horn) $310

A 20th century American carved and painted full length wooden figure of a black man, 35in. high. (Robt. W. Skinner Inc.) $2,000

One of a set of three 17th century rectangular carved oak panels, German. 50 x 27cm. $566

Late 18th century silver mounted lignum vitae goblet, 5in. high. (Lawrence Fine Art) $423

Pair of 18th century carved wood standing figures of pilgrims, carved in pine upon boxwood, 14½in. high. (Boardman) $706

English 19th century carved and polychromed ship's figurehead, the bearded figure wearing a toga, 188cm. high. $3,509

# WOOD

A small gessoed wood carving of Apollo, 4.5/16in. high. (Robt. W. Skinner Inc.) $185

A carved and painted wooden cast of a large salmon, killed by Admiral Britten on the Namsen River, the Jorum Beat, June 1899, 52in. long. (Banks & Silvers)    $1,087

A treen bucket on ebonized turned stem with brass swing handle, 14½in. high. (Lawrence Fine Art) $590

A wood figure of a Bishop Saint, Middle Rhine School, circa 1410, 31in. high. $4,558

A carved wooden ceremonial mask, possibly Polynesian, of two stylized human faces, 11in. tall. (Wallis & Wallis) $132

A tobacconist's blackamoor carved wooden figure, 2ft. 11in. high. (Whetter & Grose)    $2,610

A 16th century carved wood figure of a Saint, 40in. high. (Boardman) $1,123

A Victorian carved blackwood European smoking stand in the form of a bear, his head hinged to hold matches, 35in. high. (Stalker & Boos) $650

A 17th century bamboo, mountain carved and undercut in deep relief with figures, 12in. high. $1,212

# WOOD

Woodlands Indian burl bowl of elongated pear-shaped form, 22¼in. long. (Robt. W. Skinner Inc.) $8,750

A 19th century English treenware covered caddy in the form of a beehive, 5½in. high. (Stalker & Boos)  $250

Early 19th century splint cheese basket, New England, 20in. diam. (Robt. W. Skinner Inc.) $300

An 18th century carved wood American Military officer, 14¾in. high. (Robt. W. Skinner Inc.)  $850

Late 17th century Spanish or Southern French pair of silvered and giltwood reliquary busts, 25¼in. and 24in. high.  $717

A lignum vitae mortar and pestle, 3½in. diam. (Capes, Dunn & Co.)  $111

A 17th/18th century bamboo brushpot with contemporary applied rim and low foot supported on tripod bracket feet, 6¾in. high. $646

An early George III giltwood wall bracket, circa 1760, 1ft. 5½in. high.  $1,504

A sailorwork seed cup, the turned wood vessel applied overall with colored seeds, dated 1870, 10½in. high. $319

658

American 19th century oval tin and wood foot warmer, 10½ x 8in. (Robt. W. Skinner Inc.) $260

A carved walnut screw pattern nut cracker with double mask top, 6½in. long. (Capes, Dunn & Co.) $278

American 18th century cylindrical burl cheese draining bowl, 20in. diam. (Robt. W. Skinner Inc.) $775

One of a pair of giltwood twin-branch wall lights with pierced mask plates with feathered head-dresses, 29in. high. (Christie's) $3,205

A 17th century carved fruitwood plaque depicting the Nativity, 8.5 x 6.6cm.     $1,267

Wooden carousel rooster, mounted on spiral brass and wrought-iron post, possibly Europe, circa 1900, 48in. high. (Robt. W. Skinner Inc.)$1,800

Early 19th century English carved oak stern panel, 76cm. high. $957

A 16th century polychrome wood figure of a dog, probably from a St. Roche group, 15¼in. wide. $1,244

A baroque carved oak picture frame of molded oval form, 2ft.1in. by 1ft. 9in., circa 1700. $618

Early 19th century double handled burl bowl, probably Indian, rim 17 x 18½in. (Robt. W. Skinner Inc.)   $600

American 18th century burl scoop, with small hooked handle, 4¾in. diam. (Robt. W. Skinner Inc.)   $275

Late 18th century small cylindrical burl bowl, New England, 8¼in. diam. (Robt. W. Skinner Inc.)   $400

A walnut figure of St. Anna Selbdritt and the Virgin holding the naked Child in front of her, Malines, circa 1520, 14¼in. high.   $5,860

A limewood carving of St. Anna Selbdritt presenting the Child to the Madonna, by the Bavarian-Swabian School, circa 1500, 7½in. wide.   $12,698

Fruitwood salt container, probably England, 11in. high. (Robt. W. Skinner Inc.)   $225

A 19th century American grater with drawer below, 9¼in. wide. (Robt. W. Skinner Inc.)   $160

Late 18th century wooden cheese drainer, New England, 26½ x 26½in. (Robt. W. Skinner Inc.)   $825

Mid 14th century pine Styrian female Saint, perhaps the Magdalene, 107cm. high.   $48,840

Early 19th century American rectangular lignum vitae chopping bowl, 18in. long. (Robt. W. Skinner Inc.) $425

Late 18th century American burl bowl with ladle, 17½in. wide. (Robt. W. Skinner Inc.) $1,600

Late 18th century wooden herb grinder, New England, 4¼in. high. (Robt. W. Skinner Inc.) $500

Early 19th century pine staved tankard, probably New England, 11¾in. high. (Robt. W. Skinner Inc.) $350

A rectangular wood panel carved with the Three Sake Tasters, Meiji period, 122 x 91.5cm. (Christie's) $3,564

Six oval wooden bowls, 19th century, New England, sizes from 3 to 6in. (Robt. W. Skinner Inc.) $450

Early 19th century open mesh carrying basket, New England, 10in. diam. (Robt. W. Skinner Inc.) $450

A limewood carving of St. Barbara, Styrian Region, circa 1490, 40in. high. $9,442

A 19th century bowl with domed cover, probably American. (Robt. W. Skinner Inc.) $650

# WOOD

Half size black duck, by A. Elmer Crowell/Decoys/ East Harwich Mass., 1915, 11in. long. (Robt. W. Skinner Inc.)     $800

An 18th century lace maker's carved pine pillow, Scandinavia, the box retains old red paint and is dated 'M.S. 17..', 11in. diam. (Robt. W. Skinner Inc.)     $375

Late 19th century English boat's carved mahogany sternboard 'H.M.S. Widgeon', 57in. long.     $1,116

One of a pair of late 18th/ early 19th century Gothic Revival giltwood wall brackets, 19in. high. (Robt. W. Skinner Inc.)     $750

A carved and painted carousel horse, attributed to I. D. Loof, circa 1885, 60½in. high. (Robt. W. Skinner Inc.)$8,500

One of a pair of 18th century carved giltwood brackets, perhaps Flemish, 11½in. high.     $397

A 16th century Hungarian horseman's shield of wood covered with leather, 31in. high.     $4,404

A 19th century boxwood and fruitwood bucket, probably Dutch, 12in. high. (Christie's)     $1,339

An 18th century carved gilt and gesso Trumeau panel, France, 27in. wide. (Robt. W. Skinner Inc.)     $375

665

667